Dagrune Awakening

Heidi Marine

Dagrvne
Land of Seasons
Lonhilnai Mountain-Range
Lord Onyx's Manor
Quipar
Green Mountains
Great Red Wood
Alachor's Village
Alachor's Dwelling
Tiernac Forest
Shoone & Ruimi's Village

DEDICATION

To my dad–
Thank you for being a safe place.
Not just for me, but for anyone lucky enough to know you.

Because of you, I grew into the best version of myself.
Because of you, I had the freedom to explore who I wanted to become.

I carry you with me–in laughter, in love, and in memory.
Though you aren't here to read this story,
or meet the character you inspired,
I know you're cheering me on just the same.

This book is for you.

All rights reserved.
The Amazon Endure typeface was designed by 2K/DENMARK in 2025.
Template id: ST-414D415A-25-A01
Printed in The United States.
ISBN: xxx-xxx-xxxx-xx-x

<u>1</u>

It's Just Life

The dock creaked and groaned, bowing slightly as two pairs of feet softly padded to the end of its smooth planks. It was quieter than usual. She couldn't ignore the difference, especially considering nothing in this dream ever seemed to change. When they reached the end she drew in a deep breath—her eyes fluttering closed. They stood that way for a minute, swaying, the gentle breeze playing with her hair. He watched intently, somehow able to feel her every emotion. As if on cue, they sat down together, their feet dangling just inches from the cool water. He slipped an arm around her waist, drawing her closer. She sighed—heartfelt, from the depths of her soul, and laid her head on his shoulder. They sat in stillness, creating a perfect silhouette against the moon's pale smile. Eddies of water gently swirled around the dock. Again the breeze stirred her hair, lifting tendrils to float near his face. The strands tickled his cheek, so he tenderly brushed them back, tucking them behind her ear. He buried his nose in her neck and breathed deep, memorizing her scent and the storybook perfection of this moment. He pressed a soft kiss to her forehead. She sighed again. And he reached over to lift her chin, until they were trapped, drinking in the color of each other's eyes. She squinted. His eyes—usually warm, deep pools of brown—held a strange shadow. It was barely perceptible at first—like a faint whisp of smoke, and then it began to grow. It held her there, paralyzed in the moment, growing larger until it blotted out the familiar warmth of his gaze. Her heart quickened as it locked her in and he pulled her toward him. But when their lips met, the darkness in his eyes was forgotten as she surrendered once again to the fire of their passion.

****

Hayden's head buzzed as the dream faded into memory—and the feeling of contentment that usually came with it, slowly waned. She didn't want to open her eyes and was unwilling to leave the warmth of her covers. Maybe if she stayed this way a little longer, she could go back in and see what happened. It always seemed to end the same way… with that kiss. But maybe, just maybe—it would reveal something more.

A long, drawn-out stretch—then she reluctantly opened her eyes to let in the sun's early rays. *Guess that won't be happening today.* She thought, watching the light play with the glimmering threads she'd woven in crisscrossed patterns throughout the quilt. It reflected off the walls, dancing, shifting and spinning as she wiggled her toes. Hayden grinned to herself, fully amused with the simplicity of the moment. Her friends were always teasing: *thirty is too old to love all things sparkly*. But she didn't care what they thought. There was something about shimmer—about *light*—that had always felt important. Even if she couldn't say why. She swung her legs over and slid her feet into the size ten slippers waiting there, sitting for a moment to shake off the last of the sleep hangover. Satisfied that she was ready to move forward with her day, she launched her 6'2" frame into motion.

She shuffled toward the chair where a mountain of cotton and jeans lay in a messy pile. It was *that* chair—the one everyone pretends they don't have, where all the clean clothing land instead of making it to dresser drawers or hangers in the closet. She'd long ago given up her own pretense that she wasn't just a little bit lazy on laundry day.

Sifting through the mountain, she found her favorite pair of jeans, slipping them on as she stared out the window behind the chair. It framed a perfect view of the federal park just beyond her backyard.

She plucked a shirt from the middle and pulled it over her head. It was her day off, so she refused to endure the torture of putting on a bra. As she stepped into the hallway, she felt the soft squish of Calliope's tail–before the angry yowl of pain. "Damn cat!" she yelled, nearly tripping in her scramble to avoid pulverizing her. "What?! Don't look at me like that!" she snapped as the feline streaked down the hallway. "If you hadn't been directly in my path–you know... the one I walk *every morning*–I wouldn't have just needed to save your life."

Calliope activated her superpower the moment she jumped on the counter. She could somehow hold your gaze and be completely indifferent at the same time. It was just long enough to make a point before she broke it–stretching nonchalantly, her long tongue rolling out as a huge yawn revealed perfectly white and unnervingly sharp teeth.

Calliope had been an interesting addition to her household. Hayden had chosen the name after learning of the goddess known for her beautiful voice–it felt fitting, given the strange, haunting song that had echoed through the hills the night she found the cat. She could've sworn someone else had been out there–singing, drawing her in–but there hadn't been a single trace of another soul. Only the underweight, patchy, unkempt stray, trembling and nearly hypothermic beneath a bush, trying to shelter from the freezing rain. Now, years later, the forlorn creature had been replaced by a sleek, pampered housecat with a glossy black coat. And contrary to the tired superstition surrounding black cats, Calliope had brought Hayden nothing but happiness.

The cat meowed, flicking her tail–clearly annoyed at the extra few minutes she'd been forced to wait for breakfast. "Yup... your meow is still just as eerie as ever, ya weirdo," Hayden muttered, reaching for the coffee filters. The aroma of roasted beans filled the air as she broke the seal. The whole beans rattled dryly into the grinder, and her mouth watered as the blades mashed them into a thick powder. Once the coffee was percolating, she grabbed a can of food for Calliope, scooped it into a bowl, and tossed it in the microwave. It was only ten seconds–but Calliope wouldn't touch pâté unless the routine was followed to the letter. "There you go, your highness," Hayden mused. She chopped the warmed food before placing it on the counter. Calliope's tail stopped its irritated dance as the warmth soothed her famished stomach. "Your *Goddessness*… that's the one," Hayden snarked. "Anyway, just the way you like it," then leaning on the counter, she watched Calliope daintily work through her breakfast. "I should probably fix some oatmeal for myself while I wait for the coffee," she wasn't really talking to Calliope–living alone had just made it a habit to narrate her mornings aloud. The cat glanced up, gave a token lick of her paw, then returned to her bowl. Hayden snorted. "Well okay then. I guess I will," she said sardonically, rolling her eyes.

The smell of freshly brewed coffee wafted through the house as the dark, potent liquid splashed into her favorite mug. She poured in creamer, watching it billow as it mixed together–turning the coffee a smooth brown. A sigh of contentment escaped her lips as the first drops of morning motivation touched her tongue, leaving their delicious trails of warmth on their way to her stomach. She walked through the ornate French doors at the end of the hall and out onto a small deck. It overlooked the tree laden hills of her mountains. Well… technically they belonged to the government, but she enjoyed them more than anyone of the federal persuasion. Resting her elbows on the railing, she cradled her mug, taking a sip here and there. The hill, marking the end of her property and the beginning of protected land, dropped sharply just feet away from the solid cedar beams beneath her. Then beyond that, a ledge gave way to a brook–bubbling happily over rocks, logs, and natural debris as it made its way down from the foothills. This was her favorite part of having time off, this slow introduction into daily life.

For a moment, she closed her eyes, her chest rising and falling as she drew in deep, even breaths of the fresh morning air. That's when the dream came flooding back. Slowly she opened her heavy lids, dropping her head to rub the back of her neck. What did it mean? Why did she continue to have the same dream? She'd had it at least a dozen times before without a single detail changing. But that darkness in his eyes–it was new and unsettling to say the least. Hayden straightened, setting her mug on the railing. She mulled over the details again, trying–not for the first time–to figure out how it related to her. She didn't know this person who was supposed to be her what... lover? He seemed familiar, but she was certain she'd never met him before.

A sharp bark and gurgling howl interrupted her thoughts, jarring her out of reflection and back into reality. "Oh shit! Bérg! I completely spaced," the incensed howls faded momentarily as she hurried back through the house, her mug clattering as she dropped it on the counter. A few drops splashed out, but she would have to deal with that later. "I'm sorry! I'm coming!" She hollered, loud enough so he could hear her through the front door.

His metal bowl lived next to the food in the front closet—because if she didn't keep it inside, he felt entitled to bang the dang thing on the ground when he was hungry. He heard the ring of food kernels clattering into the bowl, and immediately started in on his jumping routine. She giggled as his ears flapped up each time his head appeared in the window. It was this way every morning, but still, the moment hadn't lost its goofy charm. Then opening the door, she braced herself for his enthusiastic greeting. She'd barely set foot outside when 160 pounds of pure muscle crashed into her, effectively spilling his food everywhere.

As she watched him eat, she thought about the day they met. He'd just been a pup, wandering alone down a remote road—yet he hadn't looked the least bit concerned about his plight. She was sure some heartless soul had abandoned him, but he'd been happy—bouncing toward her almost as if he'd expected her to be there. She wasn't sure how old he was, nor could she say exactly what breed. Her best guess? American Bulldog. But even if that's what he was, Bérg was an anomaly. There were things about him that stood out—far beyond her years of experience as a Veterinarian. For one, he seemed to understand everything she said. He needed almost no training to become a perfectly behaved member of her household. More than that, he shadowed her constantly—more attuned to her moods and needs than she'd thought possible. And then, of course, there was his physique. Jowls wider than two lumberjacks' fists. Brown eyes that bulged just enough to make you think they knew too much. And when he growled to protect her, the sound could nearly shake the ground.

The most normal thing about him was his coat—white with striking blue brindle patches, generously scattered across his massive frame. She scratched the one that looked like a paw print as he hoovered the last of his food from the dirt.

"No dog food trees for you, I guess—ya goofy goober," she teased, heaving herself off the front steps. "Wanna go check out the stuff in the barn one more time?" Bérg's tail wagged wildly in response, thunking heavily against the spindles of the front porch railing. He bounced happily alongside her as they made their way toward the barn, where the scent of freshly cut lumber and new paint gently tickled her senses. From the first time she'd imagined having a horse—and the barn she'd build to house it—she'd pictured exactly this. It rose in front of her like something straight out of *Better Farms & Gardens*—bright red with white X's. Classic and timeless. The only thing still missing was the horse, and she couldn't wait for the auction to finally complete the vision. "Hey bud," she said, her nails skimming the sleek fur on his head, "you excited to meet a new friend next week too?" He responded with a giant, slobbery kiss that enveloped her hand. "Ew, gross, dude!" she laughed, recoiling from the unexpected wet warmth of his tongue. Then she grasped the curved iron handles and pulled the heavy barn doors open.

The sweet smell of fresh hay swirled outward, enveloping them in its musky odor. One large aisle, two stalls, and a tack room made up the single-level building. The only exception was a small loft where bales of hay waited—the itchy toil of bringing them up the ladder still fresh in her mind. The largest stall was ready to go, with a fresh bed of hemp spread generously across the floor. She would have picked cedar—she loved the smell—but Mum was allergic. Bad enough, in fact, to trigger an asthma attack just from being nearby.

The second stall, which was smaller, was set aside for Bérg. It was a huge upgrade from the haphazard shelter he was used to—not that he'd ever seemed to mind. But this one had a custom doggy door and stayed much warmer. He could probably jump right over the stall door, so Hayden had decided not to waste the extra money on it. She wandered down the aisle to the tack room as Bérg busied himself snuffling around. This had become her favorite place to be lately. She took inventory daily—though it was completely unnecessary. She'd long ago committed it all to memory. Halters dangled from hooks, and blankets were neatly piled on the curved saddle horses. Shelves were lined with saddle soaps and leather treatments; underneath those were bins already brimming with healthy treats. The only thing still missing was a saddle—because everyone knows you buy the saddle to fit the horse, not the other way around. With countless hours under her belt volunteering at the auction and neighboring ranches, she was ready for this.

The faint sound of a ringing phone drifted through the open windows of the house, snapping her back to the present moment. Damn. She'd forgotten to grab her cell off the table. It looked like she'd have to call whoever it was back. *Maybe they'll just send a text,* she thought, running her hands over the bridles one last time before turning toward the house. "Only one week left, and I'll finally get to use them," she said aloud. As if prompted, Bérg abandoned his investigation and followed her out. Her feet crunched over a mixture of gravel and dry grass as she made her way back across the yard. Bérg happily bounced alongside her—until the chitter of a red squirrel snapped his attention away, inviting him into the woods to challenge the unwelcome intruder. "You're never going to catch them, 'cause you never do!" she yelled after his quickly retreating rear.

Mum's name stared back from the screen when she checked her missed calls. No voicemail or text—she never left them anyway. Mum knew her name alone was enough to prompt Hayden to call back.

"Hey, what's up?" Hayden greeted her cheerily.

"Are you free to go shopping today?" came Mum's reply.

2

About the past

Clara couldn't sleep, she'd been awake since well before her usual rising hour. Hayden had been in her dreams last night, causing her to spend her morning hours amid old fears. She shuffled her way into the kitchen, pulling the step stool out of the utility closet. It had been a gift from Hayden when she moved out and couldn't help to grab things off the top shelf for her anymore. Clara had forever joked that this was the main reason she'd adopted her, making the ladder a perfect embodiment of a gift meant as a practical joke.

As she aged, her once long black locks of youth were now cut into a shorter, more practical style. Silver was generously sprinkling among the darker strands, like fairy dust in her soft curls. As time had taken its toll on her joints, the shorter style was favored as an easier and less taxing way to care for her hair. She embarked on her morning routine, unable to shake the nagging memories her dreams had dredged up. When they refused to leave her alone, she sat down with her morning cup of tea to watch the sun's rays break over the roofline across the street.

Searing light pierced the quietness of the twilight, warming the early chilly air, effectively creating steam that rose from the blacktop to become a thin fog. Satisfied with the morning's opening chapter, she closed her eyes to revisit the impertinent first memories with her daughter.

When she'd first laid eyes upon Hayden, the small child was covered in grime. A dumpster sat outside the rear service door where four pawed scavengers were often startled in their quest for an easy meal. It was the end of a long, exhausting day. Two giant bags of trash sat patiently waiting their turn to go into the large alley bin. It was typically one of the younger employees that took care of this, but because they'd worked so hard today, Clara decided to send them home and close up herself.

She grunted, swinging the loaded bags up and over the side with all her strength. That's when she saw her, huddled and shivering in the cool summer night air. The child stared at Clara with eyes too big to belong on such a small sunken face. Her brown, scraggly, unkempt hair looked like a brush hadn't been run through it in weeks–and her frightened eyes reflected the light from inside the shop.

When she realized her hiding place had been revealed, the poor child jumped like a cornered animal. And Clara's gaze followed the sad sight of her malnourished silhouette as she scurried off down the alley into the night.

After their initial encounter, Clara made a habit of peeking out the back door every night before lock up. She would occasionally leave a sandwich or snacks so the poor girl could have a decent meal–just in case she plucked up the courage to return.

Then one evening it turned unseasonably cold for early September and she got her chance to make contact. Being particular about the process of closing out the books, she insisted on being the only one to do so. She knew that it would just be a headache to her employees, and the last thing she wanted to do was to create a work environment where micromanaging would negatively affect them.

Maybe it was the shorter September days, or the lengthening shadows that beckoned the night to hide them; regardless, this day was light as far as coffee loving customers went. She stepped out the back door earlier than usual, hugging her sweater more tightly as the night air found its way through her clothes. Tonight, she'd thought ahead enough to be prepared with a Swiss turkey sandwich stashed safely in her purse.

Exordium was a small town whose residents took great pride in its appearance. Its alleyways weren't the kind of place you would imagine—especially if you were familiar with larger cities. Here they kept them clean—only on rare occasion were there foul odors present. She stepped down from the back stairs, taking a right toward the park that resided smack dab in the middle of town. It wasn't the only one around, but it was the most popular—bringing children from even the most rural corners. She found herself wandering that way often, spending her time leaning on the fence to listen to their happy giggles and wonder what could have been, had life offered a different path.

The cool night breeze calmed her thoughts, refreshing her soul, as with deep breaths she claimed its power. So caught up had she been in her moment that she nearly missed the tentative footfall. A small arm and thin shoulder held onto a corner of the building. Her thin, nervous face cautiously surveyed the alleyway. There was a change in her from that first night; Clara could sense it. The hesitance in her flight response, those big green eyes looking at her so hopefully. Her heart felt the pressure of compassion as she used the moment to pull the slightly smooshed sandwich out of her purse, waving it in the air. "Please don't go! I have some food for you," she called out, desperately attempting to slow the child's potential retreat.

For a brief moment, she feared even such a small gesture would scare the girl away as her tiny frame disappeared back around the building. But to her relief the child slowly stepped out to inch closer, although still keeping her back solidly planted against the brick on the opposite side of the concrete. This child seemed edgy, far more than any of the other children she was friends with. Maybe her face looks a tiny bit fuller, *Clara thought to herself. Even if it was just wishful thinking, she was not one to spit at hope. "I don't want you to be scared and I don't want to hurt you. I just want to give you this food. That's all," the kind words seemed to melt a minute amount of distrust out of the sad face by the time their slow dance finally brought them within arm's reach of each other.*

She placed the sandwich in the small, eager, outstretched hands.

"Is it ok if I hang out with you while you eat?" Clara carefully inquired.

"Um, okay," the girl responded with a shrug.

Her pained eyes darted mistrustingly back and forth between the open ends of the alley and Clara.

"What's your name?" Clara asked, crouching down to make herself seem less intimidating.

"Jane" The single word was barely audible, breaking off abruptly as her voice cracked with apprehension. Her loosely shod feet shifted uncomfortably back and forth, but the quiet growl that emulated from her hungry belly made her forget any embarrassment born from accepting the charity. Without another moment's hesitation, the sandwich disappeared. The speed at which she'd inhaled it sending her into a coughing fit.

"Oh honey, I'm sorry. Here's some water to help," Clara said, holding a bottle out between them. She made an exaggerated show of opening the seal and Jane took it gratefully. Her cough subsided as the water soothed her throat. With her head tipped back and bottle in the air, her sleeves slid up revealing bruises—that until then, were mostly obscured by the cloth. Clara's anger flared as she imagined where they came from. It was irrevocably obvious now that Jane needed help. And Clara had become painfully aware that

there would be a defined but delicate balance between being too hasty, and not fast enough.

"Would it be ok if I walked you home?" Clara asked. She saw a flash of fear cross Jane's drawn features. It was all she needed to confirm this child was not in a safe place.

"No thank you. Mama and Papa wouldn't like that."

Mama and Papa? *Clara thought to herself wryly. What an odd thing for a child to be calling their parents in this decade.*

"Are you going to be ok walking home alone?" She asked, this time aloud. But Clara had pushed her luck too far. Without giving an answer, Jane took off back around the building melting effortlessly into the shadows. Clara could have sworn that a soft blue flicker followed her retreat.

Over the next few weeks Clara formed a plan. Being well known in the community, she was already acquainted with many of the neighborhood children. Because it was a smallish town, it turned out to be a simple job of steering the conversation in her favor. Most of the kid's parents frequented the coffee shop which made striking up conversations without revealing her intent easy enough. Some of them knew of Jane, but none so far knew where she came from or where her home was. From all the information she'd gathered, her best guess was a small trailer park on the edge of town. One day, after work, she began driving that direction instead of heading home.

When she pulled into the park, she pressed the brake. The streets were narrow, barely leaving enough space for cars to be parked on either side and let traffic through. Most of the trailers looked well kept. Those residents obviously cared how their homes were presented. Adorable and whimsical yard decorations filled their small patches of well-manicured grass while others displayed rows of vibrant late season flowers, whose leaves reached for the fading power of the afternoon sun. Every so often she would see lots filled with broken furniture, garbage, and various discarded items in what small yards they had to offer. These houses were dingy with vinyl siding that was cracked and missing in places. They were covered in uneven patterns where the elements had deposited dirt over time—and dull windows stared outward, their former gleam lost in layers of dirt. It was out of one of these ill-kept homes that she saw Jane come flying in a panicked rush. The screen door slammed into the house as its hinges groaned out their protest. Clara could see tears falling as she cleared the stairs and bolted toward the street. She called the child's name loudly, but for all the good that did, her voice may as well have been carried off by the wind.

With all of the detective's work she'd accomplished to find out where Jane lived, figuring out the next step hadn't really crossed her mind. But she wasn't left to wonder long when a raspy voice, laden with distain and ire drew her attention back to the stairs. The screen doors cracked wooden frame was again slammed into the siding. Now that she was this much closer, the deteriorating wood was obvious. It was barely being held together by the staples and nails that threated to scratch anyone who dared to get too close. She heard the screeching insults before her eyes came to a stop, resting on a blotchy blustering face.

"Get your useless ass back here you little bitch!" The woman shrieked into the neighborhood.

Rage, like nothing Clara experienced before, began to burn in her chest. This was all she needed to confirm her suspicions. Jane wasn't safe or well cared for here. As the satisfying warmth of anger grew, her muscles felt the full effect, allowing a dangerous sense of complete invincibility to settle over her. In her current state, she fully believed that nothing and no one could withstand the inferno that was now roaring inside. As she exploded out of the car a palpable cloud of emotion hovered around her. "How DARE you speak to a child that way," she rumbled, coming face to face with the woman.

Her restrained tone should have been a warning, a showcase that she was working overtime to make sure the rage that fueled every cell in her body didn't betray itself in her voice. And it seemed to have its desired effect for a moment, as the disheveled woman took a step backward. Clara stared defiantly into the thin pitted face. Her teeth were worn and yellow, covered in a thin layer of green fuzz from lack of care. She wore a glassy and unfocused gaze as she grabbed her greasy blonde hair, pulling on either side of the sad looking ponytail. It tightened the small wad of hair–just barely. Clara thought the gesture was meant to be intimidating, but in her current state she wouldn't have backed down for a momma bear protecting her cubs. "Excuse me, who are you exactly?" the unkempt woman spat, taking back the ground she'd lost. "I don't recall ever seeing you before or asking for your opinion! She's my kid, and I can treat her like I damn well please!"

The vocal lashing fell unfazed on Clara's ears. Curious neighbors had begun to poke their heads out to see what all the commotion was about, only to quickly move on when they realized who was responsible for the disturbance. Clara, who was no stranger to belligerent irrational people, was keenly aware that nothing she said to this pathetic, sniveling, poor excuse for a human would matter. So taking a steadying breath to calm her anger she simply replied, "Not if I can help it," then turned on her heel and walked to the car without a backward glance–confidently holding her head up and squaring her shoulders with determination.

She dove in with gusto, meeting the process head-on; long and tedious as it was. But she never gave up. From filing police reports to connecting with Healing Hands Advocates, Clara stayed committed. She held on to hope and pushed things forward whenever an opportunity arose. There was something about Jane–something Clara couldn't quite put a finger on. It gave her purpose, a deep certainty that her place was between Jane and her abusers.

The day the agency granted her permission to stay in touch, she wasted no time. With every visit, she showered Jane with love and thoughtful gifts. And as the months passed, Jane slowly began to come out of her shell. Her foster family knew Clara well, which eased her mind on the days she couldn't be there. It thrilled her to watch the unkempt, scared, and underfed child she'd met slowly fade into a painful memory. And when the documentation finally came through, making Clara an official foster parent, her friends gladly released Jane into her care.

After some time living together, Jane expressed a desire to change her name. Her therapist agreed it was a step in the right direction, but emphasized that the choice needed to be hers alone. So together, she and Clara pored over page after page of baby name books, searching for the perfect inspiration. During this time of indecision, Clara remained her biggest cheerleader. "I think I know which one I like best," the child said at last, her eyes shining with excitement. "Hayden means fire, which is perfect–because the sun makes me feel powerful, and the sun is made of fire! Do you like it?"

Clara's heart clenched at the sight of her determined little face–so earnest in its innocence. Her troubled upbringing hadn't broken her spirit. And for a moment, she held out hope that Hayden–in spite of the evil people that wanted to break her–would be ok. There was no doubt–this child knew herself well enough to make such an important decision. "Yes," Clara said softly, pulling her into a warm embrace. "I love it. And I can tell you do too–and that's the most important part," she squeezed, letting tears of relief fall into her hair. "We can't legally change it just yet, but from now on, you are Hayden– to me, and to everyone else we meet."

Sunshine warmed her face as the memories faded with the mist. She struggled a little, finally managing to push herself out of her favorite chair and return to the kitchen. Those early years had been filled with pain–which included nightmares and the strange reaction that came with them. Clara had never told Hayden—not since her martial arts instructor promised it wouldn't happen again. A promise that worked—not just to take the strange light, but to erase her memory of it too. Still, Clara hadn't given up searching for answers.

Even after the light faded, uncovering the mystery of Hayden's origins became her private mission. It was the reason she wanted to see her today. She'd finally found something. At the very least, it was a step in the right direction. Clara smiled, holding the phone to her ear as her fingers brushed the photo of Hayden with her first trophy. It was the first big goal she had ever accomplished—and the moment Clara saw 'it' click. After that day, there was no stopping the force that was Hayden. It rang four times, then went to voicemail. "She'll call me back when she sees it was me," Clara told herself. She didn't need to try again. She'd done her part. So she hung up—and waited.

3

To Go Shopping

It was nearly September. The bright, deciduous colors of early autumn dotted the landscape, scattered among the deeper greens of pine—their prickly branches dominating the woods in this part of Hayden's world. The pickup's tires hummed steadily along as Hayden breathed in Fall's earthy scent through the small crack in her window. Trading in her old car had been tough. She preferred fuel-efficient vehicles, but only a truck could handle the added weight of a trailer and animal. This one had low miles and just one previous owner, so the faint new-car smell still permeated the cab. The sound coming from the tires shifted now and again with the changes in the blacktop as she made her way toward Mum. It was a cool thirty minutes to her house, then only another half hour from there to the shops. She and Mum loved these trips into the city—where hunting for inspiration was encouraged. Whether it was for craft projects or to update their wardrobes—they could spend hours shopping.

These spur-of-the-moment trips were nothing new, but during their conversation today, Hayden thought she sensed something different in Mum's voice. She'd tried to convince herself it was just a result of missed get togethers—or work being busier than usual. There was also the barn, and getting everything ready for a horse. If she tied it all up in a neat little bow, she really hadn't had time to focus on other things until now.

As the house came into view, a gentle smile tugged at the corner of her lips. It was a small rambler with a porch stretching the entire length of the street view. The stairs met up with a walkway that was paved in flat stones, fitting together perfectly–like the pieces of a puzzle. Her lawn was impeccably manicured, although the lack of rain and colder days of Autumn had begun to take their toll. Finally, the flower beds surrounding the house and lining the driveway were blooming with Marigolds and Petunia's. Mum had spent hours explaining how she'd planned them so something would bloom in every season... except winter, of course. And Hayden was always happy to listen to her ramblings about something she loved so deeply. It kept her active after retirement–and that was more than enough for her.

The moment Hayden pulled into the driveway, all that convincing she'd done–telling herself nothing was wrong–flew right out the window. Mum was waiting on the porch. That never happened.

Usually, they'd linger in the kitchen with a pot of tea singing on the stove, taking time to relax before heading into the city. But today, Clara was already halfway down the walkway before Hayden could even shift into park. Hayden jumped out, making a goofy show of racing her to the door. Mum had needed more help lately, though she refused to admit it. She'd told Hayden more than once that she didn't want to become anyone's burden. But Hayden didn't see it that way. As far as she was concerned, if you were getting older, it meant you were doing life right. "Well, someone's excited to check out some new shops today!" Hayden said, slipping an arm behind Clara's back. She offered her other hand for balance, helping her mum ease into the seat more comfortably. Clara let out an awkward little chuckle as she settled in. *Okay... something's definitely up,* Hayden thought, careful not to let it show on her face.

Thrifting was one of their favorite pastimes. They already knew every shop in town and had mapped out the most efficient route–so they could hit them all without doubling back too many times. The familiar musty scent of used goods always sparked their creativity. It was like a treasure hunt in a minefield of forgotten things, just waiting to be rediscovered. They sifted through kitchen utensils, old bottles, vases, baskets, and books—items that now piled up in bags in the back seat.

On the way to yet another thrift shop, they spotted a cute little consignment boutique tucked just beyond the bustle of Main Street. Inside, Clara found a jacket: soft pink with embroidered, delicate bouquets around the hem and cuffs. A string of ornate buttons lined each lapel like a smattering of jewelry. Hayden had nearly given up on finding anything for herself, when she stumbled upon a simple spaghetti strap dress—deep blue, with swirling silver sparkles that splashed delicately across the fabric. A small, knee-high ruffle gave it an elegant touch. She opened her camera to get a better look at the back, admiring how perfectly it hugged her curves without feeling tight or awkward.

"Well," Clara said as they settled back into the truck, "it looks like we'll need an excuse to visit a nice restaurant now that we've got our new finery," then, just for a moment, a shadow of apprehension crossed her face. It was so fleeting that anyone else might have missed it—but Hayden was dialed in. She'd been expecting something ever since the phone call that morning. "But before we can think about dinner," Clara continued, a slight quiver sneaking into her voice, "there's one more stop we need to make. I've got some business to take care of—and they're only open until four."

Hayden didn't press her. Whatever Mum was guarding, it had to be important. She trusted her. So, without a word, she tapped the new address into the GPS and shifted into drive.

They drove down streets and past shops they'd browsed just hours ago—pulling up to a building that had clearly seen better days. The stucco siding was covered in jagged cracks that chipped away at its textured finish. Bits of the tan material had crumbled into small piles at its foundation. A sloped brown roof hung low over the sidewalk, its trim extending just far enough to cast a bit of shade over the entrance. Bold vinyl letters stretched across the front windows: **Jorden Clark, Private Investigator**. Hayden had to stop herself from asking the burning question: *What would Mum need a PI for?* But it was instinct and years of experience that held her back. If Mum wanted to share–she would have.

Hayden helped Mum out of the truck, offering her arm for support. But Clara acted as though she didn't see it and led the way through the front door. A small bell rang, singing a discordant tune with the squeak of the old hinges–hinges which Hayden thought could use a touch of oil. The smell of stale coffee hung in the air, nearly covering the musty stench of the thin carpet. Hayden coughed as her lungs tried to adjust to the strange mixture, just as a man who looked to be in his fifties, peeked out from behind a solitary door. His glasses were too big for his face, and his mop of curly hair was piled in an unruly mess. "Hi Clara, it's nice to see you again. This must be Hayden?" He asked, stepping aside to beckon them through. Once again, Hayden cast an inquisitive glance Clara's way, but Mum was still avoiding eye contact. So with no choice but to go along for the ride, she followed them into the small, cluttered office.

The vibe matched his. Slightly unkempt–yet threaded with the undercurrent of organization that only he could understand. The desk between them wasn't large. Papers were piled at the edges, separated by cheap plastic file holders. As she quickly scanned the desk, she noticed the file resting beneath his hand. "Let's get the elephant in the room out of the way first," he said, settling into the chair across from them. He pushed his glasses up his nose–a pointless endeavor, as they slid right back down. "Hayden, your mother asked me to dig into your ex-guardians past," he added, tapping the file. "Everything I found is here. It's not much, but it will at least give you a few answers."

Hayden drew in a sharp breath, her fingers tightening around the arms of her chair. She looked to Mum, who sat stiffly, her gaze fixed on the folder. "Honey, I know you said that you didn't care," Clara began, finally relenting and meeting Hayden's troubled stare. "But ever since they died... I just felt that digging into where you came from might shed some light on.. you," Hayden didn't respond right away. The hesitation in Mum's voice was impossible to miss. There was something she wasn't saying. She shifted her attention to Jorden, who offered nothing but the steady presence of a man waiting for permission to do his job.

Clara cupped Hayden's hand between hers.

"Honey, I know you've wondered so many times how you ended up in that hell hole. We already know they weren't your real parents–which, quite frankly, didn't require a DNA test to prove. So I hired Jorden, hoping he could help us find more answers. I waited to tell you, because I didn't want to get your hopes up... only for him to hit the same dead ends I did."

Her eyes pleaded with Hayden not to be upset, and Hayden felt the full weight of Clara's sincerity.

"No, it's okay, Mum," she said, her tension softening. "I'm here now. Let's hear what you found."

Clara had never done anything underhanded. If she'd gone as far as hiring a PI, Hayden trusted there was a good reason. Mum only ever wanted the best for her–something Hayden felt from the first moment they'd met.

Hayden gave Clara's hand a gentle squeeze, then turned her focus to Jorden.

"Please, I'd love to hear what you have to say."

Taking that as his cue, Jorden leaned forward and began with a question.

"What's your first memory, Hayden? I know it's a blunt place to start, but it would help to know how far back you remember."

Hayden blinked, caught off guard by the sudden cold plunge into something so personal.

"I–I'm not sure," she stammered. "I think I remember huddling under a blanket with Mama. I kind of remember her being scared... but still trying to protect me. And then someone banging on a door, trying to get in."

"How old would you say you were?" Jorden asked, his voice softer now, as if coaxing the memory from her.

"Maybe two? I'm not really sure."

Jorden let out a low whistle. "Wow. That's rare. Most people don't remember anything before five, and even that's a stretch."

Clara's grip on Hayden's hand tightened. Even with a grown daughter who could defend herself, she was poised and ready to lead with her protective instinct.

"I'd go with it," she said. "Her memory is ironclad."

The unvoiced growl from Clara didn't go unnoticed. He knew better than to challenge a protective mother. He hadn't meant it that way, but there was also no reason to defend it. So, without further commentary, he began. "I'll start from the beginning then," he said, settling into his chair. "I talked to a lot of people to make sure the details were as accurate as possible. Your ex-guardians weren't originally from this area, which made things tricky. But eventually, my search landed in a town called Euchre—the same size as this one, roughly 800 miles from here. According to their former neighbors, they tried for five years to have children without success. When it became clear they wouldn't, she fell into a deep depression, and he turned to drinking to cope with what he saw as a personal failure. Eventually, he was caught drunk on the job and fired on the spot. That loss of income led to foreclosure on their home. And then... they vanished. Packed up and left without a word. No one ever heard from them again. Honestly though, it didn't sound like anyone really missed them."

He paused to shuffle through some papers, then continued. "When they arrived here, around thirty years ago, they had a one-year-old child with them. That was you. Somehow, they had connections—friends in low places, most likely—because not long after, your birth certificate was forged. It was well done. Too well done, considering their financial situation. I have no idea how they managed it, or who helped them, but someone did," he shrugged. "From there, everything else I found came from your old neighbors in the trailer park. He became the violent drunk you knew. She started using. It spiraled. And then… there's this," he hesitated, shifting uncomfortably. "More than one person told me she claimed to be afraid of you. Usually when she was high. There was no consistency in her stories, just this repeating idea that… something about you scared her," he laced his fingers together, signaling he was done—for now—and waited.

"Afraid of me?!" Hayden's voice rang with disbelief. "I was a toddler. What the hell could make someone afraid of a baby?"

Jorden met her stare evenly. "That remains a mystery. No one had clear answers, just vague comments. Whatever happened from that point on… it's buried in your memories. I wish I had more. I've exhausted every lead."

"But… where did I come from then? I couldn't have just materialized out of thin air!" Hayden snapped, her voice thick with confusion and frustration. But she caught herself, pulling back before the emotion turned into something that might sound ungrateful. "I'm sorry," she said, exhaling. "You've uncovered so much I never knew. I really do appreciate the work you've done."

Jorden raised a hand, gently halting the apology.

"You don't owe me that," he said. "You're right—there are still pieces missing, and I understand how frustrating that is. I'd feel the same way in your shoes. But I want you to know—I left no stone unturned. I scoured every lead, and there were no reports of a missing child that matched your age or description. Nothing. Not within a thousand miles of Euchre. I promise. I checked," a heavy silence settled between them. Taking the cue, Jorden leaned forward and slid the envelope across the desk. "I've made copies of everything I uncovered. I want you to have it," then he stood and extended his hand again. "I truly hope you find the answers you're looking for," he said, his voice carrying a quiet finality.

Hayden understood. There was nothing more he could give. She stood, took his hand, and shook it with quiet gratitude.

"Thank you," she said simply.

Their ride home was filled with silence. They didn't need to say it—going out for dinner was no longer on the table. After they passed the town limits, Hayden finally let her thoughts spill out. "I just… I feel like I have so many more questions now, than I did before. Why isn't there any record of me before they found me? Is it normal for children to show up out of nowhere? Why the secrets? What were they hiding? Where did they find me? Who are my real parents?" Her voice cracked. "And now they're dead, so I couldn't beat it out of them if I wanted to. Which is no less than they deserve," she slumped in the driver's seat, feeling defeated when she should have found some closure.

"Hayd, I know, baby," Clara said softly, reaching out to pat her daughter's white-knuckled hand. "I have all those questions too. But I think we'll find out some day. When the timing is right," But in truth, she felt little conviction to back her words. Instead, she too felt the sting of defeat. This was supposed to help Hayden—not make her sink into more isolation. So Clara pivoted to the one thing she knew would ease her daughter's heart. "Do you want to come back to my place and do wine and a movie?" To her relief, Hayden's features softened and a quiet smile replaced the drawn, worried expression.

"You know what Mum? That sounds perfect. Just what the doctor ordered."

"Are Bérg and Calliope gonna be ok?" Clara asked. "Don't you need to feed them?"

Hayden's face melted into a full smile at Mum's consideration for her furry grandbabies.

"Thanks for the concern, but they'll be fine. Cal always has dry food available. She can suck up her princess routine for one night—and I set up a timed feeder in the barn for Bérg before I left."

Hayden was happy that she'd left that morning, already prepared for a late night.

"Well movie night it is then!" Clara declared triumphantly, "We haven't done one of those in a long time, so I'm really looking forward to it."

It felt comforting to settle in with food and wine. Being back at Mum's house was the right kind of self-care she needed. The wine, cozy blanket, and laughter, warmed her from the inside out, leaving her with a rosy flush on her cheeks. The movie did exactly as she hoped, giving her some time to escape from all the haunting questions. By the time credits rolled, they were holding their sides, sore from laughing through a lighthearted comedy. But as time would have it, the movie was over, leaving room for the emotional exhaustion to catch up. She sank into her old bed, and the familiar room gave her a bit of comfort. Then her breathing slowed, and dreamland took her into its confusing clutches.

4

Building Frustration

The room was small, with a vintage hardwood floor that looked as though someone had tried restoring it to its original luster—but the ravages of time and heavy foot traffic had worn away the varnish. A stove and fridge crowded together on one wall, barely leaving space for a doorway that led back out. A few cupboards lined the left side, with a sink crammed into the meager space, leaving little counterspace for practical use. In the center of the room stood a red table, its glossy surface chipped around the edges where the black, stone-like smoothness beneath shone through. Solid wooden legs formed an X, supporting the weight of the slab. Mismatched chairs surrounded it, cracked and torn, barely held together by clear packing tape. There was just enough room to squeeze between them before reaching the door. Heavy and old, the door's chipped white paint was scratched with faint streaks of color. Dirt—probably from tiny hands— smudged across the center of it, about waist high. The old glass doorknob hung loosely in its worn cradle, pitted and with small chunks missing from its once-beautiful design. The glass felt different from what she was used to. Where she'd expected sharp, jagged edges—she found only smoothness in the divots.

She tried to pull her hand back, but something held it there. Struggling, she stepped back, grabbing her wrist with the other hand. No matter how hard she pulled, her effort was useless. Something was calling from the other side of the door—trapping her. It wasn't a sound—it was more of a physical pull, drawing her toward it. The energy felt ominous. She could only watch—her stomach tightening, as she twisted the knob. The springs in the spindle squeaked in protest, the hinges groaned in agreement—and then the long, slow, gloomy creak.

The door was barely open, when the light tinkle of a bell reached her ears—strange, yet somehow familiar. The room beyond did nothing to assuage the fearful apprehension now hammering loudly in her chest. Through the darkness, she could barely make out the stairs, the green corrugated vinyl tacked to them curling up at the edges.

But as unsettling as that was, it paled in comparison to the gaps between the wooden slabs—each nailed precariously to a pair of two-by-twos, cascading downward into the yawning blackness in even succession. The darkness at the bottom merged with the dark void between the gaps.

Her hand had barely left the handle when she noticed there was no knob on this side of the door. Almost as if the room knew she'd realized it, the door slammed shut behind her. She teetered for a moment, catching herself just in time. But when her hand brushed the crumbling limestone wall, she recoiled in disgust. Then, in a burst of heat and wind, fear itself reached through the stairs, clawing at her exposed ankles.

Appendages covered in brown fur, dangerously sharp curved claws, and the scaly skin of a snake were somehow one creature. These images of terror swiped dangerously close. Her feet felt rooted in molasses as she tried to move them fast enough to evade the flesh-rending talons. All confidence in outrunning the terrifying beast vanished as the stairs began to shift before her very eyes. They grew—larger, wider, longer with each step. There was no end to them now. But still, she fought, refusing to give up on her escape.

Then she made a mistake—she shouldn't have, but curiosity overruled instinct. She wanted a better idea of what kind of nightmare this was. She froze, paralyzed by dread, as she finally glimpsed the rest of the creature's body. The space where its eyes should have been—empty, black sockets. Scores of eyes, instead, were set in an apelike face, flickering with deep, angry red flames. If she held their gaze for too long, it felt as though she was being drawn into their dark void. Its mouth was filled with sharp teeth, dripping with thick, black venom, and its body stretched out behind it—a serpentine mass, writhing to and fro as it danced angrily in pursuit.

She forced herself to turn away, but it was too late. With one final, desperate lunge, its bony arms shot between the slabs and closed around her ankle. As momentum threw her forward and the talons tore into her flesh, she crossed her arms in front of her face in a futile attempt to protect herself. Her body fell—helpless—into the infinite darkness. A feral scream of defeat escaped her throat...

Hayden awoke amid a soft whimper. Her scream had felt so guttural—so raw in its sincerity—as if her throat should be sore from her desperate cry for help. But, as always, her dream-soaked howls faded into soft, pathetic grumbles, as consciousness clawed its way back to reality. She let the room swim back into focus before daring to lift even a finger.

"Breakfast is ready, and your coffee is just finishing in the Keurig," Clara called cheerily from the doorway.

Mum's voice. It never failed to pull her out of the funk that came from the mind-fuck she was usually left with in these moments.

"I'll be there in a few," Hayden replied. She tossed the blankets down with an exasperated sigh. "I just need a moment to freshen up."

Then she sat up, cupping her face in her hands. There was something about that dream—unsettling at best. She couldn't shake the feeling—it wasn't just another nightmare. In fact, all of her dreams lately seemed to have some deeper meaning. She got up—sulking as she changed into a different outfit. When she made it to the kitchen, the smell of coffee worked its morning magic, making her feel more like herself.

Clara's motherly instincts were telling her that Hayden was anxious, but it wasn't entirely due to yesterday's discovery.

"I could tell you had a nightmare last night," she stated.

The claim hung in the air between them. Hayden closed her eyes and rubbed her fingertips firmly on her forehead. When she spoke, her voice was strained.

"Yeah, mum I did. It seems to happen after a close encounter with memories of… them," she fake gaged, emphasizing her distaste. "But it doesn't seem related… of course."

"Well I've never known dreams to have direct relevance to everyday experiences and I think dream interpreters prey off of vulnerable people. So, I don't take much stock in that," Clara said cautiously. "Do you want to tell me about it?"

Hayden tried to recount it with as much detail as possible, but dreams never seemed as terrifying in the retelling. The rooms weren't familiar and then the creature… she didn't even know where to begin figuring that one out. The only detail that kept coming back was that bell.

"Now that is a curious thing. I wonder why that specific bell made such an impression," Clara speculated.

"What do you mean by that specific bell?" Hayden puzzled.

"You didn't notice the bell above the door at the PI's office? But no matter, sometimes I think we just have bad dreams. You dealt with a lot of trauma as a child and you've always possessed a very vivid imagination. It stands to reason you'll have some pretty bizarre ones."

Clara was briefly transported back to the countless times she'd been summoned to Hayden's room in the middle of the night. She'd sometimes spend hours soothing her as she fought off yet another nightmare.

"Thanks mum. I'll just add it to the growing list of things to discuss with my therapist. I just thought since it's been twenty years, that I would be past this."

"Oh hun," Clara said, turning from the omelette sizzling in the pan. "I don't think you can put a time limit on healing. I'm quite certain something will always haunt you from those days. But being in therapy is the best way you can combat all of it."

Hayden helped Mum clean up from breakfast and made her way back home, where Bérg greeted her with the unstoppable enthusiasm of a freight train. Even Calliope showed some affection, which was a bit out of character for her. "Did you guys miss me or something?" She asked, digging in the closet. "I really wasn't gone for that long. The way you two are acting you'd think I left you alone for a whole month."

It wasn't hard to find what she was looking for. She purposefully kept it separated from the crushing weight of her other garments because it was important to keep her Gi perfectly pressed. If she were to ever appear at the academy with a wrinkled one, she wouldn't be welcomed in class. They were strict about it and she was careful to always respect the expectation. More than fifteen years in the academy had engrained in her mind that she should never challenge her professors rules.

The academy was in the opposite direction of her mother's house, so once again Hayden set out on roads that wound lazily through the foothills. When signs for the town of Lorthew began to appear, Hayden felt her usual increased sense of excitement. Although focusing on her career and building her business had caused Hayden to take a handful of years off from training, the feeling remained the same. There was just something about laying all of her frustrations on the mat that helped clear her head—which she needed today more than ever.

When training began all those years ago, Matilde had decided it was in Hayden's best interest to train solo as it seemed she was more comfortable learning that way. Over time she found the instruction to be just as helpful, if not more cathartic than therapy. When the pressures of training would overwhelm her and she found herself devolving into tears, they'd stop to meditate through the surfacing pain before continuing. Their need to pause for these moments had ended long ago, but Matilde thought it prudent to continue with their one-on-one sessions. Her keen ability to read people, and Hayden's affinity for picking up the skill so quickly, helped her to make the decision.

Matilde waited in the center of the room as Hayden hung her jacket and purse on the hooks near the door. Her long dark hair was pulled back and braided as usual. When she lifted her arm to tuck in a wayward hair, her triceps rippled, showcasing the solid muscle that had developed from years of stringent physical discipline. She had a set of piercing brown eyes that were especially adept at seeing through the emotional walls Hayden had erected to protect herself, and today was no exception. The instant their eyes met, Matilde knew something was eating away at Hayden's usual calm.

"I think today we should start off with some meditation. You're holding a lot of tension in your body right now," Matilde said, and there was no question in her voice.

Hayden bowed respectfully, pressing her hands together.

"Oss Professor," she replied.

Matilde lowered herself to the mat, bending her legs, one foot in front of the other. Adjusting her posture, she straightened, placing a hand on each knee. Hayden followed the example, preparing herself for meditation as she closed her eyes. "Before we begin, would you like to talk about what's bothering you? I can sense that it is unusually heavy," Matilde said matter-of-factly. The professor's concern for her long-time student was genuine. During these particular meditation sessions she was more likely to drop the strict instructor persona and show her caring soul underneath the tough layers. Hayden took a moment to center herself before launching into the frustrating events of the previous day. "Now that you were able to speak your truth, how long would you like to set the timer?" Matilde asked, the shadow of concern still clinging to her voice.

Hayden wasn't completely truthful. Ten minutes wasn't nearly enough, but she didn't want to take up too much time. The physical exertion was most helpful in blowing off steam–it was the part of training she needed and wanted most today. The timer went off, and though she could have used a bit longer, she was visibly more relaxed.

One of the last techniques they'd worked on was the Heel Hook when they'd trained last. It had proven difficult the first time around, and with a few years off from practice, she struggled more than usual. "Maybe you bit off more than you can chew today," Matilde observed, studying Hayden with that disconcerting gaze she'd perfected. "Why don't we go back to some basics. Your muscle memory will come back, but it appears we must work our way there more slowly."

Hayden's confidence wavered, but Matilde's observation wasn't altogether unfounded. She hadn't stopped working out, it just wasn't movements that would help her with technique. She'd stayed strong, just not fighting strong.

"I know I'm going to be sore in the morning," Hayden grunted after what felt like the hundredth time being thrown to the mat.

"Maybe my student won't take so much time off in between training sessions next time? There is a lesson to be learned here my dear."

The gentle admonition was nothing Hayden hadn't thought of on her own. It only served to make her roll her eyes internally, for she didn't dare to do it in front of her professor. It would have come off as rude in a normal situation but would absolutely be frowned upon during training. As she headed home, the previous feelings of anxiety and apprehension were replaced by a calm that permeated every cell of her tired body. Her physical therapy session had done its job to restore some of her peace.

5

It Happened on a Work Day

Hayden's sore muscles had already begun to settle in during last night's slumber, but the groans escaping her lips were more about the looming workday. She absentmindedly reached to scratch the palm of her right hand—it was one of those itches that she couldn't seem to relieve. At least it was mild enough to ignore. She'd lingered in bed for too long anyway, so she forced herself out from under the warm covers.

Anything of significance was at least an hour from home—and work was no exception. Relief veterinarians were few and far between, so she *was* in high demand. But in an area made up of small towns, work could be equally sparse. Still, the money was good, so she didn't mind. Time behind the wheel never bothered her anyway. It was calming and gave her the opportunity to sing along with the radio or listen to mystery podcasts.

Iola Veterinary Hospital had hired her four months earlier. She'd quickly found the team to be a pleasant crew to work with, which made it easier to look forward to the grueling workdays. Long ago, she'd decided that turning down contracts was completely acceptable if the vibe didn't feel right. Once, she ignored that internal warning—and it was a mistake she never intended to repeat. It was always more enjoyable to work with people who felt like friends anyway.

Tabitha, the vet Hayden was filling in for, had recently given birth to twins and wanted to stay home longer than the usual eight-week maternity leave. Breastfeeding two infants was already challenging enough without the added stress of working in a busy clinic where stopping to pump wasn't really an option. So, to avoid sending an understaffed small-animal practice into a chaotic tailspin, the hospital hired Hayden until Tabitha was ready to return.

The loud clang from the lab box was immediately drowned out by barking dogs as she yanked the back door open. The hospital also ran a boarding facility, and the kennels–situated just inside the entrance–had alerted their noisy tenants to her arrival. She took the few steps down the short hallway into the surgery prep area. This was definitely not a room she wanted to linger in at this hour; it was far too easy to get in the way.

The technicians she'd be working with were already busy–drawing blood, setting up stations, and organizing patient documents. As she passed the dental station, she noted the state of the warm water blanket. The light was on, and a motor softly whirred, indicating there would be at least one dental procedure today. She slid her fingers lightly over the counter, past baskets of blood tubes and treatment supplies. These were all tools of her trade, each with a purpose of its own.

The sound of technicians discussing labs and procedures faded as she passed through the office doorway. Carefully navigating the crush of desks and bookshelves, she reached a small closet in the back, then exchanged her jacket for a white lab coat. Her eyes grazed the familiar books stacked floor to ceiling on shelves that filled the meager wall space. Their subject matter ranged from unique surgical procedures to medical terminology. If she couldn't find information about any aspect of small animal medicine in this room, she didn't need it. In fact, she had to remind herself to bring back the one they'd let her borrow. The worn chair squeaked as she lowered herself into it. With the mouse already in hand, she clicked into the schedule. *Looks like they added a growth removal since I last looked*, she noted to herself. And as she pored over appointment notes, she took a second to acknowledge her colleagues with a quick nod. They were responsible for the morning's appointment schedule, so she likely wouldn't get the chance to greet them otherwise.

The surgery schedule looked light and fairly straightforward— as long as those three dentals didn't throw everything off. As she planned the day, Hayden caught herself rubbing irritated palms along the desk's edge. The itching had grown more persistent and had spread to both hands, making her worry it might affect concentration during surgery. She stood, rolling her chair back before stepping around it. Maybe a distraction would help get her mind off of it. The techs were sure to be waiting for her to analyze the lab work. She brushed off the sensation and stepped out, determined to move the day forward.

Four pink sheets of paper awaited her review on the treatment counter. The multi-colored pages made it easier to spot bloodwork reports in the files. She pored over the numbers, scanning for anything that stood out—values that were too high or too low. If they fell outside the normal range, it could indicate a health concern. And if it were a significant one, it could delay surgery.

A couple of Thunder's kidney values were slightly elevated, but not alarmingly so. He was a massive Lab in need of multiple growth removals. Some of the masses were affecting his mobility, making the mild kidney issue the lesser of her concerns today. She instructed the techs to highlight the findings and have the 'six-month recheck' conversation with Mom during his discharge appointment.

Alexa was her right-hand tech for the day. With ten years of experience under her belt, Hayden knew she was in good hands. In the veterinary world, one technician often filled the role of an entire OR team—so Hayden made sure they knew just how much she appreciated their hard work. Working together, they moved quickly through the routine surgeries—even making good time with the growth removal patient—while the team of dental technicians completed the easier of the three dentals. The only thing left was the procedure she had intentionally saved for last.

Grizzley was an elderly Chihuahua whose teeth were essentially being held in place by a thick buildup of tartar. He was the embodiment of the 'land shark' they often joked about. For that reason, they couldn't conduct any sort of assessment until he was fully under anesthesia. But if the odor coming from his mouth was any indication, they were in for a tough one.

Hayden cringed when realizing how involved the procedure would be—especially for a dog of his age. The fractured jaw alone would be the biggest challenge of her day... unless you counted the conversation with the owner. She braced herself for pushback, even as she hoped for the understanding that she truly had their baby's best interest at heart.

"Hello, Mrs. Shaw, this is Dr. Solara. I'm the vet working on Grizzley's dental today," she said, making sure to sound extra cheery. "I want to start by telling you that Mr. Grizzley is handling his anesthesia like a champ. However, now that we've finally been able to look inside that little rascal's mouth, we've found a few issues that need to be addressed. If you still have your copy of the estimate, we can go over everything together."

"Grizzley is my baby," Mrs. Shaw replied. "He's all I got after my Winslow passed. You just do what you need to, so I can have him for a few more years."

Hayden swallowed the instant lump that appeared in her throat.

"We have the best surgical team here," she replied evenly. "We'll get him all patched up and back home to you before suppertime."

Great. Now she was misty-eyed—and under more self-inflicted pressure to get her patient back to the person who needed him most. By some miracle, she found enough undamaged bone—more than enough for the surgical wire to hold on to. Once the tartar was removed, most of the teeth fell out during the cleaning—leaving only a few extractions. After that, it was a simple matter of cleaning up the bacteria-riddled mess. Once she was satisfied with her suture job, she gave him an injection of additional pain meds and antibiotics.

"And done," she said, immediately turning the gas down. "Wake this guy up and make sure someone stays with him. I don't want him out of your sight. His momma needs him to go home tonight."

Alexa didn't miss a beat as she took another round of vitals, pausing just long enough to raise an eyebrow at Hayden.

"That must have been some conversation. Don't worry—I've got you on this one," she said, her voice full of compassion. "I was there. You did a lot today."

Hayden pressed her shoulder blades together, stretching her sore chest muscles.

"I'm sorry, you guys. You didn't deserve that. I think I need a break."

She peeled off her surgical gown and stuffed it into the trash.

"Hey, don't worry about it. We're all a little stressed after that schedule," Alexa called after her. "You should feel free to get some air. And don't you *dare* touch those charts until you've had your break!"

As she walked back through the treatment area, the chaos of recovering patients—combined with the outpatient procedures—had fully taken over. It was a very different scene than this morning. Blankets were strewn across the floor, waiting to be re-warmed to keep the recovering animals comfortable. On the table in the center of the room, one tech held a patient while the other flushed black chunks from his ears. The tarry blackness told Hayden everything she needed to know: a yeast infection. She didn't even need a microscope to diagnose that one.

"I don't envy your workout right now, ladies," Hayden quipped as she passed by.

"Oh sure, Ms. Diana Prince! Like we don't know you could probably do this whole thing by yourself!"

The light teasing followed her down the hallway. She responded with a quiet guffaw and continued outside. They called her that on occasion—endearingly—because of her impressive height. But she didn't mind. She took it as a compliment. It *was* Wonder Woman, after all. Who wouldn't feel flattered?

Under a soft blanket of clouds, the sky darkened, amplifying the cold sting of the approaching season. "Fall is knock-knock-knocking at Mother Nature's door," she huffed, wrapping herself in a hug and spurring herself into a brisker walk. A half-hour and hastily thrown together sandwich later, she finally settled into the office to document the morning's procedures.

There was rarely enough time to take a break before she was thrown into afternoon appointments, and today was no exception. It was just four doctors, but the treatments they required kept everyone on their toes, rushing to fill requests—from labs to medications. She didn't allow herself to relax, even when appointments were over and she still had all those charts to write up. As she plugged away, turning her chicken scratches into coherent notes, the itch began to drive her to the brink of crazy. It wasn't just in her palms anymore—now the sensation was creeping up her wrists. She did her best to ignore it, and after a while, the annoying feeling slowly cooled... then faded altogether.

In the days that followed, the itching spread further up her arms, eventually finding its way to her chest. It was worse during the day, but would ease and fade as the sun went down. No rash, swelling, or redness appeared. Cold packs were her only relief. She planned to see a doctor if it persisted, but for now, she treated it as a minor distraction.

The next three days blurred by with more spays, neuters, and dentals than she cared to count. Though she didn't feel she could admit it to any of her colleagues, routine surgeries bored her, and she found herself missing the university—where challenges had come regularly. When Thursday finally rolled around, Hayden was relieved not to be needed in the evening, and she didn't risk even a second's delay as she slipped out the back door.

Sinking into the driver's seat for probably the thousandth time, she prepared for another long drive home. The highway stretched out endlessly as her eyelids, heavy with exhaustion, began to droop. She fought hard against the sleep threatening to take her over. Usually, a drive this long called for caffeine, but she knew that to allow such an indulgence would cost her a good night's sleep.

Then slowly, very slowly, as in a waking dream, she began to notice a soft glow behind the next hill. The road curved through a valley, hiding the light for a short moment until she emerged out the other side. The most beautiful painting she'd ever seen was revealed, stretching majestically across the sky. The sun hung low on the horizon as it prepared to lend its power to the moon, its glow still bright enough to send tendrils into the evening sky. They curled gently in front of a wall made of clouds, creating a stark contrast of bright light and menacing dark. It appeared briefly as though heaven's door had been cracked open. The soft hues that surrounded the sunset were more vivid than any she could recall ever having seen.

As her tires loudly protested the grooves in the road, the light on the horizon began to change. Softer and more touchable than before, she could almost see waves that appeared to be Northern lights cascading their way into the early fall sky. From the corner of her eye, something grabbed her attention. So concentrated had she been on the magnificence of the sun's farewell, that she'd almost missed what was happening directly beside it.

Here the clouds were darker; less inviting. The colors were deeper, as if warning the world that something was about to break. A flash of light, obscured by the clouds, snapped into the skyscape. Never before could she remember seeing the likeness of this. To have a rainbow's beauty pale in comparison? As she pondered the thought, her attention was sharply drawn directly in front of her. There was no mistaking the sharp angled light that ripped through the clouds this time. A brooding storm and the most beautiful sunset were walking hand in hand to introduce her to the night.

"What a perfect end to a busy day," she marveled as she pulled the car over.

This was a lightly traveled road so she needn't worry about her vehicle impeding traffic in any way.

The storm looked menacing, but she had justified her decision to be there by telling herself it was still far enough away to be safe. Thanks to the long legs she'd been blessed with, she cleared the ditch in one easy hop. Just beyond it, a hill offered a slightly better vantage point—perfect for getting the shot she needed. She told herself it was important. Without proof, no one would believe her.

Hayden lifted her device, carefully framing in the mountains, the sky, and the light show–when suddenly, a prickling sensation of electricity crawled across her skin. She cried out in surprise. From her palms to her chest, it felt like she was on fire. All the stray hairs that had escaped her ponytail during the day lifted at once. Her stomach clenched as the realization hit: she had miscalculated the storm's distance–and she was in imminent danger.

Too late, she spun on her heel, sprinting toward the car. The next moment exploded with sound and chaos. An ear-splitting snap echoed off the rocky landscape–and seconds later she saw the jagged bolt. Two trails of light forked down from the sky and slammed into her palms. She stared in wide-eyed terror as it traced up her arms, then arced out of her chest to form a glowing ring of electricity. Yet strangely, she felt no pain.

Hayden tried to move. She couldn't. Not even her pinky finger twitched. Panic bubbled up in her stomach. Her chest felt numb, her lungs frozen–yet she sensed movement in her diaphragm, which only confused her more. Still suspended in the shock of the moment, she realized something else. Her feet were leaving the ground. She was being lifted into the air.

This is it. This is how I die. How could I have been so stupid?! She thought angrily. Then it dawned on her that she was forming rational thoughts. Something that she was certain would not be the case if this were really happening. *Am I dead already? If I'm not, I'm certain that I would be extra crispy. Why can't I move? Why is the lightning going through me? Bérg and Cal will wonder what happened to me. Mum will take care of them though.*

The thoughts chased each other through her head as she faced down her mortality and pondered if this was even real or just another one of her crazy dreams. When the sun's rays appeared to reach down to earth and gently wrap her up, she thought, *dream of course*. But then she felt their warmth. The way they pacified her panic felt so real. *Am I hallucinating?* She wondered as she was lifted higher.

Suddenly, all the warmth and good feeling ended as she felt herself spinning violently through the air. Hayden hit the ground rolling. She trembled violently as all her anxiety crashed into her at once. When she tried to stand her body refused to cooperate, so she was left to stare up at the sky. A brilliant flash of nearly blinding light filled the night. When it subsided, the storm had disappeared leaving only a dark sky filled with stars. Her vision blurred and the feeling that she was sinking gently into a bed made of feathers, followed her into darkness.

<u>6</u>

Well That's Weird

"Ma'am! Ma'am! Are you ok?!" A concerned voice asked, piercing the black veil between reality and her unconscious state.

She groaned, her green eyes fluttering open. The sun was gone. The only light that remained came from a flashlight pointed at the ground next to her.

How long have I been laying here for the sun to have gone down? She wondered, bracing herself up on her elbows. Pressing fully into a sitting position, she was able to make out the face that peered through the darkness. He was a kindly looking older gentleman who's brow was wrinkled in genuine concern.

"What time is it?" Hayden asked, rubbing her sore hip.

"Are you ok?" The man repeated in earnest.

"Um, I think so. I don't feel pain anywhere besides the bumps and bruises from my fall."

"Why were you here so far away from your car? I wouldn't have known where to look for you if it weren't for your dog."

"My dog?" She asked in bewilderment.

The look of confusion pasted on her face made him hesitate.

"I hope I didn't just put a monster that didn't belong to you in your truck, but I didn't want him to get hit. To be honest, I almost didn't stop. He scared the ever-living crap outta me; standing on the road barking at me like he was. I'm pretty sure he wouldn't have left that post even if I hadn't stopped. Here let me help you up," he said, offering his weathered hand to assist her.

Hayden gratefully accepted the help, not knowing yet if her legs would fully support her weight or betray her.

I'm a decent drive away from my house. It couldn't possibly be Bérg. But what other monster of a Pitbull is there around here? She pondered.

The ditch she'd so nimbly jumped just hours before, proved a bigger challenge on the return trip, forcing her to rely heavily on him for support. As she crested the side nearest the road, two sets of headlights shone on them from the shoulder. It took a moment for her vision to adjust in the face of the blinding lights before she could see inside her truck. The sound she'd heard when she first came to, finally made sense. There sat Bérg, pawing desperately at the door. He seemed to have a personal vendetta against it, as it kept him from doing his job. His anxious warbles made their way through metal and glass. It was a sound that Hayden had never heard him make until now.

"He must be really worried. You put him in there, so I would assume that you aren't afraid of him," Hayden said politely. " I'm going to let him out now."

She pulled on the handle and as soon as the latch released, he shouldered his way out of the vehicle, practically mauling her with affectionate snuffles. Bérg circled, wagging his whip of a tail, then bowed and stretch directly in front of her.

"It's ok buddy. I'm ok! You're such a good boy to come find me," she said, bending to scratch his head.

"He certainly is happy to see you," the man noted in amusement. "Do you live close? I would assume you do because your car doors were closed. I can't imagine he opened them to get out and then closed it behind him."

He chuckled at himself, reminding Hayden of the endearing nature that was so familiar from grandfatherly figures in her life.

"It doesn't make sense," she puzzled. "I live a good half hour drive down into the foothills from here. I don't understand how he could've known where I was."

"That does seem like quite the distance for a pup to go, but not too far outside of normal for me to believe it. How long have you been here? Can you drive or do you want me to call emergency?" He offered.

"I was heading home from work…" She hesitated, trying to remember the exact details. "I left at around six and drove for about an hour. Then I… I" Her face squinched up as the memory came flooding back. "Wait.. the sunset! Did you see it? I'm sorry, I don't know your name and I must know the name of my would-be rescuer," she finished, in her best Sicilian accent.

Recognition crossed his face followed by a lop-sided smirk. He must have understood where she got that from due to his reaction, but he left it unaddressed.

"Well, I couldn't exactly leave you laying there all alone," he shrugged. "So… what you're saying is, you've been here since sunset? It's nine o'clock now. Are you sure you don't need an ambulance?!" His incredulous response rang out.

"I really think I'm ok," Hayden responded, absentmindedly rubbing a plethora of mosquito bites that had begun to itch. "I think I can make it home. I just need sleep. What's your name? I would like to thank you with it."

"Alec, Alec Porter at your service Ma'am. Pleased to meet you."

When their hands met, the warmth of his on her cold skin brought some comfort. Bérg seemed wary of Alec but not altogether unfriendly. He paced and whined, dancing until he'd placed himself directly between them.

"Well thank you very much Alec, for stopping to check on me and taking care of Bérg. We both appreciate the help, but I think we'll head home. I'm very tired and I need to crash."

Bérg, who seemed to understand exactly what Hayden had said, bounced his way over to the door. He stood, his every muscle tensed—those brown eyes staring her down as he waited to be let in.

"Can we at least exchange phone numbers so you can text me when you get home safely? If it's not too intrusive of course," he amended" It really would make me feel more comfortable since you don't want to go get checked out."

Hayden chuckled, "You sound like my Mum. Let me put it in your phone and I'll send a text to myself, so I have the number."

A relieved smile spread across his face, smoothing some of his well-earned wrinkles.

"It's good to hear you chuckle. I look forward to getting your text. What may I call you?"

"Oh, I'm sorry. My name is Hayden. But you didn't answer if you happen to see tonight's sunset," she reminded him.

"I saw some of it, but I'm afraid I was too busy at the time to really notice," he responded.

"You didn't see any lightning though?"

Alec's quizzical look told Hayden the answer before he offered it.

"No, I can't say that I did. Maybe it's just because there were mountains blocking the majority of it."

Hayden didn't want to give Alec any further reasons to be concerned, so she didn't tell him about her experience. Thanking him again, she opened the passenger door for Bérg.

The remaining stretch of their drive home was uneventful. Hayden felt stronger and more like herself with each passing mile. She pulled in the driveway, remembering to send a quick text to Alec. When they finally walked through the door she was met with the kind of yowl she'd never heard Calliope utter before.

"That makes two out of two pets making weird sounds tonight," she noted as Calliope stalked toward her from the living room.

Bérg couldn't contain himself upon seeing her, bowing and panting happily in front of the agitated feline.

"Honey I'm so sorry I wasn't here to give you your canned food tonight. How about a little more than usual to make up for it?"

Cal's ears flicked forward as she continued stalking Hayden in stiff legged circles. The agitation that poured from her was palpable. Her tiny wet nose had barely brushed against Hayden's arm when unexpectedly, small bridges of electricity reached out and snapped her on the face. She screamed, arching and simultaneously jumping back with her tail puffed out as big as she could make it. A gasp escaped Hayden's lips as an equally surprised reaction sent her sprawling backwards.

"WHAT on earth was that?!" She cried, staring in disbelief at her arm. "Maybe the lightning bolt left some static electricity? Good lord, what am I saying? I got hit by lightning and I'm alive. 'By rights I shouldn't even be here!'"

Her eyes probed the area, trying in vain to see if there was visual evidence of anything unusual. Nothing stood out. Not a burn, a scratch, or even a mark on her skin. She tentatively pulled at the collar of her shirt to inspect where the lightning had appeared to also come out of her chest. Maybe something was there? Nope. Nothing. Not a single shred of evidence to prove that the ordeal had happened at all. "So weird, but ok. Better than the potential alternative I guess. Let me get that food for you Cal, now that I know I'm not on the brink of death," she joked. Calliope threw a disgusted look her way, settling into a frantic bath as she waited for Hayden to make good on her promise. Her distrust was clear as day, with the furtive glances she cast across the counter and the displeased swish of her tail.

Bérg's automatic feeder hadn't been set up that morning, so due to the unexpected turn of events he was sure to be extra hungry. She tossed in an additional scoop as an offering of thanks to her best friend. "I bet you're famished! You ran such a long way to find me, but HOW did you find me?!" she puzzled. "It would be so much easier if the two of you could just talk," she sighed. Then, remembering how far Bérg had actually run to find her, she crouched down by his bowl that was now licked clean. "Let me check out your paws. I'm sorry, I'm a terrible mom and an even worse Vet at the moment."

Bérg reached out his paw, resting it gingerly on her leg. He softly whined, wagging his tail to tell her forgiveness was already on the table. The only spot of concern that she found was a small sore. She expertly wrapped it with gauze and ointment to protect it from further injury. Now that her babies were taken care of she could finally get the sleep she so sorely needed.

****

Hayden lay on her back staring at the ceiling when she heard the creak of the closet door.

"Is Calliope roaming the house this late? Maybe the shock really upset her more than I thought."

With plans to go check on her charge, she tried to sit up but felt instead as though she were glued to the bed. Just like earlier that night, even her fingers wouldn't cooperate when she tried to wiggle them. The door creaked again. Left without the ability to turn her head, she rolled her eyes in its direction just in time to see a pale emaciated hand emerge from the blackness. Its fingers made no sound as they each wrapped soundlessly, one by one, around the edge of the door. Her fear laden breathing increased as the realization hit. She couldn't run. The figure emerged, covered in a tattered black robe that seemed to move in a non-existent wind. A faint blue light emulated from within the robes revealing a subtle outline of the creature underneath. Silently, slowly, it glided across the room toward her bed, electricity crackling around its skeletal form. With each creeping inch more features became clear. It was humanoid in appearance with sunken eyes that glowed in an eerie blue light, and a mouth stretching from cheekbone to cheek bone that gaped open to reveal sharp teeth. These looked as though they'd purposefully been filed down to sharp points. From behind the sharpened fangs, a forked tongue flitted in and out between its thin lips which were pulled back into a foul grimace. Faintly, through the tattered cloth, the rest of its form appeared looking just as shriveled as its hands and arms had. Hayden tried desperately to move something, anything! But she was unable to change her predicament, having to watch helplessly as the figure reached the foot of her bed. It floated upward, the evil grin widening until it paused to hover mere feet over her. She tried to scream but could get no sound to escaped her lips. The only scream she heard came from the creature as its maw opened ever wider. Its clawed hands reached for her throat and a thick black ooze dripped from the ugly face taking on a life of its own. The suffocating goop began to wrap itself around her face, threatening to take what little breath she had left.

******

Hayden woke with a start. Although she knew now it was only a dream, her chest heaved with the memory of her fear. If it had been real, she wouldn't be able to move and she had just successfully stretched. Throwing her feet over the side of her bed, she turned toward the closet before losing her courage to look. The door was securely closed. Thankful that she'd confirmed the dream state, she breathed a deep sigh dropping her head into her hands. It had felt so real. More than any of her night terrors in the past. She checked the time on her phone. It was too early to get up yet.

"I have to grab some water," she said out loud, hoping it would chase the frightening image out of her head.

If she didn't wake up at least a little, the likelihood of falling back into the nightmare was high. She wandered out of her room to see Calliope sitting at the end of the hallway, as if she'd been expecting Hayden to go to the kitchen.

"Cal you scared me!" She whispered. "And why am I whispering in my own house?" she continued whispering.

The cat jumped on the counter, staring unblinking with her signature judgmental gaze, her tail swishing back and forth. When Hayden was certain she wouldn't be returning to the dream, Cal followed her back to the bedroom curling up in the blankets near her beloved owner's feet. But even with that calming presence the rest of the night offered only fitful sleep.

Even in the face of a new day, the dream did nothing but pile on feelings of helplessness. "Come on girl, it was just a dream," she self-admonished. "But I do need to shake this... and there's only one thing that is sure to help," she said, staring out over the backyard.

Then, in a sudden moment of decision, she yanked the backpack off the footboard of her bed, and began filling it with snacks and water for a full days hike.

Bérg, sensing that she was getting ready to leave, nudged her hand, interrupting her frantic packing.

"Oh no buddy, you can't come today," she replied, her voice dropping low with compassion. "The wound is still too fresh. You'll only make it worse. I just want you to avoid further discomfort bud."

Berg's ears drooped in defeat, followed by his tail. She tried to bribe him with a butt scratch and some extra treats and kisses. But he remained unhappy with the command to stay at home, making an exaggerated show of looking forlorn as he sat obediently at the top of the hill. When Hayden was sure there were enough trees between them, she cast a backward glance—just in time to see him turn toward the house. He would probably just lie down in his favorite spot on the porch until she returned.

Not far into the familiar countryside, the mountains did what they did best for her soul and she began to regain a smattering of peace. Her favorite spot was a small lake hidden in the hills where very few traveled–with the exception of experienced hikers or the occasional unlucky novice. It stayed secluded from the majority because of how far into the hills it was, and the fact that no trails led to it save the one she'd blazed.

The sun's warmth tussled with the cooler breezes of Autumn, whipping fallen leaves into miniature tornadoes before dropping them back onto the forest floor. Finally, after what felt like a longer hike than usual, she heard the swish of small waves rolling over a rocky beach. The final tree line posing as prickly sentinels, gave her just enough room to walk through their defenses. She pulled together a generous layer of pine needles into a makeshift bed, then laid down, placing her hands behind her head as a pillow.

As she lay there letting the rays soak into every cell of her body, a nearly blinding glint caught her eye. Brushing it off as a reflection on the water, she moved to scratch her face where a strand of hair had tickle her nose. There it was again... the glint. But this time it was quite obvious that it came from her arm. She reached over to brush it away, thinking maybe it was sweat. After all, she had just exerted herself by carrying the make-shift bed onto the beach. The sweatshirt that she'd clung to so desperately at the beginning of her hike, had long since been tied around her waist.

An uncomfortable warmth started at her palm, slowly traveling upward. Confused, she sat upright to stare intently as the sensation moved toward the shoulder, then her chest. It seemed to be traveling along the lines where she knew with certainty that the lightning had–last night. "What?! What is happening?!" she asked incredulously as she pawed at her arms. *As if that would have helped*, she thought. Because she was sure this was just another weird dream.

All of a sudden, Hayden felt all strength leave her body. She sat there, feeling helpless as she blinked at her arms–frozen in place by her weakened state. Then, just as quickly as it had disappeared, it returned with a vengeance–bringing with it the itching that had been plaguing her this week. This time, it was almost too intense to handle—from her palms to her chest, burning as though her flesh had been set on fire. She massaged the shimmering tracks vigorously, trying in vain to rid herself of the nearly agonizing pain.

With a sudden rush of energy, a ball of bright blue light erupted, forming between her outstretched palms. And though she was shocked, she was also relieved—because as it appeared, the discomfort in her arms promptly vanished. In a moment of panic and instinct, she shook her hands.

The light sailed away from her, finding a final resting spot as it crashed into a large boulder. The loud crack of dense granite splitting in two echoed through the tranquility of the mountains. For a brief second the lines on her arms glowed brighter and then faded before disappearing altogether. *I think I'm losing my mind. Did that really just happen or am I still dreaming?!* she wondered apprehensively. But the gentle rustle of wind, the prickle of a pine needle bed, the delicious warmth of the sun, and the peaceful sounds of nature assured her she was very much awake.

She had no choice but to rest for a while before turning homeward. Once she felt that she had regained her strength, she started the return hike, filled with trepidation. Too many unbelievable things were haunting her steps lately. *Who would believe any of this? And if I did tell someone, who could I trust not to ship me off to the looney bin? Even Mum would have a good reason.* She pondered dryly.

Her intense frustration spurred her into a brisker gait. Consumed in her thoughts, she picked her way up the familiar path. Every so often, she thought she saw a shadow flickering between the trees—but whenever she turned to look, there was nothing there.

As she neared home, her thoughts turned to her growling stomach. The idea of smelling meat smoking on the grill was beyond tantalizing, making her mouth water in anticipation. When she got home, she pulled together a simple mix of vegetables in tin foil that was placed carefully on the hot grate. Bérg stayed glued to her side, with generous amounts of drool dripping from his jowls like bouncing rubber bands. She was about half way through making the chicken breasts, to the point where she wrapped bacon around them. This was usually the part where Calliope would come running with her demanding meow, but strangely, she didn't show. It was very out of character.

"Cal! Calliope where are you?!" Hayden called out. "She can't resist bacon. Where the hell could she have wandered off to?"

Bérg's hackles raised as he took off behind the house. She could hear the echo of his deep and menacing bark, the kind he typically saved for dangerous intruders. She followed him, hoping that she could get him to stop. Unless she was right next to him when he was in this state, he rarely heard her pleas to quiet down. Then a sudden gust of wind whipped dried leaves into his face, something that didn't seem to faze him in the least. He vocalized loudly again for a moment, then his whole body began to wag. Hayden saw her tail twitching before the pitch-black sleekness that was Calliope, came strolling nonchalantly over the hill.

"What in the hell?! The whole goddamn world is going crazy!" Hayden groaned, throwing her hands up. "Since when do you wander the mountains and how the hell did you get out anyway? You're too small. Something will get you!" Cal, completely unbothered by Hayden's outburst, sashayed over to the door. She sat primly as though nothing were out of the ordinary and Hayden's complaints meant nothing to her. "It's the lack of good sleep and it seems to be affecting you guys too. I need to be bright eyed and bushy tailed for our big day tomorrow," Hayden reassured herself.

And true to her words, she plopped herself in bed earlier than usual that night.

7

To Meet a New Friend

Saturday morning brought an air of excitement Hayden hadn't felt in a while. Carefully, she backed the truck up to the two-horse trailer, bursting with pride when she did it perfectly on her first try. Double and triple checking all the connections, she stood back to survey it one last time. She wanted to be 100% sure everything was going to flow smoothly.

Inside the trailer a hanging net filled with fresh hay and a small feed bag full of grain were strategically placed to entice the expected occupant. The bag of sugar cubes she'd shoved in her pocket were just an extra measure of a sweet bribe. With all these tricks in place, she hoped they would ensure a pleasant trailer experience. This group of horses was from a rescue, so they tended to be less predictable. With no history to go on, she knew the risk of finding one that experienced trailer trauma was higher than usual.

Bérg danced around her in expectation while Calliope stared from her favorite cozy spot in the bay window. She sat like a perfect lady, with her tail wrapped around her feet, the sun soaking into her dark coat.

"Bérg, sweety. You can't come with me today. I know you're such a good boy, but there will be a lot of horses that are potentially scared of dogs. I don't want you or any of them to get hurt. You just keep an eye on things here, and make sure Cal doesn't wander off again."

Bérg looked up at her in dismay, surveying her cautiously. The enthusiasm of his tail diminished, then it drooped and stopped wagging. Hayden felt a twinge of remorse that she couldn't grant him his greatest wish two days in a row, but it was the best choice for everyone involved. She wrapped her arms around his giant neck burying her head in the softness of his fur.

"It'll be ok baby; you're still going to be my favorite."

Calliope growled, loudly hissing her protest—a sound that Hayden easily heard through the open window.

"Oh sure, like you actually care now your highness," Hayden said, rolling her eyes at the small black figure. "You know I love your aloof butt too."

A small ranch held the monthly auction just outside the city. There were corrals filled with fencing, troughs, buckets, and all manner of necessities for owning a horse. Excited people busied themselves looking at the available equipment as the auction for those items happened before the horses. Children's voices called back and forth to each other in anticipation of the day's events. Although many auctions were behind her, this time the hustle and bustle left her nerves raw—and she asked herself for the thousandth time if she was really ready for such a big commitment.

"Having second thoughts?" Came a familiar voice behind her.

She spun around to see who had addressed her and instantly recognized his face.

"Alec!" she cried in pleasant surprise. "What are the odds of running into each other so soon? Are you here for equipment? A horse?"

Alec's warm smile lit up his face. "I'm actually the auctioneer for the animal portion. I filled in for the other guy because he got sick."

"I hope it's nothing too serious," Hayden offered her concern.

"Nah, he'll be fine," Alec responded with a wave of his hand. "Speaking of... How are you feeling? You look well."

"I'm feeling just fine actually. I even went out for a long hike yesterday and I made it there and back again," she said, a twinkle of nostalgia in her eye.

"Did you just throw a quote at me?" Alec smirked. "You did it the other night too. Gotta say that I'm on board with that. Most people don't seem to recognize anything that I'm quoting. Which makes it far less fun for me."

"Well, I think we will get along just fine then," she laughed. "Not to juke the subject, but do you ever look at the horses before you have to work?"

Alec leaned nonchalantly on the fence, squinting in the face of the afternoon sun. "I do tend to familiarize myself with whatever I'm auctioning. Would you like some company while you meet some of our beauties? I can tell you their quirks if that will help," trying not to come off as intrusive, he added, "It's completely up to you, and no hard feelings if the answer is no. I know how people can get when it comes to meeting their horse."

Hayden took a moment to let the idea run through her head before answering, "You know what? I would actually love the company! My Mum wasn't able to make it today, so it would be nice to have a parent of sorts with me," she coughed to cover up her chagrin. She hadn't meant to make an age reference, but it was already out of her mouth and she couldn't take it back.

"Oh is that how it's going to be?" he asked, his tone one of mock offence. "At least no one is calling me a whippersnapper!"

Hayden was relieved that he had taken it in stride, and their shared laugh smoothed away her remaining feelings of apprehension.

Paint, roan, bay, chestnut, he looks like a dilute Appaloosa. Hayden went over the colors and breeds she was familiar with, in her head. They were all so beautiful; their graceful fluid movements, the powerful muscles rippling under the sheen of their freshly washed coats. So lost had she become in appreciating their magnificence, that she jumped when Alec's voice broke through her admiration.

"When I saw you the other night, I thought you looked slightly familiar. Have you been to these auctions before?" he asked.

"Actually, I have. I started coming about six months ago so I could have all of the necessary fencing and such before I decided to bring a new family member home. Plus, I wanted to see what kinds of horses to expect when the time did come," Hayden turned toward a different corral. "I think I'm putting it together, 'cause something seemed strangely familiar about you too. Now that I think about it, I remember seeing you work a couple of them this summer," she concluded.

He nodded. "Today should be interesting for you then. When I found you two nights ago, I was actually heading home from helping with something here," he glanced over to gauge her response.

"Why would it be interesting, and what were…?" But before Hayden could finish her question, she saw her. And beyond the shadow of a doubt, she knew this was who Alec was talking about.

A loud whiny followed by a hollow bang, came from a paddock on the far side of the grassy opening. A group hastily retreated from the fence, opening up just enough space for Hayden to see where all the commotion was coming from.

"That right there is the answer to both those questions," Alec pointed. "That mare was a handful when she was brought here. A local rancher said she just showed up out of the blue a few days ago, then started causing problems with his other horses. No one's come forward to claim her, so we thought this would be as good a place as any to find her a home."

She stood at about 17 hands and was jet black from the tips of her ears to the smooth shiny surface of her hooves. Feathers lay over each of her four hooves, then wrapped around the backside of her front legs. Her tail swept the ground, flowing as she moved. A luscious mane flipped back and forth over her neck with every toss of her massive head. She was larger than most of the other stock, but not quite large enough to be considered a draft horse. Her movements were graceful despite the bulk of muscles rippling underneath her sweat dampened coat. It took Hayden a moment to realize that she hadn't taken a breath since her eyes came to rest on the magnificence of the beast in front of her.

"Wow," she whistled, her voice filled with awe. "Now she's a quality you don't see here often."

Alec smirked. "Somehow, I expected that. And it makes complete sense after meeting Bérg."

"Now wait a minute," Hayden protested, stopping to catch Alec's eye. "I didn't say I was going to bring her home."

"Uh-huh," Alec sounded unconvinced. "I may not know you very well, but I've watched plenty of people with that exact look on their face. You're the kind of person that needs more…" His voice trailed off.

"More Cowbell?" Hayden's amused smile tugged at the corners of her mouth.

Alec grinned back at her. "I knew you'd get it."

Hayden hated when other people were able to predict her decisions. She couldn't say why, but it always seemed to rub her the wrong way. And here she was, with a total stranger that seemed to know what she was thinking. Right now, she needed to be alone with her thoughts.

"I want to get a closer look at her, do you mind if we part ways?"

She asked as politely as she could—careful not to sound offensive. After all, he had been open to Hayden turning down his offer to accompany her before.

"Of course!" He responded quickly, to her relief. "I completely understand. I have some other things I need to take care of before I start babbling anyway. I'm sure we'll meet again," then with a cheery wave, he left.

Hayden's movements were deliberately muted. She didn't want to cause any more stress to this poor animal who seemed overwhelmed with the unfamiliar surroundings. Something drew her toward the paddock where the majority of curious observers had moved on. Ideally, she didn't want anyone else's fear to affect the mood. Less people meant less emotions leaching into the atmosphere.

The stark contrast between the beast in front of her compared to the other tenants was more notable the closer she got. But something was off. If she were truly this upset her ears would have been pinned back, not to mention her frantic activity would have been enough to work up an oral lather. Her eyes also seemed to betray a calmness under the facade. And those were their own kind of unique. Hayden had spent hours poring over books and volunteering at stables to arm herself with as much knowledge as possible. There was no doubt in her mind that this horse had a tiger eye. Though that was unique enough in itself, the color was even more striking. As far as Hayden knew, bright blue did not exist as a pigment for such an iris. Then there was the eerie similarity to Calliope's.

Small careful steps brought her ever closer to the fence holding the horse captive. She paced back and forth, stomping, tossing her head, and snorting dramatically. A gust of wind kicked up, blowing Hayden's hair into her face. Her vision was momentarily obscured, and in that moment, she missed the change in the inky beast. When her hair fell back to her shoulders, she froze in her tracks. The mare seemed to be staring straight into her soul.

But the calm was short lived as she reared up. Her front hooves slammed back to the ground and dirt flew as she dug in to gain purchase, making a beeline for the fence. She crashed chest first into the weathered boards, never once taking her eyes off Hayden. The remaining crowd scattered, making a wider birth as the fence shook with the force of her powerful body. Even Hayden had been nervous, but she stood her ground, not giving even a centimeter of satisfaction to the beast.

"Thank goodness for those boards being as strong as they are," she said calmly. "Hey pretty lady! Are you truly upset, or are you just putting on a show for your audience?" Hayden could've sworn the responding whinny sounded strangely like a laugh. "Is it really so bad? What happened to you? I hope no one treated you poorly," she continued her soft monologue. "It's ok. You're gonna be ok. I want to be your friend, not hurt you."

"Ma'am, do you have a death wish?" A voice with a heavy southern accent called out from the crowd.

Hayden put her hand up in his direction, the silent gesture enough to quiet him.

"Not now, I've got this," she said forcefully, dismissing his interjection without so much as a backward glance.

Only ten feet away now. Hayden could feel the heat of her breath with every snort. The mare's neck was arched elegantly–stretched over the fence–almost close enough for Hayden to touch .

"Stop playing it up so much. You need her to like you."

The voice echoed through Hayden's thoughts, halting her slow approach. *Breathe Hayden… breathe,* she thought as her heart skipped a beat. *Someone in the audience just talked and it sounded like it was in your head. Stay focused.* She took another few steps and reached out a trembling hand toward the soft nose. *Good lord. It feels like I'm Hiccup.* But even that thought didn't sway her. She was committed to the role now.

With eyes closed, she held her hand just within reach of the mare's face–but still far enough that she could safely retreat if necessary.

"I don't understand. Is this some Earth custom?"

Hayden resisted the urge to jump in surprise. This voice sounded more demanding.

"She likes movies. I watched this one with her. You have to touch your nose to her hand," the first one replied.

Hayden's eyes flew open. Although faint, there was no mistaking it–she'd heard someone else's conversation. As her vision cleared, she found herself staring directly into the murky dark pools of the mare's eyes. There was something different about them. A shadow that seemed to be lurking just beneath the surface. Then came the soft brush of the mare's muzzle across Hayden's palm, and with it, a sudden rush—energy drawn straight from her body. Blue electricity crackled between them. With a sharp bob of her massive head, the mare reared up and resumed her pacing.

Hayden looked around, hoping that no one saw what just transpired. She scanned the audience wondering if a side effect of being struck by lightning was being able to read people's thoughts. Never mind the strange way it seemed to match up with her circumstances. *Everyone was far enough away. Maybe they didn't see the electricity, or my reaction.* This time she knew the voice was her own. *Do I just need to accept all this strange shit as normal now? If it was just animals, why didn't this happen with Bérg?*

The time had passed more quickly than Hayden realized. A quick peek at her watch. She'd left just enough time to head toward the auctioneer shelter. They always left the 'lost causes' for last, which she was certain the horse she'd just encountered would be considered. Horses were led to the auction platform one-by-one, most of them going to families that were eager to give them a place to permanently call home. Hayden was always fascinated with the speed at which the auctioneer seemed to be able to speak and Alec didn't disappoint. When it came time for the black mares auction, only one other person was raising their paddle against her. A final bid of $4000 put the high energy animal in her care. She was quite certain that her asking price was much less than a horse of this breed was worth, but it was still by far the highest offer of the day. At least the money would benefit future rescues. And in that knowledge she confidently wrote the check.

Hayden's peace offering of sugar cubes seemed to curb the horse's fierce demeanor. To her surprise, she allowed the bridle to be slipped over her head without much of a struggle. If she hadn't gone through the whole process with eyes on her prize, she would have thought the horse that walked into the trailer was a different one than she'd observed in the corral.

"What are you playing at?" Hayden whispered, eyeing her warily as she closed the rear gate.

As she rounded the trailer, Hayden spotted Alec striding across the dusty yard. He moved with purpose, his expression nearly a scowl in its intensity. She called out to him, and the moment he saw her, the scowl melted into a warm smile.

"You sure seem to have a way with oversized brutes," he grinned, raising his eyebrows in an unspoken "I told you so."

Hayden returned the smile, knowing exactly what he'd left unsaid. "All these extraordinary… friends seem to keep finding me. I feel like I'm supposed to give them a safe place to land," she dug around in her purse for the truck keys and Alec took a step back.

"Well I think you're the perfect person for the job! Good luck to you, and I hope you feel free to reach out if you need anything," he offered.

Then with a friendly handshake and a warm goodbye, they parted ways.

Over the next couple weeks, all her time was split between work and training a horse she wasn't sure would ever allow a saddle on her back. During the week Mum would stay at her place, which helped to displace some of the guilt she felt for being gone so much. Hayden made it painfully clear that Clara's only job was to give more carrots and sugar than was healthy, to try and sweeten up the big brute. Secondary regret began to creep in as she realized just how nice it would have been to take on this new hurdle after her current assignment was up. But she'd already made a commitment, and when it came to her animals she didn't believe in going back on them.

The name Tormaigh kept tiptoeing through her thoughts like little whispers whenever she let herself truly relax. So one evening, she gave in to her curiosity and decided to look it up.

"Thunder Spirit. How perfect for such a beautiful horse, and it really fits with the power she exudes. It's settled then Calliope," Hayden declared, giving the cat a squeeze and a kiss. "That shall be her new name."

One evening, Hayden had to stay especially late at work. The stack of charts on her desk told the story of a wildly busy day. She probably wouldn't make it home until well past ten. If she *had* been there on time, she would've seen two figures standing just inside the barn. Their skin was dark gray, obscuring them in the lengthening shadows of night.

The first was smaller, her long legs and lithe figure a striking contrast to the bulk of her companion. A sleek tail swished behind her, back and forth, just like a cat's. Her hands looked human—until you noticed the claws: nails so sharp they bordered on monstrous. Instead of the awkward oval shape of human ears, a pair of cat-like ones sat atop her head, constantly twitching, always alert. Her facial features were nearly human, despite the ashen-gray skin. All except the teeth— razor-sharp and built to tear into flesh.

The other creature stood several inches taller than the cat woman. A luscious mane of hair flowed from the crown of her head down to the middle of her back. Horse-like ears flicked back and forth on either side of her head, alert and restless. Her long tail, thick with coarse hair, nearly brushed the ground. More muscular than her companion, her legs bent slightly backward just above where her ankles should have been. Instead of feet, glossy hooves reflected the moonlight, while her hands remained unmistakably human. Tufts of hair adorned her ankles and wrists, with a faint trail trailing up the backs of her arms.

When Hayden pulled into her driveway at almost midnight, Calliope was curled up on Tormaigh's back. She in turn was laying down and snuggled into the generous bed of straw that Hayden provided fresh each day. "I'm so glad you two are getting along," she murmured. But neither of them stirred as they were fast asleep. "Probably tuckered out from a whole day of nothing. Next week we start trying to actually ride. Then we'll all have a reason to be tired," Before she headed inside, she called over her shoulder. "Cal, I'm still making your warm food in the morning!"

<u>8</u>

Humble Beginnings

All Calliope knew was the small village she called home. In Quipar they grew Millet and Barley. These grains had proven to be a hearty crop, thriving in their sandy soil like others could not. But since this was the 2nd summer with so little rain, the crops had begun to suffer, providing much less than the villages around them required. She'd lost track of the last time a soothing drop of rain had touched her skin. They'd tried to bring in water supply from the underground springs, but none of their tricks would matter if it weren't replenished soon.

At a very young age, she had learned that they didn't grow the crops for themselves, but rather to be brought to a hub where they would be distributed to the nearest villages. The Xard were in charge of this distribution. Being a cruel lot who carried out the even crueler wishes of Lord Onyx, this usually meant they would take more than their fair share. And in a drought, that meant the imbalance of produce would affect the people even more severely.

The Superiors had originally been a line of defense between their subjects and the ruthlessness of the Xard. But over time, the offerings from Lord Onyx to make their lives more comfortable by serving him superseded their morality. They turned into pompous, greedy rulers, whom the villagers learned it was better to keep their distance from. From their vantage point, they acted as an extension of the Xard and for their loyalty–Lord Onyx rewarded them with extra comforts.

Calliope shared a home with her parents and two brothers on the quieter side of town. She liked it that way. There was enough space for a small garden which they shared with others whenever extra could be spared. But this season with the drought persisting, they had barely enough for themselves.

The twins were five winters and one fall younger than her, making her as the older sister, responsible for their protection. And it was a role that she took very seriously. Often when provisions were especially scarce, she would slip some of her own food onto their plates. They thankfully never seemed to catch on as the last thing she wanted was for anyone to make a fuss over it. Seeing her brothers thrive was her highest priority because in the grand scheme of their simple life, it mattered to her.

They had only seen five Springs when Calliope first took them into the woods on the outskirts of town, where at the same age, she herself had started learning to trap small game. Now, five Springs later, they had become skilled enough to do the work on their own. It was how they chose to help with the growing problem of dwindling resources. The small business didn't give them much extra but with both the inventory and extra coin, they were able to help those with less means. And to her family, that meant so much more.

When they weren't busy learning to hunt, working on academics, or taking their turn in the fields, they would drift toward a small home at the heart of town. Inside lived the Lore Keeper, who spun the most captivating stories of their ancestors transforming into great beasts. Her words painted such vivid pictures that Calliope and her brothers could listen for hours, completely entranced, with the other children from the village. She always ended their gatherings with a mischievous twinkle in her eye.

"I'm so old, I remember when they were still around, you know?" she would say, her voice teasing.

"Yes, Lore Keeper, we know!" they'd reply in unison, the children's laughter rising as they tumbled into fits of giggles.

As seasons passed and their trips to the Lore Keeper became fewer, Calliope was left longing for a time before the Xard presence and the dark days they had to endure under Lord Onyx's rule. Sometimes she would lay awake at night daydreaming that the Angel Adelphiana had chosen to bless her with mastery over the shadows.

She would be a fierce Morphé and avenge the throne that King Duweot had so savagely been torn from. Then she would find a long-lost descendant and stand shoulder to shoulder as they took back what was rightfully theirs. But alas, they had not seen a morphing in many tens of seasons and the rumors of a surviving heir were just that. Rumors. And since Lord Onyx had ordered the execution of those found to possess any sort of magic, even if someone had gone through the change–she was sure it would never reach her ears.

Calliope began to feel alone as it had been some time since her friends shared in the enthusiasm for their ancestry. They'd slowly moved toward the belief that these were just stories for children. Something the Lore Keeper did to keep them entertained and out of trouble. So after losing her friends to confide in, she turned to Mother.

"You have no idea what you're so glibly talking about here. Those ideas. That kind of talk. It will bring the Xard to our door," Mother said, her tone increasing sharply.

Taken aback by the sudden shift in behavior, she went on the defensive.

"Mother," she retorted in exasperation. "Don't you think that's a mite embellished. The Xard are awful, but what do they care about these stories?"

For the first time in her short life, Calliope watched as the woman who had mastered the art of hiding emotions, crumbled into a state of grief, effectively shifting her own attitude to one of concern.

"You look scared Mother. What happened? What haven't you told me?"

Mother's legs gave out as she sank onto the couch, her face creased with worry.

"You had an aunt. She was my older sister," she said wearily, beckoning Calliope to sit next to her. "I suppose you are old enough to finally hear this, but I don't want you to say anything to your brothers. They already have enough to worry about with those thieving mongrels roaming our streets. They don't need this adding to their burden. Promise me."

"I promise Mother. I promise on the sacred Heart Of Dagrune."

Calliope closed her eyes and kissed her fingers, touching them to Mother's forehead then her own. This was their custom to show how closely they bound themselves to their vow.

"Thank you. I need you to really take to heart what I'm about to tell you," she began earnestly. "When Roeggnia was about your age she felt the same way. All she ever talked about was bringing back the days when our women were the right hand of justice. She became so obsessed that others in the village began to whisper about her," Amara balled up her fist, placing it in front of her mouth, trying in vain to swallow the lump filling her throat. "Those whispers grew into rumors that caught the attention of the Xard. Then just before her 18th Autumn, I came home from harvesting the fields to find the Xard sigil on our door," her eyes watered and her voice trembled as she fought with the weight of what she was about to recount.

"It's okay, take your time," Calliope said softly.

"I apologize. It has been many seasons since I told this story last. It never gets easier," she cleared her throat, shifting uncomfortably. "What I found when I went inside I will never be able to clear from my mind. Both your Grandparents lay lifeless in the middle of the house. I found a notice still clutched in Father's hand stained with his blood. It accused her of treason, of conspiring to overthrow Lord Onyx," her tone changed, adding a hint of deep-seated anger. "The irony of it was that she never said anything that would have given a single person that idea. She had only ever been fascinated with our history and thought it would be extraordinary to possess the Angels power. She wasn't the kind of woman that would want to start a revolution. I believe that they would have darkened her light where she stood if that were true—just as they did with my parents. I think she must have known something, because there is only ever one reason for the Xard to seize someone. Especially one so young and I'm quite certain you don't need me to say more on the subject. I'm only telling you this now to beg of you. Please be more cautious lest our family's history repeat itself."

Mother had given Calliope much to consider, and though she longed to ask more, she hesitated, unsure if it would reopen an old wound. It all made sense now why she rarely talked about them and also why she had moved from her birthplace to Quipar. That kind of trauma would most likely have put Calliope herself in the same mindset. But there was one difference between Mothers story and hers. She couldn't rid herself of the desire to become part of something bigger.

Every action they took in the village only offered temporary relief to the people—like feeding a dog with a flea infestation and expecting it would somehow rid the animal of parasites. They weren't making a difference at all. It was an assault to her heritage and their long history of bravery. She found herself imploring Adelphiana more often, begging her to see their plight and give them even the smallest glimmer of hope. But it seemed that the Angel couldn't hear her prayers as season after season, nothing changed.

As the morning of her birthday dawned leading into her 18th season of life, Calliope awoke with an odd feeling of apprehension twisting in her stomach. The sound of scratching in the main room had caught her attention. At first she brushed it off as the remnants of the dream she had just awoken from, but when it persisted, she bounced out of bed to investigate. No one else was awake, so she tip-toed as quietly as possible, not wanting to be the reason anyone lost a wink of sleep. When she reached the small door to their pantry, the usual spot where mice would frequent, she yanked it open.

"Well there was no intelligence in that," she thought to herself. "They're faster than me on my best day. Guess it's time to set some traps."

She closed the door, intent on grabbing one from the drawer on the opposite side of the room, but to her confusion, she could still hear the scratching just as plainly as before. Her movements should have at least scared it, or them, into hiding. Maybe it was time to widen her net, see if she could pinpoint where it was coming from. She walked the entirety of the small room, straining her ears to find if the noise was louder in any particular place. As she methodically moved about with no success, her building frustration got the better of her.

"Nothing that a brisk morning walk can't cure," she thought.

She stepped out to breath in the early autumn warmth. Her plan to set out at such an hour made a chance encounter with the Xard much less likely, but not altogether impossible. She kept one ear alert to anything unusual, and one on the birdsong symphony playing throughout the trees. They seemed more exuberant than usual this morning. It was proving to be an unexpected distraction as she struggled to concentrate on releasing her negative feelings. But despite her best efforts, she couldn't quite seem to settle the growing knot in her stomach.

Grass rustled loudly and the buzz from the wings of a busy bee tugged at her curiosity. How could she not investigate? More sounds that she wasn't used to hearing quite so well reached her ears. They gradually but steadily tempted her off the path where she'd promised herself she would not stray, until the chatter of metal against metal jolted her out of her investigative stupor.

"How did I..." But her whispered question trailed off as the ominous bulk of a Xard came into view. He was much farther than she expected considering how well she'd heard the jingle from his boots. So as inconspicuously as possible, she crept around the too small trunk. It would have to do, she thought nervously, since there was nothing else around that would serve as a proper hiding spot. But with every step he took nearer, she could plainly see that it would not be enough cover to avoid an encounter. Still she remained unmoving, frozen in the shadow lengthened by early sunlight. The pounding rush of blood in her ears got louder. He was within only a few steps of her hiding place now. She poised herself to run if necessary. If she didn't let him see her face and kept the wrap on her hair, she had a good chance of leaving him without sufficient evidence to apprehend anyone. But just as quickly as it had started, the ordeal ended when he walked by without so much as a glance in her direction.

As soon as his head disappeared over the next hill, she scurried back toward home, slowing only when her lungs could no longer support her efforts. As she caught her breath and rounded the final curve she heard it again, but this time much louder. The same sound that had been the reason for her abrupt departure this morning was teasing her again. She squinted, peering into the sparse offering of the nearby trees. Aha, she thought, watching carefully to match the squirrels movements with the sound. He must have had quite the pile of treasure to bury if he's been at it for this long.

She watched him idly for a moment, letting herself calm completely before invading Mother's peaceful mood. After all, she had just whispered about 'how beautiful the sunrise was.' Calliope's body went rigid, her eyes widening as the truth dawned on her. She mulled over how today, of all days, she could suddenly hear things she didn't think possible. And then there were the sights and smells that had been so distracting, not to mention how clearly she'd heard Mother's whisper just now. There could only be one explanation and it was one she feared would shatter Mothers peaceful morning.

9

Through Calliope's Eyes

Mother stood next to the washbasin, her hands gently resting on the counter. When Calliope got close enough, she could see the rising sun reflected in her untroubled stare. Having no desire to break the morning ritual, she sidled up next to her, resting an elbow on her shoulder. They stood there in silence together, Calliope patiently waiting for a break in the sunrise trance. Finally, she felt an arm snake around her waist as mother got up on tippy toes to plant a kiss on her cheek.

"Good morning dear daughter," Amara said, pulling the pot of nearly boiling water off the stove.

Amara dumped it in the wash basin, letting the heat start the process of cleansing dishes from the boys breakfast. In the time it had taken Calliope to return from her walk, they'd already made their way out to the fields with Father.

"So Father and the boys are already in the fields?" She asked the obvious.

Mother turned her attention from the dishes so quickly that her braids thwapped her in the face. There was something different in Calliope's tone, a tremble that told Mother the next words out of her daughters mouth would be heavily important.

"Out with-it Calliope. What's wrong?" she demanded.

Amara turned toward Calliope to study her face. She hated surprises, and the way Calliope's features were drawn, she worried it would be something she could not protect her from.

"I never could hide anything from you," Calliope said, a half-smile playing on her lips. "But I fear that your assumption is correct. Although calling it 'wrong' is not exactly how I feel about it."

As she dove into the mornings tale, being careful to add even the tiniest details, she watched Mother's expression grow more and more worried. When Calliope finished, Amara cupped her face between work hardened hands.

"Why does it have to be my baby. I thought it had ended with her," then without another word, she turned abruptly to yank open a drawer.

It was the one meaningless drawer that they'd dedicated as storage for odds and ends. Her hand hovered momentarily before she seemed to find some resolve, scraped a few things to the side and lifted a wooden panel at the bottom. The book she pulled out looked well worn, as if it were read often over many seasons. She clutched it tightly to her chest, her misty eyes glowing darkly with memories.

"This was Roeggnia's," she said shortly, placing the notebook in Calliope's hands. "Please guard this with your light. Whatever place you put all things that you didn't want me and Father to find. That's where this needs to go," Amara patted Calliope's hand. "That look on your face. I wasn't certain such a place existed until just this moment," she teased.

Calliope gingerly opened the notebook and began to thumb through the pages. With a gasp, she raised a questioning gaze to mother.

"Is this…" she she began heavily, "Is this what I think it is? Was she…"

Mother gently wrapped Calliope's hands between hers.

"Yes. She took extensive notes. I've read this from front to back so many times. Anything you need to know is in here," she promised.

"Most importantly, we need to keep this just between us. Not even your brother's or your father can know about this,"

Amara's words sounded ominous, making it painfully clear to her for the first time, that this could harm her family. A part of her cringed, wondering why she had wished so fiercely for something, without considering how it would affect those she loved.

"I need to go talk to the Lore Keeper," Amara said, breaking through Calliope's self-lament. "You just go about your day as though nothing has changed. It is your turn at the market stall today and you will be required there shortly. Go!"

****

The wheels on her cooling cart painfully squeaked out their protest. There was an ample supply of ruts on the way from home to the market square. Each time the cart dipped into one it pulled uncomfortably on her shoulders. The poorly maintained road made her arrive later than intended, so she hurriedly hung her wares in their designated spots. Mindlessly she went through the motions, her mind wandering often to the book hiding in her room. There had been only enough time to page through it quickly before she had to run out the door, and now all she wanted was to read it from beginning to end.

The chatter of friendly neighbors drifted throughout the stalls along with the occasional angry interaction as someone argued over price. It was a largely uneventful day with no unwelcome visit from the Xard. A relief that was felt throughout the market place. She served her usual customers then traded for a few things to fill some empty space in their pantry at home. It wasn't enough to keep them going for long, but it was better than arriving home empty-handed.

Later, after the rest of the household had laid their heads down for the night, she began to pour over the notes. As much as she already knew of what to expect from her change, there was that much and more that she had not yet discovered. By the time she tucked the journal back into its new hiding spot, it was well past her usual bedtime. She had ignored Mother's suggestion to be well rested for their meeting with the Lore Keeper the following day, but she saw it as time well spent. Arming herself with knowledge was one of the most important things she could do to advocate for her own well-being at this point. At least now she had a better grasp on how long she had before the visible changes would raise suspicion. That night her dreams were filled with the very real terrors of running from the Xard and she woke far less rested than she ought to have been.

****

"Good day Lore Keeper. May you have a meaningful life," Calliope and Amara said, bowing deeply following the traditional greeting.

"I wish you a fulfilling one," she responded with respect. "Let us gather around the alter so we may request an audience with the angel."

She beckoned them to join her as she sat cross-legged on the floor surrounded by colorful pillows. The alter was a simple wooden table, low enough to be comfortably within reach. A tray was inset deep into the middle of it, and from here they could see the glow of hot coals emanating from underneath a pot. Steam curled toward the ceiling as the water inside reached a rolling boil.

"Family, please breathe in this serenity," she said in a soothing voice as she sprinkled herbs into the bubbling liquid. "Now you must join me in speaking with Adelphiana."

She began to hum a deep guttural sound, then with closed eyes bared her palms upward. Calliope watched intently, taken aback by this side of the Lore Keeper that she'd never witnessed until now.

The smell of calming herbs surrounded them. As fragrance and the lull of the elders hum intertwined, the weight of her eyelids overwhelmed her. It was then that the humming melted into a soft voice.

"Great and beautiful one! We humbly ask for your intervention," the smell of pungent herbs swelled as she added another small handful. "We have a child in need of your protection. Please grace us with your divine presence so we may know the path she must travel."

A feeble silence followed the elders plea, stretching endlessly; taunting Calliope as she waited with bated breath. Questions invaded her sense of peace, forcing their doubt in to crowd out her hope. What if the Xard discovered them? Wouldn't that put all of their lights in dangers path?

"Do not trouble yourself with these fears," the elder reassured her softly. "One cannot see what they have chosen not to believe in. I assure you, we are safe in the Angels presence."

Calliope's eyes flew open as she realized that Lore Keeper had somehow known her thoughts. But before she could voice her surprise, a small point of light grabbed her attention, drawing her gaze upward.

"My children, I hear your request," a powerful voice whispered.

Together, the light and voice grew in intensity until it revealed the obscured figure of a woman floating above them. A veil of light covered her face. Calliope was grateful for it, as she'd often been told stories of the entrancement that could result from looking upon the Angels face for too long.

"There is a small group of people residing in the Lonhilnai mountains, toward the Demon's Star," her voice was louder now and the light wavered with the sound of it. "They are enemies of Lord Onyx, forced on the run because they dared to defy him. What is happening to you he fears greatly," at that moment, Calliope felt the full intensity of Adelphiana's gaze. "This place is a safe haven for those like you and others that bear magic."

"Will you help her find the way as you have for the others before her?" The Lore Keeper asked boldly.

"I will. And just as those Morphé were tested, so will you be also Calliope. For the heart of Dagrune will not grant passage to those who would cause it harm," Adelphiana replied.

So enraptured had Calliope been in the presence of the angel that she'd only vaguely paid attention to what was being spoken, until she heard this warning.

"What kind of test?" she asked suddenly, "how do I prepare for it, and how will I know how to get there?"

This was the first time that true fear had settled itself in her mind. There were so many things that she hadn't wanted to confront about becoming Morphé, and leaving the only place she'd called home was one of them. Then there was her family that she would have to leave behind. Would she ever see them again?

"Do not fear the journey my child," Adelphiana said, answering one of Calliope's unvoiced questions. "Your test will not be on the road, but rather at the mountains pass. Do not take this lightly. You are more important to this cause than you know."

Then without another word, the orb of light quickly retreated, taking with it her sense of peace.

Amara was agitated as she left the elder's home. "I was really hoping we could get more guidance than that," she said, reaching out to hold her daughters' hand.

"Don't worry Mother. I got all the guidance I needed," Calliope replied, squeezing reassuringly. "I could hear her voice in my head. She will show me the way. Even now, I know which way I must start out."

"But you are so young. Do you really have to face this journey alone?" Amara asked, trying fruitlessly to mask her concern.

Although she felt as much hesitation over her situation as Mother was expressing, she knew that it was important to leave her with *some* hope.

"I don't believe I have a choice. But you heard the Angel. Finding my way to the mountains is not the part of my journey that I need fear."

The cautionary tale of Aunt Roeggnia's fate gave Calliope good reason to shield the rest of her family from the truth. Looking into the tear-filled eyes of her brothers was hard enough when they thought she was moving on to find success in another village. If they knew the real reason, not only would it make them fear for her life, but it would put them in danger. The less they knew, the better. So she spent as much time as she could with them while they worked together gathering supplies.

As the day of her departure drew nearer, she felt the weight of a sadness she didn't know existed. But if they watched her fall apart, she knew they may not have the courage to press on without her. It was one small thing she could do on their behalf, before they had to say goodbye … possibly forever.

Fourteen suns had come and gone by the time they were satisfied with the store of dried vegetables, herbs, and cured meat that now filled her pack. As a final way to leave the boys with more of her knowledge, she taught them how to make arrows and rub tallow into her bow. This would prevent the wood from becoming brittle due to the elements she would encounter. Although she was not a highly skilled BowMaiden, she was at least good enough that it would give her an edge to being on her own.

Far too quickly, the twilight of her parting day crept over the village, dousing the valleys in deep shadow. After many tear-filled goodbyes, Calliope hugged her family for the last time. With only a small window of time to safely head in the direction she knew must be taken, she slipped out into the night. When she reached the edge of the woods on the North end of the village, she turned around for one last look. Then with a kiss on the wind and a tear in her eye, she turned her back with finality.

The first couple days she walked as far as her body would allow. Although she'd spent many seasons toiling in the fields, this terrain offered a different sort of challenge to her muscles. Calliope was grateful for the cover of the trees, because to travel the road was to invite danger and unwanted attention. She shuddered to think what her fate might be if she were discovered, and although the angel had told her the road wouldn't be dangerous, she still refused to let her guard down. The first couple attempts she made at a shelter were less than perfect. But by the third evening, she had achieved a satisfactory way to hide herself and a small, but comforting fire from prying eyes. With each new day she willed her sore body into motion, until by sixth sun-up her muscles didn't complain quite so much.

"Another night, another camp," she nearly jumped at the sound of her own voice. After so many days of silence it was almost jarring. Especially with the new level of auditory sensitivity that came with her change. "I'm getting better at building this shelter anyway," she voiced out loud again. It felt nice to talk, even if it was just to herself. "Mother sure knew what she was doing when she packed this blanket. Light enough to travel; warm enough for these cold nights."

She'd barely started to drift off, when the sound of rustling and snuffling snapped her senses to attention. Instantly alert, a slight movement of her hand brought it to the bow. She very slowly and quietly rolled over into a crouch, peering into the darkness beyond the flickering light of the fire. Her free hand reached for an arrow but there wasn't sufficient time to string it before the boar came into view. Calliope knew they lived in this part of the country but had thought they were scarce enough to avoid an encounter.

"I let my guard down," she thought, slowly moving away from the shelter.

The last thing she wanted was for it to run through the fire only to throw dangerous sparks onto the parched forest floor. She could see the flame reflected in its eyes. They held no fear, just a determination to eliminate this stranger that threatened his territory. He snorted, lowering his head, ready to charge as she frantically searched for the best way to move out of its path. There hadn't been any of these bristly pigs in the woods near her village, which left her no insight as to how agile they might be. Just as she decided on the best direction to dive, he kicked up dirt, accelerating faster than she thought possible for the barrel shaped body.

She released her pent-up energy and a newfound strength took her by surprise. More quickly than she'd planned, she catapulted herself toward the tree and just barely avoided a collision as she twisted her body to compensate. Boot clad feet connected effortlessly to the trunk where she pushed off, throwing herself to the side and landing in a crouch. She didn't have time to process her instinctive acrobatics, before the boar pivoted toward her again.

A quick look upward let her know where to go, and she jumped. Her powerful legs launched her high enough to grab a branch well above the ground. She used the momentum to swing herself around and land safely away from the murder pig below.

Panting from her efforts, she held onto the ample trunk, plastering herself against it. The branch she'd landed on was large enough for her to be comfortably cradled while she waited for the visitor to move on. *Well, I have no doubt this is one of my fun new abilities,* she mused. *Thank goodness it presented itself at the right time.* She closed her eyes, leaning her head against the tree. *Maybe I'll rest them for just a moment. I'm so tired.*

Calliope woke with a start to see the sun's rays scattering points of light throughout the forest. Branches and leaves cast early morning shadows over a bed of foliage that blanketed the ground. Birds began to call back and forth to each other, signaling the world to wake up. Looking down on her camp, she noted with relief that the fire had long since gone out. The dirt berm had done its job. She moved slowly, surveying her situation. As far as she could tell, the ground was easily as far away as five of her standing on top of each other.

For a moment she puzzled in amusement at how she'd slept comfortably on a tree branch for an entire night. "That must be those instincts I heard about. This will be wonderfully helpful, but now I have to get down." Last night, because fear drove her actions, she didn't have to think about how to move her body. Today, she took extra care, shifting her attention between the ground and lower branches of the tree, analyzing her courage. With sweaty palms she made her decision, took a deep breath and jumped. The ease with which she landed was a pleasant surprise and she looked back up at the branch with a grin of accomplishment. "Now I can get used to that," she said.

Each day of the journey made her feel stronger while Adelphiana's guidance led her in a steady direction. Calliope was grateful for the help as it was at least one less thing to be worried about. She passed village after village, wishing that it were a different time when she could safely explore their nuances. But when her life was quite literally on the line with every unknown encounter, she chose to carefully skirt around them.

But as time would have it, traveling for eleven suns had dwindled her supplies significantly more quickly than Mother planned—leaving her with no option except to be an unfamiliar face in a strange place. She was now grateful for Amara's insistence on packing a cloak that could easily hide most of her changing features.

With only enough coin to obtain more herbs and vegetables, she settled for the meager addition to the supplies in her pack. Although many suspicious eyes squinted in her direction, no one made a move to bother her, but she still didn't let down her guard until she again found safety in the cover of the trees. By the twentieth sunrise, the mountains finally rose in front of her and she knew without a doubt that this pass was where she was meant to be.

Calliope hesitated, then stepped through the towering doorway made of massive stone slabs. In an instant, she was swallowed by a darkness deeper than the cloudiest night. "**WHAT IS YOUR PURPOSE HERE**?" a sinister voice boomed into the darkness. Its depth caused the ground around her to tremble. Something about it sounded older than the earth beneath her feet.

"Adelphiana the Angel herself sent me. I seek solace because I am Morphé and Lord Onyx would have me killed if I don't find a safe place to hide," she clenched her fists, digging sharp nails into her palms. She would not back down in fear though her mind screamed for it.

"**PROVE YOURSELF**," again, the ground trembled at the power of the disembodied voice. "**IF YOUR HEART IS TRULY PURE, YOU WILL GIVE THIS FAWN ETERNAL REST. HE WILL NOT RECOVER FROM HIS INJURIES, SO YOU MUST HELP HIM PASS INTO ADELPHIANA'S WAITING ARMS.**"

A bright light appeared only a few paces from where she stood, illuminating a young fawn that lay bleating in pain. The small body struggled with each labored breath. She could see his ribs protruding from lack of nourishment and one of his legs stuck out at an unnatural angle. If this was one of her hunting expeditions, she may have decided to put him out of his misery. But something deep in her soul made her hesitate. A warning that she could not ignore.

Not enough food and a broken leg, she pondered, *No. I could easily help him recover*. Her thoughts were her own, but she sensed an increased anger in the energy around her.

"I DID NOT SAY TO SAVE IT! I ORDERED YOU TO SEND HIM ON TO ADELPHIANA!" The voice boomed angrily.

"No. I will not do what you ask. This is wrong, and I don't care if I'm turned away. I can save him!" She retorted bravely, then promptly pulled the cloak off her back and strode with purposes toward the injured fawn. But she never reached the poor creature as the scene around her disappeared in a swirl of smoke and she found herself face-to-face with a creature unlike anything she'd seen before.

"You passed Dagrune's first test," she said, accompanied by a shallow bow. The creatures gray face loomed above Calliope, her large ears flicking back and forth. Her luscious hair could only be described as a mane. The wavy locks tickled her eyelashes, moving each time she would blink. "My name is Tormaigh, and I'm happy to meet you," a woman's voice emulated from the creature.

"I'm... I'm Calliope," she responded hesitantly.

"I know. Adelphiana has already informed us of your arrival," Tormaigh replied, pulling Calliope to her feet. "Rest now. I know your journey was long, but your training still must start tomorrow morning. We need warriors and the Angel declares a new arrival will be important to our defiance," her eyes were clouded, but Calliope could sense the doubt she hid behind them.

"You don't trust Adelphiana?" she asked pointedly.

The woman's eyes flickered in annoyance at the impudent question.

"Don't you dare put such a thing on *me* child. I trust her. She has given me reason to; but you... you must prove yourself."

The long seasons dealing with her brothers many antics made this interaction seem familiar. The sarcasm and veiled insults were both things that she'd developed a reflexive response to.

"I'm highly certain that I'm not who you are waiting for, but I am curious how you believe that I would have made it all the way here—*AND* across the threshold without her blessing?" Calliope retorted, refusing to release the strangers gaze.

Her blue eyes stared unblinking into Calliope's brown ones, unimpressed at her defiance.

"Arrogance will not get you far with me, however right you may be. Regardless, I'm honored to take you on as my charge," Tormaigh bowed stiffly, and Calliope thought she saw the slightest flicker of amusement cross her face.

"Are… are you Morphé?" Calliope inquired.

Her entire life, she'd only ever seen drawings of their kind. With her change almost a year away, she was anxious with the possibility of what was to come.

"Yes, and I'm tasked to train you," Tormaigh nodded.

Calliope watched as Tormaigh disappeared into a yawning cavern beneath an outcropping of rock. She drew in a long breath through her nose. "Smell the flowers," she said, staring into the cave. Then she released the breath, long and slow, between her lips, "and blow out the candles. Just like Zeke taught me back home." The exercise was as effective as always, calming her pounding heart and giving her just enough courage to follow Tormaigh into the unknown.

****

Nearly four seasons had passed from the day she'd first set foot in the Keep and called it home. Under Tormaigh's expert tutelage Calliope had become quite good in hand-to-hand combat but was most proud of how skilled she'd become with her bow. Although they expected her to train hard, it wasn't always business here. So she took those opportunities to practice on her own, and as her body changed, she would work the new abilities into her routine. Relentlessly she challenged herself until the bow began to feel as though it was an extension of her body. By the time her birthday drew near, she was almost unrecognizable from the uncertain girl that had arrived not so long ago.

The day approached too slowly. She found herself often wishing to meet the Angel alone so she could more quickly find out what her Ophrahl form would be. Excited whispers could be heard as other Morphé shared in her sentiment. The only part she dreaded of her coming change, was having so many eyes on her during the ceremony. Even though it was the tradition, that much attention had always made her uncomfortable. When she'd first read Aunt Roeggnia's journal, she had imagined an intimate moment. A night under the stars to discover the true nature of who she was, for that is what would determine the Ophrahl she would be. This was a moment when she wanted... no; the correct sentiment was a need to be alone.

"Come with me," Tormaigh whispered, gently shaking Calliope awake. "We can do this without the meddling masses. Some will be upset but it's more important that you get what you want out of this."

Calliope groaned as she pulled herself out of a sleepy haze and her eyes slowly adjusted to the moonless night.

"Won't you get in trouble?" She asked groggily.

"Not if you don't tell anyone," Tormaigh replied, a playful but menacing twinkle in her eye.

Calliope wondered briefly if she had somehow read her mind. She didn't remember mentioning anything of her desires to anyone, let alone the one woman she thought it might offend. Or maybe it was just a woman's intuition. Mother had that special knack for figuring out what she was thinking also, so it would make the most sense."

"I have no intention of doing such a thing," she replied quickly. "Let's be on our way."

The peaks surrounding them were so lofty they disappeared into the darkness of the midnight sky. The two women sat face to face in deep shadow, their legs crossed. Awkward patches of grey hair were scattered over Calliope's body. She looked down to study her fingers with their sharp nails. They were strong enough that she had discovered them to be a very useful tool in helping her climb almost anything she desired.

"Sweet Angel hear our plea," Tormaigh began. "Another of your children asks for the blessing of a complete transformation."

An uncomfortable silence filled the air. It was just like the first time her Lore Keeper had called upon the Angel for help. So she held on to her patience, wondering where Adelphiana had to come from whenever her presence was requested.

"We implore you dear Angel!" Tormaigh called out again, raising her hands higher.

Calliope saw a sudden movement of clouds and the wind picked up, causing them to swirl into a frenzy.

"Hear our cry to allow another Morphé access to the power of the shadows!"

Tormaigh's mane and Calliope's hair whipped wildly as the wind picked up around them.

"My child, we implore your help," the familiar voice padded like a gentle breeze through her mind. Calliope searched the surrounding darkness, slightly disappointed that the light and form of the Angel was not present this time. "You're most important in the defeat of Lord Onyx."

It mattered not that she didn't believe where the Angel claimed she belonged, it was important to listen now. She was certain that any attempt to thwart expectations would be met with hostility, and the last thing she wanted to do was find out what that might mean coming from an eternal being.

"I am your willing vessel," Calliope found herself acknowledging. "What may I do to help our land return to its former glory."

A fresh burst of wind swirled into a funnel around her and with it came a severe tingling sensation. She screamed in surprised pain. It felt as though every cell in her body was being pulled apart and put back together repeatedly. It challenged her resolve to push onward.

"Please stop! It hurts! It burns!" she cried.

Then she felt the warmth of Tormaigh's strong hands grasping hers, and the voice that she'd come to know as a comfort, sounded for the first time in her mind.

"It's ok, I promise you can do this. It is only like this with your first change. I know you are strong enough to accept this pain, for without it, you will not become your true self."

Calliope squeezed the fingers that held onto hers. She wanted to morph, so refusing to let momentary pain stop her, she gritted her teeth to endure it. The moment she surrendered, a warmth replaced the unpleasant sensation. Her eyes slowly opened to the sight of a much larger version of the woman that had trained her so intensely, smiling back. Looking down, she could see a sleek black tail wrapped around her arms which were covered in jet black fur that covered the cutest toes she'd ever seen. Swishing her tail, she located a small puddle from the unexpected downpour that day. The moon shone brightly in the newly clear sky, reflecting it's light as her whiskered face came into view. Meowing with smug satisfaction, she congratulated herself on guessing her Ophrahl correctly.

"Now you need to think hard about a human form, sister. This will cause your re-transformation back to what you were before... almost completely. Consider the perfect balance of your human and Ophrahl aura's. You will become the image of what you should be."

Calliope pulled herself into a small ball, the intended sigh turning to a hiss. Closing off her view of the world helped to visualize a human form. But something was different. She could no longer envision the image of her fully human self. What she saw was someone more confident than she'd ever dreamt to be. The vision gave her a surge of pride and with a rush of wind, she changed into a perfect melding of her human and feline form. She would never look the same, but she didn't mind at all. The difference in her body felt incredible.

"Why would I ever want to change back into my ophrahl? This feels far more powerful," she told herself often.

Over the next few seasons, flourishing under Tormaigh's training, she became obsessed with honing her Morphé skills. With the naturally harsh terrain of the mountains, she challenged herself with increasingly difficult missions, turning her into a formidable asset to the Alchmene.

One day, during an especially difficult combat training session, Adelphiana appeared to them.

"It has come to my attention that whispers of your names have been circulating among the Alchmene governing body. I will take you to the council with me now."

She led them through a series of tunnels and when they entered the Omphalos, the place that the governing body held in secrecy, even the most resistant leaders had no choice but to accept them. Because even they wouldn't dare to question the intervention of an eternal being.

"I am your Angel, and I know to some of you, I have not yet revealed myself until this moment. My presence was otherwise required as you are not the only ones rallying to fight this evil. I would have come sooner if it were possible. However, one of your royals needs you now," a murmur of surprise rippled through the Governors and Calliope's own heart skipped a beat. The made-up scenario, the one that she had always hoped for was staring her in the face. *"She was sent to another world,"* Adelphiana continued, *"so we may better keep her safe from the evil clutches of Lord Onyx. I have brought to you the Morphé that I have deemed worthy of this task."*

Unable to hold back her curiosity any longer Calliope blurted, "Who is this in need of our assistance? I thought their lights were extinguished permanently."

"Her name is Hayden on that earth," Adelphiana replied aloud, seemingly unbothered by the interruption. "She is there in order to keep her out of the ever-probing attentions of Lord Onyx. He has searched for many seasons for a surviving heir, so I thought it safer to send her to our sister world. She has grown strong. It is time to bring her home," she allowed a poignant pause. But if anyone had questions, they did not voice them, so she turned her attention to Calliope. "She will need you to show her the way. There are many things she will not understand, for she knows nothing of the magic that lies within her."

"If my place is not by her side, what would you have me do?" Tormaigh asked, her voice echoing off the jagged walls.

"You have work yet to do here on Dagrune my child. Your time will come to train her. However, for now, your skills will serve better use with the Alchmene. And you... wise council, will make Tormaigh one of your generals," the intensity of her gaze compelled the council to lower their heads in agreement. "But you Calliope, you are the one who can gain her trust. Your Ophrahl will be accepted without question by Hayden, whereas yours Tormaigh, is one she is not yet ready for."

"I'm your humble vessel," Calliope replied, bowing in respect.

"Please stand. You do not need to bow to me," the angel said gently.

Calliope's cheeks flushed with embarrassment as she rose to her feet. After only a handful of encounters with Adelphiana, she was unsure how formal she need be. As the flush faded, she told herself that she wouldn't be making that mistake again.

"You are intelligent and your mind is strong. My guidance is not something you shall require any further. When the time comes, you will know what to do. We're counting on you."

Adelphiana's link filled her mind with one final thought.

"The magic from Dagrune and Earth aren't wholly compatible. I shall send you there as Ophrahl, but until she awakens you will not be able to morph."

"Sweet Angel, I'm honored to be a part of this," Calliope accepted, then disappeared in an engulfing rush of wind and light.

The blinding flash turned into a miserable rain that fell coldly around her on the unfamiliar hillside. She found herself in Ophrahl form, and when she attempted to change, it confirmed Adelphiana's caution. *I know, I know.* She argued with herself, *She wouldn't have told me unless it was the truth.*

After exploring for a short while, she found a bush with suitable shelter and settled there to prepare for a long cold night. Glaring at her useless paws, a wish for the skilled hands of her Morphé flitted through her thoughts. They would be much more helpful in building a shelter and fire. *But wishes are only thoughts*, she told herself as she curled up to preserve warmth.

When Hayden found her, Calliope wasn't sure it was the right person. She'd expected a strong and powerful being, but the woman who found her was compassionate. Unlike anyone in a place of power she'd encountered. Snuggling into the warmth of the woman's clothing, a feeling of safety wormed its way into her soul. Maybe staying a cat wouldn't be so bad after all.

10

How the Family Came to be

Calliope settled into life with Hayden. Since the woman didn't seem to want her wandering outside, there weren't many opportunities for hunting. So taking the only available option, she conceded to the food her caretaker provided. It took some getting used to, but her Ophrahl palate could enjoy the spoils of a hunt, whereas her Morphé wouldn't dream of eating uncooked meat. This made it easier to adjust to the strange pâté she was offered.

The sting of guilt often clouded her conscience when she'd think of all the hungry people in Dagrune—while she enjoyed the privilege of a full stomach every day. *If only I could morph so I can stay strong.* She quietly mourned to herself. *At least then, I would be making good use of all this extra sustenance.* However, she was not willing to give up completely and so turned the house into her own personal training ground. Hayden would often laugh at her antics, not realizing what purpose they carried.

There were so many foreign things here, the noises, the smells, the stuff. It was over and above what any single person in Dagrune would need to survive. The furniture looked familiar, but strange devices—machines, they were called—were everywhere. These contraptions were made for the sole purpose of completing menial tasks—the most fascinating of which was the computer. Hayden would sit in front of it for hours, arguing with herself about what to name her new charge.

After watching her do this for many nights, Calliope did her best with clumsy paws to help. It proved to be easier than she thought. Copying her observations during Hayden's searches, she typed in her name. Mother made sure her children knew how to read and write, so the task proved easy enough. With pleasant surprise, she found a being in this world with her namesake. The website was conveniently left up so Hayden would find it the next time she opened the computer.

It sure would have made life back home much easier if we had all this. The thought had crossed her mind during a particularly snowy and frigid day. *The fireplaces kept our homes warm enough, but this heat feels like it permeates everything.* She loved stretching out in front of the thing Hayden called a vent, spending hours sleeping there. Especially on the coldest winter nights.

Days turned into months while seasons came and went, turning into years. Every day Calliope tried to learn something new about this world, mostly so she could understand the things Hayden incessantly babbled on about. *She seriously needs an actual person to talk to.* Calliope thought wearily after an especially long monologue. But though it was slightly annoying to be talked *at* without the ability to converse, she always listened intently in order to better understand this woman—entrusted to her protection.

As months bled into years, and those into more seasons, she began to doubt the promise given by Adelphiana. The trust that she was supposed to gain seemed to already be in place, so why hadn't Hayden awoken yet? Had Adelphiana forgotten about her?

Two full season cycles came and went until finally one day, when she was laying forlornly in front of the vent, the wind suddenly picked up. At first she planned to ignore it because sudden weather changes were something she'd gotten used to in this part of the mountains—but when it persisted she cautiously approached the front door. Having mastered the art of opening it by hanging on the handle, the latch released easily, allowing the door to swing open. *Those look just like the clouds from the night of my first morph.* She noted.

Then, like a whisper, above the roar of the elements–a far-off voice drifted into her mind. *"Calliope my child. I'm sorry it has been so long. I had much to attend to on Dagrune."*

Calliope's heart was filled with peace at hearing her angel's voice. *"My beautiful Angel, it makes my heart warm to hear your thoughts once again,"* she replied happily. *"But I need to know. How much longer do I have to wait for Princess Hayden to awaken?"*

"I am sorry child; I do not know the precise time, but I can tell you that she is not yet ready. I have come instead to offer you another being for companionship. One that will be there for both of you in your times of direst need. He was born to a litter of guardian dogs and the differences that set him apart there, will ensure that he fits into life on Earth," her voice wavered and Calliope could feel her presence drifting off.

"And how would you have me find this companion?" Calliope asked, a sudden urgency filling her mind.

"You yourself will not need to do anything. I have set events in place which will lead Hayden where she needs to be, just as I did when I sent you," her voice had nearly faded and the tumultuous weather began to die down. *"My power is waning. I cannot hold onto our connection any longer. Until we meet again."*

As the midday sky returned to its previous calm, Calliope found herself unable to tear her attention from it. She longed for nothing more than to follow Adelphiana back to the world she loved. But she was still needed here and had to set those hopes aside so they would not distract from her obligations.

Sure enough, that evening Hayden came home with a highly rambunctious pup. His obsessive goal to make friends with Calliope turned into an exhausting marathon–testing her patience at every turn. And although she had two little brothers, she was seasons removed from dealing with their antics. She often thought about asking Adelphiana to rid her of this thorn in her side, but the promise that he would be there when Hayden needed him gave her pause.

She'd grown quite attached to Hayden, and anything that could help keep her safe; well that was just something she refused to mess up.

One day, when they were stuck at home together, Calliope happened upon a very useful discovery. She was stalking outside his kennel, trying to get him to stop whining when she opened the Link in pure frustration. Her sensitive hearing had taken as much as it could handle.

"Oh, hush young pup! You make such unnecessary fuss all the time. I can't let you out because you'll probably eat something you're not supposed to."

Feeling miffed, she began to make her way back to her favorite pillow in the bay window, when she heard a young eager voice link back.

"Oh! Oh! Oh! You can hear me! They told me we could do this but not until you let me in. Oh no. She said that would be very wrong. But now I get to talk to you. You said I could so now I can!" The broken sentences came through from the new voice.

Startled, Calliope flipped backward, her tail puffed up like a duster as she stared at Bérg in disbelief.

"Did… did you just link with me?" She asked incredulously.

"What's Link? Is it a fun game? Oh wait! That's what Mudder meant. How I talk to you! But can you get me food? My tummy is making noises."

There was no doubt now. This was coming from him. She'd heard Morphés could link with animals but had never considered any good reason to use such a gift.

****

Months passed, and she slowly began to find solace in the constant presence of her enthusiastic new roommate. At least here was another being from the home where she longed to return. And he also turned out to be a welcome distraction from the long days she'd spent alone until now. He loved the outdoors as much as she did, so they would spend hours gazing over the mountains while they discussed the many differences between Dagrune and Hayden's Earth. But Bérg, being so young when he left, didn't remember much from his short time there.

Then there was that one promise from Adelphiana that kept nagging at the back of her mind. She'd mentioned how he would fit better here than on Dagrune. Curiosity got the best of her and she asked Bérg what the angel might have meant. His answer was always the same, leaving her with more questions than answers: he didn't want to talk about it. The only thing he would say was his differences made him believe he would never get the chance to prove his worth. His duty and heritage had long been to stand at the side of the royal family as their protectors. And in this task on Earth, Adelphiana had given him back his hope.

"When did you first see Adelphiana?" Calliope asked him one day.

"She appeared to me and Mudder just before I was sent here," he told her, his big golden eyes dilating at the memory. *"She told me a princess needed my help and I was the only one who could do it. I thought I'd never get the chance to fulfill the duties given to me by my birthright. It was all I ever wanted from the moment Mudder taught me about it."*

"Well I'm happy I have someone to talk to these past years, and I'm glad that you get another chance at this," Calliope said, staring wistfully over the rolling landscape.

"I know. I miss it too and I want to go back so we can save it from this evil being. This is what the Angel told me we were supposed to do, but it's been so long. Are we ever going to get back?" He sidled up next to her, hoping that his closeness would aid in her comfort.

"I don't know. It certainly doesn't feel so to me and I tire of being in this damn cat form."

"Hey! Being an animal isn't bad!" He shot back at her, letting out a pointed sneeze.

"Maybe not for you," she retorted. *"But I'm far more capable **and** stronger in my morphé form. I miss it so much. Oh, to have hands again,"* she said, meowing forlornly.

For some time their routine went on like this until they finally received another visit from Adelphiana.

"My children, you have been so patient. I have good news! It has taken me some time to build up the energy to send Tormaigh to you as I promised. I rest in the knowledge that I will also need to help in Hayden's awakening, which is why it has taken me so long to bring her here. I know much time has passed since our last connection when I sent Bérg, but magic between worlds is difficult to transfer. The sun of this world does not hold the power ours does on Dagrune."

As usual, her introduction was followed by one of her signature pauses, giving Calliope the chance she needed to ask the question that had been on her mind for so long.

"Is that why I'm unable to morph? And not only that, but how will Hayden's awakening help me regain my ability?"

"Sweet child, I know you're anxious." Understanding colored Adelphiana's voice. *"The princess holds more power than you can imagine. Tormaigh will know how to guide her. In only a few days' time, she will be reunited with you once again."*

Calliope's heart beat a little faster in her tiny chest. When she left to be with Hayden it had been a difficult goodbye.

"I need to use my remaining energy to send Tormaigh to you. Once again, the plan is set in motion. She will be where she needs to be."

And then her voice and the usual storm that accompanied her were gone. But this time Calliope felt more anticipation than she had in a long time. Then it dawned on her suddenly and she turned abruptly to Bérg.

"Bérg! The horse auction! She's been preparing for this for months! It has to be where Hayden will find her!"

****

That same evening, a flash of light appeared to rip open the sky over a clearing in the forest just outside of Iola, where an eerie neigh from a formidable jet-black horse could be heard echoing off the mountain sides. Tormaigh snorted in annoyance as she sniffed the air.

"Unable to morph... I don't like this at all. But Calliope has been made to endure this for many seasons. I certainly can for a couple of suns."

She set off through thick groves of pine, as the smells and sounds of a nearby home drew her in. This was exactly how Adelphiana had described it. As she neared her destination, she found her thoughts wandering to Calliope.

"Only two more suns until I can hug her again," she thought wistfully.

Tormaigh was the kind of Morphé who kept her emotions under tight wraps. It was easier to fight and train others of her kind if she kept herself from getting attached. Somehow, Calliope was able to push the limits of those barriers. She had unintentionally let her guard down and found herself slowly but surely becoming quite fond of the Morphé.

"Calliope I'm here," the only energy available thus far was her Link, so she reached out, not knowing how far away her friend was.

"Tormaigh is that you?!" An emotionally charged voice responded.

It was faint but there was no mistake it belonged to Calliope.

"Yes my friend, how I have missed you. I'm sorry it took so long for me to arrive here. Much has happened on Dagrune since you last departed."

A raw urgency filled the space between them as Calliope blurted, *"My family. Please. Do you have any news of them? With no way to contact anyone for so many seasons, my heart misses them in ways I never knew could hurt."*

"Deep breath little one," Tormaigh encouraged. *"They are alive and well, but there has been an increase in unrest across Dagrune. Many people have had to flee their homes. The Xard's forces grow with each*

passing season… however, we can talk about all this when we're together again. We must keep in contact until then."

As the ranch came into view, understanding washed over her–this was why Adelphiana had sent her here. The dense forest gave way to a wide stretch of open pasture. Behind a sturdy fence, a restless herd of horses milled about; they must have caught her scent. She paced the perimeter, measuring the fence's height, calculating the distance she'd need to clear it–then, with effortless grace, she leapt over, her back hooves barely grazing the top rail.

"Well that was easy. Why do you all stay in captivity when freedom is just a jump away?" She tried to ask them..

But there was no answer. No matter how many times she tried to link with them.

"Maybe the animals are different here," she concluded.

The commotion she caused with her arrival drew the attention of the man who lived there. She decided that since it was inevitable that he would treat her like an animal, she'd give him just enough trouble to bring him to the brink of frustration. After what felt like a sufficient struggle, she finally allowed him to put the halter on. Her next mission became clear as he led her into the large stall. If she kicked the walls incessantly, there was no way he would want to try and keep her there. To her delight, it worked just as she planned, and the rancher opted to bring her to the charity auction. At least there they had separate stalls. It was there that she waited, occasionally linking with Calliope to make sure her friend didn't feel alone any longer.

Tormaigh had just dozed off for the evening when Calliope's frantic voice broke through their link, catapulting her back to consciousness. *"Tormaigh! Something has happened to Hayden. I don't know how to explain it, but I feel it so strongly. I'm sorry. I wouldn't have forced the communication unless I thought it was an emergency."*

"No need to apologize," she responded immediately, shaking off the temptation to be annoyed at the interruption. *"Use Bérg. He can*

travel quickly over great distances and has a keen sense for finding those he has bonded with. The guardian pups are well known for these abilities."

A moment crawled by. One that was far too long for Tormaigh's liking before she heard Calliope's worried voice once again.

"He's heading the direction that she drives into her job. She should already have been on her way home, so that would make the most sense. I'm going to try keeping in contact with him, but my link with him isn't as strong as ours so I hope I don't lose him."

Tormaigh thought it best not to leave her alone, working her way in as the voice of reason while Calliope seemed to be falling apart. There was a certain quality to the emotions she read through the link. Something that felt familiar. *And why shouldn't she get attached?* Tormaigh asked herself.

When Bérg finally reached Hayden, Calliope's fear was so intense that Tormaigh began to feel some of it creep into her own heart. This was only relieved once the stranger stopped to help. But nothing was truly able to put them at ease until Hayden was home and safely sl–mbering in her bed. Finally comfortable that the situation was well in hand, she settled once again into the generous bed of straw.

She had been pondering a curiosity before Calliope had rolled into her thoughts like a landslide. The man that helped the rancher bring her to this place felt familiar somehow. There was a quality about him that she thought seemed out of place on Earth, and when he looked into her eyes, she thought he'd looked surprised. If what he said to the other man held any truth, she might get to see him at the auction again. But that was still a couple suns away, so she might as well settle herself that it would remain a mystery. For a time at least.

When Hayden's plan not to rest but to take a long hike instead came front and center, it concerned both of them. But Calliope was supposed to be a cat, and Bérg took his orders from Hayden. Not the other way around. So there was nothing they could do but make sure that she didn't hurt herself further.

"Stay out of sight and sound but follow close enough to keep an eye on her," Tormaigh instructed.

"I agree," Calliope said, relieved to finally feel useful again. *"This is a great opportunity for me to loosen up my Morphé. And to see if I am still as stealthy as I was when I left Dagrune. I was quite good at sneaking up on you during training you know,"* she bragged smugly.

If Calliope were able to see Tormaigh's Ophrahl, she would have seen her roll her eyes.

"You're really going to start in before we're even face to face?" She snorted, a puff of straw dust rising up to make her sneeze. *"I see you haven't lost your sarcastic edge my dear, but I'm happy to know this world has not changed you so much."*

When Calliope told her about what happened by the lake, her former concern paled in comparison. It wasn't safe to leave the princess alone with unknown powers any longer.

"Accidental expulsion of magic is not good. Someone could get seriously hurt, but what color did you say her light was?" Tormaigh said, concern clawing at her mind.

"It was very clearly a blue light. Is this a bad thing?" Came Calliope's worried response.

"No it's not bad, it just puts a whole new perspective on things. I don't know if Adelphiana knows about this. Just let me know if anything of the sort happens again."

****

Auction day was far more hectic than Tormaigh anticipated. Everything seemed so much louder here than back home. The carriages these people had weren't pulled by beasts of burden, but seemed to be controlled from inside. Calliope told her they were called cars and trucks and the cart she rode in on her way to the auction was a trailer. New things and smells kept her curious and alert to all the people wandering the dusty grounds. If a person showed too much interest in her, she would make sure to put on a big show of just how big a problem she could be.

The moment Tormaigh laid eyes on Hayden, there was no doubt she belonged to a royal bloodline. Someone who carried themselves with such confidence couldn't be anything but.

"She's spent her whole life in a world not her own. One that held no special privilege. Yet here she is, commanding and regal in her own right."

The thought made her swell with pride. She'd had her doubts, but they were carried away as her future Queen stood confidently before her. There was no hesitation in her eyes as she faced Tormaigh down. Not a whiff of fear was on the wind that blew her hair into her face. Even when she was certain her conversation with Calliope was overheard, Hayden appeared to take it in stride.

As she settled into her new home in the barn, she noticed how much care Hayden took to make her comfortable. Though her caretaker was destined to become a powerful ruler—she was also kind, attentive, and full of quiet compassion. So, with Tormaigh's newfound comforts and her ability to Morph restored, she and Calliope resumed their training. In the present moment, it was the most effective way to support Hayden until the time was right to reveal their true forms.

<u>11</u>

Discovering the magic

Hayden was especially late coming back from work every day that week, so the two Morphé spent their time roaming the mountains. Calliope fashioned a bow out of the strongest material she could find, making the mountain terrain her range. She relentlessly practiced, turning every tree into a bullseye and every bush into a potential enemy. With her long years as Ophrahl, the previous accuracy of her BowMaiden skills had suffered and much to her dismay also, the flexibility she once enjoyed. But at least her night vision was still just as sharp. Hayden mentioned often how muscle memory worked, especially when she'd returned to her Jiu Jitsu instruction. So if she remembered correctly, it shouldn't take long to get back to her previous level of fitness.

****

"We have to tell her! We can't wait any longer!" Calliope pleaded with Tormaigh.

The concern had been weighing on her for a few days. Every day they waited to start helping Hayden with her magic was another that allowed Lord Onyx's chokehold to tighten. From everything she'd been told since Tormaigh arrived, she was certain that he suspected something. The nets that he was casting for anyone with the tiniest spark of magic, and the increase in the Xard's presence—it left her with very little doubt.

"Ugh! I hate it when you look at me like that," Tormaigh retorted, turning away from Calliope. "Although I do agree, we still need to consider what may happen if it scares her away."

Calliope strode over to Tormaigh, grabbing her by the shoulders so she had no choice but to look her in the eyes.

"Oh come on. You don't know her like I do. I promise you that she's stronger than you think. She can handle it."

Tormaigh sighed deeply. Maybe she *was* being too cautious. And it was true that Calliope had ample time to learn who Hayden was.

"Perhaps that's why Adelphiana had you arrive here so many season cycles before I did," she paused, passing her hand through her silky mane, then flexed her shoulders to the muscles on her back rippling in response. "Ok. We'll do it your way," Tormaigh finally conceded, followed by a deep sigh. "She wants to put that saddle on me tomorrow and I won't stand for it. I'll start by linking. I think that will be an easier introduction than being confronted by our Morphé forms."

Calliope squealed in approval, leaning in to wrap Tormaigh in an impromptu hug. Slightly embarrassed at her outburst, she stepped back with a flush rising in her dark cheeks. Clearing her throat, she tried to cover the awkward moment.

"You won't regret this," she promised.

****

Saturday morning arrived much too slowly. Hayden was giddy for her long-awaited first ride. She tried to force down breakfast, but her stomach was in too many excited knots and she had to abandon the effort after only two bites. The warm sunshine smiled down on her as she playfully swung her arms back and forth, her feet marching across the lawn toward the barn. Despite the weird mood she was in, she had to pause, close her eyes and breathe in the excitement of the day.

A loud bang reverberated through the barn, bringing her attention back to the task at hand.

"So impatient! Give me just a second to climb up and throw a bale down to you," she said, her hands reaching for the ladder to the small loft.

"I would really rather have some of that toast I smelled you making this morning," the sound of a voice invaded her thoughts. Hayden froze. She was sure this wasn't the first time she'd heard it.

"Toast would be a welcome break from my canned food and kibble also," the second voice was higher and held a vastly more sarcastic tone.

Now that she'd heard them both, she was certain these were the voices that had conversed at the auction. Hayden shook the thought from her head, raising her foot to the ladder.

"No, my dear Hayden, you aren't imagining it and you aren't 'losing your mind'… as you call it."

This time she slowly turned her head toward the stall, studying the mare. The statuesque way she was standing made her look like just that–a statue. Her eyes were locked onto Hayden with an almost human recognition in them. She flicked her gaze to Calliope who was frozen in the exact same stare in the barn's doorway. Hayden was used to seeing this with the cat, but the horse? She didn't think there was enough of a bond with her new charge to have that kind of connection.

Bérg's bark jerked her attention back to the ladder. He danced up to her, plopping his butt down, his out-of-control tail stirring up dust from the straw bedding. He looked up at her adoringly, then tilted his head and perked his ears. It was the look he usually gave Hayden when she was having a conversation with him. But this time, he seemed to be focused on Tormaigh.

"We can share our thoughts through a connection we call a Link," the first voice spoke again. *"And yes, I am speaking to him also right now. You can communicate with me as well, which is how I knew of your*

confusion. That's how we Morphé communicate with animals, each other, and those like you."

"I must be imagining this. Wake up Hayden. Wake up!" Hayden slapped her face lightly, squeezing her eyes shut to block out the unsettling sight.

"Why do you hit yoursell..." the stronger voice began but was cut off by the other.

"You've always been so stubborn. This is really happening. Tormaigh and I are talking to you through our Link. I can no longer wait for you to come to terms with it. I need you to see my true form."

Hayden watched in disbelief as she reconciled what she'd just heard, to Calliope's movements. She'd taken a couple small leaps outside the barn when the voice that she was starting to believe belonged to Tormaigh said, *"No, don't..."*

It was a sentiment that she felt often when it came to Calliope. And just as she usually ignored Hayden, she likewise ignored Tormaigh.

Calliope closed her eyes, bending her head as a strong wind began stirring around her. When the dust and debris settled, there she stood—a half-cocked smile of smug pride plastered on her face, one hand planted coyly on her fur covered hip. Hayden gasped and would have lost her balance had Bérg—who seemed completely unphased by the strange phenomenon—not been there to lean on.

"Take a deep breath. I know this is a lot to take in Hayden," Calliope said, trying to assuage the anxiety written on her friend's face.

"What... what is happening? I... I don't understand. How is this not a dream?" She asked with a shaky breath.

Tormaigh, anxious to change back into her Morphé, forgot herself for a moment. And in her impatience she did something she'd cautioned herself against—pushing Hayden when she should have held back.

"My dear, unless you want a face full of straw I suggest you step outside the barn for a minute while I morph."

Calliope, who could see the look on Hayden's face, realized that she may have been too hasty. So, attempting to smooth things over she retorted aloud, "Oh for… give the poor woman a couple minutes!"

"Oh… like you just did?!" Tormaigh fired back.

Calliope moved toward Hayden. Her intention had been to lend a comforting hand, but the ashen color of Hayden's face stopped her in her tracks.

"Please, I need a minute to process this. Just stay there," she said, wringing her hands.

"You may not want to do that…"

The words had barely left Calliope's mouth when a small orb of crackling blue light formed between Hayden's palms. She jumped, recoiling from it. Calliope took a step toward her, eyes wide with concern, and Tormaigh's frantic voice invaded Hayden's thoughts.

"DON'T throw it this time! The last time it was a rock which I'm sure you'll recall what happened there. Imagine what it would do to your brand-new barn," then her tone softened. *"Your magic is very strong. It's connected to heightened emotion. Lack of control can have devastating effects. Take a few more deep breaths to calm yourself, then turn your palms upward to release your anxiety."*

Her hands trembled in the struggle to control her fear, but Hayden managed to calm herself enough to do as she was instructed. The light between her palms slowly shrunk until it disappeared with a quiet snap.

"I'll step out now so you can change," Hayden said more calmly than she felt.

And as she stepped out into the heat of the morning sun, the rush of wind and swirling straw behind her whipped her hair into her face.

When Tormaigh stepped out of the barn, Hayden found herself looking up at her. It was an odd feeling, considering she was usually on the other side of that coin. She tilted her head, studying the strange forms of the women in front of her. A brief moment of clarity, and she dropped her gaze.

"I'm sorry. I'm staring," she mumbled. "I know it's rude, but I'm still trying to wrap my head around all of this."

Her knees wobbled, forcing her to lean against the barn.

"It's quite alright dear," Tormaigh soothed, a look of understanding on her smooth brow.

Hayden pushed off of the barn. "I'm gonna go sit at the top of the hill. I just need to re-center myself and then I can let my mind unravel all of... this."

She gestured wildly, walking stiffly across the gravel—Bérg on her heels. The grass tickled her palms as she brushed her hands lightly over it. It was an effective grounding technique she'd stumbled upon. She kicked off her riding boots, digging her toes into the grass and dirt, then lifted her face toward the sky. A blanket of soothing warmth covered her from head to toe, and she breathed a final steadying breath.

"Ok. I'm ready for you to join me," she called over her shoulder.

Tormaigh's hooves clomped softly with Calliope close behind as she followed Hayden's call.

"I believe that this is the part where you explain how I'm not going crazy? Please? I've had my fair share of weird lately, but this takes the cake," Hayden open her eyes, staring straight ahead. "This whole time... Calliope, I rescued you years ago. Why did I never see... this?"

She leaned to the side, draping her arm over Bérg's shoulders, caressing the soft swirl of fur on his chest.

Calliope cleared her throat, and the voice that came from her was somehow exactly how Hayden thought she should sound. "Because I've only been able to morph in this world for a couple weeks. You gave me back my power the night you awakened."

For more than one reason, Calliope's reply made Hayden turn sharp to look at her.

"This world? Awakening?" she demanded, sweeping her eyes over Calliope's strange form.

"We aren't from this earth. None of us are," Calliope waved her hand at all four of them. "Dagrune is the world we call home. And that magic that you have. It's very real and very powerful. I don't know how exactly, but you made me… well, me again," she grinned, revealing a set of sharp canines.

Hayden looked away quickly, not wanting to offend if she couldn't hide her discomfort.

"Even Bérg?!" She asked incredulously.

His tail thumped in response to hearing his name. Lazily he rolled onto his side, laying his head in her lap.

"Yes, even him," Calliope chuckled. "I'm sure you have many questions. I fear we won't be able to answer all of them, although we'll try. But first Tormaigh should tell you about who you really are and why we're all here."

Tormaigh nodded as Calliope passed the role of teacher to her. This was no small moment. She held the rare privilege–and the solemn duty–of revealing her future queen's destiny, and she didn't take it lightly. Countless times she'd rehearsed this speech in the seasons she'd waited patiently on Dagrune. So she sat a little straighter and began.

"There was a family who ruled our world with a firm but fair hand for thousands of seasons. They had the gift of the elements and therefore were chosen because they helped the many villages of Dagrune to prosper in health. Around 200 season cycles ago…"

Much to her annoyance, Calliope interrupted.

"Hayden knows time by months and years. There are four seasons in a year, but the year doesn't stop at the end of any season, rather in the middle of winter," her eyes began to glaze over as her thoughts turned inward. She tapped her chin inquisitively. "That actually makes no sense. It's always bothered me and I'm glad I can finally say it. I was holding that in for far too long."

Tormaigh's big blue eyes shot daggers and her gray lips pursed in their displeasure at being interrupted.

"Sorry, sorry. Please continue. I won't interject again," Calliope said, realizing suddenly how carried away she'd gotten.

Tormaigh snorted, knowing the promise was ingenuine at best. It may have been only a handful of season's since they were close, but it seemed that time as an Ophrahl had only served to make that part of her more exaggerated.

"Anyhow... a distant cousin of the king from those days became displeased with how far his seat was from the throne. So he followed the stories he'd been told as a child and went in search of the Heart of Dagrune. When he returned many seasons later, he never breathed a word of what he found in the Lonhilnai mountains. Slowly the family began to see a change in him, until one day his twin sister passed unexpectedly. A rare disease had taken her. After that he became a recluse, rarely leaving his home. The stories that have been passed down of the noises and sights that came from that place were chilling. Too late, the royal family discovered that he had built an army in the shadows. And when he led them in an affront on the Manor, he attacked with a type of magic they had never seen before. But he trusted his own abilities too haughtily and the Duweot's easily defeated him, forcing him into hiding."

"Hang on. What does this have to do with me?" Hayden blurted. "It's just... it sounds like you're going so far back," she stammered.

Tormaigh stopped herself from reacting like she did to Calliope. Although she may not yet know it, or accept it, Hayden was her superior. And Tormaigh took great pride in never letting her decorum slip.

"I promise. This is where your story began. It will all make sense when I'm finished."

Hayden laid back, putting her impatience aside.

"Where was I… oh yes. No one knew where he'd gone and much to everyone's relief, his small army seemed to have disappeared with him. Over the years, rumors began to re-circulate. People were disappearing in the middle of the night and they all had one thing in common. They were bearers of the gifts. Then one day, the one we now know as Lord Onyx re-emerged. His magic had become far more powerful and a much larger army followed him. With his increased strength he easily defeated them, then ordered his soldiers to hunt down any that remained of royal blood. He had no intention of letting those who would oppose him survive. He alone wanted to hold the most powerful magic and the seat of power."

Tormaigh shifted as the sound of a late season cicada temporarily derailed her. She cast a glance over the trees toward it, gathering her thoughts once again.

"The vile creatures he calls his army we learned to call The Xard. It didn't take long for the Superiors that presided over village life to become entangled in the desire for power. When faced with the choice to join Lord Onyx or flee, most chose the more comfortable option. Supposing that it was better to work with him and keep their many possessions. They turned on their own people for material possessions," Tormaigh's eyes burned with an angry fire and she ground her teeth together. "That's how Dagrune got into the predicament it's in now. With the Superiors on his side there is no one to stand between the people and the suffering he causes them. With such strict and cruel laws about magic, anyone who possesses the gifts are in danger. But even if they could use them, most cannot be used in battle. Especially against one who's power we do not know the limits of."

Hayden sat up glancing as subtly as possible to either side of her. She'd read enough books and watched enough movies to know what was coming next.

"So let me guess. This gift or whatever. You somehow need me for it? Like… I'm gonna go on some quest and… Jesus Christ! I can't even say it. This is just so damn bonkers! Would you listen to yourself Hayden?!"

She wrapped her fingers around the binder that held her hair in a ponytail, wincing as she pulled it off more vigorously than she'd meant to. Her fingers massaged her scalp as generous amounts of hair cascaded around her face. Calliope exchanged a look with Tormaigh, and her silent plea to be the one to give the truly shocking news was granted.

"Well, actually, it's more than that," Calliope said with a glint in her eye. "You are a descendant of that family. The only one who can reclaim your place on the throne. You are the rightful Princess."

Hayden froze, her fingers still tangled in her hair as she took a moment to process what she thought she'd just heard. A quiet giggle escaped from beneath her hair cave. Slowly, it grew, until her entire body shook with laughter. Then, with a loud guffaw that made everyone else jump, she threw her head back, causing her hair to tumble into a messy pile around her shoulders.

"Get the hell outta here!" she said in her best Italian accent. "A princess. A *fucking* princess. No. No. No. This is some weird-ass dream, and I'm going to wake up any minute now. Pinch me," she shoved her arm toward Calliope, who recoiled—having never encountered such a request before.

"Fine, I'll do it," Hayden said, and without waiting, she pinched her own arm. "Nope. Definitely awake. That should leave a nice bruise too."

The skin around the freshly pinched area had already begun to turn pink.

"Okay. I know there's more. Just hit me with it."

Though Tormaigh had never seen this side of Hayden, Calliope was well-acquainted with it. She knew it was just Hayden's way of processing overwhelming information, so she nodded encouragingly for Tormaigh to continue.

"Lord Onyx has lived an unnaturally long life which we believe has something to do with his unique magic. And no one has seen anything of the like until…" Her voice trailed off and she looked out over the landscape around them.

"Until what?" Both Calliope and Hayden said in unison.

"Until you. Your magic is supposed to be purple as a royal descendant, not blue."

Hayden threw her hands up, letting them flop back into her lap.

"Oh great. So now my magic is broken. Cause that makes so much sense. What is it with this color thing anyway, and why does it matter so much?"

"Well," Tormaigh replied cautiously. "The color means different kinds of energy. Some are more powerful than others which I explained before about the Royal's. The Raxyief have the power of the forest, which is green, the Gworrdikan have the power of the earth. That one is brown. And the Neidraium's is pink with power over their watery home."

"Shut! UP!" Hayden cried, her eyes wide. She found herself slipping into the intrigue of the story. A strange sense of acceptance that maybe the life she'd always known had felt out of place to some degree. "So you're telling me you have fairies, dwarves and mermaids?! You should have led with that."

The sound of Calliope's laugh made Hayden smile. Somehow, the bell-like quality fit her exactly as it should.

"Ah Hayden, no wonder you've always obsessed over fantasy type literature and movies. All these ideas came from some sort of reality, wouldn't you agree? If the stories are true, and I believe they are, our worlds weren't so dissimilar once upon a time."

Tormaigh's folded fingers turned a lighter shade of gray as she squeezed them tightly. She refused to disrespect her royalty, but Calliope was dancing on her last nerve, as usual, and was fair game.

"I would like to finish my story without more of your helpful interruptions if you please."

With an understanding of the edge she'd carved out for herself to stand on, Calliope closed her lips. Placing her hand over her mouth, she bowed to Tormaigh. In their custom, this was the ultimate promise that one would let their companion speak without interruption.

"There are more than just those beings with magic. The gifts are also granted to the commoner, but these are different. They interacting with the energy within a body, rather than the world. The Menders magic is white, its noble purpose to heal physical wounds and ailments. Sages magic is orange; their desire to create is similar to the Great Ones. They forever work to find ways to make the life of their people easier and more efficient. Their magic allows them to create the things they imagine. I could go on as there are many more kinds, but I hope that at least gives you some idea of who your subjects are."

Tormaigh, finally satisfied with the information she'd provided, placed her hand on her mouth, pulling it in a downward motion. She did this while holding Calliope's gaze, effectively releasing her from her promise of silence.

"Wow," Hayden whistled. "But… what about you guys? I thought I saw grey light when you changed. Is that your magic? You shape shift? Do all your people look like you?"

Calliope looked wistfully across the driveway, in no way focusing on the world around her.

"No, we aren't born this way. We are commoners. But long ago, our women were given power over the shadows. It is a power that is only granted if the Angel deems one of us worthy. But that is a story for another day," she resolved, bringing herself back to the present.

Hayden dropped her head into her hands with a sigh.

"This last month has been so much for me. I've learned tons about my past here, and now this? I feel so overwhelmed! I'm just some person hoping to live her life out in the quiet of the mountains. I'm no heroine," she said this while the endless worries of the last couple months ran amuck in her head.

Calliope understood all too well the exact type of thoughts that were plaguing her beloved friend.

"I know exactly what you mean," she placed a hand lightly on Hayden's arm. "That's pretty much how I felt when I found out the Angel blessed me with her gift. My whole life was changed in a moment. I had to leave everything I knew behind. It's been a lonely road, but my companions have made leaving my family bearable," Calliope smiled warmly at all three of them. "Yes, especially you Bérg."

She gave the wiggling canine a quick pat on the head, then moved her nails underneath his ear and his leg thumped in response as she found his favorite spot.

"So, this would actually give me an answer as to where I came from. With everything I found out from the PI, maybe I did just appear on a road somewhere. Then those people found me; but why did it have to be them finding me?" Tormaigh cleared her throat, attempting to draw them back to their pressing conversation. "You're right," Hayden acknowledged her. "I got a little side tracked–so... this Angel. You've met her? As in–you've actually seen her physical form and talked to her?" she asked.

Tormaigh cast a furtive glance Calliopes way.

"Of course we have. She reveals herself when necessary. Why do you ask?"

Hayden waved away the question with a dismissive hand. "Just not the way it works here, that's all. As you said," she nodded to Calliope, "a story for another time."

Hayden passed a hand over her face, trying to mentally sort everything into something that would make sense. She squeezed her chin. "My whole life I felt just a little bit out of place, no matter where I was. My therapist gave attributes to my childhood, but this makes so many things fall into place. It has to be the answer I've been searching for."

"What's a therapist?" Tormaigh asked,

Calliope leaned toward Hayden, happy that she didn't recoil in apprehension.

"Let me take this one," she winked. "They are much like our Advisors. Here, they sit and talk about tough things people are dealing with to help them heal their minds," she then looked to Hayden. "On Dagrune, their gift allows them to help those suffering pain in their mind through magic."

"Can we take a beat please?" Hayden said abruptly. She'd begun to toe the line of feeling overwhelmed again. "I need time, which will mean a hike to clear my head. I was planning on riding a certain horse today, but it appears that is no longer acceptable."

Tormaigh smiled down at Hayden.

"On the contrary my princess," she said, stretching skyward. "I would be most honored to carry a member of the royal family. However, that horrible brown seat will not be touching my back again. I accepted it when I felt I couldn't communicate with you, but this will no longer hold true," the tone in Tormaigh's voice made Hayden blush in shame.

"I'm sorry. If I'd known any of this, I would never have put you through the indignity of treating you like an actual animal. The same goes to you also, Calliope."

Calliope snorted, exchanging a knowing look with Tormaigh.

"We've discussed this at length. Any animal would be lucky to be in your care. We felt like a part of your family."

Tormaigh morphed and was once again ophrahl. With Calliope's help, Hayden was able to climb onto her back.

"I've never attempted riding without a saddle, so please go easy on me. Is it ok for me to grab onto your mane for support?" Hayden didn't know what might be offensive and therefore proceeded with caution.

"You're more than welcome to hold onto my mane. Just don't pull too hard," Tormaigh's voice sounded in Hayden's thoughts once again.

She took quickly to riding without a saddle, and the tickle of the wind in her face worked to ease some of her mental burden as they trotted along. Bérg, unable to hide his enthusiasm at getting to go along this time, ran ahead so he had more time to investigate everything. Calliope used the trees as her own personal ninja course, keeping pace with Bérg's erratic wanderings. There was only one destination in Hayden's mind, which she communicated to her newly found companions.

"I guess I can't really say you're new," she mused.

Her laugh echoed through the quiet of the mountains at the irony of it all.

They made short work of the distance between home and the lake. It was the one place Hayden went when she needed time to think—and today, she craved it more than ever. As she stared at the broken rock sheared in half by her magic, she thought about her childhood and how Clara stepped in to save her. What if she hadn't? She easily could have turned a blind eye because it truly *wasn't* her obligation. This woman had upended her life to take a chance on a kid who could have easily been a burden, and Hayden's life had been so much better for it. As her scattered thoughts began to settle, she reluctantly recognized—sometimes doing the right thing wasn't the clear and easy path. A huge sigh escaped her lips, making her doubts flit away. She knew now what she must do.

<u>12</u>

Someone Already Knew

"Cancel my classes? Why on earth would I do that?" Hayden asked, miffed that they would even suggest it. "I would think you'd want me to hone my hand-to-hand fighting skills too, wouldn't you?" Calliope of all people should have known how important it was to her, since Hayden was certain she'd overheard the many phone conversations with Mum.

"Prin… Hayden, I understand how connected you are to this part of your life," Calliope stuttered, trying to respect Hayden's discomfort with the title. "It's important, but we must spend as much time as possible working on getting you to control your magic. We know you can't give up your job right now, and frankly, your skill at sparring is nothing to be ashamed of, so this is the only logical thing to step back from."

Hayden huffed. She couldn't deny that Calliope had a point, but she had *just* started back up.

"I see your point," Hayden finally conceded, her shoulders dropping in defeat. Then an idea popped into her head, and she lifted her chin hopefully. "How about this. I would like to propose a compromise," she removed her right hand from her hip and lifted her pointer finger. "I'll go to classes for the next month while I try to figure out a way to tell Matilde I need a break. Again."

Calliope and Tormaigh exchanged a pointed look as they tried to decide if it was worth pushing the issue.

"Alright, if this is what you wish we will honor it," Tormaigh agreed reluctantly. "The only thing I would ask of you, is that you promise to focus more of your solo practice time on your magic. Although it is a part of you, it's not as easy to control as you might think. And if people are as bad as you say—which I don't dispute by the way," She corrected herself quickly as she sensed Hayden's anxiety rise. "You don't want to accidentally show them and have to explain it."

Hayden reached her hand toward Tormaigh. This wasn't the first time that she'd made the gesture when they came to an agreement. And so Tormaigh did not hesitate to grab her offered hand to seal their words.

"Deal," Hayden smiled, then her brow creased as another thought crossed her mind. "But also, that just brings to light more stuff I need to deal with. I have to figure out how I'll tell Mum about all of this," she turned in a circle, taking in the scenery as if she was seeing it for the first time again. It was funny how the knowledge that she could very soon lose it made her see it that way. "Plus a way to end my job, and this place..." Her voice trailed off as she tried to choke back tears. "I love this place so much. I don't want to leave it."

Hayden had been working so hard to shove down all the confusing emotions of the last couple weeks, that she couldn't maintain the block any longer and her resolve crumbled all at once. She crumpled to the ground as the flood of emotions overwhelmed her and finally allowed the tears to flow.

Bérg didn't hesitate—he all but climbed into her lap, whining and licking her tears as they fell. Her body shook with uncontrollable sobs as wave after wave of memory and emotion accosted her. She wrapped her arms around his giant neck, burying her face in his soft fur. When the sobs subsided, she straightened her back, wiping the tears from her face with purpose.

"Hayden, I have a suggestion," Calliope spoke up, her tone gentler than usual. "I remember a phone conversation, where your professor offered to come here to train you. Do you think it's still a possibility?" she suggested hopefully. The pain that Hayden was feeling surrounded them like a heavy cloud. And it was all she could do to hold back tears of her own.

Hayden searched her memory. Calliope was right. She'd forgotten that little tidbit. And for a moment she felt a slight lightening of her mental load.

"You know, I think that's a great suggestion," her swollen face lit up. "I'll call her and see if she's willing to come today. But you two have to be Ophrahl while she's here," she pointed back and forth between them, a warning scowl on her brow.

The phone call didn't last long. Matilde had been quick to agree to the last-minute request. With that taken care of, Hayden made the decision to also call her Mum.

"Sweety I'd love to! You know how much I love watching your sessions," Clara's initial enthusiasm faded as she asked, "But are you ok? You sound like you could use a mom hug."

Hayden fought back fresh tears. Mum always seemed to be able to tell exactly what kind of mood she was in. There was no hiding it from her.

"Thanks Mum. I think I would really like that," she replied shakily.

Clara, being the closer of the two, arrived well before Matilde. And the hug she promised did exactly what Hayden hoped it would. There was a warmth to them that no one had ever been able to replicate.

"Mum, you give the best hugs. But squeeze any harder, and you might crush my ribs," she teased.

"Well you're so tall that's about as high as I reach," Clara said as she stepped back to study Hayden's face. "Somethings going on. But I feel like you're thinking it may be better to run by your therapist first."

Hayden sighed. She should have known better than to try and hide her mood in person. She would never fool Mum when it came right down to it.

"I honestly don't know. It's all muddled at the moment and I can't even think of where I would begin anyway," she turned her face away, feigning the need to smooth down her Gi .

"It's ok, we've been here many times," Clara said, patting Hayden's arm. "You'll tell me when the time is right."

Hayden, knowing there was no need for a response, led her to the porch swing where she'd prepared the spot just as Mum liked it. The pillows propped up in the corner offered a more comfortable place to rest her back. They'd logged countless hours sitting side by side on this swing as they were now. Half that time, they would converse late into the evening while the other half they'd enjoy each other's company in silence; letting the sounds of nature do all the talking for them. And as usual, the second Clara made herself comfortable Calliope jumped onto her lap.

When Matilde arrived, they wasted no time in getting down to business. Hayden already felt as if they were behind schedule, and due to that she rushed through her meditation. They picked up where they'd left off. The techniques had become more complex, requiring greater concentration than usual. But because of everything weighing on her mind, she was finding it difficult to properly execute the instructions being slung at her. Finally, Matilde had had enough.

"Slow down Hayden, you're letting your emotions run you. I can sense your anger. This is not the way to honor and integrity and it makes you lose focus. Let's take a minute to re-center."

Hayden bowed respectfully to her Professor. She was right. Her head wasn't in it today.

"Oss professor. My sincerest apologies. I know I'm not at my best today."

Matilde sidled up to Hayden, threading an arm through her crooked elbow. Hayden's eyes were closed but still she did not shy away from the unexpected touch.

"They *are* good friends you know," she said with a slight pause to gauge Hayden's reaction. "They really only want the best for you. I would also venture a guess that your mother will understand. You should tell her."

Hayden stiffened, opening her eyes to slowly look down on Matilde.

"What friends?" she asked innocently.

Matilde squeezed her elbow and winked as a knowing smile played on her lips.

"Your companions aren't who they appear to be. I can sense it. And... I've known about your magic since your first class."

Hayden dropped Matilde's arm abruptly. She stepped back, mouth agape, glaring incredulously at her professor.

"You mean to tell me that you somehow knew about this?!" She shot at her. "But how? I only just found my magic. And if that's true, why in the world have you never said anything about it before?!"

She searched Matilde's face, looking for something–anything that would tell her she was joking. But how could she be? To joke about something so specific wouldn't make sense. As she grappled to reconcile her thoughts with logic, Matilde grabbed her elbow and began to steer her back toward the porch.

"All in due time Hayden. I will answer all your questions after you've told your mother."

Clara knew something was amiss. They'd only been training for about 10 minutes, and already they were stomping toward her, away from the sparring mats.

"You're not done already, are you? It seems like you just started," she asked, her tilted head drawing a chuckle from Hayden.

"You look like you've spent too much time around Bérg lately," Hayden teased lightly. She was trying to work up the courage to face the possibility that Mum might have her shipped off to the psych ward. After all, what she was about to tell her she barely believed herself. "I need to tell you something. It's going to sound absolutely crazy and you probably won't believe a word I'm saying. So please hear me out first," Hayden pleaded.

Clara folded her hands—a small but unmistakable sign that Hayden had her full attention.

"Ok, I can do that. What's on your mind?" She then patted the bench beside her and Hayden accepted the invitation, grabbing Mum's hand for reassurance.

"I don't know where to start. There's so much to say," she said, casting her eyes downward.

"How about you start with two weeks ago, when you started to pull away from talking to me."

Hayden raised her chin to look at Clara and a feeling of regret crept into her chest. The one person in the world that always had her best interest at heart—that's who she should have gone to first.

"I'm sorry. I just didn't know how to tell you. But now that we're here, I think this is something that you need to hear."

She began her story with the night she was struck by lightning. As the words tumbled out, she kept thinking how much crazier it all sounded out loud. Mum gave her hand the occasional squeeze of encouragement. But when Hayden revealed who Calliope and Tormaigh really were, Clara went quiet, her eyes dropping to the cat curled on her lap. The silence that followed made Hayden shift uncomfortably.

"Please say something Mum. Anything to let me know what you're thinking."

Clara, appearing lost in thought, jolted back to herself with a start, her hand returning to its idle rhythm.

"That's a lot to digest. I can't imagine how isolated you must have felt thinking you had to carry such a burden alone all this time," she leaned closer to Hayden, nudging her arm. "I knew about the magic," she whispered.

Hayden sat upright, abruptly twisting toward Mum.

"I'm sorry. There's no way I heard that right," she said with an accusatory stare. "You too?!"

Clara didn't flinch as Hayden's gaze threatened to bore straight through her. Instead she returned the look confidently.

"Honey, It's part of the reason that I tried so hard to find out where you came from. I not only wanted to find out for your sake, but also for my own peace of mind. Please don't be upset with me, but I swore Matilde to secrecy. There was just too much about this that we didn't understand. And when we were finally able to stop your magic from hurting you, we thought it was safe to assume we'd never see it again. But I'm going to let her tell you that part of your story," she concluded, jutting her chin toward Matilde.

Hayden sat forward, folding her hands, resting her elbows on her knees, and casting an accusatory glance between Mum and Matilde. "So you're in this together," she said, narrowing her eyes. "Somehow this all makes so much more sense," typically she would have tried to mask the disappointment, but although she knew Mum never did anything that wasn't in her best interest, she still felt a twinge of betrayal.

Clara lifted her chin in defiance. This moment was born of a decision she'd taken very seriously so many years ago. "I stand by my decision. I wrestled with it long enough when I made it. If you're upset with me, I've made my peace with that possibility too," the finality in her reply made Hayden snap her lips closed. The sarcastic remark she had at the ready didn't seem right to say after Clara's admission.

Matilde, intent on pulling Hayden back to the important issue at hand, cleared her throat loudly. She leaned in, resting on the porch railing.

"You were so angry when you first started your training," she said, her gaze focused on the warped boards of the porch. "Understandably so. And it was only a couple sessions in, when I started to see this blue electricity coming off of your chest and arms," she reached out to gently grab Hayden's limp hand and Hayden looked up to meet her eyes. "You were so vulnerable in those moments. Even without that magic, I knew that whatever you had been through was beyond my scope of expertise. Despite that, I tried to help, hoping that you would eventually gain control of it. But I was wrong," Matilde released Hayden's hand, folding her fingers together. "I finally took a chance, deciding that it was time to have a chat with your Mum. I was so relieved when she wasn't surprised. Apparently the same thing would happen during your nightmares. We were worried you would hurt yourself, or someone else, if we did nothing—so I planned a trip back to the place of my birth. There were rumors—stories of a Shaman that lived in a remote village in the mountains. One that knew of magic."

The dull clack of a hoof striking gravel pulled Matilde's attention toward the driveway. As her eyes landed on Tormaigh's Ophrahl quietly grazing, she let out a small gasp. "Magic to be sure," she whispered. "What a magnificent creature," then shaking her head, she jumped back into her story as if there'd been no interruption. "Until I met you, I never imagined that the story held any weight. Thankfully, it didn't end up being too difficult to track him down. And when I finally met him he didn't seem surprised in the least by your story. In fact, he seemed to know exactly what you needed. So he gave me this mixture of herbs followed by a warning. I had to get them to you in a tea as quickly as possible lest their potency fade. So I followed his instructions to the letter. After that, we never saw your magic again."

Matilde's hands rested lightly on the railing as she waited for the barrage of questions she knew was coming. Calliope took the moment to slip down from Clara's lap and saunter a few paces onto the lawn. Hayden had only known her as Morphé for a short time, but she already understood what was going through the Ophrahl's mind. She didn't even need the Link to know.

"Ladies, I don't want you to be startled," she said quickly. "Calliope and Tormaigh are about to do their morphing thing. It can be alarming at first, so brace yourself."

When the dust settled, Clara covered her mouth. Hayden could practically see her thoughts racing as she took them in.

"Where on earth are their clothes?" she blurted, eyes wide with shock.

"Mum!" Hayden admonished, " maybe a little rude?"

But Tormaigh's hearty laugh cut off her reproach. Her tone held a strong air of amusement.

"Now, how exactly would clothing survive a shift into Ophrahl? I'd shred anything I tried to wear, and Calliope would just vanish under a pile of fabric. This is what we Morphé look like. We don't need clothing—our Ophrahl side is more than capable of keeping us warm. All the perks of being human, plus the benefits of the beast," she said, her chest swelling with pride.

Color crept into Clara's cheeks as she tripped over her tongue to apologize.

"Clara, your apology is sweet but not needed. For those who have never witnessed magic, we can be quite shocking. I would, however, like this one to stop circling us," she said, snorting at Matilde.

Unfazed by Tormaigh's annoyance, Matilde finally came to a halt, satisfied with her investigation.

"You have questions," Matilde stated. "Now would be the time to ask them."

Tormaigh smiled down on Matilde, sensing the kindred spirit of another warrior.

"I do," Tormaigh nodded. "This person you call a Shaman. Did he have any unusual features or do anything you might see as ritualistic?"

Matilde rolled the end of her braid through her fingers, a far off look in her eyes as she pondered the question.

"It was a long time ago, so I'm trying to bring back a mental image of him," she closed her eyes, swaying as she searched her memories. "I'm not seeing anything out of the ordinary physically—but... he did seem to rub his chest a lot. Oh right—I remember now. After he rubbed his chest he would brush off his arms–like this," she said, demonstrating the motion.

"So there have been more," Tormaigh whispered under her breath.

"More what now?" Hayden asked, leaning forward earnestly. "Please, I really don't want any more secrets. What do I need to know?"

Tormaigh held back a sigh. This development was as much a surprise to her as it would be to Hayden.

"Princess, it appears you weren't the first one from our home world to come to this one. It would seem that one of our own Advisors made it here. And he appears to be able to harness his magic still. I'm nearly certain that he put magic in that tea. And we need to find out what it did to you."

Hayden felt the weight of her secret whisked away as the conversation ebbed and flowed well into the evening. They shifted easily between discussing the world of her birth and the one she currently called home. She smiled often, her eyes shining as she witnessed two of the most important people in her life joining in, as if they were discussing the weather. For the first time in a long while, she felt completely at peace.

When it was time to part ways, Matilde's embrace lasted longer than usual.

"When will I see you again? Is this our final goodbye?" Hayden asked, wiping a tear before it could fall. "I'm sorry… you shouldn't have to see me this weak," she sniffed.

"No," Matilde replied sharply. "Don't you ever let anyone tell you that emotions are a weakness. You've been to hell and back. You only become weak when you try to pretend those emotions aren't an integral part of you. Besides, I have a feeling we'll cross paths again down the road. Reach out if you think there is anything I can assist you with."

As the headlights disappeared from view, Hayden felt a distinct sense of loss. But it wouldn't be the last time she'd feel that sting. Her circle of friends was small, but what it lacked in numbers, it more than made up for in quality. There would be no easy goodbyes.

13

Practice Practice Practice

Hayden threw herself headlong into work. She needed something to feel normal, something mundane. But that luxury stayed just out of reach. Even her job seemed determined to upend her peace, with an unusual number of last-minute emergencies piling up.

As the week drew to a close, a new, frosty bite crept into the air—a warning that winter in the mountains was drawing near. The only trees still clinging to their brittle, dying leaves, was the majestic oak.

Friday arrived too quickly, catching Hayden in a tangled web of anticipation and dread. Today, they would officially begin teaching her to control the magic. A few wispy clouds drifted overhead, guiding them toward the clearing they'd chosen. Bérg paced nearby, ears alert—he was the designated lookout, and he took the role seriously.

With Tormaigh's background as a general of the Alchmene, she naturally claimed the role of mentor. Calliope, on the other hand, offered to provide moral support—though Hayden suspected Calliope's definition of that might differ from her own.

"The first thing we need to address," Tormaigh began, "is how you will allow the magic to flow through you, without letting it consume you. You were caught unaware because of your emotions the last two times—we cannot allow that to happen again. Now it's time to learn how to harness it and make it do what you desire," she instructed Hayden to sit down and extend her hands out, palms facing skyward. "Can you feel it?" she asked, hardly waiting for an answer. "The sun's energy isn't as warm in this world, but that's still where your magic comes from. You have to open yourself to its power," Tormaigh paced, hands clasped behind her back. She'd lost count of how many times she'd been at this beginning stage with a new pupil. It was so familiar now, she could almost do it in her sleep. "There's a reason time in the sun feels so refreshing," she continued. "But the planet's most vital star will never force its power on you—that's why you have to let it in."

Hayden had always loved the feeling of the sun on her skin and today was no exception. She raised her chin to welcome its warmth, determined to put even the smallest detail of Tormaigh's instruction into practice. All it took was a simple thought—a yes—then a surge of energy washed over her. "Whoo-eeee!" She yelled, springing to her feet. "Where has this been all my life?!"

She dropped instinctively into a defensive stance, throwing a half-hearted flurry of punches at an invisible bag to warm up for a sprint. She reached out, balancing lightly on her fingertips—then exploded forward—arms and legs pumping in perfect rhythm. She was closing the distance to the far tree line much faster than she'd thought possible. *If I can run faster, maybe I can flip better?* The thought had barely crossed her mind before she gave in to the chaos. Hayden dove forward, executing a perfect front handspring—then another, and another. She landed cleanly on her feet, just inches from the edge. Without missing a beat, she spun to face Calliope. "How 'bout them apples?!" she shouted across the clearing.

Calliope's smile widened, slowly revealing her sharp canines. She snorted at Hayden's challenge.

"Pretty good for a newbie!" she razzed back.

"Alright alright ladies," Tormaigh called out, beckoning Hayden to rejoin them. "Now that you've had your fun let's get back to the business of that energy you just experienced. Although it feels endless now, it will only take a little of your magic to drain it. You must keep that in mind. The moon only reflects the power of the sun—it cannot carry it—therefore it cannot restore your magic. Conserve when you can."

Hayden settled into a meditation pose, her hands resting lightly on her knees. She welcomed the sun again, shivering as its power sent a tingle through her body. She could feel it soaking into every pore, every cell—bringing with it an energy unlike any other.

"Now, you must find a memory—one that makes you wildly happy. Once you have it, hold on to the emotion connected to it."

Hayden dug deep, sifting through her memories in search of the perfect one. A blush crept into her cheeks. She'd found it—and she knew it was exactly the one she needed.

It was her first kiss. She was 17 and that boy treated her like she was the only person on the planet. The whole thing played out like something straight out of a romance novel. Their first kiss had been wild and passionate, but when he moved away...

Tormaigh pat the ground between them to get Hayden's attention. "You aren't focusing on the positive. I want you to only hold the feeling of happiness in your mind."

Hayden's eyes fluttered—she adjusted herself, intent on making a good impression with her first attempt.

"Ok good. Now hold onto that and open your eyes," Tormaigh instructed, her voice betraying a proud smile.

Hayden did as she was told. She'd only seen her magic twice before, but it had never looked like this. She gasped, her mouth falling open in awe. From her hands to her chest, small, angled points of light were emanating from her skin. It looked like electricity, but she felt nothing more than a faint buzz—as if her cells were quietly vibrating. She moved her arms, twisting and turning, watching as the light danced across her skin.

Tormaigh and Calliope looked on in amusement.

"That must have been some kiss," Calliope whistled.

Crimson crept back into Hayden's cheeks.

"That was a bit private maybe?" She countered shyly.

But the distraction had done it's work. The light on her body slowly faded, then disappeared.

"Will I always have to stay so mentally engaged when I'm trying to use this? It seems a bit counterintuitive if I have to do this much work while trying to defend myself. Or worse. Someone else," an image of herself, drained of strength and magic in the heat of battle flashed through her mind.

"We just started training. There's no need to worry yourself about that yet," Tormaigh soothed. "You will get stronger with time. Basing anything off your first attempt is bordering on madness. Imagine..." she paused, tapping her chin in thought. "Imagine if you had lost confidence after performing your first operation. Nothing you put your hand to will be perfect at first."

Hayden nodded. A part of her subconscious absorbed the advice, but another—the stronger side—shoved it to the back of her mind. She'd gotten used to being counted on, so she would treat this much the same as everything else she put her hand to.

"The next emotion I want you to focus on is mirth," Tormaigh went on. "You will notice a slightly different manifestation of your magic. I need you to understand... whatever emotion you're working with will make it react with your mind and body differently."

That didn't really make sense to Hayden. Weren't mirth and happiness the same, if not at least adjacent? But she tossed the thought aside. If there was one glaring point gleaned from the many years under Matilde's tutelage, it was to trust the teacher's process. So she again settled herself into a state of focus, and this time a picture of Mum popped into her head.

They were trying to shovel the sidewalk after a significant amount of snow had fallen. Two feet of the unusually heavy

stuff sat atop a layer of ice. With less-than-ideal footing, they
kept slipping. Unable to stay on their feet, they eventually
dissolved into laughter. So lost were they in their giggles that
Mum lost control of her bladder—which left them rolling
weakly on the ground, in the throes of even more laughter.

She had to giggle at the memory, and when she opened her eyes, the light twisted and swayed as if stirred by a gentle breeze—though she couldn't feel it on her skin.

Tormaigh encouraged her, "You're doing well," she said. "Now see if you can make the energy do something you want it to. It can be anything."

Hayden, more than eager to oblige, raised her palms to the trees surrounding them. She had to fight down the creeping notion—that feeling that she was trying to copy what she'd seen in movies. But neither Tormaigh nor Calliope seemed to share her sentiment. They instead, appeared to be riveted to her every move. So, concentrating on a rather large pine, she imagined it swaying in the gale force winds of a hurricane.

At first, nothing happened. She stared down the tree, brow furrowed in concentration, silently pleading for it to move. Then, as if it heard her unspoken command, it suddenly leapt into motion, thrashing wildly to and fro. With a cry of surprised triumph, she dropped her hand into her lap. She half expected to feel her strength drained—but instead, she felt as powerful as ever. "So I don't need to create the ball of light to make things happen?" she asked, studying her hands.

"No. Definitely not," Tormaigh confirmed. "The orb is made with the emotions that are more difficult for you to control. Once we've practiced enough, and you figure out how to regulate your minds hold over the magic, only then will I have you try again. For now we are going to keep it simple. Manipulate one of those branches. Bend it. You will use it as a sling shot to send Calliope... hmmm" she turned slowly, scanning the clearing. "Right... there."

Although Calliope seldom appeared as Ophrahl these days, Hayden still found it difficult to see her as anything other than the small cat she'd taken on so many years ago—and the vision of her being impaled on a branch due to Hayden's tenuous grasp on her magic felt all too real. But then again, after spending the past couple weeks watching her display an otherworldly ability to manipulate her body in tight situations, that fear quickly vanished.

Calliope sauntered confidently up to the tree, springing onto a branch with barely any effort. Her anticipation was nearly palpable as she honed in on her target, muscles tightening as she readied herself to launch.

"Ok, here goes nothing," Hayden breathed, wiping her sweaty palms on her sweatshirt. "It's too late to sign the safety waver. You sure about this Calliope?"

But Calliope was locked in and ready. Without even the tiniest flinch, she hissed quietly. "I was born for this."

Hayden took a deep breath to calm her shaking hands. The first time she'd asked the tree to let her in, and it had—that had to be how this worked. It still felt strange to ask something inanimate to work with her, but Calliope was waiting, and this seemed to be the key. She reached across the distance with her thoughts and magic, and the branch trembled—bending easily to her will.

Heartened by the tree's cooperation, she tightened her hold, steadily pulling the branch toward herself. But with the added pressure, an odd sense of strain began to bleed into her magic—almost as if the tree itself were in pain. Hayden relented, letting the branch ease into a more comfortable position as she carefully released some of the tension. It should still have enough snap to send Calliope across the open space. "*Ready, Calliope?*" she asked through the link. "*Three, two, one... and GO!*" With a whistling swish, she let the branch fly.

Calliope exploded into action. With a wild cry, she sailed across the short distance, digging her claws into the trunk of a massive pine. The tree quivered, swaying as she curled her body around it—bark flying as she kicked off.

Hayden watched in awe at the effortless way her body flowed, twisting between the branches. Then, with a final huff, Calliope hit the ground running and was back at Hayden's side in no time. Her breathing was steady, and not a drop of sweat touched her brow.

"Show-off!" Hayden said, sticking out her tongue playfully.

Calliope smirked, a hint of shameless pride in her voice. "Cat, remember? No one moves like me."

With a glint in her eye, she flopped back down and buried her nose in her latest favorite story, already lounging as if nothing had happened.

Hour after hour rolled by the constraints of time forgotten as they worked through a multitude of emotions. With each one, her magic shifted—both in how it behaved and how it felt. Tormaigh used the branch's movement as a baseline to highlight those changes.

When it came to emotions like frustration, annoyance, or embarrassment, she found it much harder to make the branch cooperate—almost as if her inability to focus directly affected the living thing. In contrast, emotions like sadness, loneliness, and shame brought a complete reluctance to move. Even though she could feel the magic flowing through her, it had no effect.

As much as she wanted to keep practicing, the long day had begun to take its toll. Her last few attempts had failed, and she knew it was time for a breather.

"I'm getting kinda tired. Can we take a little brea—"

But Hayden never got the chance to finish the question. She slumped forward into the brittle grass, bringing Tormaigh and Calliope to her side in seconds.

Calliope pressed her ear to Hayden's chest.
"What happened? Is she okay?! Did you know this could happen?!"

She sat back on her heels, satisfied by Hayden's strong heartbeat, her eyes searching Tormaigh's face for an answer.

Tormaigh dropped to her knees beside Hayden.
"How did I miss this?" she asked in bewilderment. "I would've given her a break sooner if I'd known. But... she didn't say anything."

"Yeah, well," Calliope smirked, patting her shoulder. "Welcome to Hayden's world. She'll never let you know when she's struggling."

Tormaigh grunted, shifting into her Ophrahl.
"*Yeah, well,*" she said, mimicking Calliope, "*I'm not sure what's worse—* ***that***, *or a student who can't stop complaining about every minor sniffle.*"

Calliope heaved Hayden's limp body, carefully rolling her onto Tormaigh's back. As Tormaigh got to her feet, Calliope held tightly to both her mane and Hayden.

Bérg trotted alongside them, tuning out their argument—or whatever it was. He whined occasionally, concerned by the state his master was in. He trusted his nose; he could smell death when it was near, even if it were still days away—and she wasn't anywhere close to that.

But it didn't stop him from worrying.

At least they were headed home—and to Clara. *She* would know what to do.

****

The bedroom slowly came into focus. She could see the afternoon sun lazily streaming through her window. Shadows from the pine just outside wave slowly at her from the wall. A small pile of clothing was draped over the foot of her bed and trailed onto the floor. She made a mental note to tidy up, but for now she just wanted to stay snuggled under the warm covers. Then a thought dawned on her. Why was she sleeping in the middle of the day? She threw off the blanket.

"What a dream!" she whistled quietly. "I could write a best seller off of that weirdness."

"Hayden?!" Mum called from the living room. "I'm on my way. Don't you *dare* get out of that bed!"

There was an urgency—an almost irrational concern—in her voice. Clara strode through the doorway with a cup of tea in hand and worry written plainly on her face.

"Mum, I'm fine!" Hayden said, puzzled by the reaction as she took the tea that was promptly shoved into her hands. "And even if I weren't, *you* of all people shouldn't be helping me out of bed."

But Clara, acting as though Hayden hadn't said a word, turned toward the hallway and bellowed Calliope's name at the top of her lungs.

"Now how is the cat gonna..." Hayden began, but her words trailed off, replaced with a groan as Calliope appeared in her Morphé form.

"So I didn't dream all of it, then. A part of me keeps hoping it's that. How long was I out?" she asked, massaging her temples.

Clara sat beside her, resting a hand gently on Hayden's arm. "Twenty-four hours since you passed out," she said, her voice much softer now that Hayden seemed to be acting more like herself. "Tormaigh promised it was safe to just let you sleep. If it were up to me, you'd be in a hospital bed right now. How are you feeling?"

Hayden swatted Clara's hand away as she reached out to feel her forehead.
"I feel normal. Not tired at all, actually. Are you going to stop fussing over me and let me out of bed now?" she asked sarcastically, heaving herself off the mattress.
"Is Bérg okay? I vaguely remember a lot of whining."

Calliope walked as close as she dared—ready to lend a steadying hand, but far enough back to dodge one of Hayden's swats if it came to that.

"He's fine," Calliope replied, "and waiting patiently for you outside."

It was time to talk to Tormaigh. Whatever had happened, Hayden was sure she held the answers.

She crossed the lawn to where Tormaigh sat–legs crossed, her unusual blue eyes fixed on something in the distance. Hayden settled down beside her.

"Your mother told me about your guardians," Tormaigh said quietly, "and what you endured in their care–how that affects your drive for success, and your reluctance to ask for help. I am truly sorry, Hayden."

She bowed, pressing an open hand to her chest.

"No one should have to go through that. However... if I *had* known, I might've tried harder to check in with you during training," her gaze shifted to meet Hayden's. "I'm not entirely unfamiliar with the need to appear strong in the face of adversity. But you have nothing to prove to me. Following that path again could be dangerous. Some magic," she added, her voice wavering for a moment, "if you're not careful... it could end your light," she fell silent, the weight of the warning hanging between them.

She could sense it in Tormaigh's caution–she was hesitant to resume training. But Hayden, eager to continue learning, persuaded her until they reached an agreement: they would pick up again the following day. But only on one condition–Hayden had to promise to do nothing but rest and refuel in the meantime. She readily agreed. It was a small price to pay, and Mum was more than willing to wait on her hand and foot anyway.

They were up in time to see the sun break over the hills. Its rays scattered across the land, casting deeper shadows where the light couldn't reach. Hayden threw on a pair of sweats, a plain tee, and an oversized sweatshirt. It was only practical to be comfortable for a long day of training. As they made their way to the clearing, the few scattered clouds in the sky proved nearly more engaging than Tormaigh's monologue about how much easier training would be under the full influence of the sun.

They moved quietly along the forest floor, carpeted with fallen pine needles. The musk of decomposing leaves puffed into the air as they kicked through scattered piles. Hayden had pulled her arms inside her sweatshirt—even their brisk pace wasn't enough to counter the morning chill.

She was grateful when they finally arrived.

Tormaigh, noticing her discomfort, gave quiet instructions on how to accept the sun's warmth—something that would make it easier to focus on the lesson ahead.

"Let's start today with feelings of serenity and calm," Tormaigh, it seemed, would be wasting no time picking up where she left off. "I want you to understand that none of these emotions are wrong to use with your magic. Each has its own unique merits, strengths, and weaknesses. As you familiarize yourself with how they manifest, you will start to understand when and where they will serve you most."

Then choosing a light breeze as Hayden's baseline for the day, Tormaigh helped until she was confident that a little freedom was in order.

Hayden had gone from coaxing the wind to offer even the smallest breeze to forming small funnels—tiny tornadoes that whipped up piles of leaves and sent them swirling around Tormaigh. She remained perfectly still, almost statuesque, as the leaves danced around her. Feeling bold, Hayden turned her attention to Calliope, who was already snoozing in the crook of a tree. But the prank never landed. As the distance grew between her and the object her magic was manipulating, she felt a sudden drain on her strength. The wind faltered, and the leaves dropped heavily back to the earth.

"You did very well," Tormaigh encouraged. "And as you just discovered: the farther your magic extends from you, the more strength it takes to maintain. But do not be discouraged. I can already see how much more control you have than on your first day. If you continue down this path, you'll soon grow strong enough to forge a way back to our beloved Dagrune."

Hayden's smile faded. She dropped to the ground in front of Tormaigh, stunned. That was something she thought their Angel would handle—*not* her.

It had never crossed her mind that it could be up to her... or that her magic might be capable of something so monumental.

"You can't be serious," she groaned, the weight of it all settling over her. "How do you even know that's possible?"

Tormaigh's voice softened.

"Hayden, I know all this responsibility can feel crushing. But Adelphiana made it clear: *you* are the key to helping us return home. She wouldn't have said so if it weren't true.

Yes, she's powerful. But she has limits. Don't trouble yourself with all of it now. In time, everything will become clear."

It had been a few hours and they'd taken plenty of breaks. Hayden had vowed not repeat her rash mistakes of the previous day. So when Tormaigh granted her the opportunity to work with a stronger emotion, she jumped at the chance.

"I want you to draw on fear. It can be quite unpredictable, so I need you to stay focused—stay in control. When you have the memory you want to use, make sure you let go of the details, and just hold onto the *feeling*. Don't get lost in it," she warned, then raised her voice. "Calliope! Time to wake up. We need you here!" Her call carried, successfully nudging Calliope out of her slumber. "You've known Hayden for longer than I. If she starts to lose control, you can help to calm her."

Hayden nervously chewed her lip. "Well now you're making me worried," she confessed sheepishly.

"I'm giving you cautions, nothing more," Tormaigh said. "I just don't want you to go into this unprepared. I failed you once. I would not be pleased with myself if I were to repeat that blunder."

With Tormaigh's caution fresh on her mind, Hayden settled in to find something she could use. One *could* think it would be an easy task, drawing on the memories of *her* childhood—but when the options are many, coming to a decision can prove difficult. Eventually she landed on one, closed her eyes and buckled down. She would isolate the emotion.

Hayden lay face down on the floor, her hands folded together behind her. The wooden boards pressed uncomfortably on her nose where silent tears pooled. At least it was a distraction from the smell of rotten garbage, *she* thought. *The trash hadn't been emptied in over a week again, because if she didn't do it–it didn't get done. She wanted to squirm away from all of it, but knew that if she moved even one muscle from this position, it would only cause pain from the wooden handled brush to be inflicted twofold.*

The reason for her current punishment? She'd made the mistake of asking Mama for help with her math homework. The class had just started learning about the value of coins. One of her worksheet questions was: how many pennies are in a dollar? Her teacher didn't tell her how many cents were in a dollar, at least not that she recalled, so she had no point of reference.

The sound of cloth moving against itself, and the creak of a floorboard sent a terrified surge to her little heart. Mama was coming back for another round.

"How many pennies are in a dollar?" Mama asked with a hateful sneer.

She'd lost count of the number of times this exact scenario was intentionally played out. It didn't matter if she answered incorrectly or not at all. It always ended the same way. CRACK! The brush hit her on the head. CRACK! This time it was her back, then her buttocks. Mama seemed to relish every blow she inflicted on the small body.

After what felt like hours, Hayden began to feel numb in places that had been struck what felt like hundreds of times.

"When you stop lying to me, this will stop. This is your own fault."

But Mama's words were as far from comforting as they could possibly be.

Hayden's eyes opened to the sight of her light dancing angrily.

"Good. You've found it. Now hold that and see how the wind reacts."

Tormaigh's reassurance was perfectly timed. Hayden felt a little calmer as she closed her eyes to try and concentrate. The moment she saw the dark behind her eyelids, she felt herself being drawn back in. But this time she couldn't seem to pull herself away from it.

Hayden stood in front of the dingy mirror tenderly touching her back where bruising had already begun to show. Pinpoints of blood seeped through her thin shirt. She'd finally guessed the right answer and Mama had ordered the 'little bitch' to get out of her sight. How many times had Mama hit her to cause bleeding in so many places? She could barely sit down because there wasn't a single part of her buttocks or thighs that weren't covered in swelling and bruises. Tears welled up in her little eyes. Angry tears.

She couldn't shake the anger clawing at her chest, growing to an almost painful intensity. Why did she have to endure such horrors? What did she do to deserve having a Mama that had to hurt her like this? Her seven-year-old self hadn't been angry enough. The injustice done that day was unacceptable. Someone had to pay, and in this moment it didn't matter who.

"Princess, no!" Tormaigh screamed, betraying her usual calm in the face of Hayden's change.

Hayden's eyes flew open, revealing pupils blacker than a moonless night, her magic flickering darkly within them. Calliope and Tormaigh looked on in horror as her face twisted into a chilling smirk, her body rising effortlessly. The light that once danced between her hands and chest crackled across the entirety of her body.

Then suddenly, the wind roared, surging until it grew to a frenzy.

"She's blocking me from linking!" Tormaigh shouted, the wind doing its best to drown her out. "If we can't get through to her, this could turn deadly!"

But despite their combined efforts, they couldn't get through. The winds assault forced them backward. Tormaigh dug in, her hooves finding purchase. She held Calliope's hand as they worked together, battering at the door of their link. But Hayden was unfazed, rising higher—her expression morphing into a cruel, mocking smile.

Just as they began to lose hope of ever getting through to her—a deep, furious snarl tore through the trees. In a massive white blur, he burst from the forest, and in a matter of strides—closed the distance. With no sign of slowing, he launched into the air with his powerful hindquarters—straight into Hayden.

His shoulder slammed into her chest, the full force of all one hundred and sixty pounds of him, sending her flying backward. She crashed into the ground, the impact expelling every last ounce of breath from her lungs. With her concentration broken, she could no longer maintain the magical storm and it vanished as abruptly as it had come.

Calliope and Tormaigh collapsed, panting from the effort. And Bérg, though the immediate danger had passed, remained alert. Only when he was sure Hayden had returned to herself did he relax, lying down to rest his head gently on her stomach.

14

Catching Feelings

"Never - use - anger," Tormaigh panted.

The second the storm dissipated, they'd collapsed, their chests heaving from the exertion. Hayden stared wide eyed, her hand clamped tightly to her mouth. She didn't try to move, not even after recovering her ability to breath normally. The only comfort she found was in the weight of Bérg's head as his forgiving brown eyes searched her face. She couldn't shake it. That sick feeling in the pit of her stomach from nearly hurting her friends.

"I'm- I'm so sorry," she stammered, shame creeping into her cheeks. "I didn't mean to. It-it…it just took hold of me. I couldn't make it stop. I saw you guys. I knew it was you. I tried to control it, but it's… it's like it was this thing," here she hesitated, her hand hovering over her chest. There was a difference in how she saw that moment now. But she could still understand it through both sets of eyes and wasn't sure how to feel about that. "but it wasn't me? Or it was? I don't… I can't… I'm sorry."

She pursed her lips, feeling annoyed at her own ramblings—at the sound of her own voice. If it was affecting her, it certainly had to be irritating them.

Tormaigh sat back on her hocks, still trembling from the effort. If there was one thing she knew, it was darkness and shadows— which was only in part, because she drew her own magic from them.

"Hayden, you didn't hurt us," she began hesitantly. "But you need to listen to me very carefully. When you use your magic you are digging into the deepest, most powerful parts of your emotions. What we saw just now has always been a part of you," Tormaigh watched helplessly as Hayden fought back tears, knowing she had to break through the spiral of self-pity. "Princess! Look at me!" She commanded.

As Hayden abruptly pushed herself into a seated position—drawn by the sharp urgency in Tormaigh's tone—Bérg let his head drop into her lap.

"We all have that dark place that we want no one to see. And anyone who pretends otherwise can't be trusted. But the problem here lies in the nature of your power. I believe we've witnessed a glimpse into what you could become—if you let it take control."

Hayden absentmindedly rubbed her chest where Bérg's shoulder had connected. She was lost in thought—remembering the promise she'd made to herself when this all started. The whole idea was to see it through no matter how tough the going got. They let her sit in silence as she surveyed the disturbed earth around them, her thoughts of self-doubt vying for dominance.

"Well I made quite a mess here, didn't I?" she observed, rubbing her neck aimlessly. "But quitting isn't in my nature, no matter how much I don't understand. So if you still feel comfortable being my teacher, I'll happily take all the pointers I can get," her response held a finality that even Tormaigh couldn't ignore.

The sun had just hit its peak when they were finally back to resting on her laurels. It was the term that Hayden had given to the position Tormaigh made her sit to practice. It was amusing to her only, but it helped separate training here, from training with Matilde. The last thing she wanted was to, in any way, take reverence from those years at the Academy. This had to feel different, so she'd borrowed the term.

At first Hayden felt like a fisherwoman, only allowed to catch and release her magic in short bursts. It took some time, but she finally felt she'd earned the right to use deeper emotions to call on the magic without fear of losing herself.

Hayden grinned in triumph as she allowed her deep-seated anger to entwine with the light on her body. And for the first time, she felt comfortable admitting that it had always been there, simmering beneath the surface. There was nothing she'd encountered in therapy that had given her this sense of control over its power—she hadn't thought it was possible—until now. Her eyes danced with excitement as a small orb began to form between her palms. But before she could make it grow, she felt a massive draw on her energy, and was forced to let it fade.

Hayden squeezed her eyes shut until the frantic pounding in her chest settled back into its usual pitter-patter. A deep breath filled her lungs as a cold, clammy sensation crawled across her skin, raising goosebumps and lifting the fine hairs on her arms. She let the breath out in a long, steady sigh, then slowly opened her eyes.

"Ummmmm... ok? That's definitely not what I expected," she said with a gasp. "Hello?" her own words answered back, overshadowed only by the sound of water lapping at the dock. She turned her head as if on a swivel, taking in the scene.

The boards she sat on seemed to be worn and warped by the elements, weeds rustled like paper as a barely perceptible breeze played with them, and a strong deja vu was calling. She'd been here before. She was certain of it. "It's not Tranquil Lake," she argued with herself. "There's no dock there," the dock shook gently and the quiet pad of a silent footfall reached Hayden's ears.

Did Calliope somehow follow her into this weird dream? Or whatever it was. She relaxed her crossed legs. From there she pressed herself into a stand and spun around in one smooth motion. A move that she was very proud of mastering. Her intention had been to pounce on Calliope, announcing how she 'couldn't sneak up on her,' but the words stuck in her throat and her mouth fell open in shock. The person standing there was not Calliope. It was the man from her dream. The one that she'd spent so many months wondering after.

He stepped toward her and instinctively she took one away from him. The smile that had been sparkling in his eyes wavered.

"My love! Why do I see fear in you?" His wrinkled brow betrayed the concern he failed to keep from his voice. And for a moment Hayden felt guilt for being the cause of it.

"Who are you?" She asked, balling her hand into a fist. "I've seen you in my dreams," her eyes swept the shore line behind him, realizing with certainty that she'd crossed it many times. And beyond that were the stairs leading to the cabin. She'd never been inside because her dream had always started at the top of the hill. But even so, she could see its details, right down to a lamp that shone weakly through a lone window. Her nose wrinkled as she turned her attention to studying him. Somehow, she knew this was where he belonged. Standing there awkwardly, waiting for her, his brown eyes emanating concern and his mop of dark hair spilling onto his forehead. It looked wildly unkempt as though he'd just run his fingers through it.

The man laughed and the sound of it filled her with a warmth that offered relief to her chilled skin. "Oh come now love. You mustn't joke in such a way. You know quite well who I am," he strode forward with his hand out, reaching for hers. "Let us sit by the campfire. You look cold my love."

Mesmerized by the moment and drawn into to his irresistible gaze, she reached out to accept his hand. But they never met as the scene abruptly dissipated in a swirl of mist. And with a start, she found herself face to face with Calliope.

"Hayden!" Calliope yelled, snapping her fingers between them. "Oh thank goodness! She's with us again," she breathed, tossing the statement past Hayden to Tormaigh. Placing her hands on Hayden's shoulders, she gently shook the remaining fog from her brain. "What happened? You went white like you were going to pass out and then you just froze. Your eyes were cloudy and we couldn't rouse you," she sat down in a huff. Everything about her body language screaming that she'd been scared. "Then you just jumped up and spun around. I didn't know what to think," Calliope's tail swished, dancing just as it did when she was Ophrahl. "Don't you smirk at me!" She said, shaking her finger.

Hayden's shoulders lowered. She removed Calliope's hands as the last shreds of the visions aura faded. It was the only description that kind of fit into the strange experience anyway. She shook her head replying, "I'm sorry. But you're not the only reason for that. I'll tell you what happened, but we should multitask. Let's walk and talk," Pointing toward the sun and it's waning light, she worried that it had fallen lower on the horizon than she'd planned when they set out that morning.

As they picked their way back up and down the familiar path, she recounted the details of her short experience. Highlighting how uncanny it was that she could swear it was all real. "What about dream walking. Do you have people that can do that in your world?" The idea hit her as she reached into the cobwebs where memories of all things fantasy resided. "But wait... that can't be right. They visited the dreams of other people. Not their own," she corrected herself.

Calliope exchanged a bemused look with Tormaigh before squashing Hayden's idea. "No, people do not deal in dreams where *we* are from," the emphasis on 'we' was pointed. She tired of Hayden's avoidance in embracing Dagrune as her own. "I fear the only thing I've observed that may have been similar, was when our Lore Keeper called to Adelphiana at the start of my journey to become, well... all of this," she grinned, proud of her movie reference, as well as her success in getting a smile out of Hayden. "Even so, she did not disappear into her mind as I believe you did."

Failing to provide further insight into her vision, the conversation slowly moved to less puzzling subjects. But even as they spoke of other things, she found her mind drifting back to how she'd felt when she let herself look into his eyes. It was safe and warm, even though she'd been shivering from the cool of the night... in the dream of course.

They drifted into silence. And Hayden's mind did what it did best when faced with such immersive quiet. There was something she'd been meaning to ask, and hadn't remembered until now. It would help get her mind off of the failures she'd faced today. So she expertly maneuvered herself between Calliope and the others, slowly pulling her away.

When she felt certain they were out of Tormaigh's earshot, Hayden bumped playfully into her shoulder.

"I saw that by the way."

Calliope cleared her throat, suspecting what Hayden referred to, but desperately hoping she was wrong. She'd meant for it to go unnoticed. "Saw what exactly?" she said, feigning ignorance.

"You know what I'm talking about," Hayden said with a wink. "The way you reacted when Tormaigh grabbed your hand. Even through that gray, I saw you blush. You like her, don't you?"

Calliope turned, keeping her expression hidden. When she answered, Hayden thought she heard a catch in her voice—subtle, but enough to confirm the suspicion she'd carried since their first argument. She hadn't fully understood it then, but looking back, the energy between Tormaigh and Calliope had been palpable.

"She has no time for frivolous feelings. I will always be her student. I doubt she will ever view me any other way," Calliope replied, squaring her shoulders.

Hayden laid a hand gently on Calliope's arm. It felt strange touching her skin. Although that particular place on her arm wasn't covered in hair, there was still a difference from her own. It was tougher, closer to leather.

Calliope responded in kind, placing her hand on top of Hayden's. They walked this way, arm in arm, their feet moving together with each step as Hayden gathered her thoughts. It seemed to be a vulnerable subject for Calliope, so she needed to choose her next words carefully.

"Liking someone—or loving them—these should never be considered frivolous feelings," she began thoughtfully. "Now I don't want to grand stand or anything but I do have a few extra years of experience than you on the subject," she squeezed Calliope's calloused hand. "Do you think perhaps she feels the same? Because I happen to know that sometimes people outside the situation, often see it long before you do."

Calliope's nails clacked as she ran her thumb over the other four fingers. "I don't know. Is she not hard to read?" she asked, her trademark sarcasm creeping into her voice.

Hayden smiled, intimately aware of the familiar tactic. She herself also used it as a shield against admitting vulnerability. "Well yes, you're right there. But I saw her when she got off that trailer. She may have been a horse, but I could tell almost instantly that you two had a unique bond. I just thought I'd gotten lucky with my little tribe getting along and here it turns out that it was all divinely orchestrated."

Calliope pursed her lips. "You know," she teased, a hint of mischief in her eyes, "you're not bad, as far as replacement mother's go. Although," and Hayden looked over just in time to see mischief turn to sadness. "This is one of those things that I always wished to discuss with her. And now I don't know if I will ever see her again," a lone tear slipped down her cheek but she was quick to flick it away. "Let's talk about something else. This isn't something that can be resolved now anyway. No matter how much you want to fix everything all the time."

It was clear that Calliope was drawing a line in the sand. Hayden had a solid rule: never push a boundary once someone has set it. So she smoothly shifted the conversation to other things, making a silent promised to herself. Sometimes these things just needed a little nudge—she would become matchmaker once again. After all, it *had* worked out pretty good for her friends.

******

"Another week done," Hayden exclaimed as she plopped down on the couch.

The softness of the suede welcomed her into its embrace, giving her aching body much needed relief. She was exhausted after yet another busy week at the clinic, having difficulty recalling if she'd gotten enough sustenance amidst seemingly infinite cases. It had been such a blur. The endless piles of charts had been the stuff of nightmares. She could see the horror movie title now. *Night of the Killer Medical Files,* she thought. But no... that sounded too sterile. Too... doctory. She rubbed her forehead, as she tried to reign in her increasingly bizarre thoughts.

"Mum, do you want to live here?" She blurted suddenly.

There were probably more tactful ways to ask, but exhaustion had weakened what was left of her decorum.

The thought had been going through her mind all day. They were getting nowhere with the next quest–she might as well start tying up the real-world loose ends. She snorted aloud. That word again. She'd started using 'quest' ironically–an attempt to keep fact and fiction separate. But her favorite genre of literature had landed itself squarely in her lap. She could ignore it no longer.

"Hun, I've been thinking about that very thing lately," Clara replied in her usual cheery manner. "I want to have that discussion, but I have something to tell you first. I just can't hold it back anymore."

Hayden pushed herself to the edge of the couch. The tone in Mum's voice held apprehension mixed with joy. Even without tapping into her ability to feel emotions she could tell that whatever this was, was more than important to her.

"Okay, I'm listening" She said attentively despite her exhaustion. "Don't tell me. You're dating someone," she said it lazily, laced with a southern drawl to punctuate her witty 'guess.'

A wall of mirth passed, just as Clara burst into laughter. It wasn't so much physical, as there was this sense that it surrounded her. She fought to maintain control as its influence elicited a quiet giggle.

"Wait… I guessed right? That was supposed to be a joke," her eyes welled with happy tears as she gave in and joined in on Clara's laughter. "Are you serious Mum? I'm so happy for you! He must be some special guy if you broke your promise to yourself for him," Hayden cringed, immediately regretting bringing it up as Clara's joy flickered briefly.

It had taken years of of gentle prodding before Clara would opened up about why she'd never gone searching for love. It was a tragic story. One that Hayden wished had played out differently.

They were high school sweethearts who showed their love so openly that harmless jealousy from teasing friends would often find its way to them. But love hadn't been enough for his family. They came from old money and thought themselves to be better than those with less. His parents eventually demanded that he choose between her– someone they deemed a nobody–or them.

Without a second thought, he packed his car with a few belongings and followed her into the small town they would come to call home. For love, he'd given up his inheritance and everything he'd ever known, never once looking back in regret. They were married for five bliss-filled years, and in that time, opened the coffee shop in Exordium. It brought the kind of community to town that it sorely needed, becoming a place of repose for many.

But there was another, more dangerous being that found jealousy for their love. Fate found a way to get her cruel claws in to tear it all down.

He'd stopped on the side of the road one rainy night to help a family change their tire. The driver from a passing car was distracted and struck him. He spent three pain-filled days in intense surgeries, but in the end Clara had to say goodbye to her biggest love. From then on she vowed to never give any

*future relationships a chance lest fate come knocking at her
door again.*

"So what's his name?" Hayden asked, worried that she'd
overstepped by bringing it up.

Clara cleared her throat. And to Hayden's relief she could detect no
sorrow in her answer.

"It's ok Hayd. I know what you're doing, but you shouldn't worry
yourself. I came to an understanding with myself. It's just..." Her eyes
dropped shyly to the wooden spoon in her hand. She pushed the stir
fry around, barely able to concentrate on cooking. "When I met him, it
felt like something inside healed a little. I told myself, 'Clara don't you
ignore that!' But I honestly don't think I could have, even if I wanted
to."

Before Clara had finished explaining, Hayden closed the
distance between them, wrapping her in a warm hug. "Mum, you
know you don't have to explain yourself to me, I've always wanted
you to fall in love again someday," she stepped back to lean on the
counter as the smell of smoke prompted Clara to turn the burner
down. "You deserve to be with someone who makes you this happy.
What's his name? Or maybe I'll have to eventually call him Dad, so it
doesn't matter anyway?"

Clara giggled, reminding Hayden of the first time she'd done
the same with her friends. It was the universal sign of a major crush,
and Mum had it bad.

"Alec Porter," Clara said with a gleam in her eyes.

She turned her head too quickly, leaving Hayden unable to hide her
shock.

"What's wrong? You look like you've seen a ghost," she said, turning
to face Hayden.

Hayden chewed her lip, anxiety creeping into her thoughts. "I
know him. He's the guy who helped me the night I was awakened. And

he was also the auctioneer at the charity place where I got Tormaigh," she shook her head at the mistake. "I mean *met* her."

"Sweetness, look at me," Clara took Hayden's hand. She'd been here many times over the years, watching as her daughter worked through yet another worst-case scenario. It was one of her most predictable thought processes. "I know. He told me about both times. I can assure you that he came looking for me on purpose, but the intention was never to try and get me to fall for him. He wanted to meet the woman who raised such a strong daughter. His words." Dropping Hayden's hand, she busied herself with gathering dishes for dinner so they could enjoy it before it got cold. "I guess you must have mentioned the coffee shop. That's how he found me," she stretched, trying to get her hands on the bowls, but they were just out of reach. Hayden leaned over Clara, pulling the desired dishes off the shelf. "Thanks dear. So anyway, my heart went all crazy when I first talked to him. And we ended up spending hours just talking. We honestly didn't talk about you that much."

Clara's explanation gave her a small reprieve from all the reasons to be suspicious. Though she couldn't ignore how strangely this man had entered their lives, she let herself drop her guard—just for now. Mum was blissfully happy—finally. She had to trust that she could handle it on her own.

So she put on her best cheerful voice and said, "Well good! You needed a distraction from *me* being distracted. Perfect timing if you ask me. He can fill those hours that I once did," her light hearted response did exactly as she hoped. Clara's smile said it all. "And next time you see him, tell him hi from me."

Eventually, when her eyelids grew heavy and the weight of sleep became impossible to ignore, she excused herself with a reluctant smile. A long week of training loomed ahead, and rest would be as vital as any meal.

"Sleep tight, my angel," Clara said, pressing a kiss to her forehead.

A soft smile played at Hayden's lips. Some things, it seemed, never changed. But how many more moments like this remained in this chapter of her life? As her eyes drifted shut and sleep tugged gently at her thoughts, she held onto that question, and the quiet resolve to make the most of each one.

<u>15</u>

Unofficial Goodbye

The next couple of weeks dragged by. Things at the clinic had finally quieted down, but any extra time was quickly swallowed by longer, more intense training sessions. Instead of rest, her days blurred into work and magic, with little space left for herself. She missed lazy weekends curled up on the couch, binge-watching old favorites while wrapped snugly in a cocoon of blankets. Still, the effort was starting to pay off. Her magic lasted longer now; she could sustain the orb with far less strain.

That progress gave her the push she needed to keep going, even when self-doubt crept in. And so far, there had been no more flare-ups of wild magic, a victory she didn't take for granted. She'd also started to recognize the different threads of energy in the world around her. The wind hummed lightly, the rain carried a restlessness, and the earth held a slow, almost sleepy thrum. Everything had a voice, and the older it was, the more stubborn it seemed.

Then, one day during a rather extensive training session, they stumbled across something unexpected. Something, that, to Hayden's surprise, was even new for Tormaigh.

"This boulder is being especially uncooperative," she complained, her hands shaking slightly with the effort. And when no one responded, she shifted her focus only briefly to gauge why, surmising from the look on Tormaigh's face that she hadn't been clear enough. "It doesn't want to work with me today," But Hayden could see that her 'clarification' hadn't helped.

"I'm sorry, run that by me again?" Tormaigh said, her request slipping into a question. "What do you mean it doesn't want to?

 Her puzzled eyes darted between the boulder and Hayden.

"Well," she said, stalling, "basically it's like a stubborn old man. You know the type—curmudgeonly, terse, tired, that kind of thing. It has that ancient energy that likes to give me trouble."

She gave up trying to get the boulders attention and turned fully to Tormaigh instead.

"You look perplexed," Hayden stated plainly. "Am I correct in assuming that you have no idea what I'm talking about?"

Tormaigh paused, unsure of how to address this. It was true that she'd never heard any of her students say such a thing, but then again, she knew magic existed that she'd not yet encountered. Lord Onyx was proof of that. "You're right. I've never heard anyone mention arguing with a non-living object. But your magic is truly unique, so I'll take your word for it," her fingers drummed a beat on the ground. This new territory meant she would have to consider a different approach. Methodically she probed her memory for a solution, but she couldn't come up with anything. So unsure of how else to proceed, she encouraged Hayden to use force. "Just try to push past the resistance. Grandpapa can usually be persuaded," she instructed.

For the first time, Hayden felt a strong sense of contradiction. That pesky inner voice was urging her not to proceed, that Tormaigh had no personal experience so she couldn't really know if it was the correct path. But on the other hand, logic reminded her that she was the student and Tormaigh was the instructor. A life full of learning from experts had taught her to trust their guidance. So with a wish in her heart, she re-engaged with the stubborn energy that was the boulder.

"Ok, here we go," she said, taking up a wider stance. "As if a stronger base has anything to do with my magic," she scoffed quietly.

The boulder wasn't massive, but still heavy—too much for even a tractor. It left her wondering if its weight was causing her struggle, or if it was a part of her growing suspicion. She used all the tricks that Tormaigh had given over the weeks and dug deep, reaching into the basis of her magic. Then just as she was about to open herself to the suns power, it conveniently slipped behind a wall of clouds.

"See, even the sun doesn't want me to do this," she grumbled through her teeth, glancing covertly at Tormaigh to make sure she hadn't been heard.

The force of resistance from the jagged mass was again quickly becoming unbearable as she pressed forward. Except this time, to her relief, she was able to overcome it. The ground trembled as the boulder moved. The earth caved, breaking into dust around it as the huge weight rose upward, clearing a hole that the dusty clods of earth eagerly took over. Hayden grit her teeth, fighting the desire to give up, pitting her will against that of the boulder.

Hell Yeah! She thought to herself as she felt the strength of her magic grow. It was working. She looked on proudly, it had moved a couple inches, then six, eight, and now it rose to a foot above the miniature crater in its wake. Then gradually a feeling of unease began to creep over her. The hint of a warning that must not be ignored. But Tormaigh's instructions had been clear; she was expected to raise it to twice its current height. She snapped her teeth together as she made the decision, releasing a feral yell and putting everything she had left into the effort.

The sharp sting of pain exploded in her head, followed by the sound of a thousand silent screams filling every thought, every forgotten crevice of her consciousness. Instead of raising as she'd planned, the boulder disintegrated with a thunderous clap, raining harmless debris over them. With the energy ripped from her grasp, Hayden fell breathless to her knees. She stared blankly at the ground, waiting for the attack on her mind to subside.

"What just happened?!" She grimaced, not daring to look them in the eye.

Here she was, yet again, on the other side of magic that had gotten out of control. Just when it seemed to be within her grasp too.

"I'm not certain, but I don't like what I saw," Calliope hovered next to Hayden, preparing to help if the need arose. "I saw a flash of darkness in your eyes just before the rock turned to dust."

She helped Hayden to her feet and they brushed what they could from their bodies, the dust puffing into little billows as the breeze carried it away.

Tormaigh was at a loss as she also found herself on the other side of yet another mistake. Until now, she'd never encountered them when training a new student, but with Hayden they seemed to be piling up. Her confidence wavered as she was faced with the idea that she may have taken on too much with Hayden's power. It was unsettling and she didn't relish the fact that it affected her in such a way.

"Hayden. You were in pain. What was it this time?" She asked, wishing it were a question that didn't have to be voiced. "It was pain that was yours alone. I could not sense it through our link, no matter how I tried."

Hayden closed her eyes trying desperately to remember every detail. But it was in vain. The harder she tried, the further it slipped away.

"It's all getting so fuzzy, but I think I remember there was someone screaming. Lots of someone's. And..." She massaged her temples, wishing it would pull the memory to the surface. "All I know is that I can't feel that energy thread anymore. Like... like I killed it?" She sighed, tapping her forehead to emphasize her next point. "The only thing still there; whatever that was—it wasn't good and I won't be doing it again. And I think... somehow, it all ended up here," she said, patting her chest.

There was a sense of sadness in the thought—one that she was certain did not originate from her. She stared unblinking into the trees, as if they would somehow absorb the sorrow. But instead, she felt it retreat, waiting in the dark recesses of her emotions, lurking there until she could call on it once again.

****

Things were going so well with training that Hayden took a much-needed break. If there was one thing she admitted to missing the most, it was hanging out with her girlfriends. Even before life had been flip turned upside down, they'd only been able to see each other every couple months. The responsibilities of adulthood had seen to that. Between vastly differing careers and their young children, they had to sacrifice something. And the coveted girls night had drawn the short straw. But there was no reason to dwell on it because they had a pact. They would *not* allow life to take them from one another.

Hayden leaned close to the mirror, putting the finishing touches on her eyeliner. Tonight she would make sure to give herself the perfect cat eye. They wouldn't be able to tease her this time. She stepped back to spray a bit of product in her hair. It was the final touch except for the earrings that were still on the sinks edge.

"That's as good as it's gonna get," she giggled to herself.

But that quote certainly didn't fit here. It wasn't just the makeup, it was the dress from the thrift shop, the shoes, and matching jewelry. She faced the hallway mirror—the only one in the house tall enough to see the whole picture. She twirled, admiring how cute she looked tonight. Mum had worked too hard instilling self-appreciation for her to pass up the opportunity. *Don't let anyone make you feel shame for seeing your own beauty, but on the flip side, don't elevate yourself above others for it either.* It was sound advice. And in a world that seemed to easily confuse that with some vilified version of pride, she carried it close. After a couple more poses to make sure every wrinkle was smoothed and every hair had its place, she paused one last time to admire the sparkle of the moon stones that hung from her neck and ears. Another little nugget of perfection from Mum.

The parking ramp had four levels, the first of which was full. The digital sign said as much anyway, and she wasn't about to waste her time driving through to find out.

"Level three it is," she said, pulling the steering wheel to the left.

The only open spots that remained were near the back of the lot. Hayden preferred that anyway because it was easier to maneuver the truck into places with fewer vehicles. With keys in hand, she let her head fall back on the headrest. Time was running out and she had to figure out what to tell them tonight. As of yet, everything she'd thought of had seemed either too passive or too aggressive. These were the friends that had seen her through so many struggles and stayed, even during some of her more selfish stages. They were the only people outside of Mum whom she would have considered entrusting with this unbelievable information. Every foreseeable reaction had run through Hayden's head, and she was afraid of each and every one. There wasn't a perfectly happy ending to this, no matter how she tried to spin it. Reluctantly she opened the door, fumbling with the thought that this would solidify all the events from the past couple months into reality.

The elevator lobby told a story of neglect. It was clean enough, but missing tiles every few feet and large faded green letters denoting the ramp level gave it the feeling of a New York Subway station. It was complete with tags from many graffiti artists, both amateur and pro. She took a picture of the floor and row, not willing to trust her memory after a late night out. Beep beep, the truck chirped as she hit the lock button twice. Zip zip, went the sound of her necklace as she zoned out, dragging the pendant back and forth along the chain. So lost in her thoughts had she become that she was caught unaware when a voice slurred just over her shoulder.

"Nice truck you got there."

Hayden jumped, accosted with the stench of cheap vodka and the unwelcome presence of a stranger, far too close for comfort. The smell. The feeling of him breathing on her neck. It made her shudder as she took a large step sideways. Her eyes watered and she nearly gauged as the overpowering smell of body odor mingled with alcohol rolled off him in waves. His bleary eyes travelled up and down her body and her skin crawled at the leering smirk that played on his lips. She gulped, swallowing the familiar feeling of dread that arose when it came to meeting men who reminded her of Papa.

"Thanks," she replied tersely.

There would be a zero percent chance of riding the elevator with that level of creep. So in a split-second decision, she yanked the stairwell door open, sprinting up the two floors to Restaurant Bay. He was too drunk to follow her, she was sure of it. So she allowed herself to catch her breath, pausing long enough to straighten her dress and regain composure.

The encounter was all but forgotten when she passed under the bright yellow awning where paintings of flower bouquets with roses, sunflowers, and gardenias scattered across the vinyl. In large gold letters, the words "Garden Party" seemed to flow effortlessly around them. The ambiance was ever cheery as a bright yellow theme pervaded every corner of the place.

"Solara, party of three," Hayden let the hostess know. "The other two-thirds may have already arrived."

She stole a cursory peak at what was visible of the dining floor. So far it didn't look too busy for a Saturday night, but that didn't mean it would stay that way.

"I know right where they are. Follow me this way please," the hostess said, beckoning Hayden to fall in line behind her.

Hayden zoned in on the click of the hostess' shoes, finding it nearly impossible not to judge her choice of footwear. With a job where the woman had to be on her feet all day, she couldn't imagine how uncomfortable that had to be. She herself preferred the comfort of sneakers and cute flats. Not only did her career and hobbies demand it, but she also preferred not to add even an inch to her height.

Her eyes drifted to her own shoes. They were simple strappy sandals, with ties that wrapped around her calves and ended in a bow just behind her knee. But that wasn't what had drawn her to them. It was the sequins. They covered every inch of the straps, catching the light to sparkle in the most deliciously distracting way. How lucky she felt when she found them.

She heard the squeal even before rounding the corner. Faith was doing her best to make Hayden blush with embarrassment. It was just a silly rivalry they'd kept up since high school, but tonight, it meant just a little more. She returned the favor, putting her heart and soul into the Forrest Gump wave, pulling her lips back into a ridiculous grin to add effect. That was the game. Hayden had forever been the easiest person to embarrass while Faith was equally easy when it came to giggles. Whoever broke first was the loser, and Faith seemed to lose every time.

"Get over here you!" Faith demanded in-between giggles. She drew Hayden into an embrace, then practically shoved her toward Sadiki.

"You look stunning babe!" Sadiki beamed, catching Hayden before she could trip.

Sadiki, her oldest friend, the one person who had seen Hayden through it all. They'd made a pact when they were neighbors in the trailer park, not just to make it out together, but to also make something of themselves. She stepped back to study Sadiki's expression. Was it her imagination, or had she received an extra-long hug from the person that liked being touched even less than herself?

Hayden shuffled through the narrow aisle. "Let's sit!" she said, suddenly noticing the server. "We've kept this poor guy waiting long enough."

After he'd taken orders for drinks and apps, they got right down to the business of catching up.

"Sadiki, that afro is looking on point tonight girlfriend! How do you do it? So many hairstyles. So little time." Hayden asked, casting a covert glance toward Faith.

"Oh I don't know about that," Faith chimed in. "I think it's less pointy and more round...y," she tilted her head as her words trailed off.

Hayden laughed. Faith had always been the one to seek out puns in conversation. So much so that Hayden would intentionally set her up for the spike. "Nailed it!" She grinned. Just then the server returned, expertly balancing three glasses of wine. He took their entrée requests and left them to their chatter. "Look at the two of you! No frumpy mom life here I see," she said with a wink. "I honestly don't know how you two do it. I don't even have kids and my career seems overwhelming sometimes. And here you are. Just super moms one and two, raising schmiglets and making it all look easy."

Sadiki placed her elbows on the table, encircling the glass with her long slender fingers. "Like I always tell you. Coffee during the day, wine when the kids are in bed or when I get a night off. And tonight is my night off, so cheers to that!" They raised their glasses together, each making a toast of their own.

"Something's different about you." Faith said, shaking her forkful of salad in Hayden's direction. She wrinkled her nose and squinted, surveying her closely. "I can't quite put a finger on it. If I didn't know you weren't seeing anyone, I'd suspect pregnancy glow," she ducked, shielding her face as Hayden dipped her fingers in ice water and flicked it playfully across the table.

"Oh no you don't!" Hayden slung back, "You know I'm perfectly content being single and childless right now," she rolled her eyes to emphasize the point.

"I know," Faith giggled, tossing her blonde curls. "You know I kid."

Their banter continued, and though she was having a good time, Hayden stilled grappled with the real reason she'd come out tonight. Would it really be so bad if she chickened out, didn't tell them, and just disappeared one day? But the moment the thought crossed her mind she knew that it would be an impossible guilt to live with. Pushing the thought away, she re-engaged with the conversation, not wanting to spend the night dwelling on 'what ifs.'

"So this glow..," Sadiki prompted, bringing the conversation back around. "Is it your horse? I know you were excited about that. I didn't know one person could use so many exclamation points," she teased. "But I think it's more than that. There's something else. You exude a certain je ne sais quoi that I've never seen in you before."

"Yeah!" Faith agreed, "that's a good way to put it."

Hayden raised an eyebrow. They were leaning shoulder to shoulder, cheek to cheek, staring her down. Acting as if their pretense at judgement would in any way wrangle something out of her if she didn't want to share. And even if she were to tell them what to attribute her little 'glow-up' to, it couldn't be here.

"I'm just in high demand at work right now," she said, trying to guide the conversation to safer waters. "I've barely been able to catch my breath because it's client after client after client. Can you glow when you're overworked? Because I don't feel very shiny lately."

She took another sip of wine and thanked serendipity when their food arrived just in time to save her. By the time they were settled and had taken their first bites, the distraction was enough to move them along to other things, and conveniently their conversation turned to work.

Sadiki was a busy Air Traffic Controller—a career that made perfect sense after a childhood spent obsessed with airplanes. Hayden had been over the moon for her when they'd gotten the news that she was the top candidate. They'd celebrated, crying tears of joy over drinks that night because she was the first to make good on their pact. Against all odds, through every challenge, and over every hurdle that came with being a black woman, she'd overcome them like they were nothing.

"I completely sympathize," Sadiki said with a deep sigh. "I'm mandated to a certain number of hours, but the powers that be had to petition for an increase until they hire someone new. I barely have anything left to give the kids when I get home." For a moment, Hayden saw the mask slip and she could see the exhaustion reflected in her eyes.

"You don't have to pretend with us," Hayden said softly. "I can't put myself in your shoes, but I still think you're killing it as you juggle everything," she took a bite of steak, letting the excuse give her time to form the next thought. "Is that husband of yours still holding things down at home?" Hayden finally asked, a glint of warning in her eye.

"Oh don't you worry. He's still good and scared of you. And he wouldn't dare to do anything that would land him on your bad side," Sadiki replied with a short laugh. "But in all seriousness, my raise giving him the freedom to quit that dead end job and do his woodworking art full time; it was one of the best things to happen to us. He's finally seeing his dream come to fruition, and he gets to spend more time being dad. It's what he's always wanted."

Faith smiled, leaning over far enough to nudge Sadiki's shoulder. "Fun twist on the old stay-at-home mom schtick," she said.

"Speaking of stay-at-home moms, and art, and following your dream, how's *your* new business going?" Sadiki grilled Faith, eager to remove herself from the center of their attention "I've been thoroughly enjoying all the designs that you keep sharing in the chat. If only you had discovered your talent *before* I got married, I would have paid you handsomely to make my dress."

Faith straightened, a quiet pride in her eyes. She'd only discovered her talent after taking an impromptu sewing class—one that had taken Hayden and Sadiki some time to convince her to try. When they produced their first projects, the instructor had pulled Faith aside and offered to take her under tutelage. Up until that point, she'd been stuck in low paying jobs. Her parents didn't have money for college, and refusing to be a burden on them, she'd started working straight out of high school. What was supposed to be just a year, turned into a few as the possibility of college slipped further and further from her grasp. On the brink of giving up, the new found talent stepped in just in time, and saved her—giving her purpose as she absorbed every detail, took every instruction to heart, and practiced often late into the night on her old sewing machine.

"Well, prom season is approaching, and you know how crazy *those* moms can get."

She pulled out her phone and began scrolling through her pictures vigorously. "But when I can get a smile like this out of a girl, because of a piece of clothing... it makes it totally worth it."

She passed the phone, and as Hayden and Sadiki leaned together to look at the photo, they smiled—remembering the way they'd felt wrapped in satin, sequins, and lace so many years ago.

After hours of good food, even better conversation, and a couple bottles of wine, they decided it was time to move onto the dance floor. But by the time midnight rolled around and their glasses of wine had worn off, they were ready to call it a night.

"I'm up way past my bedtime and my feet are *killing* me," Faith complained, her shoes dangling from her fingers. "The universal sign that we've had a good time," she grinned, raising them higher—adding weight to the statement.

They were back in the elevator after a brief protest from Sadiki and Faith. *They* claimed that Hayden didn't need to walk them back to their cars. A protest that was quickly squashed when she reminded them of the years she'd spent perfecting a certain martial art.

"Ok you're totally right!" Faith conceded. "I'm sure we'll both feel safer with you there. You can fight and I'll just use my gift of talking ears off to keep them at bay. It'll annoy them so fiercely that they'll run for the hills. So yay teamwork!"

This sent them into peals of laughter and as the elevator doors opened, that nagging obligation hit Hayden again. She had to find some way to tell them before they parted ways.

"This has been way too much fun," Faith said, her voice bright with laughter. "I wish it weren't already over," her face fell slightly, giving pause to the moment. So Hayden, finding it as a potential opportunity, opened her mouth, heart pounding. But she never got the chance when a gravelly voice slithered from the shadows.

"Oh I agree. Ladies as pretty as yourselves shouldn't stay all cooped up."

Hayden instinctively moved to put herself between the faceless voice and her friends. She could hear Matilde's instructions—*Your absolute last resort will be to fight your way out. But most importantly, never ever turn your back on a potential threat.* She strained her eyes, trying desperately to separate a form from the shadows.

"We're just trying to get home. Leave us alone," she said firmly.

Her skin turned clammy as a second voice rose behind them.

"I think we should keep partying. It's only midnight you know," it said.

Then her blood ran cold when a whistle cut through the dark from a third direction. Things had just gone from bad to worse. One opponent would have been a breeze, two a challenge—but three? Maybe on her own, but here she found herself reluctantly cast into the role of protector.

"My friend knows Jiu Jitsu," Faith squeaked. And Hayden cringed, biting her lip as she willed her talkative friend to keep quiet for once. She squeezed her hand, hoping that the silent reassurance would bear the message.

"Oh I see..." the voice sneered, "little lady can do some kicks can she?" The mocking belittlement was meant to unnerve her, anger her, make her do something that would take her focus. But all of the training, both in self-defense and magic had unbeknownst to Hayden, given her the tools she need in this moment. "What are you gonna do?" he continued, stepping into the light, "there's three of us. You don't amount to even half of that."

At the very least, he'd been successful in one thing. She could feel her heart pounding loudly, but it wasn't out of fear as he'd planned. Instead it emerged from a growing sense of anger. How dare they try to hurt her friends—to hurt her? She wasn't weaker and she knew it. But they didn't. A strong sense of obligation whispered to her.

She was going to make sure they thought twice before doing this again. Tonight she wouldn't back down.

"Sadiki, please call the police. They're gonna want to know where to find three very unconscious and banged up little boys," she threw the insult at them, fully aware that it would elicit anger.

"What are you doing?" Sadiki hissed, her eyes widening in shock at the bold words.

"Don't worry, I've got this," Hayden whispered over her shoulder.

Like a coward, the man behind them lunged—only to find she'd already seen it coming. With a swift sidestep and a spin on her heel, she slipped between him and her friends. There was just enough time to plant her other foot before she drove her hand upward, the force surprising even her. They heard him grunt as his momentum gave strength to her blow. His head snapped back and the grunt turned to a scream as blood gushed from his nose, his knees buckling under the force of the unexpected attack.

With no choice but to focus on his bleeding nose, the distraction gave Hayden her chance. She grabbed a fistful of collar and belt, sending him scrambling toward his cohorts. At least now they were all in front of her. It all happened so fast, that by the time their friend landed, sprawled out next to them, they only just had time to react.

"Who's next?" She taunted coyly.

An enraged snarl came from the leader as they advanced together. She ducked and weaved, deflecting punches intended for her face, keeping them fixated on her until she could see an opening. Then, with laser focus she saw it. Chop, her hand landed a blow on someone's throat which sent him coughing and gagging to his knees. Then with a pop, a well-placed cuff to the final opponent's ear. If she did it right, it could create a vacuum, causing his eardrum to rupture. And she must have succeeded, because he started a string of expletives that would disappoint anyone's grandma.

With her focus taken by the skirmish, she made her first mistake. A shriek from Sadiki brought her spinning back toward her friends. There he was, face covered in blood, his hand wrapped around her throat, pulling the frightened woman backward. As he backed up slowly, the dim lights reflected his sinister intent, and being all but too familiar with the horrors there, it sent her over the edge. If he got Sadiki out of sight… Hayden shuddered inwardly as rage, pure and unadulterated coursed through her body. The feeling grew, threatening to rip through her every vein.

"Get your filthy rotten hands off my friend," she growled menacingly. "I'm giving you one chance and one only," she stared unblinking into his eyes, daring him to ignore her warning. And just as he'd proven moments before, his cowardice resurfaced as he took another step backward, his hand unrelenting in its grip. "Big mistake buddy," she snarled. And as soon as the words left her mouth, all the built-up rage erupted from her chest to her palms.

Gasps of surprise and awe fell on deaf ears as she honed in on her target. She took a step toward them reaching out for his thread–his life force–the energy that she craved. But when he resisted, that feeling she once promised to never again entertain crept into her magic. This was different. He deserved to be turned to dust after everything he'd done, if that's even the way the magic worked. But even now, with anger driving her, she couldn't bring herself to cross that line. Still, she could do *something* to make him comply–so she pushed her will more forcefully and suddenly found herself surrounded by his consciousness.

Though she could still see the world around her it was through a different lens. Foggy and obscure, playing hints of memories that were difficult to piece together. But there was one thing for certain, a cord of malice and hatred wove itself through everything. If there was any good here she wasn't sure it could be found. His retreat wavered, his steps sluggish as she locked onto the energy with a vise like hold. Finally she saw his grip on Sadiki's neck loosened and she took her chance. As she lunged, she freed herself from his mind. Left with nothing but fear, he released Sadiki from his grasp, turning to flee down the ramp, the others hot on his heels.

"Are you guys ok?" she asked after making sure their attackers wouldn't be coming back.

Faith rushed to Hayden, squeezing her with every ounce of strength she possessed. "Are *we* ok?!" she thundered, "How about are *you* ok? Or a better question; WHAT THE HELL WOMAN?!"

Now the heat of the moment had passed, Hayden began to see what things must have looked like through their eyes. Just a few short months ago, she might've had a very different reaction than Faith.

"Sadiki, let me see your neck!" she demanded, slipping into doctor mode. That was at least something which could help bring some normalcy back to the moment.

"It's fine, he wasn't really squeezing hard. I just froze," Sadiki replied, brushing away Hayden's hand. "Is your truck close? I think our night out might not be over yet. You, young lady, have some explaining to do," she pointed her finger in Hayden's face, then fell into line as they scurried toward the truck. "Drop us at our cars, and then we'll meet at the park just off the swimming hole. You know the one," Sadiki demanded.

Hayden nodded, knowing enough not to challenge her friend when she was in momma bear mode.

"Welp, I guess that explains the 'glow,' huh?" Faith cut in, unable to hold back any longer after Hayden finished recounting the whirlwind of the past few months.

Sadiki sat in silence, gazing across the water. Hayden had heard plenty from Faith, but Sadiki had been quiet–to the point that she worried her friend felt betrayed somehow.

"Sadiki. Please say something," she pleaded.

With a sigh, her friend finally spoke. "All this time and you have to go and one up me? I mean–girl! Magic?! Goddamn I'm so jealous!" And the light hearted tone did exactly as intended, granting Hayden a reprieve from the guilt. "I don't understand any of this and I barely believe what I saw with my own eyes," Sadiki continued, "but if this Dragoony or whatever, is where you come from. Don't you feel obligated?"

Hayden stared through the glass at the sliver of moon peeking out from behind the clouds, torn between loss and–yes–the obligation that Sadiki spoke of. Her necklace, caught in its gentle glow, cast an almost imperceptible shine.

"I wish I could just go on with my life here and forget all this happened," she said, resting her head. "And I don't even know if I have the ability to come back once I make it there. How can she just expect me to rip out the roots I planted here after all these years?"

"Ah... the Angel lady," Faith clarified. "Yeah that seems a bit much. But don't godlike people not understand time really?"

And just like that, laughter burst out of them unexpected but needed, releasing the sadness, the fear, the apprehension of life dealing its cruelest blow. It had found a way to separate them after all.

With two o'clock in the morning quickly approaching, they had to say their goodbyes. Hayden turned out of the parking lot and headed for home. If she'd looked in her rear view, she would have seen a figure, grey with piercing blue eyes that reflected the moonlight. And as it slipped through the shadows, she might've wondered why it followed the same path they'd taken just hours before.

16

Murder or Justice?

"Wha' the hell man?! I tol'djya. Though' I was clear as the nose on yer face. Find a easy score—**EEEAAASYYY**," his mocking drawl of the last word hung in the air. "Instea'djya find these big bitches an' the one tha' canno' stop talkin.' Then one o' them turns ou' electric. Did'jya find a demon robah,' cause **WHA' THE FUCK WAS THA'!?**"

His voice got louder, more enraged, until he was screaming the final words. But his recently accosted throat cut short his rant, sending him into a coughing fit.

"Well shit Pete, I'm not really sure how I coulda predicted that. I was surprised, same as you! But talk into my right ear, cause my left is useless as hell right now," he sneered. "You're not the only one who caught some pain back there."

The third man had kept quiet from his crouched position for long enough. He exploded upward, spittle flying as he laid into them.

"Oh shut up you whiney ass bitches! Neither of you dick heads would be here if it weren't for me. You didn't feel what I did," he said smugly. "She put me in some kind of fog. I swear I could feel her in my head. But I was stronger and I got away," he puffed his chest out, filled with self-importance. "She might've killed us all if I didn't," his bragging echoed off stone, brick, and pavement. These were the sounds of an empty parking lot in the industrial park. He'd chosen this spot because it offered concealment from nosey neighbors or the law. "Then you two shit for brains have to go and get lost," he said, though conveniently leaving out the fact that fear had made *him* run the wrong direction. "Now we have to go back for the van. We didn't wipe it down so we can't leave it there."

He was mainly worried that if they didn't get moving soon, it would be too late and the van might be discovered.

"Oh look at Seth, always thinking he's the hero," this time it was the man who gingerly massaged his ear that cut in disdainfully. "You're SOOO BRAVE that you froze up when she went all nuclear. I saw it in your face; you were scared shitless. Nice nose by the way, how's it feeling you ugly fuck?!"

His insult drew the intended rise and Seth advanced angrily.

"Sam, you ungrateful prick!" Seth countered shakily, trying to control his voice despite his rage. "And you too Pete! When I found the pair of ya,' you were digging through dumpsters for your next meal," he shook his finger in their direction. "Taking money and shit from these people was supposed to be easy, but the two of you constantly fuck things up. Those girls would have been a nice bonus too. One for each of us," he said, with a hint of smarmy regret.

They devolved into a heated argument, flinging insults and dodging blame as precious minutes ticked by. Someone had to step in as the voice of reason, so Seth whistled, high and shrill to get their attention.

"Let's just get back to the van," he said curtly. "Either way we didn't score anything tonight. And if any cops were there, they pro'ly be gone by now."

Conceding to follow Seth's lead, they made it through the deserted streets more quickly. And just as they were about to step into the shadow of the ramp, a tree shook in the darkness.

A long, exaggerated inhale was followed by an otherworldly voice drifting from the tree. "Oh yes... you've got something here, don't you?" she murmured, almost delighted. "The aroma of fear. The taste of it–such fun to play with, isn't it?"

As the realization that it was a woman they faced dawned on Seth–a smug, delighted smirk tugged at his lips. "Couldn't get enough the first time and had to come back for more, huh?" he said, every word dripping with slimy intent.

"Ohhhh.... You've never met the likes of me," the voice cooed. And in unison, they jerked their heads to the right, as this time it had clearly come from inside the ramp. "She did you a favor and held back," it continued, low and threatening. "But you won't get so lucky with me. Do you want to know what it feels like to be completely helpless?" she hissed.

By this point, her voice seemed to come from every direction, leaving them to spin in circles, desperate to pinpoint where she was.

Then, without a sound, a creature unlike anything they'd ever seen dropped from the ceiling, landing between them and the exit. She stood calmly, staring them down, the confidence in her eyes sending shivers through their spines. She was nearly six feet tall. A soft gray fur covered her body and a long sleek tail twitched behind her in annoyance.

They hesitated only a second before propelling themselves into motion. They fled in terror, her laugh, chilling and ominous, following them as their feet pounded the pavement. They ran toward the safety of the van, trying their best to ignore the strain it was putting on their injuries.

"Where the hell'djya ge' the goods man?" Pete accused Sam, gasping for air. "I trus' you with one thing and smokes are laced with, wha'... LSD? I di'na ask for this trippy shi' tonigh,' bro."

"I swear they're from our regular," Sam defended himself feebly. "If somethin's new, it's on them."

Their flight came to a screeching halt when she dropped from the ceiling–again–landing directly in their path.

"If it's a game of cat and mouse you want," she said, stretching lazily. "I'll play along," her smirk sharpened and she took a step forward "But you three? You're more like cockroaches. Only a true parasite would think intimidating women counts as some kind of accomplishment. Would you agree with my assessment?" She tilted her head, voice dropping to a purr. "You should apologize. Maybe then you'll earn a sliver of redemption before you die."

Her casual disregard toward them, peppered with the not so veiled threat, settled their growing fear into the pit of their stomachs.

"Leave us alone you… you demon!" Pete choked, "we di'na do nuthin.' Sides, the bitch was kinda scary but whatever you is? Ha! Am I s'posed to be scared?" But the attempt to convince himself that he was tough fell flat as his voice betrayed him. So in a final attempt to regain some courage, he pulled a knife from his pocket, expertly flicking his wrist to snap it open.

A laugh escaped her throat, high and wild, somehow more threatening than staring down the barrel of a gun.

"Cute," was the only word she uttered. And when she raised her hands to her waist, they could see her nails, razor sharp and ready. "You boys haven't been very nice to people. Especially the women you ambush," she poised herself to strike as they began their advance.

"None o' that is any yer business kitty cat," Pete said, regaining some composure.

Her stomach turned in disgust at the condescension that oozed from him.

"Oh I disagree," she countered. "You tried to hurt my friend, which made it my business. My name is Calliope. I thought you should know— since mine is the last face you will be seeing," she mirrored his tone, laying it on extra thick to drive the point home.

Then tiring of the banter, she flew into action. They cried out, one after the other, as pain erupted where her nails found their mark. Pete swung wildly but failed to land a blow as she melted unscathed back into the shadows.

"Do you know where I am?" She laughed, the sinister sound bouncing through the empty space. "You'd better run," she whispered loudly.

Now completely petrified, they fled through the exit, their eyes straining to pierce the darkness as they ignored the sting of fresh wounds. They didn't slow until they reached the boulevard. Gasping for breath, they clutched at their wounds, where blood had begun to seep through their clothing.

"How does it feel to be on that side of fear for a change?" Her voice followed their retreat, laced with revulsion. "I could feel what she did, and she was right. I couldn't find a shred of goodness."

Before they had a chance to compose themselves, she materialized again—slicing her way through them. Cries of pain rang out, nerves screaming in agony, as they were driven into a circle with their backs to each other.

"Bitch! I will end you," Sam grimaced, biting off the bitter words.

"That might work with your other victims," she sneered at the hollowness of his threat. "But we all know it's not true. I'll be the only one ending anything tonight."

Soundlessly, an arrow flew from the dark and buried itself in Sam's chest. His face froze in disbelief. He staggered, tripping into Pete and Seth, shoving them forward. They turned on him, ready for a fight—but irritation twisted into horror as they realized what they were seeing. Sam opened his mouth to speak, but only a fading croak escaped. He collapsed, his eyes still wide in shock staring blankly as his blood soaked into the ground.

"She has a fucking bow and arrow?!" Seth cried in disbelief. "You're on your own dude."

Then he scurried away, trying to put as much distance as he could between him and the shadowy demon. When he didn't hear her following, he slowed to a walk as the deep gashes on his side and upper thigh began to take their toll.

Pete's feet had turned to lead. He should have taken the opportunity when Seth did, but at this point, he wasn't sure if it mattered. He had to face the fact that she could out maneuver him no matter what he tried.

"You should beg for your life," she goaded him, unbothered by Seth's escape.

She'd deal with him soon enough.

"Pete don' beg," he said flatly. Then gripping his knife more tightly, he willed himself forward. Slowly they circled each other, each looking for the other's weakness. His clothing soaked in blood, his agony obvious as she forced him to work through the pain. "Pete. Don.' Beg," he growled, biting off each word.

Tucking and rolling forward, he aimed for an angle that might avoid her dangerous nails, then swung his knife low, slicing at her ankles. But her reflexes were lightning-fast–she sprang forward, easily avoiding the blade. Before he could turn back to defend himself, she was on top of him, knocking the knife out of reach. She grabbed his neck, shoving his face into the dirt, blood welling where her nails pierced his skin. In one fluid motion, she pulled an arrow from her quiver, plunged it through his neck and turned her back, not staying to watch as he choked out his final breaths. She would not be leaving a witness who might bring trouble to Hayden's door and she could still smell the remaining life. Tonight, she would finish her hunt.

Flitting in and out of shadows, she found him leaning against a brick wall clutching his wounds. He tried in vain to bolt when she appeared next to him. Even if he could have gotten away, he was severely weakened from blood loss and wouldn't have made it far.

"From me–there is no escape," she purred. "The shadows are good friends of mine, and they told me what you've done when you thought no one was looking. But tonight, you stumbled into your biggest blunder. You tried to hurt someone I love. I know what your intentions were and there was not a shred of nobility in them. Why do people like you hurt others? I never understood."

But though she held his life in her hands and at her mercy, the light was dim, and she could see no remorse in his eyes. It was written clearly on his face—he was determined to hold his villainy close until the end. His eyes reflected back a deep-seated darkness from which there was no return. For a brief moment, she marveled that there were beings in this world just as dark as the one that terrorized hers. She slowly wrapped her fingers one by one around his throat, leaning in to whisper directly into his ear.

"You deserve this end," she hissed, then ripped through the soft flesh of his inner thigh with her free hand.

He tried to struggle against her, but his blood loss had weakened him. She watched as the darkness slowly left his eyes, and when he went limp, she released her grasp, letting him fall. Returning to the other bodies only to collect her arrows, she slipped off into the night toward home.

****

"CALLIOPE!" Hayden's frantic cry catapulted her out of a deep slumber.

Since she'd revealed her Morphé, she now took up residence on the couch.

It was early Tuesday morning. Hayden was making her normal preparations for work when the news article popped up on her daily feed. "What the hell is this?!" she asked, her cheeks flushed.

Calliope did her best to hide her smirk. Hayden looked comical with one hand planted firmly on her hip, holding the phone just inches from Calliope's face. Calliope knew that it would be in poor tasted to laugh just now, so she focused on the headline. **Triple Homicide Baffles Local Law Enforcement**, it read. Pictures of their faces were posted at the top of the page.

"Okay? What does it have to do with me?" she yawned, feigning ignorance.

"Oh come on Cal! Arrow wounds and lacerations matching a feline profile. You really expected me to think this wasn't you?!"

Calliope was slightly taken aback at Hayden's level of disgust.

"Why are you upset?" She asked, deciding it was better to lean into the truth. "I stopped evil before it could hurt anyone else. Why is this a problem?"

She sat up, rubbing the sleep from her eyes.

"Because we don't dole out vigilante justice here!" Hayden snapped back.

Calliope's gray ears twitched as she raised her brows.

"Vigilante?" She said, her inflection denoting confusion.

Hayden began to get frustrated as her imagination conjured every possible version of this being traced back to her. She stamped her foot, aggravated at having to explain when she was already running behind.

"We have certain procedures that must be followed here. Justice requires they get a fair trial in front of a jury of their peers," she paused, reigning in her expectations for someone who hadn't grown up here. "Do they not do this in Dagrune?"

"Well I guess it used to be something like that, but not in my lifetime," Calliope said, folding her hands in her lap and shrugging. "I'm sorry. I wouldn't have done it if I knew it would upset you. It was meant as a favor.

Hayden stepped back, slightly deflated from her initial angst. She hadn't expected an apology, but now that she had one, it didn't feel right.

"I'm not gonna lie, I'm a little relieved they can't hurt anyone else, and what's done is done. But damn woman! Did you have to be so brutal?"

Calliope crossed her legs, relaxing into the corner of the couch. "I didn't do anything worse than they did," she said indifferently, playing with a loose thread in her blanket. "In fact, I was most likely nicer than they were to most of the people they hurt."

Hayden pinched her nose, blowing out a long breath as she tried to get a grip on the situation.

"Please stop, I don't want any more details. Plausible deniability and all that," she rocked back on her heels, jumping as she checked her watch. "If I don't leave now, I'll be late for work," then pivoting in exasperation, she yanked her purse from its hook, shouting over her shoulder, "Don't kill any more bad guys while I'm gone!"

But when she got to work, she found it impossible to escape the touchy subject. It was another day in surgery with her favorite tech Alexa, and their conversation inevitably turned to the hottest news of the day.

"Good riddance to bad rubbish," Alexa said from behind her mask. She was holding the clamp on a vein that wouldn't stop bleeding when she brought it up. "But I really want to know who, or what, killed them. You would think Green Arrow was hanging around. But not just him. He's probably got a pet from Krypton that Super Girl gave him."

Hayden laughed at the irony that she would bring up something supernatural, thinking only to herself–*more like grey arrow.*

Eventually, interest in the subject died down and began to focus on her approaching departure with Tabatha's return.

"I'm happy she's coming back, but this place just won't be the same without you," Alexa admitted dejectedly. " I wish there were some way we could keep you both on," she stood over the sink, rinsing the tray of surgical instruments that had finished soaking in disinfectant, the clink of metal on metal drowning out her words as she dumped it onto the drying rack.

"It's ok," Hayden said, still writing vigorously. "I really have enjoyed my time here, but I have other things I need to move on to."

Alexa raised an eyebrow, smirking at words she knew were left unsaid.

"Alright then, keep your secrets," she said, stealing a glance at Hayden as she scribbled her surgery notes.

When Hayden pulled into the driveway that evening, she saw Tormaigh towering over Calliope giving her a piece of her mind. She knew what it was about, but was too far past tired to care, let alone get involved. Tossing her dirty scrubs in the hamper, she found herself torn between anticipation and remorse. This was merely the first of a handful of lasts that she would have to face in the upcoming weeks. So she donned her favorite pair of pajamas, then dug in the freezer for some form of comfort.

"Oh hello my old friend," she said, grasping the half-eaten carton of rocky road. "Girl dinner is waiting," she smiled, content in the moment, trying her best not to think about what was to come.

Piles of pillows and knit blankets welcomed her into their cozy embrace as she fell back with a satisfied exhale.

"My house. My rules," she said, addressing the container sitting coldly on her lap. "Bowl schmowl."

Then taking a huge spoonful, she began to nibble on the chocolate bits around the edges. With a few clicks of the remote, the comforting sound of a woman narrating to a dark screen made her relax just a little bit more. This was the extended version, so tonight was going to be a late one.

<u>17</u>

The Beginning of the Beginning

Hayden's days as a relief vet at Iola Veterinary Hospital had finally drawn to a close. Although it had only been a handful of months, she found it difficult to say goodbye to the friends she'd made along the way. They felt real in the moment, but the truth was, they rarely lasted past her employment. She opened each door, wrote each chart, and put down each scalpel, thinking of how it was just another last.

This time was different though. It wasn't just the last of her experience at this clinic, it was quite possibly the last time she would get to do any of it. The day turned into a blur. So many cards. So many goodbye hugs. Then there was the generous pot luck that they'd somehow kept a secret from her. But the most difficult thing she faced by far was saying goodbye to Alexa. She was the one person Hayden could truly imagine forming a real connection with.

"I know we've only known each other for half a year, but it feels like it's been so much longer," Alexa had said.

And though Hayden agreed, she had to maintain an air of detachment. It was the only way to keep another person off of her 'need to know' list. One less person to hurt with her disappearance. And as the miles stretched behind her on her way home that night, she knew in her heart that she would never cross paths with any of them again.

Training had reached a new level of difficulty. They expected her to fight to win and not just to spar—a development that went against everything she loved about Jiu Jitsu and her own moral code. It created a mental battle that had been ongoing since she decided to follow her obligation to Dagrune. She found herself less passionate about learning their style of fighting, which reflected in her waning effort. Between growing her magical strength and honing her fighting technique, it felt like another full-time job. At least she was grateful that there was no nine-to-five to contend with the growing workload. It all seemed perfectly timed, so she mentally added another scratch to the tally of strange seamless coincidences.

"You're getting better and your reaction time is decreasing, so that's a positive," Calliope commented one day.

When Tormaigh had caved to her relentless requests to be the teacher, she'd been over the moon excited.

"But why do I feel that you aren't putting your all into it?"

"I don't know," Hayden replied, sitting down with a shrug and a humph. "Maybe it's because I feel like my life has been upended. I have no real direction except for you guys training me, and we have no idea how we're even supposed to get back to Dagrune. Not to mention, no one has heard from the Angel," she plucked at the browning grass, rolling it between her fingers. "Do we wait for her? Do we wander around until I figure out how to get us back there? Is there some doorway or something I'm supposed to magically find?" Her teeth clicked together with an ironic grimace at the unintentional pun.

"I've been pondering the same things," Calliope admitted, watching Hayden carefully.

A sudden gust of wind whipped her hair into her face just as Bérg barked a warning from up the hill, prompting Tormaigh and Calliope to morph. It wasn't a common occurrence for hikers to wander through their training grounds, but it happened enough that she didn't need them to tell her anymore. She sprang into action, straightening the picnic blanket as Bérg made his appearance in the clearing. They all took up their places. Bérg offering himself as a pillow and the Morphé women lounging in their Ophrahl forms as if they were on a leisure, late fall outing.

"What a crew you have with you," the man said in obvious awe.

He'd only been mildly startled to see them as he broke through the tree line. He must have heard Bérg's warning.

Hayden sized him up as she peaked over the pages of her book. His boots were well suited for rugged terrain and although it was an unusually warm day for fall, Hayden could see a jacket tied to his pack. His pack was large, but not large enough to hold a tent. If he was a camper, he was certainly traveling light.

"Yeah," she responded, feigning laziness. "We really enjoy it out here. It's good for the animals to experience this kind of freedom... OW!" The exclamation slipped out involuntarily. Calliope had clearly taken offense. *"Really?! You KNOW what I meant,"* she linked, "Do you camp often?" She asked him, the friendly intent of her inquiry doubling as a ploy to find out if they need worry about him.

"It's probably my last camp out of the season," he answered, not slowing his stride. "I love being out here, but these old bones don't do so well with the snow and cold anymore," he laughed, waving briefly before he disappeared on the far side of the clearing.

Old?! She thought to herself. *He couldn't have been much older than me.*

As soon as they were sure that he wasn't hanging around, the two women once again melded to their Morphé forms–continuing their conversation as though there'd been no interruption.

"I too, have thought long and hard about this, and I think I may finally have some direction," Tormaigh paused dramatically in her usual way, something that had begun to grate on Hayden's nerves lately.

"And?!" She prompted, trying fruitlessly to keep the urgency from her voice.

"And I think we need to go find this Shaman Matilde told us about," she finished.

Hayden's eyes lit up as she exacted a loud slap to her forehead.

"Oh my god you're right! It was staring me in the face all this time! He provided the herbs to block my memories. If he can somehow restore them, maybe I will remember something that could help us out. It would at least point us in a better direction than none at all."

"You linked my thoughts exactly, Princess," Tormaigh agreed.

Hayden cringed for the umpteenth time at the title. No matter how often she asked them not to use it, they never seemed to listen.

"There are so many logistics to consider though," Hayden began to ponder aloud. "When we find out exactly where he is, how do we get you guys there? I don't want to travel alone, but the two of you can't exactly hop on a plane as yourselves. While I could fly with a cat in a carrier..." a hiss from Calliope cut her off. "Exactly," she continued. "Mom isn't in the greatest state of health, so flying would be too hard on her, and I don't feel right about asking Matilde to come along."

"Let's just tackle one problem at a time," Tormaigh admonished. "You're getting yourself agitated before we have a chance to even look into where you need to go."

Hayden laid back, resting her head once again on Bérg's back.

"You're right as usual," she sighed, letting the warmth of the sun sooth her. "I'll get in contact with Matilde and find out where he might be," then her face twisted into a wry smile as the realization dawned on her. "Damn, she was right. That wasn't the last time I would see her."

Another piece of the strange puzzle seemed to fall into place as her nerves gave way to a sudden sense of purpose. With that renewed direction, she could no longer focus on training.

****

"Mum, I'm so happy to hear your voice! How are things going with Alec?"

Hayden had called to solidify plans for brunch. This was the first time she would be hanging out with Alec in any official capacity, and for reasons she couldn't quite place, she was a bundle of nerves.

"Oh you know—he makes me feel young again," Clara tittered. "Maybe it's all those walks we take, but I've noticed that my joints don't hurt as much lately."

Hayden's brow wrinkled with the realization. Mum was right. She *had* noticed a change in the ease with which she moved.

"As I've always said," she replied, slipping once again into professional mode. "Moving is the best thing you can do for those arthritic joints."

"Yes—yes hun, hush. You're not my doctor," Clara teased gently.

They met at the old inn as planned. Located in the center of town, it had been a community staple for decades. The owners were good friends of Clara's—and what began as a professional relationship had long since turned into a deep friendship. The building, a former Victorian home, was covered in aqua blue cedar shake siding. Though the pine log porch was a recent addition—added after the original failed a safety inspection—it still echoed the building's Victorian charm.

They picked their way through the delicately designed metal tables and chairs scattered across the porch, heading toward a small glass room that graced the side of the building. It glinted in the sun, inviting them into its warmth despite the cold bite in the air.

"So many good places to sit here, how will we choose?" Alec asked, a hint of playfulness in his voice.

"I think patio season is over for me. The greenhouse looks pretty nice though," Clara parried.

Hayden stifled a laugh.

"You two are already joking like a weird old couple. But you can't fool me! I know we have a reservation," she raised her eyebrows, joining in on the lighthearted banter.

Alec feigned an air of offence. "Hey now, be careful with that old guy stuff," he nudged her gently, "And you can't call your mom old either," then with a self-satisfied grin, he took Clara by the elbow and let her lead them to their reserved table.

NeuUlm Inn was renowned in the area and rightfully claimed its spot as a popular destination when it came to high-quality brunch. The bubbly they served was one of its well-known draws. Here, no one would be judged for getting a little tipsy before noon. They shuffled themselves into their seats where champagne glasses awaited them, the bubbles already popping and splashing invitingly.

"It's good to know people in high places," Alec said, his eyes dancing with mirth. "We get the best seats in the house AND the good stuff already waiting for us."

Clara smiled, throwing a wink his way, also squeezing Hayden's knee.

"Only the best for my two favorite people," she said sincerely.

Hayden could see how happy Mum was, but despite the observation, her skeptical side still fought for dominance. This seemed to happen far too quickly. Especially when she considered all the coincidence that surrounded their meet cute. But now was not the time to voice concern. Mum needed her support and not her jaded sense of trust.

"I haven't seen that look on your face in a very long time," she said, trying not to let her doubts creep in.

Brunch was buffet style. The first table was heated, offering breakfast meats such as sausages, eggs, and even a juicy cut of perfectly marbled prime rib. The second was filled with every salad imaginable from the crisp, lettuce-heavy type, to spiraled noodles that marinated in a savory oil dressing. But Hayden's favorite, by far, had always been the dessert table. The first time Mum brought her here as a child, she'd been hesitant, unable to believe the offer to take as much as she wanted wouldn't be revoked. But it never was. She gave herself a stomachache from the sugar, yet Mum never got upset. That was the first time she allowed herself to hope that Clara might actually be different from the tyrants she'd once called parents.

"Ernie! Ruth! It's so good to see you!" Clara said, pushing her chair back and nearly springing up to hail her long-time friends.

Hayden blinked slowly as she also rose to greet them. It had been a good while since she'd seen Mum move that quickly. But it was soon forgotten when Ruth wrapped her in that signature rib crushing hug she was so good at, and planted a kiss on her cheek with a loud smack.

"Will it be the usual for you Hayden?" Ernie winked, not needing an actual answer.

Back when the dessert anomaly had worn off, she'd gotten more adventurous in her food choices and had found a new favorite. But it wasn't something they offered at the buffet tables. This was a special order.

"You're the only one who makes it just the way I like it," she said, returning the gesture.

"You got it kiddo!" he replied enthusiastically.

And the warmth of his affection washed over her in a familiar wave. These two were the only people she'd ever had the privilege of calling grandparents.

When the omelet arrived, it was exactly as she remembered. A blanket of eggs wrapped around wild rice, sautéed onions and spinach. Roasted tomatoes were also mixed in with a delicious spice blend. But the ingredient that gave it that special something was the cream sauce. She'd never been able to duplicate it, and Ernie would not divulge the family's secret recipe.

After Ernie and Ruth left them to enjoy their food, they settled down to the business of friendly chatter. If there was any way she could scope out the kind of person Alec truly was, it was over bubbly—the perfect catalyst for lowering defenses and loosening tongues.

"How are things going with your crazy crew?" Alec asked, opening the conversation between bites of hashed browns. "She let you ride her yet?"

A wry smile crept onto both Clara and Hayden's faces. But they had to curb their desire to exchange a knowing glance lest it was too obvious.

"Oh definitely!" Hayden replied, a hint of amusement in her voice. "We love to go on long hikes through the foothills and Bérg loves having her as a companion."

Alec's surprise flashed across his tan features and he raised his eyebrows.

"That horse lets a dog get anywhere near her?" His forkful of eggs benedict was paused halfway to his mouth as the image teased him. "Well I never would have seen that one coming," he said, shoving the generous portion into his mouth.

They took their time, slowly sipping sweet bubbly and talking about the changes that life always seemed to bring. Between Hayden finding herself in limbo—although she was careful with how she addressed it in present company—and Alec practically inviting himself over for a game night, she felt that the conversation had stayed in a fairly safe boundary. After paying their bill despite protests from Ernie and Ruth, they headed back outdoors for a short walk through town. But it was short lived as the fringes of old man winters attention was upon them. They hadn't prepared for the wind, which was making it more difficult to talk anyway, so they agreed to head back to Clara's for a game of cards.

As they pulled into the driveway, she noticed the sleek design of Alec's car. Though cars weren't an obsession of hers, she could appreciate and acknowledge when others took pride in their vehicles. And one as nice as his was sure to fall into that category.

"Wow, that is one perty looking Buick you've got there," Hayden whistled, taking a lap around the silver monstrosity.

And the way Alec's face lit up with pride told her the hunch was right.

"Oh yeah! This baby would leave a lot of cars in the dust," he beamed, running his fingers lightly over its curves. "I named her Jasmine."

"I didn't know we were still naming cars these days," Hayden teased.

She regretted the ribbing almost instantly when the proud glow in Alec's eyes dimmed for a second.

"Well it means something to me," he defended himself.

Laying her hand gently on his arm, she tried to amend the mistake.

"Oh no, I'm sorry. I was teasing you. I didn't intend to make it sound snooty."

But when she touched him, he tensed and quickly pulled away. His response left her puzzled as she watched him walk briskly toward Clara, passing her to offer a supportive arm when she got to the stairs.

Hayden followed her mother up the walk, distracted by the strange interaction–trying to understand why he'd reacted that way. Her focus, usually hypervigilant when it came to keeping Mum safe, had slipped. And in that moment, she heard a cry of pain as Mum tripped, her toe jamming against a raised slab of concrete. She careened forward, throwing her arms up to protect her face. Hayden knew she was too far away to help, but she jumped forward anyway in a desperate attempt to catch her before the fall could do any damage. Only one thought raced through her mind. *Help Mum!*

Then, as if on instinct, she opened herself to her magic, and flung her arms out, reaching frantically for Clara's energy. By the time Clara's cry had reached Alec's ears and he'd spun around to see what the commotion was about, Hayden had already set her back on her feet. She quickly composed herself with Clara leaning heavily on her arm as she grimaced in pain.

"Mum, are you okay?" She asked, concerned.

But even without the unique sense that stemmed from her magic, she didn't need an answer. Mum's pain was written on her face.

"No," Clara said, panting hard as she tried to hold her composure. "I think something might be broken or at least sprained really badly."

Alec hurried back to them, and all the while Hayden scrutinized him to see if she could get a read on whether or not he caught a glimpse of her magic. Thankfully, it didn't appear to be the case.

"Here let me help you up to the porch."

He didn't wait for her permission, just scooped her into his arms as if she weighed nothing.

Hayden watched in awe as he walked with ease up the stairs and waited by the door for her to catch up. If she'd had any doubts about how he felt for Clara, it dissipated in that moment. The concern in his voice was all the evidence she needed. Not only that, but the power that their love held was as obvious as the energy between them felt as though it had multiplied tenfold.

They helped her inside, making sure she was as comfortable as possible under the circumstances—in her favorite easy chair.

"Let me get a look see," Hayden demanded.

She pulled off Clara's plain black flats, revealing a small spot near the joint of her little toe that looked like it might be darkening in color. The shoes were soft enough. It was completely plausible she could have broken the toe. She flipped into emergency mode, not caring that Alec might still be harboring offence from their previous tense exchange.

"Let me go get some ice and some bandage material. Alec, you see if there is any damage to the ankle. A gentle massage is all you need to find pain," she barked the orders. "Then have her move her foot around so she can tell you if the movement is compromised at all."

She quickly made her way to the kitchen, grabbing a gel pack out of the freezer and moved on to the bathroom. She was never gladder than today, on her insistence for Clara to keep a kit of basic medical supplies there. It was just a small plastic storage container, so she snatched the whole thing out of the drawer and jogged back down the hall where she saw Clara leaning her head back. A couple extra pillows were propped behind her–courtesy of Alec.

"Let me go make some tea for you," Alec offered tenderly. "Is your stomach feeling okay? If it isn't, I can make a tea for the pain *and* that."

Clara smiled, regarding Alec with a look of adoration. One that shone through her pain.

"Some tea would be pretty soothing right now," she said, wincing involuntarily as a fresh wave hit her. "My stomach's fine. The massage seemed to help."

When Alec came back from brewing the tea, Hayden noticed it wasn't the usual bags Clara kept in the cupboard.

"Changing up your tea routine I see," She noted more to herself than the others.

Clara's laugh made her relax a little. If she was laughing through the pain, it was most likely bearable by now.

"He's taught me a whole new way to drink it," she said with her eyes still closed. "You should go in there and check it out."

"Okay, but let me wrap this gel pack on your foot first."

When she was confident nothing else could be done, she went into the kitchen. Jars of dried herbs and flowers sat on a brand-new shelf she assumed was installed by Alec. Chalkboard stickers were labeled with what was inside. Items such as orange and lemon zest, chamomile, and basil were written in Clara's flowing script. The whistling teapot was still there, but now there was a smaller one sitting next to it. This one was ceramic and light blue, covered by a glossy sheen. Bumps were in even patterns over the entire outer surface and a metal handle fell to one side. There was some tea left underneath the small metal strainer carrying a mixture of herbs. Its tantalizing smell made her pour a small cup for herself. She felt much more relaxed as she made her way back to the living room.

"Your setup is no joke! Is tea a hobby of yours?" She addressed Alec, happily noting fresh color returning to Clara's cheeks.

"Actually, it's one of my businesses," he replied. "I make different herbal tea mixes and sell them online."

"He didn't really give me a choice," Clara interjected. "Installed the shelf and brought over all the stuff for it. It's quite an improvement…"

"Over the tea dust?" Hayden grinned, glancing at Alec to see if he caught the reference.

"Oooh! Good one! Ducky would be proud," he returned with a toothy smile.

Hayden was relieved by the banter, knowing that the earlier tension between them seemed to have fluttered away.

The tea mug in Clara's hands was one Hayden painted when the adoption was first finalized. It was a simple design of hearts and flowers, with the words 'thank you' written in block letters above it. Hayden smiled fondly at the memory. It had been one of joy and trepidation. But nothing on that day so many years ago, could have sullied the feeling of safety that she'd dared to allow herself.

"Let me take a look at your toe Mum," Hayden commanded, carefully unwrapping the bandages.

To her surprise, there was no discoloration and the toe looked normal.

"How does it feel? Can you wiggle it?"

Clara obliged, seeming to have no difficulty moving the injured digit.

"Huh…" she muttered, staring suspiciously at the toe that only moments before was causing her a decent amount of discomfort. "It feels completely fine. Maybe I just haven't felt pain in a while."

"Well I'm glad to hear it!" Alec exclaimed, almost too enthusiastically. "You two still up for a few games of cards?"

He moved toward the dining area not waiting for an answer. Then opening the card drawer, he pulled out two decks and began to shuffle them. Hayden exchanged a pointed look with Clara, shrugged, then led her to the table.

They played a couple games of Golf before Hayden found the right moment to excuse herself.

"I have some things I need to get done today, but I'll call you," she said, turning to Clara. "I would really appreciate a chat later."

"Ok honey," Clara said, giving her a knowing look. "I should be available around seven tonight."

Back on the road, her fingers followed the familiar path of taps on her screen. She'd dialed this number so many times in her life, that she probably could have found it with her eyes closed.

"I thought I might hear from you pretty soon," Matilde's voice answered. "What can I do to help?"

"What would it take for me to get some information about that Shaman you went to visit way back when?" she asked.

Hayden heard the rustle of papers before Matilde's reply.

"I thought you might need it someday, so I saved everything and just found the folder a few days ago. I'm happy to meet you somewhere and give it to you," she offered. "It would be good to see you again."

"Are you available tomorrow?" Hayden asked.

<u>18</u>

Memory Triggers

*Jane stared out her window, the hum of tires on the highway nearly hypnotic. But she didn't want to fall asleep, not when she knew they were headed to Little Laughing Falls. It was rare to go on one of Mama's adventures, so to pass the time, she'd invented a game to play by herself. Today the letter she picked was **H**. She was only up to ten—noting to herself that it was far fewer than when she counted vowels. The game worked—and before she knew it they were pulling into their favorite parking lot.*

The 170-acre state park seemed huge to a city girl such as herself. It felt like acres of freedom when compared to the concrete she'd gotten used to. When they stepped out of the car, the sun wrapped her in the only kind of hug that she knew. Something about it made her feel more hope than she dared, that today might be a good one.

"Come on, let's get moving!" Mama said, sounding annoyed.

"Coming Mama," she replied.

Jane quickened her pace, knowing that at any moment, something could easily upset her. Usually, Mama allowed her to wander a little bit when they were here, but she didn't want to test the waters—at least not yet. It would be better to wait until Mama's mood was more obvious.

At first the path wound through an even mix of leafy trees and pines. They made the perfect environment for plants that fared better in the shade. The faint, distant buzz of a mower drew her attention, and the sweet pungency of fresh cut grass reached her nose. She inhaled, feeling another sliver of sadness melt away. Next to an impending storm, that smell was hands down one of her favorite things about summer.

"Can I pick some of those flowers so we can put them on the table?" she asked, pointing at brightly colored blooms mere feet off the path.

"I don't think we're supposed to take flowers from a State Park," Mama replied thoughtfully. "Why don't we stop at a regular one on the way home and pick some dandelions or something.

Oh good. I think she's having one of her good days, *Jane thought in relief.*

Thoughtfulness toward anyone or anything other than herself was a rare occurrence, so maybe today would turn out alright after all.

"Okay!" she replied cheerily, skipping ahead.

Birds called to each other from the trees, flitting about, unfazed by the familiar human presence. Jane excitedly pointed out a hummingbird. It hovered over a flower, its body shimmering in rays that peeked tenaciously through the leafy canopy above.

"Oh!" she exclaimed, her eyes wide with discovery. "Look Mama! That's why we don't take them."

She chattered with excitement at each butterfly, crouched to examine beetles, and marveled at a rare garden snake. Eventually, the dirt path opened up into a large field. A hill loomed in front of them, leading down to water that splashed over rocks in a very shallow creek. A few blankets dotted the flat ground nearer the water where adults lounged within sight of the children at play. Some screeched with laughter as they rolled down the hill, while others walked around in the water, bending down occasionally to inspect the offerings of the creek bed.

"Can I roll down the hill?" Jane asked. She desperately wanted to join in the fun the other kids were having, but she knew better than to do it without permission.

"Yeah, go for it! I'll time you," Mama said, to her delight.

Jane laid down, squeezed her eyes shut, and left the rest to gravity. Smiling and giggling she would readjust every time she found her feet pointing downhill.

"One minute! Record time!" Mama yelled.

Her feet landed heavily as she put one foot in front of the other. Years of coping with drugs had left her muscles weak and stringy, making it more of a struggle than it should have been for a woman of her age. When they reached the creek they pulled off their shoes to dip their feet in the cool wetness of the water. It felt good on such a warm day.

"Should we walk down to the river or the falls first?"

The fact Mama even asked her opinion made Jane feel a little warmth and extra relief in the pit of her stomach.

"I like the sand walls by the river. Can we go there first?"

Jane loved carving pictures in the soft rock, but it usually crumbled away too quickly, taking her intended artistry with it in a shower of sand. Mama led the way, following the path as it crossed and recrossed the creek. Sometimes the bridge was made of boards, while others were logs that offered only precarious footing.

"Put your arms out like this Mama," Jane suggested, noticing Mama's struggle. She floated her arms upward to demonstrate. "It helps you to balance."

Along the way she kept her eyes peeled for the perfect rock. Sticks always broke too easily. And it was well known that the best rocks were along these banks anyway. Suddenly she saw it—poking out of the mud, beckoning to her. It was perfectly sharp at one end, yet still smooth enough to sit comfortably in her hand. Grasping the carving tool tightly, Jane climbed the well-worn footpath, made by a thousand pairs of feet before her.

Mama looked on from below, completely uninterested in vesting the effort. So Jane carved as fast as she could, casting glances over her shoulder to the path below. She had to time it just right, because Mama's patience might run out before she'd had her fun. She stepped back to admire her efforts, reveling in the feeling of peace she felt whenever they did this trip. Then she abruptly turned her back and her smile faded as she clamored back down to the main path. They continued onto the edge of the river where the path ended, and for a moment paused to watch the water flow by.

"Ready for the falls?" Mama asked, spurring Jane forward.

So back they went. Over the winding path, past the hill, then up an incline. There they came upon a flight of stairs, switching its way up a very steep hill. The crumbling steps left piles of pebbles and broken old cement, which was only rivaled by the rotting boards that framed it all in. Here, the creek went from shallow to deep and turbulent as their view opened up to the falls. A pillar of water flowed over a rocky ledge, then cascaded into a deep pool below.

They could see boulders, smoothed over by decades of abuse from the water, disappearing into the frothy darkness. A black gate hung haphazardly just to the side of the stairs. Its hinges were nearly rusted through. If the ground weren't providing support, it would have happily detached itself from the fence. Holding on to the gate for dear life, by one screw—an equally rusted sign read: **Danger! Keep Out!**

Beyond the gate the footpath narrowed. It was dangerously close to the eroding soil of an edge that dropped sharply into the angry water below. In contrast, a steep hill rose to the right, ending at a stone wall that separated the thick vegetation from the sidewalk beyond.

"No one's around. Let's climb over the gate and go behind the falls," Mama whispered, her hot breath brushing her skin like a warning.

It took everything in her not to shy away from the feeling of that breath. It never failed to make her want to recoil, but she couldn't let Mama see her do that. So she tried her best to cover it up—allowing the real fear she felt, to lend its aid. When Mama got an idea like this in her head, there was nothing she could do to change it. So obediently and without protest, she climbed the gate. Thankfully, the helpful arms of small saplings offered their assistance—guiding them safely to a rock shelf behind the thundering water. She tried to hide her fear as the powerful roar threatened to drag her into the dark pool below.

When Mama finally turned back toward the gate, she stifled her outward manifestation of relief—but it would be short lived. With horrified realization, she watched helplessly as Mama began to ascend the steep hill toward the wall. Jane's mind raced, thinking of what a fall down the hill would mean. She couldn't help the thought that it looked like a difficult swim, even for someone who might be good at it. And she had never been taught.

"Come on, this should be fun!" Mama encouraged.

"She has to be able to see that I'm scared," Jane thought. But she knew that hope was futile.

So with no voice of reason to stop them, they began the harrowing climb. Loose dirt rolled down the hill with each step. The trees, which were sufficient to help them on the path below, felt as if their shallow roots would give way with every tug. Her heart beat faster with every sound of rolling dirt and every snap of the thin branches. Then it happened. The ground, softened by recent rain gave way, causing her to teeter for a moment before the dreaded backward motion of her body. They were halfway up the hill, high enough that a fall would have sent her careening without hope into the water below. She clawed backward, but there was no ground to catch her.

"Jane, take my hand!" Mama barked.

She felt calloused fingers reaching out to brush hers.

I should be in the water. Why am I not in the water? *Her thoughts churned.*

She could feel branches pressing into her back. Had they somehow caught her? After only a split second of hesitation, she reached out so Mama could pull her back onto her feet. As soon as she left the safety of the branches, they sprung back into place. When her eyes met Mama's, she could see a mix of anger and relief on the sunken face.

Why would she be mad at me for falling? *Jane wondered.*

Though it felt as if centuries had passed since Jane reluctantly scrambled over the gate, they finally reached the wall—only to be faced with another dilemma. It was too high to climb over from their position. Panic filled her chest again as she began to consider the possibility: they would have to turn around and climb back down the steep slope. Then with a shrill cry, Mama surprised Jane.

"Is anyone up there?! We need help!" she screeched.

Grateful that Mama had at least thought to call for help, Jane waited with bated breath for someone–anyone–to respond. Then, suddenly, a kindly face appeared over the wall.

"How in the world did you get down there?" He asked, a look of shock stretching his sharp features.

He reached over to grab Jane's outstretched arms and pulled her to safety.

"Can you lift Mama too?" Jane asked with concern.

Something about the stranger made her feel instantly at ease. Maybe it was because he'd just saved her life and she was relieved to be out of danger's unforgiving clutches? At any rate, he was kind, with an easy manner that made her feel like she was in safe hands. An idea that was nearly foreign to her.

"Don't worry, I'm going to get her out of there," he assured her, turning to a couple walking by. "Hey buddy, can you give me a hand here? There's a woman down there I need to pull over this wall."

"Of course!" The other man responded.

They each grabbed one of her arms, supporting her weight, her feet scrambling to find footholds. When she was safely over the top, the three of them leaned against the wall to catch their breath.

"Is everyone ok?" The first stranger inquired.

Mama's confirmation was lost in the sound of the other strangers wife, fussing over her like a mother hen. Jane felt uncomfortable, unused to that level of care and attention from an adult. Before they left, the kind man crouched down, whispering just loud enough for her to hear.

"I'm so sorry, I'll try to fix this."

She didn't understand. Why would he need to apologize when **they'd** been the ones in need of his help? Mama thanked the couple and they headed back to the car. The adventure was over for now.

Their drive home was uncomfortable at best. Jane could feel something brewing in her mother's head, but try as she might, nothing came to mind of any wrongdoing on her part. She'd known enough to prepare herself for this possibility before the day even began. After all, this wasn't an uncommon occurrence. But despite knowing that something unpleasant was coming, she couldn't help feeling a little sad that there would be no pretty dandelions on their table tonight.

"Go get in the tub," Mama ordered tersely when they stepped into the house, "and leave your clothing on."

Jane silently obeyed. She was just about to turn on the water when Mama walked into the bathroom, her blotchy red skin proving just how angry she was.

"Don't touch that handle. Sit down," she spat out.

"Mama, what did I do?"

The sting of Mama's hand connecting with her face sent her sprawling backward. Her head hit the tiled wall making hot tears spring unbidden to her eyes. She couldn't help it—the pain made it happen involuntarily. But Mama had a strong rule. She could never cry during 'learning time,' which was the name Mama gave it so she could be subtle with her threats in public.

"Don't lie to me. You know exactly what you did, and you're gonna sit here until you tell me. In fact..." She paused, the slow change in her expression making Jane shudder. Nothing good ever followed one of those looks. It meant she was coming up with a new way to put fresh fear into the cowering child. "I'm hungry and there isn't much food in the house. You would make a great soup... which is what will *happen if you don't apologize for what you did," an evil twisted smile spread across her face. "I'm gonna get started with this butter."*

Only then did Jane notice the spoon in her hand just before she proceeded to smear the generous portion all over her hair.

"Just call out to me when you're ready to come clean," she cackled cruelly.

Knots twisted themselves in Jane's stomach. She went over every second of their time at the park, trying in vain to come up with what triggered this treatment. She cried quietly to herself, quickly wiping away the tears when she heard Mama coming back.

"A little salt and maybe some pepper would do the trick," she sneered, adding them to the greasy mess of her hair.

Time simultaneously crawled and sped by too fast with every return trip Mama made. Each time she came back with a different seasoning, chattering glibly about the vegetables she was cutting up to put in the 'Little bitch soup.'

"I told you before to stop with the witch stuff and you keep choosing to disobey me."

It had been nearly two hours of the routine fashioned to terrify her into admitting something she didn't even do. When Mama said this, the realization finally hit her. The trees preventing her fall were there only when she lost footing. That had to be it. Sure, it wasn't normal, but she didn't understand why Mama reacted this way. Strange things did seem to happen to her every once in a while, but how could any of it be her fault? Then she reminded herself that when Mama was in one of these moods, it was better just to agree with her. Even if it was a lie. She hated lying, but sometimes it was the only tool she possessed to survive learning time.

"I'm sorry Mama," she admitted insincerely. "I didn't mean to. I don't know how it happened," she allowed tears to well up in her eyes.

While they weren't allowed when Mama was causing her pain, tears of remorse were. So she used them when they provided the most benefit. This typically made Mama believe that there was a sincerity behind her words that wasn't necessarily there.

"Fine. I never want to see it again, otherwise it will be worse for you next time," she stormed out of the room, calling over her shoulder, "wash all that shit off. Supper is ready and you'd better be here in fifteen minutes exactly!"

Without waiting even the tiniest second, Jane turned on the water, hurrying as quickly as possible through her shower. Tossing the wrung-out clothing in the hamper, she threw on a new outfit, then practically ran to the kitchen. There on the stove was a pot, boiling with some fresh vegetables and chicken Mama had picked up at the food shelf earlier that week.

****

Hayden's abrupt movement upset Calliope's nap. In a rare time when she wanted to be Ophrahl, she'd curled up on the couch. Morphing in the house would be a poor choice to make, so she instead linked with her annoyance.

"I was having such a nice dream. What was that about?"

"I have to call mum!" Hayden cried, intentionally ignoring Calliope.

Reaching for her phone with trembling hands, Hayden barely had time to dial the number by the time Calliope returned from her morph.

"Hey Mum, I need you to come over. Now. Alone. Please, this is really important and I don't want to discuss it over the phone," she demanded.

"I'm on my way," Clara answered shortly.

Hayden was forever grateful when it came to how quickly Mum would jump to her aid when asked. When she arrived, she practically ran into Clara's waiting arms.

"Hey kiddo, what's eatin' you up?"

Her hug was exactly what Hayden needed, though worry still wove through every fiber of her being.

"I'm not gonna mince words Mum. I was going through the information Matilde gave me, when a picture triggered that memory at Little Laughing Falls," she paused, weighing her words. "I... I... know I told you the story, but there was one thing I left out... kind of," she pulled Mum toward the back deck where Calliope and Tormaigh waited, elbows propped on the railing as they gazed out over the landscape.

"The guy who pulled us up from the rock wall," she said, coughing to buy a moment before revealing the truth. "It was Alec," she cringed at the cutting words aimed at the one person she'd never want to hurt. "I knew he seemed familiar–besides seeing him at auctions before," her thoughts churned, a burning question at the tip of her tongue. "Mum! How was he there when I was a kid?"

It landed heavily and Hayden searched Clara's face for the anger that was sure to be there. She was, in a way, accusing the man Mum loved of something. Even if she didn't know what that something was.

Clara's eyes reflected her struggle. Hayden knew her well enough to see it. And then, in a subtle shift, the swirling turmoil turned to a calm purpose. If there was a way to keep the two halves of her heart whole, she would find it.

"Ok Hayd. What would you have me do? Do you want me to ask him about it? Coincidence or not, there must be an explanation."

Hayden's anxiety relented. It was a better response than she'd hoped for

"Honestly, no. I don't think so," she answered in relief. "This is something that I need to do. But I want you there," she stepped back, turning to lean her hip against the smooth railing. "I don't want you to feel like I'm doing any of this behind your back."

"Oh please!" Clara tsked. "You know better than that. I chose you first. And you'd better believe that no man will ever be make me forget it."

A smile crept across their faces, each rooted in its own sentiment. Hayden's shone with a quiet trust—one that she'd built with Mum despite the ashes of her childhood betrayal. For Tor and Cal, it was admiration; they couldn't help but reminisce on the strength of the women in their own villages. That a woman of Earth could carry herself the same way felt like a beautiful, unexpected echo.

Hayden held fast to the idea that this was a new thread of promise. Maybe it was the exact push forward they needed... yet again. Because somehow, she had a premonition of hope that Alec could be a missing strand in the unfinished tapestry of her mysterious beginning.

<u>19</u>

Back to Her Real Beginning

Jurtah groaned—her pain nearly unbearable—as she crouched on the cabin floor. She tried to brace herself, but the weight of her swollen belly threw her off balance. Her hands slipped, and she rocked forward onto her knees. The last thing she wanted was to be sprawled helplessly on the floor. The feeling of the smooth stones beneath her palms might have caught her attention any other time, but in this moment, the contractions demanded every ounce of focus.

The baby had finally decided it was time to make an appearance, and for that, she was more grateful than ever to have found a trustworthy companion. His offer to bring her to his hidden dwelling in Tiernae Forest was more than she could have hoped for. He never questioned her request for secrecy, and she had never volunteered to explain. Still, she trusted him—because he had trusted her first.

He was a Mender. She'd seen it the moment they met—that soft, barely perceptible white aura that gave them away. With him it shone a little brighter exposing him as a practicing wielder, despite the danger. Eventually, he shared the truth with her—unprompted. He still didn't know about her own magic, not yet at least. But just knowing she had a brother in arms made it feel less lonely.

Alachor stood at the stove, impatiently tapping his fingers. He gave the pot full of water a menacing stare—it should have been boiling already. Her muffled groans had him on edge. She was losing strength. If he didn't get the tea to her soon, the mending magic would be less potent. "Finally," he muttered, snatching the pot from the coals. Carefully, he poured the boiling liquid over a cheesecloth full of herbs. Then pumping the wooden faucet, he refilled the pot, placing it back on the heat.

"Let's get you over to the bed while that steeps," he suggested gently. The last contraction had faded, leaving her panting–but granting just enough will to move across the tiny dwelling. Slipping his arm beneath hers, he counted aloud so she'd know when to rise. "As soon as you're more comfortable, I'll get you that tea," he promised as he propped pillows beneath her head and knees.

"Having a laugh, are we?" she teased, amused by the irony of finding comfort in a moment like this.

Alachor returned cradling a mug, roughly hewn out of tree bark. The aroma of mixed herbs rose with the steam, curling into her nose as she inhaled its soothing warmth.

"Another of your handmade wonders?" she asked weakly, rubbing her thumbs over the smooth surface.

He nodded with quiet pride. Everything in the cabin–even the structure itself–had been crafted by his own two hands. He'd harvested the forest's simple offerings to build it all, but only ever took what was freely given. Though he didn't fully believe the old stories–that spirits haunted those who harvested from what had not yet fallen–he preferred to err on the side of caution. Anything he used had to be dead already. It was a rule he never broke. And so the forest accepted him–where others with less care had succumbed to its shadows.

Jurtah began to grow restless again–the first sign that another contraction was coming. She readjusted, finding herself once more on her hands and knees. But this time, the straw filled bedding offered a more comfortable resting place for her sharp joints. She lurched forward, her body tightening as a fire grew between her thighs, threatening to tear her in two. Then slowly it began to subside, until finally she was able to stop her rhythmic panting. She collapsed to her side, chest heaving, left to tremble in exhaustion. Then digging for a shred of motivation, she willed her hand toward the mug in Alachor's hands. He'd rescued the tea from falling just before the contraction surfaced.

"Please," she panted lightly. "Work your magic."

She grasped his hand, pulling it to her belly.

The aura around him intensified, then shimmered into visibility as it danced across his skin. He closed his eyes, bracing for the crushing wave of pain he knew was coming. It was the only way he'd learned to use his magic—he had to *feel* the pain before he could mend it. That was the cost of his specific gift, a sacrifice he was certain the Angel had designed to keep his kind humble. He drew in a deep breath, then opened his magic. Pain crashed into him, and for a moment, his resolve wavered as he gritted his teeth against it. It was all he could do not to grip her belly too tightly.

He reminded himself that she'd been suffering this agony for more than a day, so he certainly could bear it—for a moment—for her sake. He sensed the herbs, using his light to guide their relief where it was most needed. His breath grew heavy as he synced his rhythm with hers. Slowly, the space between their breaths lengthened, and with it, the pain began to ease. Finally, he removed his hand. And as the connection broke, the room returned to view.

"The sun's going down. You've been at this all day," he stated, massaging her feet. It was the only place she'd tolerate his touch anymore. Her nerves were frayed and her temper short as the process took its toll. "Maybe you're due for another head check? Baby must be getting close."

She nodded, beads of sweat dripping down her brow.

"Go ahead. Just help get this thing out of me," she agreed.

He checked, dropping the sheet with a defeated grimace. No progress.

"Let me think for a minute," he said, rapping his knuckles on the bed. His head hung low as he searched his memories. There had to be something the high midwife taught him that might help. Exhaustion was one explanation. Then again, he remembered a time when a second baby had been trapped behind the first–but no, it didn't fit here. "That's it!" He snapped his fingers as it dawned on him. Hurrying to her side, he probed every angle of her belly and a triumphant grin spread across his face. "It's head isn't positioned all the way down," he announced. "This might cause more pain, and for that I'm sorry, but I need to do it, or you may never have this child."

"I–don't–care… just do it," she replied wearily.

That was all he needed to hear. He got to work pushing and probing until with a soft whimper, another contraction took over. He waited patiently, letting her crush his hand to help her through. When it passed, he examined his work.

"Got it," he whispered. "Please let this be it."

And for the first time in a while, he heard a sigh that wasn't marinated in pain. Her hand flew to her face, but he saw the lone tear slip down her cheek before she could wipe it away.

Morning dawned, and through the soft sounds of a forest emerging from slumber came the sharp cry of a newborn taking her first breath.
"She has your eyes," Alachor said, placing the naked child on her mother's chest.

He stepped back, folding his hands with quiet reverence, watching with a soft smile as Jurtah's eyes filled with tears of relief and joy. Upsetting this moment was the last thing he wanted to do–but they both still needed tending.

"Jurtah," he said gently, "I need to take care of the birth cord, and you'll need to push again. The rest still needs to come out so we can bury it."

She nodded, reluctantly surrendering the child to Alachor. Though her body was weak after nearly two days of labor, her heart surged with a love so fierce, she knew she'd never let go.

Alachor made quick work of cleaning the squirming newborn, then returned her to Jurtah—cozily wrapped in a soft blanket. He'd bought it during his last trip to his home village, a gift meant for this moment. The way Jurtah had looked at it—like she couldn't quite understand why someone would do such a thing—made him feel something more than pity. It was clear she wasn't used to kindness from strangers.

"What will you name her?" he asked, once both mother and child were clean, fed, and resting.

"Farren. After her father," Jurtah whispered. "She has his strength."

Her eyes fluttered shut. She fought the buzzing in her head, but the pull of sleep was too strong. Alachor adjusted a pillow beside them and then quietly settled onto his makeshift bed on the floor.

Alachor was the perfect caretaker, making sure they were settled before tending to his own needs. A single day turned into a handful by the time they slid into a routine that seemed to work for everyone. He couldn't help with Farren's meals but was more than willing to watch her while Jurtah slept. And in this way, she quickly regained her strength. But her renewed strength brought with it a restlessness—the need to move on. She'd lingered too long in this place.

"I'm going to have to leave soon," the words fell harsher than she meant, slicing through the quiet of a rainy afternoon.

She stood in the open doorway, gazing down the moss-covered walk. The light patter of raindrops on leaves of every size added the wildness of Rax magic to the forest's already enchanting song. She closed her eyes, wondering what it might have been like to meet one of the gentle Raxyief. But Lord Onyx's cruelty had driven them away many moons ago, and now, like so many other magical beings, their stories lived only in whispers, half-remembered dreams, and fading songs.

Jurtah blinked away the sentiment, pushing off the doorway to face Alachor. He'd been crushing the herbs for his pain relief tea when the pestle went quiet. But his hand hovered for only a moment before he resumed his task.

"I don't understand why you would have to," he stated over the clink of the mortar. "The people in my village would be more than happy to take you in." With a loud clack, he set the pestle on the counter. "But that wouldn't work. You had her here for a reason," he resumed his preparations, tying up the cloth before dropping it into the mug. She took a steadying breath to prepare herself, then pulled out a chair.

"You shared your secret with me, so I guess it would be my turn now," she said, tapping the wooden seat.

"I need to be here right when the boiling starts," he dropped a couple more chunks of coal underneath the pot to prove his point.

"If that is what you wish," she conceded. "I hope you will forgive that I haven't been completely honest with you. No one, outside of my own flesh and blood knows, other than my love Farren of course," she paused to look at her baby, resting peacefully in the safety of her basket. "I fear that I've come this far now and can't take it back, but somehow, I know I can trust you. You've proven that to me. To us."

Alachor finally turned, tearing his attention away from the water. Her tone—everything about how she was building to something. If she already knew his secret, it had to be something bigger than that.

"You know that I will guard this knowledge well for you," he promised.

"I'm a direct descendant of the Duweot family," she said in a rush.

Her eyes stayed fixed on the floor. After everything Alachor had done for her, she wasn't sure she could bear it—if what she saw in his face was betrayal. He shifted uncomfortably, keenly aware of his role in this moment and the news she wouldn't have shared lightly.

"No place to call home for your whole existence," he murmured, shaking his head sorrowfully. Then quietly he moved to the chair–the tea could wait for a moment. Right now she needed his reassurance that he was the person she'd put her trust in. "Look at me Jurtah," he reached out gently, a finger under her chin to lift her face. "I can't imagine how hard that life has been. But listen to me– whatever shock I feel from what you've told me… it *will not* outweigh this: you are safe here. You are seen."

Jurtah's eyes welled with tears. After Farren, she'd been completely alone, almost forgetting what it was like to have another person to lean on. And now, with an infant, that life felt so much bleaker. Then like the walls of a dam giving way, all her uncertainty spilled out. Her shoulders shook with sobs as a thousand tears fell. Alachor reached out without hesitation to pull her into his embrace. By the time she sat back to wipe her face, his shirt was soaked.

She clicked her tongue, feeling guilty for having soiled his garment. "Oh no. Look at what I've done to you," she sniffed.

"I couldn't care less about that. You just told me the lineage of the Good King lives on. Because as I'm sure you're aware–most everyone believes that none survived. Why don't you tell me more about that while I finish this tea," he moved back to attend his boiling pot.

"You have no idea how heartening it is to hear someone refer to him by that name so boldly," her hands twisted together in her lap, "I–I g–guess that I don't know where to start. I know you have questions, so why don't you ask?"

Alachor paused, thinking. He'd spent so many hours imagining this exact moment–praying the old blood had not truly been extinguished. Now that it was here, sitting in his home, he found himself stunned.

"Well," he said slowly, "how about we start at the beginning. Who survived? And how has your family remained undetected?"

Although Jurtah had told her father's story hundreds of times, this was the first person outside the family that would be receiving it. Gone were the great halls filled with script that told their story–all the way back to the first King. The one that had found favor with the Angel and was granted power over the elements. She was all they had left and that was a heavy burden to bear.

"My grandfather, a cousin to the head royals," she began, finding her voice. "was merely an infant when the Annex happened. His nursemaid had taken him on a trip to a small village near the Manor to visit her family. Because he was so young, he was not required at the Council and therefore was spared that gruesome fate."

Alachor walked the mug over, placing it in her hands as he sat down once again.

"Go on," he encouraged, trying not to sound too eager.

"His nursemaid loved the Duweot's dearly and when news of the Annex reached them, she knew what to do. He only survived because of her sacrifice–because she left her family behind to save him," she paused to take a sip of the tea and gather her thoughts. Although the story was very familiar, she hadn't granted it the power of words in some time. " He lived until his light was extinguished in his 75th season cycle–that spring when the flood claimed so many. It was something our family's collective magic could have easily prevented. You would have been only a child when it happened," Alachor nodded reassuringly. "He stayed true to the compassion that was taught in our family, saving many lives from the turbid waters before they claimed him. My father was convinced that he found his final resting place there, because no one ever found him–alive or otherwise."

She grew restless, the desire to pace too overwhelming. Alachor, understanding the place he'd put her in, sat back to allow her room in the small space.

"My mother went to Adelphiana's star the day I was born, so my father ended up raising me on his own. He taught me the way of the nomad–the only people that took us in without question. I learned how long was too long in each village and how to slip out unnoticed if there was any suspicion. I also learned to trust no one," she paused her nervous march to give him a look, heavy with many things left unsaid. "When the completion of my 20th season cycle rose, we parted ways. He'd taught me all he could about survival and it was much easier for us to avoid questions when we were apart. We could never tell anyone who we were for fear of our secret finding the wrong ears. Some would rather sit in good standing with the Lord Onyx, than to protect the side of good," she finished, sweeping the mug off the table before she took up her place next to him again.

Alachor leaned forward, resting his elbows on his knees as he stared at the floor. Moments ago, he'd clung to nothing but a wisp of hope. Now, he had proof–tangible proof–that Lord Onyx's reign might actually end.

"Did your grandfather or your father have any magic in them?" He asked tentatively.

At the very least, it was well known that only some in the Duweot's line could wield it.

Jurtah nodded, "they did, but the fear of being discovered was too great. So from lack of use, it grew weak within them," she gripped her mug securely with both hands, then shoved it toward Alachor.

His confusion lasted for only a moment before the steam disappeared and hot liquid became solid ice. He stared at her arms, marveling at the purple shimmer that mimicked his own. Then she released it, and steam once again rose from the tea.

"Elemental magic?" He whistled in awe. "I'd heard the royal family commanded it, but it has always been difficult to separate lore from fact."

"Yes," she confirmed. "It's the reason all peoples trusted us with our rule. We kept the lands fertile and the rivers in their banks," her eyes drifted toward the window, chasing something only seen in memories that were not her own.

Feeling the weight of her confession, Alachor teased her in hopes to lighten the mood.

"So do I bow, or curtsy?" He asked, the light hearted twinkle returning to his eyes.

"Most certainly neither!" she smacked him lightly, a smile playing on her lips. "I'm rather envious of you though," she continued. "You have such skill. I don't know how I would have made it through this first week without you," her eyes dropped to the mug in her hands, and she sighed. The deep soul rending type. "I can barely maintain mine for long enough to even cool a drink."

He placed a hand gently on her arm, his voice quiet with understanding.

"It took a long time to get here, you know. There are many partially healed animals wandering these woods because I wasn't always so good at it," her eyes brightened at the imagery and he dropped his hand, satisfied that he'd distracted her from self-doubt. "But I've also had the seclusion of this place," then he wrinkled his brow. "You know, there are more out there than you realize. You can trust more than just yourself. I pray to the Angel that knowing this gives you hope."

Jurtah's striking green eyes flicked to his face. He had never once made her believe he'd lead her wrong—not then, and certainly not now.

With the sun below the horizon and the rain clouds moving on, a clear sky made way for the moon. Its soft light scattered over the forest, casting a gentle glow even through the thick canopy above. Jurtah woke Farren to feed her, and over their meager meal, she offered Alachor one last confession.

"I knew before you told me," she said, tearing off a chunk of the dry bread. "My strongest magic is being able to see it in others. I'm just glad you felt comfortable enough to tell me."

Alachor folded his hands, studying Jurtah's face.

"So it wasn't just coincidence—or *Her* intervention that brought us together," he said gently. "It was your intuition. Your magic. Don't forget that."

Fourteen suns into their stay, their supplies had dwindled faster than he'd prepared for, forcing a trip back home to restock—a journey he could no longer avoid. Although she reassured him many times that she and the child would be fine on their own, a small part of him wondered if they would even be there when he got back. But her journey was her own. If she wanted to leave in secrecy, it was her choice, and it was one that he would understand completely—given his newfound knowledge of who she was. So he grabbed his small pack and set off.

As usual, he noticed small changes. It was something that he had only begun to notice once he became more familiar with his secluded spot in these woods. A new bush here, a tree that seemed to age overnight there. The oddities had grown on him as a unique charm—but more importantly, they seemed to be the very thing that kept the area safe.

"Pfft, ghosts," he scoffed. "Too many suspicious people in these parts."

The thicket eventually gave way to the rolling hills of the countryside. He stopped for his usual meticulous scan of the surrounding area. If even a single sapling had been broken by careless feet, he would have aborted the mission and returned to try again another day. But all was clear. Staying close to the forest's edge, he quickened his pace—slowing only when the cover of Tiernae finally thinned. He glanced over his shoulder often, unwilling to let a black-clad member of the Xard catch him unaware. Not that it was likely. He came from a long lineage of Trailfaders, as adept at vanishing without a trace as they were at avoiding discovery in the first place. Still, if anyone saw him on the road without a travel certificate... well, he didn't care to dwell on what might follow.

As he neared the village, he noted the length of the shadows—he'd made good time. It would give him that little extra that he needed to get back due to the brewing storm. Lifting the floorboard that kept his meager supply of perishable food extra cool, he filled his pack with what remained. Then, without so much as a backward glance, he made the journey back to Tiernae. Thunder rumbled a menacing warning, while lightning cracked overhead—but he wasn't worried. The rain felt refreshing, each cold splash grounding him as it struck his bare skin. He welcomed the cover it offered—few would venture out to tempt fate in weather like this. Least of all the Xard.

He reached the edge of the forest, a feeling of dread sinking into the pit of his stomach. There in front of him, like an insult to the protection he'd enjoyed for so many seasons, was a trail of crushed and broken vegetation. His heart quickened, his feet following suit, as with every step he confirm that it led straight to his dwelling. Trotting as fast as he could without taxing his lungs too heavily, he reached the thicket that hid the small dwelling.

The acrid smell of fresh smoke filled his nostrils, causing the hair on the back of his neck to stand up. He broke into a run and just as he crossed the edge of the clearing, tripped over something that sent him sprawling. As he rolled to recover, he saw the familiar garb of the Xard. He'd tripped over one of their lifeless bodies. When he saw the blackened ruins, he fought back angry tears, allowing himself to mourn the loss of what had taken so many painstaking seasons to build. Then swallowing his trivial sorrow, he burst into action again jumping over the bodies of two more Xard that lay just a couple paces from the door. He wondered briefly how it could be so far from its frame before his search for Jurtah and Farren pushed all other concerns from his mind. Heavy beams from the collapsed roof felt as light as sticks as he tossed them aside, ignoring the pain of burning flesh as he searched. No additional bodies. That meant they escaped.

He surveyed his remaining belongings, searching for a sign, a shred of torn cloth, anything that would assuage what remained of his fear. But anything that might have given him hope had long since been turned to ash. So he turned to the only other skill he knew, following every piece of broken underbrush, every crushed blade of grass that could lead him to them. He took heart that the clumsy wanderings of the Xard did not seem to be present any longer. That meant his previous suspicion was correct, that the Xard laying lifeless back at the dwelling were the only ones that had come for them. Finally, and with a quiet cry of victory he found them. Shivering behind a wall of vines, her body curled around the infant cradled warmly in a sling.

"Are you hurt?" He asked, shrugging off his coat and draping it around her.

"We're ok," she replied, teeth chattering.

"What happened?! How did you kill the Xard?"

He was asking out of curiosity but found himself completely unprepared for what she said next.

"No, it wasn't me. Farren did it."

A look of disbelief crossed his face. She was far too calm to have said what he just thought he heard.

"Excuse me—what?! Did I hear you right? An infant who's only seen fourteen suns just killed three of the infamous Black Xard? But how?!"

He'd never heard of anyone getting their magic earlier than eighteen season cycles, let alone a mere infant. But maybe it was different with the royal family. It very well could have been since so much about them had been lost to rumor.

"She... her magic light is blue," Jurtah replied, sounding more bewildered than sure of herself. "I don't know what to make of it. When they broke into the house, I thought we were dead. She got upset when they tried to take her from me and then made this ball of magic light that sent them flying out the door when it hit them. They never got up."

"Wow! A blue light?! I don't like how familiar..." He began.

But didn't get a chance to finish before Jurtah cut him off sharply.

"I know how it sounds," she said, placing her hand on his chest. "He's the only one I've ever known to have blue magic. Their only connection is me. I don't understand. I thought he got it by some horrible means. But my sweet baby..." she squeezed Farren a little tighter. "She hasn't been exposed to anything from Dagrune's heart."

She may have needed rest, but the uncertainty of how the Xard had braved a storm *and* the dreaded Tiernae Forest, had him on edge.

"We have to move," he said, loathing the need for it. "I don't know how they knew I was here. But it's no longer safe for us."

"We?! You can't leave your home behind!" She protested.

But Alachor was firm in his decision.

"I lost my wife many seasons ago and she was the only person in the village I ever truly trusted. There is nothing left for me there."

She could sense that further arguing would do no good, so she parted the vines, stepping into a cool breeze. Then suddenly she turned to Alachor, wrapping her arms around his neck. He encircled her in his, feeling the warmth of an unbreakable friendship bloom. And together they set off, following the shimmering lights of fates new direction.

<u>20</u>

A Difficult Goodbye

Motherhood was both simpler and more complex than she'd ever expected. There were many days when she'd lament not having a place to call home. But the fond memories of her own childhood on the road offered hope that it would be okay. Her father had become an expert at making every day feel like an adventure and she wanted to give Farren that same life. At least until she grew old enough to figure out the crueler side of it.

"You seem lost in thought. Anything I can do to help unravel those tangled musings?"

She jumped, his voice jolting her back to the present.

"I was just thinking about my father and wondering how he made it with a newborn," she said, following the scattered light on a path rife with tree roots. "It must have been such a struggle in the beginning–losing my mother and then not getting to mourn her because he had to focus on me. At least I had *some* time to get used to the idea," she swallowed the next words, not ready for that level of vulnerability yet.

And sensing her hesitation he let the silence stand.

Skirting the edge of yet another village, they followed the fading light of the setting sun. With his prowess as a Trailfader and her instinct to remain unseen, they made the perfect duo–each teaching the other everything they knew.

"I know a man that lives in a village about a day's walk from here," he said, breaking the awkward moment. "He wields the magic of the Sage."

They parted the dark blue-green fronds of the Wandering Ferns that shielded them from prying eyes, maneuvering carefully around their delicate cap clusters. The moving roots could hide footprints, but a single crushed cluster meant death for the fern—and a trail their enemies could follow. And since they weren't on the road with papers, well the Xard wouldn't hesitate to grab them. A strong gust of wind parted the ferns behind them, blowing Jurtah's long dark locks into her face. She smoothly pulled them back, wrapping them securely into a high bun—tying it expertly using only the strands of her hair.

"He can help us with travel papers," he continued. "He decided long ago that he would channel his craft into illusions. And he's quite good at it."

Jurtah tilted her head curiously.

"I've never come across a Sage before. I wonder what their aura feels like," she caught herself, reeling back the wandering thoughts. "We'll want to agree on a story, on the off chance that we're questioned," she continued. "And I am fully prepared to go the obvious route. It would be believable at its core."

Alachor nodded. He'd been thinking the same but was unsure of how to tactfully bring it up.

"It will give us a bit more freedom to travel openly once we get in the village. They're less likely to stop a young family. I've witnessed it enough to be confident in this," he added.

And true to his word, when they arrived, few seemed to notice them. Barely anyone cast even the briefest glance in their direction. Still, Jurtah's breath came easier as they put distance between themselves and the village entrance. Once she could concentrate on more than their survival she began to do her usual assessment. The produce fields looked too sparse to feed the villagers, let alone supply the Hub. Distant silhouettes of children and adults moved among the rows, tending to crops. It was late in the day–they should have been home, playing and enjoying the carefree days of childhood. She shook her head to rid herself of the image, trying in vain to stuff down latent feelings of anger.

"Children shouldn't have to work to survive," she whispered angrily, only just loud enough for Alachor to hear.

Her hand involuntarily moved to cradle Farren's head, wondering how she would feel if her only choice was to make the child work when she got old enough.

"I have to agree with you, milady," he replied.

And once again he saw a glimmer of the formidable leader this woman was capable of becoming. She no doubt would have ruled fairly no matter the challenge.

They hurried to the heart of the village. There, they were able to blend into the crowds of customers making their final sales. Again, she frowned, knowing how heavily the merchants were taxed. People just trying to make an honest living were being taxed out of hope–the simple goal to be free of poverty. The quiet murmur of the market square faded as the streets narrowed. Houses were more closely crowded together here, creating dark alleyways. She could see the piles where those without a home found shelter and her attention was drawn sharply to the sound of a deep rattling cough.

"This wouldn't be happening under the right ruler," she grimaced, balling up her fists. "Everyone should get the basics. A nourishing meal and a warm bed to rest their head in every night. I see this in every village, and season by season it's only getting worse."

Alachor slid his arm through hers, massaging her hand until she loosened her grip.

"You're right to be upset about all of this. The sharp edge of starvation stays just within reach for most. But some day you will rise up and change it all. Until then, let's do what we can and focus on our next step."

They walked arm in arm until Alachor brought them to a halt in front of a set of warped stairs.

"We're here," he announced.

A soft glow illuminated the room behind a worn door—the light peeking through its wooden gaps drawing bright lines in the dirt. Behind it, muffled sounds of a lighthearted conversation drifted out softly.

"Follow my lead," he said, raising his hand to knock.

The timing couldn't have been more perfect. Farren had just begun to fuss as they were walking into the market square. She was probably just hungry. However, without fully understanding what had triggered her magic back in Tiernae, Jurtah found herself nervous about being outside when the child was upset. She suspected it was her sense of danger—but she couldn't be sure.

Alachor knocked. Three quick raps, then kicked some dirt off his boot on the doorway. He followed that with two slower knocks, then stepped back. Standing straight, he faced his right palm forward and his other back. Jurtah, always one to pick up on subtle cues, straightened her back and mirrored his stance. There was some commotion followed by the sound of shuffling feet before the door was jerked open. Out popped the face of a woman whose cheeks were flushed with exertion and the brightness of her youth. A welcoming smile graced her delicate features. Jurtah wondered at how her eyes twinkled with such a fervor for life despite the grim reality of their collective existence.

"My friend, how long it has been since our last visit!" Alachor greeted her enthusiastically.

Her eyes swept them up and down, and a slow recognition dawned.

"Oh my dears, isn't this a pleasant surprise!" she bubbled happily. "You're just in time for supper and from the sounds of it your little one could probably also use some. Come, come! Let us catch up on lost seasons!" Her energy was contagious, putting Jurtah instantly at ease.

The room felt cozy despite a small draft that snuck through the door's imperfections. Simple furniture was scattered throughout, yet the room still managed to look organized. Though the space was modest and the outside looked questionable, the inside was clean and well kept. A fire danced in the stove beneath a pot, bubbling with the savory smell of potato soup. After so many days on the road with cured meats and raw vegetables, she couldn't stop her mouth from watering in anticipation of a hot meal. In a chair not far from the fire, a short jovial looking man sat with a wooden stir spoon in hand. Bulging muscles rippled underneath his brown skin and the subtle smell of cured meat hung about—clues that pointed to him being the village butcher. But what drew her attention most was the orange aura that surrounded him—shining more brightly than even Alachor's.

Until now, she'd tried desperately to avoid interactions with other Wielders, but here she stood in a room with three of them. No—she corrected herself—there were four.

"Are you alright dear? You look a little peaked," their concerned hostess asked.

Jurtah brought her eyes back into focus, only then realizing that she'd frozen in the moment.

"Oh no ma'am, I'm fine. I'm just overdue to feed Farren. It tends to get a little uncomfortable if you know what I mean."

She hoped her reasoning would distract from whatever odd look must have crossed her face.

"I'm sorry, but I *don't* know what you mean. We only wed a short while ago and don't aim to have children for some time," her cheeks flushed as she cast a sly glance toward her husband. "Anyhow, maybe someday, but enough of this ma'am nonsense. You can call me Ruimi and that handsome hunk of a man over there is Shoone," she beamed, pointing her chin in his direction.

Her wink drew a hearty laugh from Shoone.

"You embarrass me dear heart," he said, winking back.

Then he leaned over the soup to stir it, moving the pot just enough so Jurtah could see how much was there. She winced, realizing they would be sharing their meager rations. Somehow, she also knew it would not only be impolite, but pointless to protest.

After dinner, Alachor regaled them with the string of events that led them to their door. But still, he left out any mention of magic, using words that must have been a silent code between friends. After exchanging a pointed look, Shoone excused himself, closing the bedroom door behind him. She heard the squeak of wood and metal, then a thunk as something heavy hit the floor. Farren, who'd been napping peacefully, woke suddenly. She stirred, reaching out her chubby little arms, stretching and cooing in delight. Jurtah felt the familiar warmth that came with being close to magic as it was wielded. But this energy felt different from anything else she'd been around.

I can see and feel magic. I wonder if Farren can too?

And then, as quickly as the feeling had come, it faded away.

The repeat squeak and thud from the bedroom brought her back to the present. Shoone filled the doorway, a look of smug accomplishment proceeding him as he strode toward Alachor, holding In his hand a rolled piece of parchment.

"Would you like to check it first?" he asked, placing it in Alachor's eager grasp.

"I trust you," he replied without hesitation. "I know you're very skilled in your craft. Now here is your payment as agreed upon," he reached into his pack, pulling out a worn parchment of his own. "However, I hope it's not too intrusive that I must ask to stay the night. We're tired and it would be comforting to have a softer place to rest than the ground."

"We wouldn't have it any other way," Ruimi smiled approvingly.

And for the first time since their flight from Tiernae, she felt a sense of comfort and safety that had long eluded them.

They were well on their way out of the village with refreshed supplies before the sun peeked over the horizon. Amid many futile protests, the generous couple had insisted on packing some of their precious food, claiming they needed it more. They scanned the road in earnest for landmarks that would lead them toward Shoone's gate.

A quick left between two run-down homes, then a right underneath the twisted gate. You must follow that to the bushes with large purple thorns. Please be careful not to tear your clothing on them as it could be tracked by magic.

As they carefully maneuvered through the thick vines, Jurtah began to sense the same magic they'd encountered the night before.

"It's here," she whispered to Alachor. "I can feel it, just as it was at your friend's home."

Alachor was hesitant, but Jurtah instinctively knew what she must do. Sensing the strongest point of magic, she reached out confidently, the familiar cold tingle affirming her suspicions. At her touch, the tangled vines rolled back to reveal a small gate, and as they stepped through, the greenery returned—sealing behind them as though it had never been disturbed.

They walked in silence until they were a safe distance from the village. Jurtah wondered at the network of resistance that she hadn't been privy to until now. And so, she allowed the tiniest glimmer of hope to surface.

"That truly is some amazing handywork," she said, after Alachor gave her the travel certificate to inspect. "If only my father hadn't been so afraid, maybe he could have helped in some way," she rolled the parchment again, tapping it back into its prominent place in the pack. "Do you mind if I ask what you gave to him in return?"

"It was my home," he replied simply. "I'd already made up my mind before I came back to Tiernae, that the two of you would need me more than my village did. Then I saw the charred remains, and it wouldn't have mattered anymore whether or not I found you—with or without your lights."

His admission that he hadn't been forced into a companionship, made her feel happier. It seemed they weren't the burden on him that she spent every day worrying about.

Days turned into seasons as they travelled from village to village. Some felt safer than others, allowing them to reside long enough to see the turn of a season. Larger villages, however, usually meant a heavier Xard presence, driving them to shorten their stay. Her ability to see and feel the magic in other Wielders gave them an advantage when it came to dealing with strangers. In their few close encounters with the Xard, she began to realize that the stories of captive Wielders were true, making her ever more grateful for the special gift. No matter the encounter, the magic in the parchment served them well. She could see a change come over the viewers face, almost as if it placed them in a short trance.

Their friendship grew, often leaving Jurtah to smile at how Alachor treated Farren as his own daughter. They watched the child grow in strength, from walking earlier than expected, to how quickly she picked up on speech. The inevitable result of a growing child meant an increase in material needs, so they ended up exchanging healing teas for a donkey. They worked together to build her a cart, then found old scraps of cloth which they braided into a comfortable harness. After Jurtah's attempt to name her, Farren's ability to articulate language morphed the name to Kleeng, so the handle stuck. The child seemed to form an almost magical bond with the animal. They would often find the two of them snuggled up together, whether in the villages or on the road. And trying to separate them in those moments only resulted in upsetting both Farren and Kleeng

Farren was nearing the end of her first season cycle. She'd only shown her magic a handful of times, some of which seemed tame enough. But the power Jurtah saw that first time, was not repeated.

One morning, as they were packing up to move on to the next village, Jurtah found herself lost in memories of the child's father. She'd spent many suns trying to shake them from her thoughts, but when they made their way into her dreams, she was no longer able to hold back the deluge of emotion. She found herself crying uncontrollably as the wall she'd built so carefully crumbled to dust.

"Please let me at least be a listening ear," Alachor offered, sensing a familiar pain. "I know how hard it is to deal with it in solitude. I'm here. I can help if you would just let me," he pleaded.

"I just miss him so much!" She began, after catching her breath. "We were both supposed to be there for our child, but the Xard took that chance away from us," the more she talked, more of her sobs faded into sniffles. "He distracted them before they could find my hiding place. Somehow, I think someone like me was there. One who could sense magic's energy. His was always stronger than mine, so they went after him. And like a coward, I hid," she passed a calloused hand over her face. "He was an Advisor. It's not the kind of magic that could have saved him. If only mine was stronger he might still be here with us today. We shared such a strong love bond, I don't think I will ever be able to fully heal."

If there was anything Alachor understood—it was this. His own loss had taken many heartrending seasons to come to terms with. Yet he still struggled with the pain from time to time.

"The only advice I can give you, is to hold onto the feeling of your bond. It will carry you through many challenging times. Dwelling on his fate, blaming yourself for surviving, holding back that tide of emotion—it will only drag you into darkness. You don't always have to be so strong you know."

Jurtah leaned over the small table, head hung low, her tears falling silently to disappear into the wood.

"I just wish he'd used his gift to get into their heads and make them leave," she said angrily, slamming her palms into the table.

The gesture startled Farren who'd been watching her intensely from her first sob. She toddled over, placing a gentle hand on her mother's leg.

"Momma sad?" she asked.

Jurtah picked her up, giving her a kiss on the cheek.

"Yes, Momma is sad. But you know what?" She pushed Farren's brown hair away from her eyes. "One of your super special hugs would help make it better."

And without hesitation, Farren wrapped her little arms around Jurtah's neck, gritting her teeth and grunting–putting all her might into making Momma feel better.

"You know we can't do that," Alachor replied softly, after watching the tender moment play out. "It would have affected him just as negatively as the recipient. I believe we've already observed the path that would take him down, and I think that would have been a worse fate."

She nodded, conceding to what she knew to be true. It was a dangerous path, to control another being. One that her father had warned her about as far back as she could remember. If it could do what he described... her stomach turned at the thought.

"We really need to get moving," she said, to bring herself back to their reality. "If we leave too late, they might not let us out of the gate and I don't believe we should linger here any longer."

The cart was packed, ready for the next leg of their never-ending journey. And Farren was perched in her usual spot, busy with the wooden puzzle that Jurtah had carved for her. When the gate came into view, they saw two Xard lounging lazily on either side of the road, their raucous laughter making Jurtah's skin crawl. They were clothed head to toe in black, the only contrast a vivid red sigil of Lord Onyx emblazoned on their chests. Their swords hung from a specially fashioned belt that doubled as a whip when they chose to use it. And then there were the boots–gleaming buckles securing them, shiny metal molded over each toe. She held her composure, even as the memory of one of those boots cruelly slamming into her lover's side threatened to overwhelm her.

"The Nomads are finally moving on to leech off another village," one of them sneered, heaving himself onto his feet.

She nearly snickered when he drew himself to his full height as he was barely tall enough to reach her chin. She handed over the travel papers before he had the chance to request them, but that didn't stop them from trying again.

"At least you and that whelp of yours aren't our problem anymore," the other chimed in.

And this time Alachor cleared his throat, moving his hand to cover Jurtah's clenched fist. The silent gesture was all she needed—the reminder to not to give them what they were looking for.

"Is everything in order?" she asked, ignoring their insults. "Are we free to go?"

"I don't know Heitsch, what do you think. Should we let these mongrels leave our quaint little village?"

Heitsch lounged like a man with nothing to fear—one leg stretched out, the other propped for his elbow. He didn't bother to stand. His eyes darted between them, a flicker of contempt in their soulless depths.

"I say good riddance," he finally said with a dismissive wave. "Let the compost rot somewhere else."

As the wheels on the cart once again rolled forward, Jurtah cast a glance over her shoulder at Farren. She was still concentrated on the puzzle, happily oblivious to the almost ritual humiliation they faced. And so they continued through the gate with their heads held high, knowing the greatest insult they could throw at the Xard was one of indifference.

Once they'd put some distance between themselves and the village, Jurtah was finally able to let down her guard.

"Where would you like to go now?" She asked, "we could skirt around the next cluster of villages and head into the Green Mountains. It might be smart to spend some time away from people for a while."

The namesake given to the Green Mountain range was deceiving at best. The craggy cliffs were harsher and less forgiving than the meadows and woodlands they were used to. There, villages were farther apart, which meant less travelers to contend with and the opportunity for undisturbed nights out under the stars. It was the logical next move.

Farren's day of birth quickly approached. And though Jurtah searched diligently, the barren landscape offered little in the way of gift material—until they reached the base of the mountains. The giant trees of the Great Red Wood stretched high into the heavens, their upper branches difficult to see beyond the mist. When she dug her knife into the massive trunk, she realized that the soft wood could provide exactly what she needed. So cutting out a chunk, she carved it into small beads that she then strung together with threads, pulled from the ropes they used to tie their bags.

She braided the ends together, then burnt them, so they wouldn't unravel. Then, on a whim, and in the dead of night, she had an idea. Even if her magic weren't strong, she could still give Farren something priceless. And so she worked into the early dark of morning, weaving her protective love and magic into the fibers.

"I'm sorry I couldn't give you something more on your big day, baby," she apologized as Farren unwrapped the gift.

But Farren, used to their wandering life, saw only a pretty trinket.

"Tank ew!" she said, giving Jurtah a cheerful grin.

Then she plopped to the ground, rolling the bracelet on and off her wrists.

As the terrain became increasingly rocky, the giant trees soon disappeared— leaving Jurtah to long for the safety of their vast trunks. She could still see their branches in the distance as they climbed. With every step forward, the ever-increasing steepness of the mountain pass and the narrowing road began to make her feel unsettled. The unforgiving ascent of the mountains around them not only blocked out the fading sunlight but also left them vulnerable and exposed despite the rising walls. Just when she thought to suggest turning back to try again in the morning, the sound of crunching on the road ahead formed an instant lump in her throat. She tried to swallow, looking frantically to Alachor for support. They were out too late and that meant trouble if the wagon ahead was driven by the Xard. With no choice but to face the danger, they steeled themselves for the inevitable confrontation. And with a sinking sense of dread, it rolled around the bend.

There, sitting on the driver's box, was their worst fear. As it came to a stop, the subtle hint of an earthy aroma escaped from underneath the sheep's wool covering. Jurtah leaned casually against their cart, hoping the non-threatening stance would be enough to make the Xard ignore them. But the way his eyes lit up with ill intent brought her hope crashing down.

"What do we have here?" he asked eagerly. "A couple of travelers out too late? I guess we've forgotten the Lord's laws, haven't we now?" he jumped smoothly from his seat and advanced on them, his tone mocking their very existence. "Why don't you show me your papers, lovelies?"

He stopped, his face merely inches from hers, his acrid breath and sneer revealing teeth that hadn't been cared for in far too long. Before she could stop herself, she recoiled from the foul-smelling creature. Alachor reached into his pack, not waiting to be asked again. He shoved the parchment between Jurtah and the Xard. The man took it slowly, still locked onto Jurtah's gaze. She didn't waver, accepting the challenge of wills. Finally, he dropped his eyes to the papers, studying them with intent.

"Well well, it looks like everything is in order. Except…" He drew out the last word, studying Jurtah intensely. "Weren't the women of the old royal family exceptionally tall?"

The knots in Jurtah's stomach tightened, causing her meager dinner to almost make a reappearance. She couldn't back down—couldn't show her uncertainty. Not after that claim.

"Perhaps it's your stature that leaves you wanting and not my height," she retorted too quickly.

The boldness of their stare down had given her too much confidence. She felt Alachor stiffen beside her and knew what he was thinking without any words. *Now was not the time to anger the Xard.*

And he was right—she shouldn't have. The man grabbed her roughly, yanking her closer. And this time she tried not to gag as the stench from his unwashed body hit her.

"You think you're pretty funny, huh? Well were just gonna have to see what the master thinks," he sneered.

Chaos shattered the mountain's stillness, splintering the reverent quiet into panic and fear. His companion, who'd been silent until now, erupted into cheers—spurring him on, bolstering his already bloated sense of self-importance. Farren screamed, sensing her mother was in danger, while Alachor pleaded on their behalf. Jurtah fought the vice-like grip on her arm, crying out for Farren as her child's terrified screams tore through her. But the appeal to compassion fell on deaf ears. He had already decided who she was—the promise of a reward for delivering a surviving royal too great to ignore.

But he'd missed one crucial detail: the strength of a mother protecting her young. Jurtah grabbed his hand, trying desperately to pry it off her arm. And in her uncertain fury, she released a wild burst of magic. He cried out in pained surprise, forced to release his grip. Clutching his hand, he stared in shock as his skin reddened, swelling in the perfect shape of a handprint. Jurtah used his hesitation, whirling back toward her screaming child.

"I told you she was one of them royals! See?! Purple!" he screamed, drawing his sword.

Realizing they would never be rid of danger if these men lived, Jurtah slid to a halt and rounded on them. She searched the thickening mist for threads of moisture to gather them with her magic. With a flick of her wrist she sent a barrage of icicles flying toward the two men. He forgot his injured hand for a moment when he lunged, deflecting the shards with his sword—but some found their mark, sinking into the soft flesh of the Xard still standing by the wagon. He grunted, then slumped forward, his last stunned breath slipping soundlessly past his lips. Jurtah stepped backward, her feet moving fast—but not fast enough.

A loud bray from Kleeng echoed off the mountain walls as he lunged forward again and this time the sharp blade slid cleanly into her shoulder. She cried out at the sudden pain as blood bloomed from the fresh wound. He yanked the sword free, rearing back, preparing for a second blow as the commotion from Kleeng grew. She turned to run, the wound taking its toll—making her stumble as it drained her strength. Her eyes found Alachor—his face an ashen mask—as the white-hot burn of the blade slicing open her back drove her to her knees. She reached a trembling hand toward Farren, tears welling in her eyes.

The wide-eyed fear on the small angelic face erupted into terrified screams at the sight of her bloodied and broken mother. Then slowly—almost imperceptibly—her expression changed. It melted her fear turning it to the hurt and anger only a child could know. Jurtah fell forward, using every ounce of will she had left to crawl toward her child. Then the blue light erupted on her tiny body, raw and visceral in its infancy. The wind picked up swirling into a frenzy as Farren's face became a mask of rage.

"Please Alachor! Protect her. You need to run!" She croaked.

But the wind drowned out her weakened voice. And as her vision began to fade, she saw a wavering wall as if a body of water had appeared between them. Through it, she could see a long smooth rock with broken lines evenly spaced in the middle. Trees could be seen swaying in the wind of a late-night storm. Then, a blue orb—seen only once before—burst from Farren's chest, disappearing into the heart of the sword wielding Xard. It sizzled as disbelief flitted across his face. Then he too collapsed in a heap. Alachor stood frozen in stunned silence.

As the last of Jurtah's strength waned, enveloping her in the warmth of the inevitable, her tired eyes took in Kleeng, Alachor and Farren. The donkey's frantic brays disappeared into the shadows and with a thunderous clap Farren and Alachor vanished. The last thought that tiptoed through her mind was the regret that she wouldn't get to see Farren grow up. Then she sank into the welcoming embrace of the darkness.

21

Mystery Adds Clarity

The short sofa was turned at an angle in the modest living room. Despite the comfort it offered, Alec could only bring himself to sit on the edge. He clasped his hands tightly, showing the white of his knuckles as he leaned forward, resting on his knees. His voice trembled with the uncertainty of someone who'd just delivered some difficult news.

"I was so confused," he continued. "One moment I was holding you on Dagrune and the next we were shoved through a wall of thick, viscous liquid. I felt you get ripped from my arms and then I find myself in this completely different world. I'm sorry," he finished softly.

Clara, who'd been on the edge of her seat through the entire retelling, flopped back into the couch.

"Wow," she exclaimed softly.

Hayden had been standing in front of the fireplace, her hands shoved in the large pockets of her jean overalls. When he said that final 'sorry,' she walked over to sit on the sofa next to him, letting out a slow breath through rounded lips.

"That's a lot," Hayden said after the soft whoosh. "But I feel like you're blaming yourself for something—which is completely unnecessary."

"Oh?" He asked, raising an eyebrow and turning toward her.

"Oh come on now. You know it wasn't your fault," then with a playful backhand on his arm, she said "I wouldn't be my Mothers child if I blamed you for it– which from the sound of it, includes the one who gave birth to me."

Alec smiled. It was good to hear her talk about Jurtah–it was almost healing in a way. He glanced over at Clara, who just shook her head and pointed back at Hayden.

"Besides," Hayden went on, "if the last few months have taught me anything, it's that *anything* can happen when it comes to magic," her amused snort startled Alec–he twitched like he'd been shocked. "I'm sure someone's written that in a book somewhere," she mumbled, then suddenly lit up. "Oh! I'll be right back!" Then she jumped up, trotting toward the kitchen.

When he looked to Clara for some explanation, he noticed her eyes, shining with delight at the interaction that had seemed so natural.

"You'll get used to it," she assured him. "I think you'll find that little girl, turned into so much more than you could've imagined."

He shook his head, his thoughts riddled with doubt.

"I don't know Clara. From what you've told me–what she went through was horrifying. If we hadn't been separated, I would have given her a much better life. She deserved that much."

"Stop," Clara commanded, her tone harsher than Alec was used to. "Hayden wouldn't want you playing that game with yourself," she sat forward, doing her best Hayden impression. "In the game of what–ifs, there are no champions."

Alec grinned.

"Yeah. That does sound like my tenacious little Fire Berry," then noticing confusion in Clara's expression, he clarified, "I called her that on Dagrune. Jurtah thought it was adorable. But I'll explain what it means later."

He peered in the direction that Hayden had gone, wondering what was taking her so long to find.

Hayden leaned on the counter, staring at the small card box. It was filled with things that she would never consider getting rid of. She'd jokingly referred to them as her Horcruxes because each one felt like a little piece of her soul. She needed this moment to breathe—to process everything she'd just learned about the missing chunk of her life. Laying a tentative hand on the box, she thought about what life she might have lived if her mother had never stumbled into the Xard that day. Then, in a moment of renewed clarity, she rolled her eyes at the redundancy of her own musings.

"Your number one rule girl," she admonished herself quietly. "Let's go ahead and bring that back down to earth."

And before she could change her mind, she jerked it toward her, prying the top off with her fingernails. There it was—just as she remembered and exactly as he'd described. Snatching it off the top of the pile, she hurried back to the living room.

The tiny bracelet lay in her open palm, drawing a quiet gasp from Alec.

His eyes flooded with emotion. "You still have it," he whispered reverently. "It's the only part of her that still exists."

Hayden returned to the sofa beside him, sensing his struggle to keep the overflow of emotions in check.

"Can I please hold it?" he asked abruptly. "I-I know it's a strange thing to ask, but that's the last strand that connects anything to her."

Hayden regarded Clara—that protective part of her wondering if she was reading into Alec's reaction. But Clara's expression was one of compassion and she nodded to Hayden, silently communicating that she understood.

"I've missed her every day for the last 30 years—and not one goes by when I don't wish I hadn't frozen like an idiot."

"Hey Alec, you don't have to do that to yourself," Hayden said with quiet warmth.

Then placing the bracelet in his hand, she gently curled his fingers around it.

For a brief moment he remained motionless–fist clenched, eyes squeezed shut. Slowly, he uncurled his hand, opening his eyes to let the bracelet's memory bring him back. Tears slipped effortlessly down his cheeks as the final moments of his friend's life replayed like a haunting reel. Two more fell, breaking past the dam of his steely resolve. They splashed onto the bracelet and suddenly he felt a change. There was a low thrum, then a soft purple shimmer glowed into the rope fibers. The thrum grew, and the light intensified– transforming the air around them into something they could feel– vibrant, alive, and uplifting. He dropped the bracelet and recoiled, afraid of what it might mean. The moment it left his hand, everything returned to normal.

"Did anyone else feel that?" he asked, his eyes wide in disbelief.

He blinked at Hayden who sat stiffly beside him, eyes glued to the bracelet. Bérg was guarded, his hackles raised, a low uncertain rumble in his throat. And Clara simply appeared confused as to the reason for their sudden change in demeanor.

"I felt it too," Calliope called from the bedroom.

The soft pad of her bare feet echoed down the hallway before she strolled nonchalantly through the doorway. She flicked her tail, deliberately brushing it over the arm of Alec's chair as she passed. Her appearance was sufficient enough to distract them from the unexpected surge of magic–leaving Hayden to roll her eyes at Calliope's love for dramatic flair. Alec, however, held her gaze, his expression unreadable.

"I never thought I'd live to meet a Morphé," he said, looking on with quiet intrigue. "Nearly ninety years on Dagrune without so much as the hope that you were still around. And now, I find the unique privilege of running into two of you."

Hayden exchanged a puzzled glance with Calliope—until realization dawned. He was talking about Tormaigh.

"Yes," Alec said, noticing the shift in Hayden's expression. "That would be correct."
He nodded slightly. "I knew the second I saw her eyes—that she must've been here for you."

Hayden shook her head again, marveling at the strange, invisible threads that were pulling them all together.

Calliope dropped gracefully, her movements fluid as she folded her legs beneath her. She was ready to impart her knowledge, but Hayden was still reeling from Alec's strange truth. She had to know if he was teasing— or if he truly meant what he said.

"I'm not sure which one confuses me more," she said thoughtfully. "The fact that you just claimed to be over one hundred, or the idea that my mother was nearly sixty when she gave birth to me."

Alec smirked, recognizing the same resilient spark he'd once seen in Jurtah.

"Well—the women of Dagrune often wait to have children well into their fifties. Not always, but there's no reason to rush into it when you're looking at roughly two-hundred years," his eyes flicked to Clara, understanding the weight of his admission and how it might affect her.

But she remained amused, keenly aware that this was something to take in from a distance. And so she responded with only a warm, supportive smile.

"Mum!" Hayden called out, breathless with mock incredulity. "You're dating someone almost fifty years older than you?" Then jerking her thumb in Alec's direction, she followed it with a sarcastic quip. "Cradle robber, this one."

Clara blushed, a quiet chuckle escaping her throat.

"Well I certainly couldn't tell," she winked.

And for a moment, Hayden almost regretted the teasing, forgetting that it was a parent's job to embarrass their child—something her mum excelled at.

Calliope cleared her throat, attempting to rein in their wild tangents.

"If I may, I think we're getting a bit off subject," she said coolly.

Hayden, taking the hint, sat forward, giving her undivided attention back to the issue at hand.

"There are stories that have been passed down by my people," she began, her voice thick with memories of those who had gone before. "Stories of Tokens—objects that can be imbued with protective magic. This particular craft is powerful, but only if a mutual bond already exists between the giver and receiver. That bond can then be woven into the object. And when united, it becomes a force of protection unlike any other."

She nodded in Alec's direction. "It seems this one reacted to you... which is interesting, because I thought it would have been made for you, Hayden."

Alec covered his mouth as he studied the bracelet now resting in Hayden's grasp.
"She never told me any of that," he whispered—then angled toward Hayden. "I don't know why, but I *know* she made that specifically for you. Whatever just happened... I can't explain it. I suppose it *is* possible that we were connected more deeply than I thought," his face was strained with the uncertainty of it. "She was always in doubt of her magic, but did wield it far better than she gave herself credit for. And here's your proof," he motioned to the bracelet.

Hayden chewed her lip, psyching herself up to ask the difficult question that perched on the tip of her tongue. The one that had haunted her from the second Mum mentioned they were seeing each other. She squeezed her eyes shut tight, inhaled sharply, and blurted, "Did you date Mum to get to me?" Then she met his unwavering gaze, holding it so she could read his face as well as his emotions.

"No," Alec said without pretense. "I sought your mum out because I wanted to meet the woman who raised you to become exactly who you were meant to be."

He sighed, scratching his face as he gathered his thoughts.

"I loved Jurtah, but not in the way you think," he said, staring at his hands. "The bond we formed over those seasons was very special. We needed each other, though she never would have admitted it. And that's all there was to it. We were friends. Nothing more."

His eyes misted over—the weight of a thousand memories pressing on his heart. And then he raised his gaze, seeking out Clara.

"Now Clara. You healed something in this old Mender that I thought was already fixed. When I told you that I lost my beloved wife, I was telling the truth. She just wasn't from the world you know."

And Hayden could sense a sincerity in his words that satiated her worry.

The screen door slammed with a sharp crash. Everyone flinched—everyone but Calliope.
Tormaigh's broad frame filled the doorway as she stepped inside, her gaze sweeping the room until it locked onto Alec.

"I have heard your story, as Calliope relayed it while you gave it life," she said, bowing her head in respect. "It is good to see you again. By the Angel, our paths align," then stepping further into the room, she added, "Would you prefer that I call you by your Dragunian name?"

He regarded her for a long moment, noting the subtle similarities between her Morphé form and the Ophrahl he'd met on that wonderfully fateful night.

"I've become accustomed to Alec," he replied. "I'm fine with you addressing me as such. And I believe a thank you is in order. Because of you, I was on the highway at the right moment to find Hayden."

Tormaigh smiled and nodded in agreement.

"Adelphiana is wise when she orchestrates events. It is no coincidence that we've all found each other—it had to be done without raising suspicion."

And with that nugget of wisdom, an idea popped into Hayden's head. An obvious plot twist that she just couldn't ignore.

"You just might be onto something Tormaigh!" Hayden exclaimed, snapping her fingers at the revelation. "This could solve my conundrum about going to see Matilde's Shaman. I never wanted to travel solo. Since you know all about Dagrune—wouldn't it make sense to have you go with me?"

Her excitement anchored itself in resolve, wrapping the rest of them in its infectious clutches.

"As long as everyone in the room is comfortable with this," Alec agreed, "I would consider it an honor to accompany you on this journey."

When there were no protests, Hayden allowed herself to relax back into the sofa with a sigh of purpose—the path ahead of her once again clear.

As their discussion drew to a close, the sun's absence cloaked the mountains in shadow. Alec opened the door for Clara, helping her into the passenger seat. But before he could make it back to the driver's side, Hayden surprised him with a hug.

"You've given me something priceless today," she said, taking a step back. "The stories of my mother mean so much more to me than you can possibly imagine. I spent my childhood wondering why my parents didn't want me. Then today, you helped me to see just how wrong I was," her hand came to rest over his heart, her eyes shining with gratitude. "A broken-hearted little girl found some peace amidst the pain tonight. And that was all your doing."

"Thank you," he replied, his voice thick with emotion. "I'm so relieved I could finally bring you some happiness after missing my chance at the falls," he squeezed her shoulder, and in the gesture, Hayden could feel his heartfelt sincerity.

22

Answers, or no?

Hayden rolled the beads between her fingers, staring blankly through the triple-paned glass. She'd tried everything to coax the magic from the old rope fibers again, but even her cleverest efforts had failed. It remained an ordinary bracelet–unimpressive to the naked eye. Maybe what happened with Alec was the only magic it had left–that was her running theory anyway. Her keys dangled from the bracelet, jingling softly as her fidgeting became more intense.

She'd granted herself *some* grace for being nervous, since this was her first time flying, but she was now being faced with a whole new dilemma. Stuck in a giant tube–miles from the earth–with roughly one hundred people whose heightened emotions felt like hot needles to her brain. It was a problem they hadn't run across before. If only she'd realized how raw the energy would feel, she wouldn't have trapped herself in such a small space full of stressed-out strangers. And then, as if on cue, Alec's voice cut through her meandering thoughts.

"What's on your mind?"

She snapped her head to the right, then followed his gaze down to her restless hands.

"Oh, um. Loads of unchecked feelings, and nowhere to escape from it," she answered tensely.

She gripped the arms of her seat, focusing on the ugly pattern and how it clashed with the even worse carpet. No matter how she shifted, the seat jabbed uncomfortably into her back—which was only slightly less aggravating than the complete lack of leg room. They were only halfway through the five-hour flight, and already, she wanted to pull her hair out.

"Hey, Alec," she tapped his arm, her focus drifting to the wing as it sliced through the clouds. "Please tell me more about my mother."

The sun blazed against the white canvas of soft billows that surrounded them, compelling her to narrow her vision. It was strange to hover above clouds she'd only ever seen from below. And with a gentle squeeze, Alec assured her that he was there for her.

"Hmmm… where do I even start?" he murmured, pausing to gather his thoughts.

The squeal of a contented child drifted down the aisle. He smiled, resting his head as it prompted memories of her at that age.

"Your mother was the happiest when the two of you were goofing around," his eyes dilated as he returned to Dagrune once again. "She took joy in each new thing you accomplished. From rolling over, to walking, to running, and then climbing. Your first word was "up" when you were about eight months old. She always said you would be wise beyond your years and I believe that you've proven her right. Your ambition to excel at everything you do shows itself quite impressively."

Hayden remained fixed on the clouds, letting the visions his words created play out like a movie. They were vivid. She opened her eyes a little more, the brightness no longer stinging her with its sharpness. She saw herself. Happy. Bouncing toward Mamma. Babbling with excitement at every new discovery. The warmth of it wrapped around her, returning a sense of calm to rattled nerves.

Then the pilots voice crackled over the intercom, jolting Hayden out of her trancelike state. There was rough weather ahead and they were likely to experience turbulence. *Great!* She screamed in her head. *And just as I was beginning to find some sense of calm.* She folded her arms, digging her fingernails into her flesh as the weight of increased anxiety tested her already frayed nerves.

"You said your gift is connected to emotion," Alec whispered, noticing how her body language had shifted.

Hayden had never faced anything like this. She didn't have an answer. This was so different than any of the other situations when her magic had gotten out of control. She dug her nails in harder. It hurt, but the pain distracted her from some of the crushing weight in the atmosphere.

"I don't know," she replied, grinding her teeth.

Then, in a quiet act of instinct, Alec wrapped his hand around hers.

"Use my energy to calm yourself," he whispered. "I know you learned how to meditate with the martial arts training. So use it."

Hayden knew he had a point. Any unchecked magic released into a space this small—with so many people—well that would probably end in tragedy. She slowed her breathing, settling on one of her favorite visions to center herself.

"Ah… a glass of vino by the fire while snowflakes fall gently outside," she whispered. "Little puffs of wind make them swirl past the window panes. They have frosted art on them. I love seeing each new masterpiece Jack Frost is working on," her voice held an edge of nostalgia. "Calliope's Ophrahl curled up in my lap, keeping me warm next to the fireplace."

Alec patted her hand reassuringly.

"You're doing great. Keep going," he encouraged.

And his prompt spurred her to another memory. Another place of calm. Her breaths evened out, the clammy haze beginning to subside. It was helping.

She'd just begun to whisper through another memory, when the plane shuddered violently, drawing sharp cries of fear from terrified passengers. Her fingers curled into her arm, finding a fresh patch of skin to distract her magic. Again, the pilots voice came through the speakers.

"Hello folks," he said in that practiced, soothing voice. "I know this can be an unsettling experience, but I've definitely been through worse. Please stay seated with your seat belts fastened. We should be through this in no time."

Just as the intercom clicked off, they dropped into an empty pocket of air. The passengers gasps turned to screams as chaos settled over her like an angry cloud. It rose, vibrating painfully on her eardrums. Then, as if things couldn't get any worse, a man stumbled out of his seat, swaying drunkenly down the aisle as the ragged air buffeted the plane. The high-pitched shriek of a panic-stricken woman followed him.

"Karl! Karl! Get back here! You're not supposed to be out of your seat! Stop him!"

But before anyone had time to act, the plane shuddered again, plunging them into a second freefall.

The man had made it up the aisle to just a few rows ahead of them—leaving Hayden to look on in horror as he was thrown face-first into the ceiling. She heard the sickening crunch as his face struck, blood spattering over the curved upper reaches of the plane. Then gravity slammed him back down violently. He took on the likeness of a ragdoll, limp and unresponsive as his body narrowly missed the seats. Cries of *"Someone help him!,"* and *"Is there a doctor here?!"* rose from worried passengers, but no one moved to unbuckle themselves. She, like everyone else, was frozen with indecision—caught between helping a stranger in need or preserving her own safety.

Suddenly, the absence of warmth from Alec's arm registered. He was getting out of his seat.

"No! You'll just get hurt too!" She cried, grabbing his elbow.

But he pulled away, yanking it from her grip.

"I can't sit here and watch this," he called over his shoulder. "Someone has to help him!"

"I won't be able to help *you* though!" she pleaded in a fierce whisper.

But he was beyond earshot. And though she worried after him, she knew that his instinct as a Mender would compel him to disregard her protests. She wondered helplessly how he would be of any help if he too became a victim of the air pockets.

Alec yanked his belt free, moving carefully down the aisle toward the man's motionless form. He wrapped it around his thigh and, as he came within reach, lashed it to the arm of the closest seat–securing it to the strongest point. There was just enough time to lock his arms around Karl when they hit the next pocket. The force of gravity worked against him, trying its best to rip Karl from his grip. Pain shot into his hip as the belt went taut. He fought with every ounce of strength as they hung suspended, just a couple feet off the floor. Then the plane leveled–and Alec's hand slammed into the floor, cushioning Karl's head from the impact.

The second they were back on the carpet, Alec released him. His hands flew to the belt, unfastening it from the chair. With a sinking feeling, Hayden realized that he meant to drag him to the nearest empty seat. No one else was moving and he needed help. She clicked her seatbelt open, snapping the keys onto her belt loop and charged into the aisle. There was no telling when the next drop might happen, so time was everything. She ignored the frightened whimpers of the other passengers, her only goal to get the three of them to the safety of a seat belt.

"Are you ok?" She asked nervously, scooching around them to a more accessible position.

"Nothing a little tea can't handle later," Alec grimaced.

Karl moaned and began to stir, gingerly raising his hand to cover his battered nose. He winced as he returned to consciousness and the pain began to swell.

"Hey Karl," she addressed him firmly. "We're going to get you secured."

Exchanging a look with Alec, she nodded toward an empty row ahead, then slipped her arm beneath Karl's. And then, like something out of a bad movie, the shaking began. Hayden's heart plunged to her stomach. It was going to happen again. She looked around frantically—Karl was barely conscious, so they couldn't just leave him to his fate.

It started in slow motion—her feet lifted from the floor, her hands scrambling to grab whatever was anchored within reach. She'd arrived face-to-face with the knowledge—either she was about to be in a world of pain, or worse, reveal to everyone that she wasn't normal. She squeezed her eyes shut and braced herself—waiting...and waiting. But instead of pain, she felt herself set down gently. Then the intercom crackled to life, cutting through her tangled thoughts and prompting her to open her eyes.

"Ladies and Gentlemen, this is the Captain again. We've come through the worst of it," he paused, leaning into the drama. "If you look out your windows, you will see us leaving the clouds responsible for our little mishap. And my flight crew told me about the heroic act of the gentleman and lady in the aisle," a buzz of excited chatter rippled through the cabin, but the captain wasn't finished. "We're close to our destination, so the injured gentleman will get the medical care he needs. Please join me in a round of applause for our two heroes. They deserve it."

And instantly, the cabin broke into loud cheers, covering up the quiet click of the intercom.

Hayden, uncomfortable with the attention, looked to Alec—only to find him staring her down, his expression full of meaning.

"Hayden! Can you check his face please?" He asked, his eyes pleading with her to move.

It was all she needed—something to ground her.

"Can you please move your hand so I can assess the damage?" she asked.

But he kept his hand in place, eyeing her warily.

"You a doctor or somethin'?," he mumbled through his swollen lips.

"A Veterinarian actually, but I can at least look," she answered confidently. "Does anything else hurt? You took a pretty bad fall there."

"No," he grunted. "Just my damn face bein' on fire is all."

After a gentle thumb massage and closer inspection, she determined the only injury was likely a broken nose. With Alec's help, they guided him back to his seat, where his wife sobbed in relief, thanking them over and over as the flight crew took over.

True to his word, the pilot announced their descent into the airport soon after. Deboarding the plane, they were met with more accolades from fellow passengers thanking them for stepping in to save a stranger. Karl, surrounded by a concerned crew, gave them a grateful wave as they passed by.

"Check your phone," Alec prompted. "I think you're gonna want to see it."

She held her thumb down, switching off airplane mode. The familiar ding of an incoming message chimed. She swiped down to her notifications and tapped Alec's text.

You must have activated the bracelet during that last bit of turbulence. But I don't think anyone noticed. Just like your Mum didn't notice back at your house. We can talk about it when we get settled in tonight.

It said.

But after the exhaustion of a five-hour flight and the anxiety it had caused, she wouldn't let it bother her when all she wanted was to get to their rental and sleep.

Their Habitation Station came into view just as sunlight faded behind the nearby mountains. There were other homes around, but theirs was surrounded by trees, giving them more privacy than she'd hoped for. The house wasn't fancy. It was just a simple two bed, two bath set up that she'd picked so no one had to sleep on a couch. As they settled in, she felt the cares of their ordeal begin to melt into the past. And with the squeeze of their troubled experience fading, she felt better about granting Alec the request to discuss what had happened. She fell back into the oversized chair, releasing a deep sigh.

"So what did I do? What did everyone see?" she asked, her head lolling back lazily as she stared at the ceiling.

Alec chuckled—watching her fondly. More things that reminded him of Jurtah.

"Well… I was preparing to put myself between Karl and another meeting with the ceiling—and then this wave of violet light came from you. It spread through the cabin," he paused, a curious expression masking his face. "And when it did, the way the plane leveled and how you seemed to float in the air—well, it just felt very magic driven. Whatever that was, it stopped that whole free fall in the most perfect way."

She opened her hand, studying the indentations from the wooden beads. She didn't even remember grabbing hold of the bracelet—but that wasn't the weirdest part. The impressions were still there though a few hours had passed. Even the marks from her nails were gone, with the exception of the three places where she'd broken her skin.

"I don't think I actually did anything though," Hayden said, her tone thoughtful. "And that purple… my magic is blue. My mother's was purple," she closed her hand back into a fist. "Maybe it was the protective power of the Token. But it didn't react to you this time. And here I thought that you'd used the last of the magic in it," her lips spread into a smile—the kind that easily found its way to her eyes. "Looks like she made it for me after all."

Hayden wanted to forget about it. She hated the fact that more questions had surfaced, no matter the comfort that was layered between them. This was the first vacation she'd taken more than a few hundred miles from home, and she wasn't about to waste it. So she proposed a change of scene.

"Let's play some cards since this is getting us nowhere. It would be good to get my mind off of all these unanswered questions anyway."

And understanding where her frustrations had led her, he went along with it.

"You got it Princess!" He said enthusiastically, smirking when it made her cringe. "Yeah, your mother hated that one too," he laughed.

They were only a couple hands in before face splitting yawns began to sneak up on her, turning her eyes into leaky faucets.

"Maybe you should get some rest kiddo," he said, his voice tinged with fatherly warmth.

"You're not my dad," she teased. "You can't tell me what to do!"

But he was right. And as her head sank onto the feather-down pillow, she thought of how nice it was to have him around. He was as close as she'd ever come to having a genuine, caring father figure. A soft smile led her into dreams of Mum—happier than ever, laughing at a joke Alec had told. She'd never seen her light shine so bright.

Tap tap tap. A soft knock on the wall made her eyes flutter open. She breathed deeply through her nose, spreading her limbs into a starfish pose. A pterodactyl-like scream escaped her throat as she stretched out her cramped muscles. The rumble of beating wings startled her into motion, as her loud screech scared the woodpecker away. Her travel bag was at the foot of the bed, so she rolled over to it, rummaging through until she found her workout clothes and toiletry bag.

"Quick brush of the teeth and hair, then a nice morning jog," she narrated. "And I don't even have to leave my room to get to the bathroom... noice!"

She rushed through the routine, eager to explore this new world. To go from, never having left her state, to flying into an island in the middle of the ocean—it was kind of a big deal. She made quick work of tying her running shoes and pulling her long hair into a secure ponytail. This was non-negotiable. It had to stay off her neck when she was exercising.

"All ready," she said to the mirror, pointing at herself with finger guns. "Let's conquer this thing."

And with one last look over her shoulder, she made her way outside.

She was still in the mountains. And although they weren't hers, she felt perfectly at home. She'd just traded the soft look of the pine tree laden hills, for a more tropical fern-like aesthetic. Even the birdsong was similar, with the exception of a few louder warbles. She started out at a brisk walk, following the tantalizing smell of salt in the air. *Maybe I won't jog after all.* She thought, her more adventurous side taking over. *I can't enjoy the new things when I'm fighting to breathe anyway.*

"Well I agree with me," she smirked, slowing her pace to that of a leisure stroll.

Hayden now had a new destination in mind and it involved digging her toes in the sand. She oohed and ahhed her way down the street, pausing at every new flower and strange looking bush. But it wasn't until she came upon a tree with a large red bloom that she had to stop. She slid her phone out of her running belt and with a couple swipes, pulled up the lens. Sweet eddies of perfume swirled from the flowers as she snapped the picture and waited.

"Ah! Here it is," she cried triumphantly—holding the phone up for comparison. "Red Maga. They're quite pretty—and such delicate little flowers."

There were only a few more houses to pass in the little neighborhood—before she would get to see the number one item on her bucket list. The Ocean. To swim in its warmth—it was something that had always whispered through her mind. But she'd never felt its pull as strongly as she did today. As the breeze picked up there was a slight shift from salt to fish. The boardwalk ended, turning into a sea of soft white sand. She took off her shoes, wiggling her toes through it, on her way to the water. The ebb and flow of waves pulled her closer. This was so much better than hearing it on a white noise machine.

"I could get used to this," she said, closing her eyes to draw in a deep, satisfying breath.

And then, in a moment of reckless delight, she tossed her phone and shoes to the side–dashing toward the water. The small waves splashed up to her knees before she had to slow down. She waded out a few more strides and plunged beneath the surface. A pleasant blanket of warmth surrounded her. *So this is what swimming could have been.* She thought. *Maybe I would have been a better swimmer if Tranquil Lake had been this kind to me.*

Hayden looked around at the bits of vegetation floating past–slightly disappointed that she hadn't immediately seen schools of colorful fish. Thinking that maybe they were farther out, she followed that thought into deeper waters. And to her surprise and utter delight, she found herself at the edge of a coral garden bursting with color and life. Her chest tightened–her lungs begging for air, so she swam for the surface.

One exaggerated gasp, and a few panting breaths later, she swallowed another lung full of oxygen. Back down she went, to the fronds of sea anemones waving among the sharpness of the coral. Her hand brushed past one in the shape of a paddle and was surprised to find that it felt more like a sponge.

Whenever she felt the need for a breath, she would swim up for it and then right back down to continue exploring. There were many kinds of fish–from itty bitty, to fat bellies and pointy heads. Even some that reminded her of Nemo's friends. As she swam over a large coral shelf, the garden ended and a field of tall grass opened up before her. It swayed in the push and pull of the ocean, occasionally exposing the bony curves of a seahorse.

Hayden looked toward the surface, noting with pride that she was about twenty feet below it. Her eye was drawn to the lazy movement of a sea turtle as it moved through the thick grass. Then the clicks from a pod of dolphins that swam around her, curiously tapping her with their noses. She would have giggled if she'd been breathing air–which reminded her to go get more of it. They followed her up, only swimming off once she'd stopped panting.

Her watch buzzed twice—the indication that she'd gotten a notification. She tapped on the text from Alec. **I'm worried about you. Where did you go?** Frowning, she pressed the side button, bringing the display back to the home screen. She'd lost track of time, which would bring her woefully close to messing up their timeline. A couple more taps, and the smile emoji was on its way. A quick emoji text was better than making him wait any longer. She cast her attention back toward the beach. And though it felt like she'd swum for miles, it only took ten minutes to reach the shore. Then grabbing her phone and shoes as she ran by, she pressed her thumb firmly on the call back button.

"I guess I'm getting that jog in after all," she mused, breaking into a trot.

The sun had almost completely dried her hair by the time she burst through the front door of their rental. A quick shower to rinse the salt from her hair, then her soggy clothing on the washers fastest setting. She could lay them out to dry in the car so they wouldn't have to wait for the dryer. They *were* looking at a long drive anyway. She ran a brush through her hair and tossed her remaining things unceremoniously into her small backpack. As they drove through the small town and onto the highway, she felt her mood darken a little, watching the ocean fade in the rearview. She kicked her seat back, trying her best to focus on the happier reasons for this trip.

The drive seemed nearly as long as the airplane ride—and the consecutive days of cramped travel were beginning to take their toll on her muscles. They took one break at the halfway point, to give them a chance to stretch their legs, but Hayden didn't want to linger. She was too close to getting some of those long-coveted answers. They rolled to a stop at the end of a narrow road, lined with trees whose branches were twisted together into a canopy. Anything beyond that was clearly a footpath.

"Looks like this is where we get out," she said, pointing to a sign.

It showed a car with a red circle and slash through it—no translation needed.

"According to Matilde we should expect about an hour hike up the mountain. Got those hiking legs on?" she teased.

Alec didn't skip a beat, "Well, they're gonna have to work–these are the only ones I got."

He slapped his knee in true old-person fashion, and Hayden had to laugh.

"You've definitely nailed the dad jokes in your time here," then she refocused, slipping back into quest mode. "Shall we follow the yellow brick road to where x marks the spot?"

Hayden started off through the canopy of branches. Passing under those arches only added an extra layer to the shroud of mystery surrounding this Shaman.

"It's like a whole different world here," she said in reverent awe. "From the ocean life to the kind that flies."

Alec let out a hearty laugh.

"Oh the absolute irony for you–of all people–to say *that*."

They slapped at their exposed skin as mosquitoes took advantage of the easy meal. The only two, really–there wasn't another soul on the path. Wispy clouds drifted overhead, but none offered relief from the blazing sun. And the humidity? It worked overtime, soaking their shirts in sweat. The higher they climbed, the more often they stopped–for water, for air, for any excuse to catch a breath. Still, they pressed on, eager to be done with the branches that whipped at them from every side. At last, they stumbled onto a wider road that opened just beyond a small convenience store. Armed with her translation app, Hayden marched confidently up to the woman behind the counter.

"Hello, I was wondering if you might help us find someone," she said, pressing the button to translate when the woman began to gesture that she didn't understand.

"Hola, me preguntaba sí podrías ayudarnos a encontrar a alguien," the app echoed.

The woman's face lit up. She chattered excitedly, her words tumbling out while Hayden listened through the translator. By the time their conversation ended, Hayden felt like she'd made a friend. They exchanged a wave as Alec and Hayden headed off in the direction she had pointed.

Their final hurdle was the steep hill that began where the footpath ended. It was another person they'd met on the path who told them about it. The natural steps made the ascent easier than they'd anticipated. And as they neared the top, they passed a garden full of vegetables of all kinds. The plants were in neat rows, without a weed in sight. Whoever tended them was meticulous. Just beyond that, they were met by a white fence, with a wide-open gate. Hayden hesitated—now that she was here, the idea that this might actually lead to answers felt suddenly daunting. Alec saw her struggle and offered his elbow.

"I don't think I can give you courage," he said softly. "But what I can do… is drag your stubborn behind to that door," he finished in a rush, that signature twinkle in his eye.

She laughed—an unsure, nervous sound as they ambled side by side up to the door.

"I don't know what to expect," she whispered, breathless. "What if I don't like what I discover on the other side?"

"We've come this far," Alec encouraged. "There'll be no sense in turning back now."

So with a decisive grunt, she raised her hand to knock.

<u>23</u>

Memory Lane Pain

The door swung inward and Hayden stepped back as the man emerged, leaning casually against the doorway. A flicker of recognition passed through his hazel eyes, but it was so fleeting, she wasn't sure she'd seen it at all. *This can't be the right person,* she thought, taking in his unruly red hair and smooth complexion. He looked, at a bare minimum, a few decades younger than he should have—at least according to Matilde.

"Hola amigos," he greeted them. "What can I do for a couple of travelers such as yourselves?" His voice was warm and inviting, hinting at mirth that bubbled just beneath the surface.

"My name is Hayden, and this is Alec," she answered cautiously. "I'm *so* sorry… I'm not sure we're in the right place. The person we were looking for would be… older than you are."

He chuckled, pushed off the doorframe, and straightened to his full height.

"Not exactly the first time I've heard that," he said. "If you're looking for the one they call 'The Shaman,' I am present and accounted for," he stepped back with a flourish, beckoning them inside. "But I'd prefer if you called me Ardis—though I'm afraid you've caught me in the middle of making dinner. Still, it would be my pleasure to have you join me."

Alec and Hayden exchanged a look. With an hour-long hike back down the mountain and two days of travel fatigue behind them, they were in no position to turn him down.

They removed their shoes before following him down the short hallway. It opened into a room where tapestries, rich in color, graced the walls–offsetting the simple furniture. Vases of all shapes and sizes crowded shelves, covering nearly every inch of wall not already claimed by fabric. Whether they were carved from wood or forged in a kiln–their handcrafted quality and artwork were exquisite. Hayden couldn't take her eyes off the intricate needle work and the detailed pictures–staring in open mouthed awe at each new discovery.

"Beautiful, aren't they," Ardis said, his voice closer than Hayden had expected. She resisted the urge to step away from him, not knowing if it would be offensive. "This is how my patients pay me," he added, brushing his fingers down one of the more elaborate pieces. His eyes glazed over with the weight of a memory–but he shook it off quickly, his smile returning. "And I wouldn't have it any other way."

After politely refusing their offer to help with dinner–insisting they make themselves at home–he scuttled off to the kitchen.

They'd barely had time to get settled when Ardis returned. He untied his apron, hanging it on a hook just outside the kitchen.

"So–to whom do I owe thanks for the pleasure of your company?" he asked, crossing his legs and perching on the arm of the sofa.

"Her name is Matilde," Hayden's reply flew off her tongue, and for a second, she felt the warmth of color rise in her cheeks. But she stuffed down the embarrassment. She didn't have time for that anymore. "She would have come by roughly twenty years ago about one of her students," Hayden went on. "Matilde grew up here. Talked about it all the time, so I'd imagine she would've mentioned it to you," Hayden waited, searching his face for the flash she'd seen when he first looked at her. But it wasn't there.

"Many travel here. I *am* sorry, but I will need more details than that. Children who've grown up on this island often returned to see me," he uncrossed his legs and slid down onto the cushion. "Is there anything more revealing? Any further details?"

It was then that Hayden found a moment of clarity. It was a charade–he was feigning ignorance.
The recognition she'd seen in his eyes–it hadn't been her imagination. He knew about her magic, but he had to be sure. So she rubbed her palms together, gathering her courage into a ball of light. It's glow reflected in her eyes, expanding with the orb as she pulled her hands apart. A proud grin tugged at her lips–she'd come so far from that day by the lake. Then, with a steady breath, she severed the connection between magic and emotion. The orb dissolved, drifting harmlessly through the walls.

A whistle escaped Ardis' lips. "It seems my mistakes have come back to haunt me," he sighed, tenting his fingers in thought.

"What do you mean by that?" Hayden asked, the satisfaction she'd felt unraveling slowly.

There was something in his tone–something she couldn't quite place. It wasn't menacing, but it didn't exactly scream 'good' either.

"What do you remember? When was the first time you recall using your magic?"

The way he scrutinized her was unsettling. And though the question seemed harmless enough, it carried a weight she could feel in her chest.

"A couple months ago," she answered.

He ran his hand over his face in frustration.

"Damn it! I was right. I should have been there when you drank it," as the words left his lips, she felt a shift–a subtle lean into heavy regret. And for a moment, he seemed older, more like the man she'd expected at the door. "Sending magic like that... time-lapsed magic–it... can change things. I never should've done it. It was only supposed to take what was directly tied to your mental anguish. But now..." His voice dropped lower as he grappled with his failure. "Now it seems I've not only dulled your magic—but erased your memory of it too."

Hayden chewed her lip thoughtfully. That would answer the question of why she couldn't remember anything until after the storm—despite Mum and Matilde insisting they'd seen it firsthand. She picked at the skin around her nails—a bad habit she'd acquired over the years when dealing with stress.

"So... is there any way to get those memories back? Because—" she added quickly, seeing the doubt behind Ardis' eyes. "I don't think I'll ever fully understand my magic without them," she turned to Alec, who gave her an encouraging nod. "And I need to understand this bracelet. I think there's something in those memories that might tell me how it works."

She pulled her keys from her bag and held them out to him. Ardis' eyes widened as he pushed himself forward and took them gently from her outstretched hand. He rolled his thumb over the beads—and just as it had happened with the tapestry, his eyes seemed to glaze over. Hayden watched in concern—until, with a sharp breath, he rejoined them. And without an explanation, she began to understand how his magic worked. Part of it anyway.

"I haven't seen handywork like this since..." his voice trailed off as he handed the keys back to Hayden. "I want to help however I can. But business must wait until after dinner," he pushed himself to his feet, retreating again to the kitchen. "Please find a place at the table," he called out. "I'll have the food out shortly."

As if on command, Hayden's stomach rumbled in response as the mouthwatering aroma reached her.

A hint of garlic and cilantro rose with the steam, torturing her already famished stomach. Still, she waited—hands folded in her lap—for their host to take the first serving. But the sound of something tapping on glass caught their attention.

"Excuse me," Ardis said, shoving his chair back. "She always seems to know when I have company and loves to meet new people. I'll be right back."

He returned to the kitchen and a moment later they heard the dissonant twang of rusty springs as he slid the old window open. With a loud squawk, a bright green parrot announced its arrival, fluttering to Ardis' chair. She stretched her wings, and the fading sunlight glimmered over her feathers, sending waves of blue and purple iridescence cascading through them.

"Meet Cafie," Ardis beamed, his face glowing like a proud parent introducing their favorite child. "I rescued her from the clutches of a thrush when she was just a baby. She comes and goes as she pleases."

Cafie tipped her head toward Ardis when he said her name.

"Dinner!" she croaked, bobbing her head up and down. "¡Cena lista!" Her excited dance continued until Ardis produced a small plate, set it on the edge of the table, and dropped a handful of peanuts onto it. She happily flapped to the place setting, wrapped her claws around a shell and got to work. Just as she found success, she stopped with the nut grasped in her beak. Puffing up her chest, she let out a loud squawk. "Your turn!" Ardis laughed, and the sound of it woke a sudden feeling of contentment—the kind that was so encompassing, there was nothing, in this world or hers, that could upset it.

And when the moment passed, and dinner was served, she almost felt a sense of cold in its absence—despite the heat of the dish in front of her.

Alec and Ardis enjoyed lighthearted reminiscing over dinner. Hayden didn't mind being out of the loop—she was more than happy to sit quietly, absorbing everything she could from the tidbits of their stories. With every new detail, she'd begun to feel closer to the world she'd been born in. The way they talked about it—it just made her want to return. Her thoughts were interrupted by Cafie's creaky voice.

"Clean up! Squawk! Everybody clean up." With a flap of her wings, she got to work, carrying napkins and silverware into the kitchen.

Hayden flipped a smirk in Alec's direction. Amid Ardis' protests—and not to be outdone by a bird—they jumped in to help.

"Many hands make light work," Hayden said, feigning superiority. "Aunt Ruth and Uncle Ernest always said so."

But, in truth, she had a bigger goal in mind. Something that she wasn't ashamed to admit was a priority. She knew that the sooner dinner was cleaned up, the sooner she would get to the part where Ardis could help her.

Cafie had settled onto her perch at the top of an elaborate tree, packed with activities meant to spark a bird's natural curiosity. Some were hand-carved, others molded from plastic. Ropes, fidgets, and pop-its dangled from various perches. Hayden would've loved to spend hours watching her play, but today, her attention was on the pile of pillows in the center of the room—and the familiar whistle of a teapot reaching its perfect temperature.

"I do remember Matilde," Ardis admitted, rounding the corner with a steaming mug of tea. "You were right. It was a visit I'll never forget," his voice took on an edge of nostalgia. "You were her first encounter with magic. Quite possibly her only one—except for me, of course. And when she revealed that your light was blue, I was immediately concerned."

"I know," Hayden cut him off. "You aren't the first person to tell me as much."

"But…" He raised an eyebrow, motioning for her to settle in with the pillows. "I can see that you have a good heart. And although not everyone may agree with me, I believe it's not magic that defines the wielder, but the wielder who defines the magic."

She took the mug from Ardis, mulling over what he'd said.

"I hope you're right," Hayden sighed, dipping the tea basket in and out of the water. "But you weren't there the first time it took over. I don't know—if it happened again—will I even be able to control it?" Her eyes darkened for a moment as she placed the basket on a saucer. She blinked, pulling herself back to the present issue. "So—you said these are herbs that will make me sleep?"

"No, it's not sleep. It's a meditative state," Ardis knelt down next to her as she took her first sip. "In order for me to guide you through these memories I don't want you distracted by anything. It allows you to retreat into your mind with your full concentration."

Hayden swallowed nervously, flashing a look toward Alec.

"Okay. I think I'm ready. Bottoms up?" Then she raised her mug, tipped it back and drained it to the last drop. "How long will it take to..." she went silent, squeezing her eyes shut as a wave of nausea rolled from her stomach to her mouth. She swayed and the world started to melt, dripping into a swirl of colors that galloped around her.

Alec put out a steadying hand and they worked together, guiding her down to the bed of pillows. Ardis placed his hand on her forehead, the yellow shimmer of his craft beginning to glow. Then Alec watched as that same light crept into Ardis' glassy stare.

****

"Don't be afraid," Ardis' voice was all around her— calming—echoing through the darkness. "I'll be here if you need me, but you must ask. To tread on the sacred field of memories is a boundary I will not cross unless it is your wish."

Hayden opened her eyes to an absolute darkness. It pressed in around her, suffocating in its totality. Then, a pinpoint of light flickered in the distance. She pushed herself to her feet and stumbled toward it. The sound of her footsteps echoed, reverberating back in sharp waves. Then in a sudden rush, something shoved her forward and she found herself standing in the middle of Mama and Papa's bedroom. That old familiar feeling of vulnerability gripped her throat, squeezing until she thought she might choke. To be standing in this place again... she'd worked so hard to put it all behind her. The feeling of rising bile was overwhelming—until a soft whimper caught her attention.

"No!" Hayden whispered fiercely.

The sound had come from a tiny pile of worn-out pajamas. Beneath it was the long-lost memory of a shivering, helpless child. Moonlight spilled through the dingy bedroom window, casting the shadow of a cross on her tiny forehead.

"That's right," Hayden gulped, tears springing to her eyes. "Mama used to make me stand by her bed if she was still mad at me when she went to sleep. How could I have forgotten? She made me do it so often."

The thin carpet had done nothing to protect her from the cold wooden floor underneath. Only once, in an act of impulsive defiance had she tried to go to bed, and they'd made sure she would never want to try it again. So when her head would drop in exhaustion, she'd curl up on the rug and fall into a restless slumber. Jane shifted, and a polished wooden bead on her wrist caught the moonlight. Her arm slipped into the pale beam and Hayden watched as the bracelet shimmered softly to life. Then with a final tremble, Jane stopped shivering, sighing in the welcoming warmth of relief.

"Now I remember!" Hayden gasped, clapping her hand over her mouth. Then the tears spilled over. "It always felt like someone was covering me with a blanket," and the gentle pulse from the bracelet seemed to glow in response—covering her in its tender comfort.

The room wavered and she instantly felt a shift in energy. There was a sudden burning pain. Not the physical kind, but the kind that had buried itself so deep, she'd forgotten how raw it was. Her pulse quickened and the crushing weight cracked her carefully built inner fortress. Whispers of self-doubt escaped, swirling around her like the heavy tendrils of a vine. They squeezed, climbing until she felt the breath leave her lungs.

The blue light hurt. Her magic had never felt this way before. And then it dawned on her—she hadn't learned to control it yet. A quick glance around—she was back at the

Academy—it must have been around the time that Matilde first started training her. Hayden could feel the overwhelming anger eating at her.

She was always so angry.

Her ears perked up as the sound of screaming tore through the small studio. The kind of anguished cry that could rip a person apart. And then she realized—the screams were hers, and she couldn't seem to stop.

Memories bombarded her—relentless in their attack. Every slap, each new bruise, every degrading word—from her appearance to how smart she was. Mama never held back. And then she began to feel a change. The whispers were quieter, the vines were loosening, and her light didn't sting anymore. Something was taking the pain, dulling it to a place where she could process. The bracelet was clasped firmly in her hand. It always seemed to find its way there when she needed it. She could remember it now. She could remember them all. Every time she needed comfort in her loneliest moments, it had somehow provided it. That day at the falls— she could now see the soft burst of purple just before the branches caught her.

Hayden crashed to her knees as the darkness swallowed her again, the tears streaming unchecked down her cheeks. After everything Matilde had done to help her, it was a cruel twist. She'd inadvertently taken the one thing from Hayden that had carried her through the agony that was Mama.

She let out a feral screech, pounding her fists in the dark. Why did it have to happen at all? Why couldn't she have just stayed with her birth mom? The questions churned. And then she caught herself. This isn't me, *she thought.* I don't wallow in self-pity. *She sniffed, running a finger under her nose. This was something Matilde could never know. It would break her. No matter the burden of it, Hayden would take it to the grave. And just as she was ready to call out to Ardis to bring her back, the blackness relented in a blinding flash of light.*

The deep growl of thunder followed her onto a road. It was a place that she had no memory of. Lonely, in the middle of the night–maybe it was symbolic somehow? The faint sound of fabric, tearing at the seams, made her spin around. It started slowly, just a dark thread. Then it opened wider and Hayden could see a man that looked just like Alec holding a baby. His face was frozen in shock as a blue orb erupted from the infants chest. Then with a thundering crash, the scene disappeared, leaving Hayden staring at the small child. If this was a memory, then that would be her just after... And the bile rose again, but this time she couldn't hold it back. She retched into the ditch. Because knowing that she couldn't do anything to change this moment–it had sent her over the edge.

Farren's tiny face was streaked with tears. Hayden knelt in defeat as she watched herself crying, knowing there was nothing she could do to stop this from unfolding. The headlights came into view and the car rolled to a stop. Before the woman had even stepped out, Hayden knew who it was.

"Babe! How do you think she got here? There's no one around."

That stinking breath. The fake sweet voice. The vacant eyes– devoid of even the tiniest shred of love. Hayden felt her rage building. Seeing it play out like this... she was going to lose herself in it. "Ardis!" She cried frantically. "Get me out of here!" And with a rush she gasped, breaking through the surface of her memories.

*****

Hayden opened her eyes to find herself staring at the ceiling. She wrinkled her nose, trying to remember how she'd gotten here. Oh right, the tea. Ardis said it would help her meditate. She propped herself up on her elbows, shaking the last of the dizzying, emotional roller coaster from her head.

"Everything felt so real," she breathed, wiping a hand over her cheek. "But it's dry. And..." Hayden patted the pillows around her. "No vomit."

Then she paused, looking out from under her eyelashes as the rest of the room began to materialize. The darkness was slowly relenting–until, all at once, it rolled back, leaving her panting for air.

When she was once again fully present, she felt a crushing grip on her hand. Alec was squeezing so hard that her fingers were turning white.

Hayden! Are you ok?" he asked, his eyes wild with concern.

She tapped his arm, drawing his attention to the vice-like hold he had on her.

"I will be once I have my hand back?" she winced.

He released his grip, mumbling an apology. Then, needing a moment for composure, she excused herself to the bathroom.

When the latch clicked, she leaned heavily on the door–sliding to the floor and resting her head with a soft thunk. She had to get away from the prying eyes of the two men who seemed intent on stepping into a fatherly role. She knew why Alec felt that way, but they'd only met Ardis a few hours ago–yet he wore that same look. That strange mix of pity and guilt–although it made zero sense coming from him.

She forced a sigh, wondering if Ardis had walked through the memories with her, though he'd promised he wouldn't. Still, they were waiting on her, and if she didn't pull herself together soon, they would come knocking. So reluctantly, she moved to the sink, turning on the faucet to splash a bit of cold water on her face–hoping it would calm her racing thoughts. And it did, but only slightly. She took one last look in the mirror, tucking in a few hairs that had escaped her ponytail, and braced herself for the barrage of questions that was sure to be heading her way.

Hayden had barely stepped-foot back in the small living room when Cafie glided from her perch. Her wings brushed Hayden's face as she landed lightly on her shoulder, nuzzling affectionately into Hayden's neck.

"You met Cafie the dinner guest," Ardis explained with a light laugh. "Now meet Cafie the therapist," Hayden bent her finger, running it over the smooth feathers on her chest and Cafie purred in response. "She always seems to know just when to fly in," he said softly.

Cafie's calming presence settled over Hayden, lending the nerve to ask the question that had been gnawing at her. She cleared her throat, looking Ardis square in the eye.

"Did you see anything? Follow me into any of those memories?"

She stared him down, searching for the tiniest cringe of guilt—anything that might give away what his words wouldn't. As she expected, he denied it. And when she could see no lie in his eyes, she simply nodded, finding her way back to the couch.

"So—" Ardis began, treading as carefully as he knew how, "Do you want to talk about any of it?"

He was sitting uncomfortably at the edge of his chair. Alec, who'd just returned from putting the last of the pillows away, looked on in quiet curiosity.

"Well—I think I got what I needed in the way of knowing how this trinket works," Hayden answered, rolling the beads through her fingers. "And by that, I mean—I don't make it work. It just does," she shrugged, settling casually into the couch. "It gave me what I needed to get through some of my more difficult moments. And for the time being that's all I want to say."

There was a finality to her tone that neither man wanted to challenge. So Ardis, with decades of experience in smoothing over awkward silences, slid into an offer for them to stay for the night.

"Might as well pull all those pillows out again Alec."

The playful jab did exactly what it was meant to—disarming Hayden enough to release her pent-up tension.

The wine glasses clinked together—their painted stems poking through his fingers, looking like a colorful bouquet. Because—like everything else that adorned every nook and cranny of this place—they were hand-painted. And as Ardis was excited to point out, they were also made by the glassblower in his little village.

They toasted to Dagrune—Hayden wondering, not lightly, what Ardis' story was. How *had* he come to Earth in the first place? But just as he respected her wish not to dive into her memories, she respected his secrets. And so the conversation stayed light, lasting well into the evening.

When they were settled in for the night, and her eyes could barely stay open—the moon peeked out from behind a cloud. It seemed brighter here—shining gently through the window. She could see her reflection and the cross on her forehead from the small panes blocking some of its light. In a flash of memory, she saw herself as a child—cold, uncertain, and scared—that same cross resting on her little face. Then the image disintegrated to dust, leaving her to look into the eyes of the woman who had overcome that past. She had her piece of comfort now, and it gave her the courage to do what she knew she must.

<u>24</u>

The Veiled Case

"Paul!" Captain Richard barked, his sharp tone laced with venom.

The Captain's door was wide open—but even if it hadn't been, the giant windows left nowhere to hide. Paul stiffened, flooded with the dread of being summoned. This was only his second year working for the FPD and already, fear of the captain was installed in his psyche. Forswear had never been a place he'd planned to settle for long. The small town was thick with small-minded views that he longed to escape. But somehow he was still stuck here a full year after his plan to move. And a small part of him knew that this job was the reason.

"On my way Captain," he called out, forcing a polite tone.

Since his little slice of hell was at the far end of the small office, he had to pass every one of his colleagues in his walk of shame. Those who didn't keep their heads buried in work offered looks of quiet pity in support, so they too wouldn't end up on the chopping block. He leaned against the doorway, hoping for something that didn't require more than the exchange of a few words. But his hopes were dashed when he was ordered to sit. He pulled the chair away from the desk, noting—not for the first time, the sharp contrast between its stiff discomfort and the Captain's cushy throne.

"Why has there been no progress on the triple homicide? I haven't heard anything new on it in a couple weeks," Captain Richard bellowed.

Paul tried not to let the tactics get to him. But when the villain in his story thrived off of everyone knowing who was in trouble, it was nearly impossible.

"I'm sorry Captain, I've had a few other cases come across my desk," he answered, trying to add a note of professionalism to his voice. "With no new information, I was focusing my time elsewhere."

Paul knew he was being used. He still held the title and pay of an officer, but the captain was slowly pushing him into detective work. He kept claiming that he was working on hiring a detective, but all of *that* paperwork seemed to somehow pile up in front of Paul. Asking for a promotion and bump in pay had gotten him nowhere. The Captain had simply made up a lie—an insult to Paul's intelligence.

"We're a small-town force and I don't have the funds to give a big pay increase," He'd said.

But it wasn't true. The expensive mahogany desk between them was all the proof he needed. It had conveniently been delivered around the same time as Captain Richard's claim. He blinked, realizing that his mind had wandered during one of Captain Richard's famous belligerent rants.

"I don't pay you to make those decisions, I pay you to follow orders!" Richard spat. And Paul flinched as it cut into his resolve to defend himself. "The sooner you realize I'm right and there's some coven of witches hanging around, the sooner you can close the case."

This wasn't the first time that he'd made the remark, and it took everything Paul had to hold onto his professionalism in the face of blatant sexism.

"Sir, I'm not so sure we can pin this on fairytales and conjecture," his voice was commanding in spite of his self-doubt. "I need more information, which I won't have until I hear back from the medical examiner."

"Don't get smart with me!" The captain growled menacingly. "That was a planned ritual if I've ever seen one. They called something sinister up from the depths of hell, mark my words."

Paul wanted to argue further, but he couldn't afford to lose this job. He'd already picked up a second one bartending on the down-low just to keep up with his bills.

"You're right," he conceded, exhaustion creeping into his voice. "I'll move this case to the top of my priority list."

The pandering worked. And Paul was relieved to see a flicker of disappointment cross the Captain's face. He'd clearly been geared up for a bigger fight.

"Fine. Get back to work then," the Captain scoffed, waving Paul away with a dismissive flick of his hand.

Paul trudged back to his desk, mulling over all the other cases that would now have to wait. Those cases had actual family members waiting for answers. But sure—he had to push the real criminals to the top of his list. All for the Captain's weird fantasy.

"Richard," he said scornfully under his breath. "Fits though. He *is* a giant dick."

He cast a glance around and when he was certain no one heard what he said, he dropped into his chair with a quiet huff.

The open file stared back at him. He ran a hand over his face, searching for some new insight in the pages he'd read a hundred times already. The autopsy report still hadn't come in. It was the one piece he could count on to push the investigation forward. An investigation that made him question, for the first time, the oath he'd sworn to uphold. Because whatever, or whoever, had ended the slew of crimes these three men committed—they deserved a medal. Not a manhunt. The town was better off without the scum of Forswear being allowed to wreak unchecked atrocities on the innocent.

He tossed the folder on his desk in frustration, staring off into the far corner of the room. There had to be something he could do to make it look like he was working on it. What was it now? At least a week since he touched base with the coroner? He should definitely call again. His hand hovered over the phone momentarily.

"I can fill more time with it if I go see her," He mumbled under his breath.

So he grabbed his coat—his need to escape the stale office just as strong as the need to appear busy. As inconspicuously as possible, he scurried through the door to freedom. The sound of raucous laughter followed him down the hall, making his skin crawl. The Captain seemed to be on a personal phone call, so he would be unlikely to ask where Paul was going.

The morgue was about twenty minutes from the station, giving him time to reminisce over the day he got the call. He'd already felt uneasy when it came in—because who wouldn't with three dead bodies? It was a rare case for a small-town department to deal with. Then, there was the initial shock when he came upon the scene, and he'd promptly lost his lunch. Upon closer inspection of the wounds, his first thought was an arrow. But their search turned up empty. The claw marks—the arrows... nothing added up. Unless of course he considered the full moon that night.

"Don't they have to eat their victims to survive though?" Paul said aloud.

He rolled his eyes at himself, cringing in disgust at how much it sounded like the Captain's claim. He needed to focus on reality and getting a win—so his boss could swoop in and take all the credit for the hard work. At a bare minimum, he could solve it with science. That at least would be something he could discreetly throw back in the man's face.

The morgue was in a bleak and uninviting building. It had a sterile atmosphere, but that did nothing to stop his imagination from dredging up the smell of death. He pulled back the heavy metal door, hesitantly approaching the window. A red button lit up on the wall with a sign to the right of it reading: **RING ONCE FOR SERVICE, MULTIPLE RINGS WILL WAKE THE GHOULS.**

Paul laughed out loud as he respectfully pushed the button once. He appreciated the dark humor. How could anyone working a job like this live without it? Then a woman who looked to be in her fifties, briskly strutted around the corner. Her glasses were a size too large for her face—and her hair, pulled back in a tight bun, was covered with a surgical cap. The apron she wore was clean—much to Paul's relief.

She peeled off her disposable gloves and tossed them unceremoniously into a trash he couldn't see.

"How may I be of service, sir?" She asked, her tone polite but stiff.

Paul had taken in her details, comparing them to what she sounded like on the phone. And it matched—perfectly with the all-business persona he'd gotten used to.

"My name is Paul," he replied, feeling a little awkward about talking through the window. "I'm the detective on the triple homicide case. I hope it's ok I came down instead of calling again."

Her sternness melted into a smile, and for a moment, she reminded him of one of his favorite elementary teachers. A no nonsense school marm type that everyone else was afraid of. He, however, had found her to be all bark and no bite.

"I was just putting the finishing touches on my report. You came at the right time. Do you want to come back with me?"

A buzzing sound followed by a click unlocked the door to his left. It appeared that she meant it as a statement, not a question.

The room was lined with doors—each of which had a small keypad. After casting a cursory glance around, he thought it safe enough to let his guard down. The fresh smell of bleach burned his nostrils, but he was grateful for the reminder that no bodies were on the autopsy tables. He'd had enough of seeing those for a good while after the scene in town.

"I appreciate you seeing me with no notice, Freyja," he said with a grateful nod.

His tone was apologetic. He hoped it would disarm any ill will she might hold from his unannounced visit.

"I don't mind," she replied. "I'm typically more concerned about someone showing up if I'm actually in the middle of an autopsy. Most people don't have the stomach to see what I do."

That was the opening he needed. Something grounding and relatable.

"Gonna be honest," he said, running his hand through his dark, curly hair. "I'm glad I didn't have to see anything."

She tossed a half-amused smile over her shoulder.

"If you want to pursue a career as a detective, you may want to get over that."

They'd reached the computer. She quickly found the document, sending it to print. A whir, followed by the smell of hot paper and ink, replaced the bleach.

"I can go over it with you if you'd like," she offered. "I know the format can be a bit confusing sometimes."

Paul was more than grateful to accept her offer. There were medical words that needed explaining–and a professional was a much better resource than a search engine.

"I also took the liberty of sending it to your email," Freyja added.

She went over the document with him, patiently filling him in on details that were outside his scope of expertise. And when he felt satisfied with the new information, he expressed his gratitude for the hospitality, shook her hand, then begrudgingly headed back toward work.

Every mile that took him closer to the office, his apprehension grew. Maybe he could buy a little more time if he stopped at the crime scene. It *was* related to the case after all. And more time outside of that stuffy building was a win that he needed right now–especially after the humiliation he'd just faced there. So with the autopsy report firmly in hand, he pulled into an empty parking spot. The arrow wounds—he'd at least been right about that. But there had to be something he missed—some clue that could lead him down the right path. His boots crunched on what remained of the brittle grass.

"Let's see," he said, ruffling through the pages. "Here it is. Slivers of wood… blah blah blah… defensive wounds—the fatal wounds," he rambled on, reading to himself as he skimmed the report. "The slivers in the wounds. Definitely something I can look into. Could be something. Could be nothing."

But he couldn't find anything in any of the information that seemed relevant to *this* place. The rest was pretty spot on with what he guessed initially. So there had to be something else here. Something they'd thought wasn't important the first time.

"More details. Look deeper into unrelated objects. Expand your search area. What did we miss?" He recited.

One foot followed the other as he turned absentmindedly in a circle. There was that tree—right by the ramp. It had a good vantage point, high enough to get a fresh perspective of where the first two bodies had been. He started toward it, mumbling with amusement.

"Dad would have laughed," he said, letting the fond memory cloud his mission for a moment. "You'll never have a career in climbing trees," he shook his finger in the air, mimicking the mock sternness his dad used to find so funny. "Well Dad, looks like you were mostly right. I may not have a career *in* climbing trees, but I do have climbing trees *in* my career."

Stretching up onto his tip-toes, he grabbed the lowest limb.

"Let's see how those muscle-ups are working," he muttered, shifting his focus back to work mode.

A couple of hops to gear himself up, then he jumped. His motion was fluid, the execution perfect as he popped up, his feet landing lightly on the branch. Hand over hand he climbed, glancing back now and then until he felt high enough. Then he pulled out his phone, carefully cradling it in one hand, and opened the camera.

Paul pinched and zoomed with his camera—checking every detail of the place. Nothing. A deep sigh of frustration and the phone went back in his pocket. It was safer there for his descent of defeat. He turned to face the tree and as he lowered his foot, it slipped. His heart slammed into overdrive as he found himself scrambling to grab anything that would keep him from a paralyzing fall.

"Holy shit!" he grunted.

The breath exploded from his lungs as he landing chest-first on another branch. He wrapped his arms and legs around it, holding on for dear life.

"Mother…" he hissed, cutting off the curse before it passed his lips.

Slowly, he loosened his death grip and pushed himself upright, pressing his back against the trunk. He stayed there, catching his breath and calming his trembling muscles. When he opened his eyes in preparation for his final descent—there it was—right in front of him. Claw marks that matched the ones on the bodies.

"The plot thickens," he muttered sarcastically, pulling out his camera to capture what he was now sure was evidence.

Paul climbed the rest of the way down, and once his feet were firmly on the ground—opened the photo to compare it with the autopsy report. The marks were identical.

He trudged back to his car, mulling over what the next steps were.

"Nature experts," he mused, logging the idea into his mental notebook. "Trees and wildlife."

With a lead to chase, the station's usual tension didn't weigh on him quite so much. He strode confidently through the doors and settled at his desk, his fingers already flying across the keyboard. A few clicks later, he paused at a title: **Dendrologist**. *Exactly what I need.*

"Kent Hayashi," he read the name off the website. *"No one closer, huh? Not even in these mountains,"* he muttered, eyeing the contact info skeptically.

But it was his only option, so with confident anticipation, he dialed the number.

"This is Kent, how may I share the wisdom of the trees with you today?" came the whimsical greeting.

Paul was pleasantly caught off guard. A tree expert that wasn't a stick-in-the-mud. He thought ironically. He hadn't expected that. So he explained who he was and what information he was looking for.

"Why don't you send those pictures to my email," Kent requested. "And as far as the specific cedar wood you have there—it's actually a tree found in your area. But sadly, due to a disease about forty years ago, we're looking at a species that is exceedingly rare," he paused for dramatic effect. "But if you dare to look hard enough, they can be found in the mountains—outside of town limits."

It felt good to have a lead to chase again. A carrot to dangle in front of him, pointing him in the right direction—or at least the general vicinity. He planned to celebrate with an easy tv dinner and a movie. But the next day he woke with a start—the morning alarm buzzing on his wrist. He'd fallen asleep.

"Story of my life," he said, heaving his tired body off the couch.

He went through the motions, running the razor over his chin. Then his second alarm went off. He had to move faster so he wouldn't be late to work.

A cup of coffee—an email from Kent. Everything seemed to be falling into line. He wasn't at the office yet, but something told him he was on the right track. He just had to convince Captain Dick to let him follow this lead. Paul rehearsed his lines, tweaking his message so it would land with authority.

"I need to get a Sample so we can confirm that it's here," he'd offered. "Then when I find out where some of these rare trees are, we'll have a smaller area to search."

With a grudging and surly agreement from the boss, Paul made his plans–happy for an excuse to go hike the woods he'd grown to love. It was the only place where he felt truly at peace. Being in nature did something for his soul he couldn't quite put a finger on.

25

Adventures of the Cold Kind

The late-morning air filled his lungs. Its sharpness brought that metallic taste to the back of his throat—a sensation he still wasn't sure he'd ever get used to. But nothing was going to bother him today. Not out here. Everything felt fresher, less chaotic than in town. He smirked, knowing he'd gotten the rare privilege of being paid for this little excursion–something that Captain Stingy Pants typically frowned upon. But his reasons were ironclad, so there was no stopping him.

The sound of crunching gravel changed to a soft clomp as the ground turned into a blanket of leaves and pine needles. And with the weight of work being lifted from his shoulders, Paul began to relax, his mood tempered by the quiet authority of the mountains.

His path dropped steeply then took a sharp left. Instead of following the bend, he ducked and weaved between the dense branches to follow his usual route. Keeping to a familiar path would most likely be the best way to find the elusive White Cedar. He couldn't remember seeing any before–but then again, he hadn't been looking. As he stepped out of the tree line, he felt the shift. A subtle change, that if he didn't feel so connected to the earth, might have gone unnoticed.

There was a different kind of energy in the air–palpable– almost as if he could gather it up and use it. And just like it happened every time, his smile widened as the last of his cares melted.

"It's good to be back," he said, breathing in the scent of decaying foliage.

He kicked at a pile of leaves, grinning in delight as the sound sent a shiver down his spine. The ones that were still whole, sparkled as the sun revealed the frosty patterns still clinging to them.

"Port Orford White Cedar," he read aloud, glancing again at the picture to refresh his memory.

Their needles were more fern-like than the typical fir in this area, which would at least make it easier to spot. But when hours passed without so much as laying eyes on an actual fern, his confidence faltered. The sound of buckthorn swishing harmlessly over his Carhart only added to the tension in his clenched fists as he passed yet *another* unhelpful grouping of trees.

"Maybe this wasn't your best plan dummy," Paul sat down in a huff. "I should probably check in with the captain anyway, so he knows where I'm at," he mumbled.

But when he unlocked his phone, he discovered that no amount of raising it overhead or moving to higher ground helped to add bars.

"I'm gonna need a drink after the earful I'm getting tomorrow," he predicted ruefully, dropping it back in his pocket.

As he pondered whether or not to give up for the day, he pulled out his compass. It had been a gift from Mom and Dad on his fifteenth birthday—one that hadn't led him astray yet. He rubbed his thumb over its bronze case. They knew he loved antiques, so they'd found one—tested by the passing of time. And his Father, in his usual way, waxed poetic. Giving Paul a nugget of advice that he'd carried ever since—both literally and figuratively. Partly because he'd had the words etched into the case after he passed.

"A compass may always point true north, but it's your heart that decides which way your feet will go."

Paul smiled softly.

"Alright heart. You heard the man. Lead the way!" he crowed.

As he moved forward with renewed purpose, he had a thought. Kent had mentioned something about the trees thriving in wetter ground—and if he remembered correctly, there should be a lake nearby. So with one eye on the compass, and one on the horizon, he set off in its direction.

Paul broke through a final line of trees, and the lake opened up before him. His breath caught in his throat at the untouched perfection that surrounded it.

"I made it," he breathed, taking in the scene. "I *should* have time to stop and enjoy this. Even if it's just for a few minutes."

He eyed the field of boulders ahead, hesitated for only a second, and stepped forward. He hopped from rock to rock, placing his feet more carefully as their surfaces grew smaller and smoother. When he stepped off the last of them, his feet sank into a beach filled with the smoothest stones he'd ever seen. Paul waded through, enjoying the scratching sounds as they slid against each other.

It was late enough in autumn that a thin layer of ice had begun to form along the shoreline—not thick enough to walk on yet—it'd take a few more nights below freezing for that. Then he felt the quiet nudge of a memory. All those camping trips spent at the water's edge, skipping rocks with his parents. So he gave into the nostalgia and picked up a small stone, found its balance, and launched it as far as he could across the smooth surface. *Kerplunk.* It broke through the ice a hundred yards out. A few more stones whizzed over the surface, sliding and spinning until they too, fell off the fragile edge of the ice shelf. Satisfied with his little side quest, he was just about to move on when something caught his attention.

It was a boulder—nothing unusual about that, given the piles he'd just climbed over. But it was at least a few hundred yards from where it should have been. The strangest part—it was broken cleanly in half. He approached it, his curiosity winning the internal argument between investigating or moving on.

"It's not a clean break," he observed aloud. "Looks like Hulk got his fingers in there and tore it in half," he ran his hands lightly over the ridges, and as he did, he saw an impact point. "Whew!" He whistled. "Maybe it was Stark with *those* cracks. Or is it?" he asked, tapping his chin. "Seems there would be scorch marks if it were *that*. So couldn't be lightning either."

He continued his slow circle, peppering the air with empty guesses. What could have caused something so dense to crack open so easily?

"Another mystery for the books I guess," he sighed and wondered for the hundredth time why so many strange things seemed to find their way in his path lately.

After taking a few pictures to study later, he conceded that it was another puzzle that would most likely go unsolved. Besides, it was getting late and he'd already lingered too long in this place.

Paul glanced nervously at the waning sunlight. He had to find something soon. Showing up to the office empty-handed wasn't an option—not after all the effort he'd spent convincing Captain Richard this trip was worth it. A squirrel screamed at him from the safety of its nest, and he spun to face his accuser.

"My apologies, good sir!" he called back sarcastically, "If you could just point me toward this tree I would get out of your..." The words died in his throat. There, just beneath the nutty herald, was the exact species he'd been searching for. "Praise Jesus and thank you little squirrel man!" he answered gratefully. "Yep! Pictures match and everything."

He shoved the paper into his pocket and flipped his hatchet, catching it smoothly by the handle.

"Best not to tempt the mountains without your finest tool at hand," he quoted—this time, a saying from his mother. "I might just now be realizing that my parents are closeted poets," he reflected, wrinkling his brow.

The sharp blade sliced cleanly through a few smaller branches, which he then shoved in his pack and headed back toward the car.

The freshly chopped branches plumed just above his head, giving him the swagger of a piney peacock. Paul felt accomplished, which meant that he could finally let go and enjoy his time out here. The animals seemed to echo that feeling, suddenly more active than before. Squirrels skittered through the trees, their bushy tails twitching as they chased and taunted one another. A porcupine lumbered slowly through the underbrush–the one animal he was sure to politely gave an extra wide berth. And with a rustle of leaves, out popped a fox, it's bushy red tail drooping momentarily as it cautiously surveyed him. Sensing no danger, it nonchalantly trotted back into the trees.

Crack! Went the sharp snap of brittle wood.

An involuntary hesitation slowed his stride as he peered into the shadows beneath the trees. His heart jumped into his throat. Not fifty feet away was a freshly broken branch–and it wasn't small. The sight spurred him into a quicker pace, hoping that whatever had been there had no interest in him.

As he hurried on, he measured the sky, stacking his fingers between the sun and the horizon.

"Four... no, five fingers," he muttered, squinting with one eye. "That gives me about an hour to get back to the car before I lose all sunlight."

He cast a wary glance upward. Although the radar had shown no signs of a storm this morning, the clouds that were rolling in seemed to have missed the memo.

Then–snap. Another branch.

"Just your mind playing tricks on you, Paul, old buddy," he said aloud, trying to drown out his nerves. "That wasn't a shadowy figure and talking might scare it off."

But it didn't work. His heart and his feet thudded to a halt as a cougar stepped from the trees. It held its head high–those unsettling yellow eyes staring straight into his soul.

"You have *got* to be kidding," he said, keeping his voice low. "Just my damn luck."

He slid a foot slowly back, then the other—cringing at every inch he moved in the wrong direction. He'd already been in a time-crunch, and this would only make it worse—if he survived it of course.

"So far so good," he whispered, a bead of sweat tickling his brow.

She twitched her tail, watching him curiously. So far she didn't appear to be in a mood to attack, which gave him heart. But nonetheless, his hand hovered near the gun he desperately hoped not be forced into using.

"Hey pretty kitty," his soothing voice lilted. "I hope you already had a nice lunch today."

She lowered her head, flicking and turning her ears to catch the sound.

"I have to get back to my car, but I'll never reach it at this pace. Do you think you could go find something else to watch for a while?"

Another few steps back, but this time she took one of her own toward him.

"Oh no kitty, wrong direction. Please go the other way," he begged.

His hand shook as he released the snap that secured his gun to its holster.

"Please don't make me use this thing. I want to be left alone just like you do."

She padded forward a few more paces, sniffing the air. Paul's heart was now pounding a loud and irregular beat as he moved the gun into his hand. He placed his finger alongside the trigger, his every muscle on high alert.

Just as he thought his chest might explode, something drew her attention. Something that *he* hadn't been able to hear. She pricked her ears, breaking their stare-down as her head swung toward the sound. It was just the distraction he needed. His heart pounded wildly. The gun jumped in his hand, and a single shot buried itself in the earth between them. Whatever she'd heard, combined with the blast, was enough. She hissed, leapt, and vanished in a streak of fur and fury. He reholstered the weapon as fading echoes ricocheted into the distance.

"Man… fuck *that*!" He cried, panting and dropping to one knee.

Desire to wait until his panic subsided was strong, but his instincts—born of countless hours in the wild alone—were stronger. So on legs that felt like jelly, he forced himself into a jog. His lungs burned as he raced to make up for lost time.

Minute after long minute dragged by until he reached the edge of a large clearing. Visibility here was good enough that he allowed himself a much-needed break. If she were still coming after him, he'd be able to see her from here. His heavy breathing slowly subsided, and as his brain switched from flight to logic, he realized he'd lost his bearings—nothing his tried and true compass couldn't fix. But in yet another frustrating twist, he stared in disbelief at the erratically spinning needle.

"Just my luck," he groaned dejectedly. "I had no idea there were iron deposits around here."

He leaned against the closest tree, scanning his surroundings for anything that might point him in the right direction.

"Wait," he pushed himself upright, his eyes lighting up. "I've been here before," he snapped his fingers as the vision of that scene resurfaced. "That lady and her animals—they were right there. And I think I came through the far side."

Now that he had his bearings and a familiar path in front of him, he returned the compass to his pocket. But just as he was about to set off, a pattern of deep scores in the rough bark of a nearby trunk caught his eye. He chewed his cheek, furled his brow and found his way to the pictures he'd taken just days before. Yep. It confirmed his suspicions. It was an exact match.

"No way is my luck this good," he said hopefully, running his fingers over the marks.

Click click click. A few new pictures, then he opened the gallery to do a side-by-side comparison. There was no mistaking it. They were identical.

"How the hell did a cat travel all the way from here, take out one of my… victims, then come back? Do they really have that big a territory?"

A sharp, cold gust tugged at his scarf.

"Shit," he muttered, casting a worried glance at the sky.

The clouds had closed in—sometime amid all the distractions—swallowing what little daylight remained. He yanked up his hood, the thick material shielding his ears from the worst of the wind, and pulled his scarf tighter to cover what skin he could.

The sky darkened and the wind whipped into a frenzy, bringing with it more of his mother's sage advice.

"Someday, you may find yourself in a predicament where your know-how must turn into know-now. Trust your instincts. Don't let panic gain the upper hand. And please, don't overestimate your skill. Arrogance will only get you killed."

"Yes mother dearest," he acknowledged wryly. "I'll be sure to keep my head."

The thick flurry of snow and angry wind had reduced visibility to barely a few yards, slowing him down even further. If he kept going, the arrogance his mother warned against would be his undoing. He had to find somewhere to hunker down and wait out the storm—and fast. He no longer had a choice.

So he ducked into the next grove of trees, where the angry howl faded to little more than a whistle. Without wasting a second, he grabbed his hatchet and got to work. Each swing sent a dull ache through his fingers, but the exertion helped thaw the numbness creeping into his toes.

He gathered pine branches and dragged them toward the largest tree he could find—one with low, sheltering limbs already forming the frame of a rough cave. Beneath it, he scraped together armfuls of pine needles, layering them thick across the frozen ground until he had a crude bed and enough to bury his legs and feet.

Minutes dragged into hours, and as the temperature plummeted, so did his resolve to avoid a fire. The risk of giving away his position to its more dangerous residents, no longer outweighed his need to survive. He groggily reached into his pack, pulling out his bag of Vaseline covered cotton balls. When the fire greedily caught the excess wood, he checked his phone to make sure the texts had gone through.

"Maybe I should've told more than one person I was coming out here. What a colossal idiot," he said, shaking his head at his own poor planning. "Time to go over the list of cold facts now. Rule number one: Find shelter. Mission accomplished. Rule number two: Conserve energy and don't sweat. Looks like I messed that up already—but on to three anyway. Never fall asleep when alone in the cold. The chance of not waking up is far too real."

As he listed off all the things that he should do to keep himself safe, he began to feel the weight of the hike, his panicked retreat, and his fight with the harsh weather. Warmth dragged his heavy lids closed as he melted into the musky pine floor. His last visions before he drifted off were of raking claws and a pair of blue eyes that stared unsettlingly into his meager shelter.

26

A Stranger In the Woods

Hayden gazed out the window at the clumped snowflakes pelting the truck. It was their first winter storm of the season—a bit late, which probably explained its fury. When she'd checked the app before their flight, it said nothing would hit until morning. Yet here they were, forced to slow down as sleet turned to snow and the temperature plummeted. Storms arriving earlier than radar predicted were nothing new. After thirty years in the shadow of, or among these mountains, she'd learned to expect the unexpected. Maybe that's why the events and conversations of the past few days didn't feel so surreal.

She smirked, amused by the dots she was connecting. Talking with Mum always helped her string them together. Her thoughts drifted to Matilde. Would that be the last time she ever spoke to her? Matilde's parting words came back to her—something about Hayden getting wings so she could fly.

She glanced at Alec... or Alachor. She wasn't sure what to call him anymore. Then she cleared her throat, breaking the silence.

"This storm looks like it's getting serious," she said.

Alec nodded, unwilling to take his eyes off the slick road. He had to get them both back to Clara safely—though, if he was honest, it was mostly selfish. Two days without her had been harder than he expected. He gripped the wheel, trying to hold back his anticipation. Beside him, Hayden shifted anxiously in her seat, just as eager to get home. They pulled in just as the wind rose to a howl, tearing at their light jackets as though they weren't even there.

"I'd hate to be caught out in this mess," Hayden shouted over the roar of the wind.

The screen door slammed back, yanked from her grasp as she lost the fight with the storm. They burst inside in a flurry of snow and cold, stomped off their boots, and peeled off their freezing layers. Warmth wrapped around her as she stepped into the living room, where a fire crackled in the hearth.

"Mum!" she cried, bounding across the room.

She threw her arms around Clara and squeezed until she heard a grunt.

"You're frozen solid, honey," Clara squeaked through the bear-like grip.

Bérg's nails clicked and clacked on the tile as he danced, waiting as patiently as he could for his moment. When Hayden collapsed by the fireplace, he took his chance—wiggling wildly, circling her in excitement, and covering her face in wet kisses.

Alec had waited respectfully, standing back to let Hayden have her moment with Clara—but in truth, he felt more like Bérg. He just hid it better. As soon as there was an opening, he stepped in. Clara's eyes lit up, mirroring his own joy. He lifted her off the floor, and she giggled, squeezing him tight when her feet touched down again.

"Have you been lifting weights while we were gone?" he asked, pretending to inspect her arm.

"Oh, Alec, don't tease," she said, smacking his shoulder with a laugh. Then, even though it wasn't her home, she slid easily back into hostess mode. "I've got cider and hot chocolate to fight the cold. Hayden, can you check with Tor and Cal if they want some?"

Hayden opened her mind to the link, grinning from ear to ear. Mum had used the old nicknames she'd given their friends, and she could already hear Tormaigh's grumbling protest.

But her smile faded when she realized she couldn't sense Calliope.

"What is she thinking, being out in a storm like this?" she asked Tor, her worry bleeding into the link.

"Don't worry," T

or assured her. *"She should be back soon. Part of her training with the Alchmene focused on survival in harsh conditions. She's smart, with razor-sharp instincts. She'll find her way back."*

But Tormaigh wasn't as calm as she sounded. Calliope had closed her out of their link that morning—which might have been fine if the weather hadn't turned deadly. She wouldn't tell Hayden yet, but she'd already reached out more times than she wanted to admit—with no luck.

The guilt of resting while Mum worked began to set in, so Hayden followed Clara to the kitchen. The three of them chatted about her trip over a tray of snacks that were already laid out in the center of the counter.

Alec leaned on the island, quietly observing Hayden's animated storytelling. She spoke with her whole body—eyes wide, hands flying, her voice rising and falling with emotion. She moved just like Jurtah. Passionate and magnetic. But there was something else too. A flicker of someone he couldn't quite name.

"I just wish Cal were here so I could talk to her about this bracelet," Hayden said with a dramatic sigh, one hand on her hip in thought. "She seems to know more about it than the rest of you Dagrunians."

She rambled on—until her words began to slur, and her excited chatter ground to a halt.

Clara had been busy at the counter, cutting more vegetables— though there were plenty out already. When Hayden's rambling story trailed off, it took Alec snapping his fingers in Hayden's face and calling her name for Clara to realize that something was wrong. She spun around. Hayden stood frozen, still locked in the last sassy pose she'd struck–her eyes unfocused and jaw slack.

Clara rushed to Hayden's side

"Alec, what happened?" she asked frantically.

"I don't know," he replied, his panic bubbling just beneath the surface. "She just zoned out. I've never seen this before."

Bérg whined, sidling up to Hayden's legs, his big brown eyes filled with the same concern they had. Then with a single sharp bark, he bounded to the front door. A blast of wind followed by the sound of thundering hooves announced Tormaigh's arrival.

"Give her some space," Tormaigh said calmly, entering the kitchen. "She's caught in a DriftLink."

Bérg had become calmer now that Tormaigh was present. Sensing Clara's anxiety, he shoved his way between her and Hayden, nudging Clara toward Alec. And it wasn't until Alec wrapped his arm around her waist that Bérg relented. Clara smiled down at him, scratching his head gratefully.

"Thanks buddy. I'm ok as long as she's ok," then casting a glance up at Alec, she asked, "What's a DriftLink and is it dangerous?"

"You have nothing to worry about Clara," Tormaigh replied, laying a soothing hand on her arm. "I've heard of but never encountered it. Someone with unfinished magic is calling to her."

Clara again turned to Alec, searching his face for answers. But he just shrugged, pointing her back to Tormaigh.

"She's the expert on this one. Links aren't my forte–they seem reserved for only a special few."

Tormaigh grinned, nodding. "Special indeed. But to answer your question–not much is known about unfinished magic. Only that it exists. And while it's rare in our world, it would be even more so in yours."

Her gaze stayed fixed on Hayden as she searched for an opening in the Link. But much to her dismay, she couldn't get through. Whoever was trying to reach Hayden commanded her full attention.

A few excruciating long minutes later, Hayden's eyes cleared. She dropped her hand to her side and cast a confused look around the room.

"How the hell?" she exclaimed, drawing in a sharp breath and jumping back when her eyes landed on Tor. "How did you get here?!"

"You don't remember anything?" Tor asked slowly.

Hayden shook her head, looking from one face to another.

"I was talking about our trip and then you just appeared out of nowhere. Why?
What happened?"

Alec exchanged a look with Tormaigh, then explained what they'd seen.

"Huh," she said, chewing her lip in thought. "It appears that I've lost that time," she paused and sat down on the nearest stool. "But I also all of a sudden have this nagging feeling that we need to get to Cal. And soon."

****

Clara stood inside the French doors, peering through the darkness beyond the outside light. It reflected off the flurry of snowflakes, making them glow as they cascaded past the window. Her breath fogged up the glass as she willed the storm to slow down. It was only going to put everyone searching for Calliope at greater risk. Her feet shuffled nervously. Standing here, staring down the blizzard, wouldn't change the fact that they had to go on this rescue mission–if that's what it even was.

She wandered back into the kitchen, where Alec started instructing her on how to help him prepare his calming tea.

"You always seem to know just how to distract me, my dear," Clara said with a soft smile.

Alec dropped the spoon he was holding and turned to take her hand. "I'm sure they'll be just fine," he said, lifting her chin so she'd meet his eyes. "Those three are more than well equipped to handle what's out there. You're allowed to worry–but try not to let it consume you."

She sighed and squeezed his arm. "I know you're right. But it's so hard having to stay behind. I feel useless, tucked away in this cozy house while they're out there fighting the mountains–at night–in a blizzard."

A deep bark from Bérg brought their attention to the front door where Hayden was busy stuffing emergency supplies into her rucksack. She'd initially told him he couldn't come because she didn't want to worry about him on top of everything else. But he'd insisted. Asking Tormaigh to relay a message.

"I may not be like my kin on Dagrune, but I'm nothing like the dogs of this world either. I am Dagrunian. My place is by your side. The Angel was clear that my job is to protect you, and I will not be kept from doing as she asks."

Hayden understood. She was asking him to step away from the one place he felt that he truly belonged. And she knew that feeling too intimately to ask it of him.

"I would never deign to question the Angels instruction–or your loyalty to your birthright," she'd conceded. She then leaned down and pressed a kiss between his eyes. "But no matter how badass of a warrior you become, I reserve the right to give you those any time I want," and to demonstrate just how serious she was, she grabbed both sides of his massive head and gave him a dozen more.

. They stood at the edge of the steep hill–Bérg trembling in anticipation, Hayden bundled in layers against the cold, and Tormaigh looking every bit the majestic Ophrahl. Hayden couldn't help but think of *The Black Stallion*–that first time she'd seen him on screen. Tormaigh looked every bit the part, but somehow, even better–as her feathered legs, mane, and tail billowed in the wind. Then Hayden started laughing. It began as a quiet snicker, building until her body shook and she was nearly out of breath.

"What's so funny?" Tormaigh finally asked.

"Oh, I'll explain it to you sometime when we're not so pressed. But his name was Alec too."

Then Hayden, filled with a renewed sense of urgency led the charge. And they half-walked, half-slid down the hill and into the trees.

Progress was slow. The wind was strong, the snow thick, and visibility near nonexistent. Even with Bérg's superior sense of smell, they couldn't find a single track–Calliope had covered her trail too well. Thankfully, the Link spared them from having to shout over the storm, and they were able to communicate easily between the three of them.

"He says he keeps getting faint traces of a familiar human scent," Tormaigh relayed. *"But he's having trouble placing it."*

They kept to the familiar path toward the training grounds. When they arrived, Bérg suddenly paused. He lifted his head and sniffed the air. A low whine escaped him as he began to dance in place, zeroing in on the whole reason for their mission–he'd finally caught Cal's scent.

"I guess we're headed that way then," tor agreed.

And encouraged by the sign that Calliope was near, she tried to reach her again.

"Tormaigh! How did you find me?" Calliope sounded breathless, but excited to be connected again. *"Forget that,"* she said quickly, shifting gears. *"I found something, and I'll definitely need your help. Where are you? I can guide you to me."*

Tormaigh morphed, the tiny whirlwind that usually accompanied her change lost in the frigid howl of the storm. Though the thick hide of her Ophrahl was better suited for the cold, their link was stronger when they were both Morphé. When she reopened the connection, it was easier to follow the familiar threads of thought she'd grown used to over the seasons. As the draw toward Calliope deepened, she picked up the pace, her hooves finding purchase in the snow as Bérg kept his nose to the ground. He'd caught Calliope's scent—and now, he was on a mission to get to her as fast as possible.

The small break in the closely grouped trees was exactly where Calliope said it would be. The three of them ducked beneath the protective branches, grateful to be out of the worst of the wind. The temperature was still dangerous, but without the constant buffeting, it was at least bearable.

Up ahead, they spotted Calliope—hard at work, weaving a flat contraption from a nearby pile of branches.

The cold clamminess of her sweaty layers and the lingering anxiety from the DriftLink incident hit Hayden all at once.

"Calliope!" she snapped. "We were worried sick! And you're just out here having—what, arts and crafts time? In *this* weather?" She spun in an agitated circle, gesturing wildly toward the sky.

"I know you're mad," Calliope said evenly. "And you have every right to be. But look—he's the reason I was out here all day. I was following him," she tilted her head toward a makeshift structure.

At first, Hayden saw only an odd pile of branches. But as her eyes adjusted to the dim light, the shape resolved into something more deliberate—a shelter. A compact, cave-like structure built with expert hands. Even with her survival training, Hayden wasn't sure she could have made something so seamless. She squinted, trying desperately to part the shadows with her piercing gaze.

Then she saw him—curled up in the heart of it, covered in a blanket of pine needles. Hayden gasped. Without a moment's hesitation, she dove through the doorway. A sigh escaped her lips when she found the steady beat at his wrist. Then it began to grow stronger—a pulse that traveled to her own heart until it filled the air around her. She was in sync with the rhythm. Something about it felt familiar, yet distant. A voice called to her, lost in the darkness of uncertainty. This was magic that she hadn't felt before. But it was so faint that—

"Hayden!"

That had to be Tormaigh's voice. But why did it sound so far away?

"HAYDEN!"

This time it was stronger. Pulling her away from the faint voice beyond her consciousness.

"No," Hayden whispered. "I need to help him."

Then in a rush, she was face to face with Bérg. He'd crawled into the cramped space and was nudging her urgently.

Calliope peered at Hayden through the doorway, her brow furrowed with concern. A small fire crackled nearby, filling the air with the thick, acrid smoke only pine needles could make.

"Finally," she breathed, dropping her shoulders as she released pent up tension. "What do you remember? Anything?" She leaned in, offering her hand.

Hayden turned to find the blanket from her pack draped over the man beside her. She cast a curious glance at Calliope as she accepted the help and crawled out of the shelter.

"Yes, I did," Calliope said, answering the question before it was asked. "All one-thousand heat packs you brought are activated and placed on his heart, arteries, and extremities," she met Hayden's gaze, wagging three fingers in her face. "Now tell us what happened. You were entranced for about five minutes."

Hayden glanced between Tor, Bérg, and Cal. They all wore the same curious expression—one she was certain was mirrored in her own eyes.

"I heard a voice, I guess," she said with a shrug. "I've heard it before, I think. But I can't be sure. I'm sorry, I can't remember anything more."

Calliope heaved herself to her feet, only mildly satisfied with the answer. Beneath her was a stretcher—cleverly crafted from the same pine branches she'd been weaving earlier.

"So that's what you were working on," Hayden said, dragging a hand wearily down her face. "Now I owe you an apology."

"Nah," Calliope said, elbowing her in the ribs. "But if you want to make it up to me, you can provide shelter for the poor guy."

She grinned—one of those sarcastic, toothy smiles that made it impossible not to smile back. And sure enough, Hayden did.

They made an unusual procession—the unconscious stranger draped over Tor's withers, Hayden riding behind to make sure he stayed there, and Bérg curled on the stretcher pulled by Cal. He'd growled in protest when Hayden insisted, but her worry overrode his pride. She was right—his paws weren't used to the cold yet. As they neared home, the wind finally began to ease. Hayden kept trying to coax the man back to consciousness, but the only response she got was the occasional stir and a soft mumble—then he would slip back into his catatonic state.

"Mum!" Hayden called out, bursting through the door in a flurry. "Throw some blankets in the dryer!"

Clara took one look at the unconscious man and turned on her heel toward the laundry room. Alec followed closed behind, filling his arms with load after load of pillows. He stacked them near the fireplace, fluffing them into a cozy nest.

"Who's the guy?" he asked.

Hayden hovered near him, warming her hands near the flame—her newest patient nestled in a cocoon of blankets and pillows.

"He's the one that pulled me into that DriftLink thing," she stared into the fire, bracing herself for more questions.

But they didn't come. Instead, Alec stepped away from primping the make-shift bed and laid a hand on her arm.

"We'll navigate this together. All of us," his gaze bore into her, softening her defenses.

"Okay," Hayden quipped, stepping back from the pile of uncertainty that now filled her living room. "Let's table that and make sure this guy is ok."

The thermometer read 96.8°F. Only one degree lower and he would have been in danger of hypothermia. Hayden was confident the steady rotation of fresh blankets from the dryer would help reverse the drop in his body temp. He'd be better off in a hospital—amid nurses, monitors, and actual doctors. But thanks to the storm and several feet of snow, *she* was the only option he had. Snatching her stethoscope from the hook in the kitchen, she knelt beside him and pressed it to his chest. His heartbeat was strong. That was something, at least.

She straightened and rose to her feet—but when she tried to step forward, her foot got caught up in a pillow. She careened backward, practically collapsing on top of her guest. Then all of a sudden, like something out of a horror movie, he sat up, clamped his hand over her arm and squeezed until she winced from the pressure.

"The veil is torn," he gasped. "The door is opening. You must go soon."

Hayden's head buzzed, the same heartbeat she'd felt in the trees swelling—filling her consciousness with its eerie rhythm. She struggled against his grip, but even with the strength of the Duweot bloodline coursing through her veins, she couldn't free herself.

"You must find it soon," he rasped. "You must not miss it. Find where the veil is thin," his eyes looked empty as he turned—slowly, eerily—in her direction. "Find the veil!"

Then he exhaled sharply, slumped back into the pile of blankets—and started snoring.

"Whelp! I'm out," Alec said, theatrically dusting off his hands before turning on his heel and walking stiff-legged toward the door. Hayden burst into laughter, breaking the tension of the strange moment.

"Phew! Glad that worked," he said, wiping an imaginary bead of sweat from his forehead. "But as much as I hate to be the one to say this, I think we need to pay close attention to that."

He nodded toward the stranger, smoothly moving to Clara's side. Her reaction to the bizarre interaction hadn't been lost on him.

"You're not wrong," Hayden agreed, fatigue from a day filled with travel and rescue beginning to take its toll. "Why don't we all find a place to sleep for the night. Mum, you and Alec take my bed. I should probably be the one to sleep out here with my patient anyway."

Calliope and Tormaigh returned to Ophrahl—Calliope curled into her cat bed, and Tormaigh in the barn. With the house quiet once again, Hayden drifted into a sleep, filled with the restlessness of the day's events.

The sudden movement of her head slipping from her hands jerked her awake. She'd fallen asleep sitting up.

"Right. Living room. Patient," she mumbled blearily.

The man stirred slightly, but he remained deep in slumber—reassuring her that her footsteps wouldn't wake him. Tiptoeing across the room, she paused at the window. She'd only been asleep a short while, but in that time, the storm had passed.

There was something *magically beautiful* about the aftermath of a winter storm. She swayed in the silvery shafts of the midnight moon, eyes closed, feeling its ebb and flow.

She felt different. Like the door to something new had quietly unlocked.

She opened her eyes, and in place of her usual magical light, a softer glow flowed with the moonlight. It illuminated the room, shining just as brightly as the power she drew from the sun.

Then Hayden heard a gasp, and a gentle knock at the door of her link.

"Hayden!" Calliope called, her internal voice filled with awe. *"You have moon magic?!"*

27

Back to the Every Day Stuff

Sounds of a slurred mumble came from the pile of blankets near the fireplace. The fire's greedy flames had long since diminished, leaving trails of glowing embers etched into the smoldering logs. The man sat up to rub his eyes, clearly disoriented. But to Cal and Hayden's relief, it seemed he wasn't actually awake. He laid back down, returning to his previous state of slumber. The distraction was just enough to break herself away from the influence of the moonlight. And as she left the trance-like state, the baffling new glow faded.

"For about the umpteenth time, I find myself asking the question," she whispered. "What the fuck was that mess?"

She'd gotten used to the feeling of her magic, but whatever happened in the face of the moon felt different. It wasn't less powerful, just a different kind of connection.

"I'd ask you to explain, but it didn't feel dangerous, and I really do need to get some sleep," Hayden murmured to Calliope, her words slurred with exhaustion.

She stumbled toward the couch and collapsed, letting her heavy eyelids take over for the second time that night.

****

"Bérg!" she cried, frantically.
The swollen river threatened to breach its eroding banks—
roaring around logs and boulders jammed into the shoreline,
that despite the water's violent pull refused to give way. From
across the river, she glimpsed his drenched head now and
then, bobbing toward her—barely visible as he fought to keep
it above the churning surface. He surged past, missing her
outstretched arms by inches as the current dragged him
farther downstream. She could see how desperately he swam
toward her, but every effort only seemed to push him away.
His pleading eyes locked onto hers as the river swallowed him
whole.

"I'm sorry! I couldn't save you!" she screamed.

Tears streamed down her face, falling into the raging river.
The moment her tears touched the surface, the rapids stilled—
as if soothed by the depth of her sorrow.

A glint caught her eye upstream and though her heart
still ached from watching her best friend get swept away.
Only a few rocks blocked her path. Then a few more—and a
few more. They sprang up in an endless stream, as if
determined to test her patience.

"Damn to hell these stupid rocks!" she snapped. "I just want
to see what that was!"

Whether out of pity or tiring from their petty game, the rocks
relented, finally letting her stumble into a small inlet. There,
draped over floating debris, was the familiar gray form of
Calliope—her bow still strapped tightly to her back.

She rushed into the water, dragged her to dry ground, and
collapsed in grief—cradling Calliope's lifeless body. Angry,
painful sobs tore from her throat. She threw her head back,
ready to scream at the sky.

But something caught her attention, cutting off her lament mid-breath.

A small boy stood on the opposite bank, staring past her with wide, unblinking eyes. In his hand, he held a staff easily twice his height. Slowly—effortlessly—he raised it, pointing at something behind her.

At first, Hayden didn't care to look, too bogged down by the weight of her grief. But when she glanced down, Calliope was gone.

She twisted around just in time to glimpse a strange ebb and flow of red fire vanishing behind a distant hill. The light flickered once more, then faded completely.

She spun back toward the boy, ready to demand what had just happened—but the child was no longer there.

In his place stood a tree unlike anything she'd ever seen. Its oddly colored branches curled toward the sky, twisted like pipe cleaners wrapped too tightly around a stick. And as if that weren't strange enough, massive flowers—each the size of a Volkswagen Beetle—bloomed above it, their wide petals slowly unfurling, as if beckoning her closer. Then the river suddenly vanished, taking with it the pain in her chest, and lump in her throat.

Now she was in an abandoned building, hanging precariously over the edge of a cliff. Hayden was already in the middle of it—too far to run if the foundation gave way.

She tipped her head back, mouth agape, marveling at the perfectly spaced black pillars that soared overhead. They supported a single massive stone slab that served as its roof. Everything about this place felt uninviting—from its cavernous vastness to its oppressive lack of color.

She felt herself pulled unwillingly, farther from the safety of solid ground. An unseen force drove her forward, then slammed her into a wall. All breath left her lungs in a huff as she stared into the misty void below.

Her hands tingled and her lungs filled with a strange emptiness—like she didn't want to breathe, even if she could.

Though the stone barrier was tall, she could still see the stress lines in the beams and wondered how they held **her** up— let alone the crushing weight of the structure around her.

She scanned the skyline, taking in every peak, every valley, every tree. Her unusually sharp vision caught the occasional glint of mountain streams and lakes. Then she began to notice—where there should have been echoes of birdsong, there were none. Not even the slightest wind whispered through the trees.

Here, there was no color. Everything was touched by the bleak shadows of gray and black.

A cold shiver ran up her spine. The feeling that something else was in this vast empty space with her. Reluctantly, Hayden turned to face it. Her heart lurched into an uneven rhythm and her feet turned to lead. The tattered black robes. The skeletal features. The evil grin stretched ear to ear on its unsightly face. And the blue, pulsing light—it was all familiar. Where had she seen them? She'd faced this enemy before, but something was blocking her from remembering.

"What do you want?!" She called out frantically.

As the last of her courage bled away, she dropped harshly to her knees. The creature stared at her—soundless—the black void of its eyes boring through her. It didn't speak. It didn't move. It only fed the overwhelming terror pounding in her skull.

"Wake up. It's the only way!" she screamed.

Just for a second, a vision of her bedroom flickered between her and the creature. And in that flash, Hayden remembered that she had to get back there.

"Stand up you idiot!" She said through gritted teeth.

But her body didn't respond. And with that realization, the panic she'd been holding at bay crashed into her— overwhelming and complete.

Then the bullets came.

They ricocheted off the pillars, passing straight through the creature as if it weren't even there. Still, it held her in its unrelenting, dead-eyed gaze—mocking her fear, reveling in her helplessness.

She struggled again, willing her limbs to move, to flee, to do anything. That's when the pillars began gliding toward her—swimming through the floor, which crumbled into sand ahead of them. The closer they came, the smaller they shrank, drawing the massive ceiling slab lower and lower, stealing what little breath she had left.

The barrage intensified, the bullets singing past her in a menacing chorus. Then they found their mark.

Two holes tore through her. Then three. Then four.

She stared, stunned, at the bloodless wounds.

With a sickening crunch, the weakened beams gave way. The last thing she saw was her own limp body tumbling over the cliff's edge into the misty blackness.

Above it all, the creature hovered effortlessly, its sharp teeth glinting in triumph as the broken stones and shattered wood rained down into the valley below.

******

Hayden twitched, her entire body caught in the violent re-emergence from the dream. She sat up, rubbing her eyes, trying to rid herself of the lingering memory—sorting nightmare from reality. She could still feel the sadness of her emotional hangover in the pit of her stomach, even though—in reality, she knew Bérg and Calliope were alive and well. But something about it remained unsettling. Was it supposed to mean anything? Up until the last few months, she would have brushed it off as yet another nightmare her mind conjured from real-life experiences. Now, she wasn't so sure of herself.

Her eyes shifted to the pile of blankets. They were tossed to the side with no stranger in sight. The sound of silverware clinking and the soft murmur of conversation drifted from the kitchen. Then the unmistakable smell of bacon filled the air, reminding her that she hadn't eaten in almost twelve hours.

"Of course Mum's cooking already. And why shouldn't she?" Hayden mused, pushing herself off the couch. "She got a new test subject— trapped by a couple feet of freshly fallen snow."

Clara flitted about the kitchen, somehow still able to master the familiar stare-down she reserved for her newest victims. The man's hand trembled nervously as he lifted a fork cradling his first bite. Hayden smirked. *Mum must have whipped up a new recipe with that look on her face.*

"She's up!" Clara exclaimed as Hayden stepped out of the living room. "Paul, this is Hayden. Hayden, Paul," she nodded between them, making sure to catch Hayden's eye. "He's a detective working the case of the triple homicide a couple months back. Isn't that right dear?"

Clara flicked her gaze to Paul, and he offered a tight smile, avoiding eye contact.

"Pleasure to meet you," he said, holding out a hand. "I don't know how you found me out there, but I'm quite sure If you hadn't, I would've been toast."

He looked up at her and she looked down at him. Hayden could always tell if a man felt intimidated by her height. But Paul held her gaze without flinching. She smiled back at him, relieved that she didn't need to diminish herself to make him feel better.

"You look much better than when we brought you in last night," Hayden dropped his hand, stepping back to size him up. "Do you remember anything from the time you fell asleep until you woke up this morning?"

She reached out, palm up.

"Hand please, then remove your socks. I need to check your toes too."

Paul looked to Clara for assurance just as the bedroom door squeaked open. Alec emerged, trotting down the hall to join them. Clara shrugged, planting a quick kiss on his lips before responding.

"Better do what the doctor says."

She then busied herself making up a plate for Hayden and Alec as Paul obediently peeled his socks off.

"Satisfied?" he asked, wiggling his toes at her.
Hayden nodded, accepting the plate from Clara's outstretched hands. Then she smothered her pancakes in peanut butter and topped them with a generous pour of maple syrup.

Paul's account of his hike the day before ended with a harrowing story about a cougar.
"Ever run into one out there?" he asked Hayden.

"Well, certainly not like you have. You're just lucky, I guess," she said, dipping her bacon in the leftover maple syrup.

"Not so sure I'd slap a 'lucky' label on that just yet," he snorted.

Bérg whined from the doorway, waiting as patiently as possible. Bacon was his favorite treat. Even though he drooled in anticipation, he wouldn't dare break Hayden's rule: no entering the kitchen during mealtime unless invited.

"Okay, here you go, buddy," Hayden finally relented. "You earned this one."

The plate clinked as it hit the floor. His nails skittered against the tile as he launched into motion, and they laughed as he practically dove headfirst into his prize.

"Wait a minute," Paul said, tapping his chin in thought. "You wouldn't happen to have a horse, black as the midnight sky, would you?" He stared at Bérg as recognition washed over his face.

"Yes," Hayden confirmed, studying him for a confused moment. "She's the only reason I got you home last night."

"Well that certainly answers some pressing questions."

Paul threw his head back, and the deep baritone of his laugh made them all smile. He got up, moving around the counter to gather the dirty dishes.

"The idea of you carrying me all the way here just didn't make sense. But that's actually not why I asked. I thought I recognized Bérg."

He turned on the water, waiting for the steam to rise as it reached scalding temps, then sighed as he let the scorching water run over his hands. Hayden opened the cupboard next to him and handed him the bottle of dish soap and a rag.

"I was hiking last week, and I passed you lounging in a clearing with Bérg, your cat, and your horse. It was the same clearing that I hiked through today. What a strange coincidence."

"Strange coincidence indeed," Hayden agreed, leaning against the counter, her arms crossed—a look of quiet reserve settling on her face. "I remember someone hiking by that day, but you weren't close enough for me to recognize you. I suppose my little ragtag crew would have made quite the impression."

Their conversation switched to more practical things as Hayden conceded to being snowed in.

"Not sure how work usually goes for you," she said, herding everyone to the living room, "but you may as well settle in for a day or two. Not only is this the first storm of the season, but the roads around here are last priority for the county. That wind probably did a pretty solid job drifting them over, so you won't be able to get to your car until the plows come through."

She wasn't stoked about having a detective in her house for that long—especially considering how close to home his case was to them. But he didn't have anywhere to go, and she wasn't about to kick him back out into the cold.

"I guess I have no choice then," Paul said, pushing down the sense that he was imposing on them. "If I'm stranded, the chance to take a shower and wash my clothes would be greatly appreciated. But only after I call my captain," he tapped his screen. No bars. He sighed—a deep, frustrated, exasperated breath.
"I should have known. My cell service sucks up here. He's probably been trying to get ahold of me for a while. Do you have a phone I can use?"

"You're welcome to mine," Hayden said without missing a beat. "Service is decent—had to make sure I picked the right provider, living this far out."

Calliope wandered down the hall with Paul, purring as she snaked between his legs. She wasn't going to let him out of her sight. A small part of her felt responsible for bringing him into their house. He was the one person who might find a connection between Hayden and the lives she herself had taken. She wasn't worried he'd suspect her in her current form, but she'd been there when he found her marks on the tree at the edge of the training grounds. And when he mumbled his suspicions out loud, she could tell that he was smart. It was only a matter of time before his investigation led him back to their door. So it was imperative she eavesdrop on his conversation—just in case.

Pretending to be fully engaged in a bath, she paused momentarily at the sound of the angry voice on the other end.

"How could someone berate him after everything he'd just been through?" she puzzled. *"Hadn't he already suffered enough?"*

"I don't pay you to sit in front of a fire and drink hot chocolate!" The unpleasant voice screeched.

"I know sir. I can make it up by working the weekend," Paul replied, resigning himself to taking the abuse—yet again.

He tapped the end call button and stared out the doors at the end of the hall. Calliope could sense him trying to keep his emotions in check, not wanting to bring that energy back to the others. His voice dropped to a low growl.

"You don't pay me for a lot of things," he said, his jaw clenched.

Then he turned, dragging his feet back down the hall to rejoin the others.

"Your boss sounds like a terrible person," Clara said boldly when Paul rejoined them. "I could hear his awful rant from here."

"You know, just between us–he really is," Paul replied, relieved he didn't have to keep up some ridiculous farce.

He was tired of always feeling the need to defend a man who didn't deserve any grace–especially one who offered none to anyone else.

"None of my colleagues like him either," Paul continued. "He's a broken-down relic who needs to retire and leave the rest of us alone," he gave a half-smile. "Anyway, a nice hot shower should wash away some of the negativity... along with this stink."

Steam puffed from the bathroom door as Paul emerged looking refreshed, the scent of Hayden's favorite body wash trailing behind him like a floral cloud.

"Now that I smell like roses, would it be rude of me to take a nap?" He asked, sounding more relaxed. "I know I practically just woke up, but I still can't seem to shake the run-down feeling. And I have this whole day where I'm not obligated nor am I able to be any particular..."

Clara cut him off with a wave.

"Oh goodness, not at all dear! You don't have to explain yourself. You're no bother to us in the least."

Hayden's bemused smile widened as Clara glanced her way with a look she knew all too well. To the untrained eye, it might have seemed friendly enough–but Hayden had spent years on the receiving end of that expression. She knew exactly what it meant: she didn't have a say in this. Once Paul was tucked into the guest room, Clara practically dragged Hayden to her own bed.

"If you thought he looked tired, you should take a look in the mirror. You all had a long ordeal last night and didn't get enough rest. BED!" She barked over Hayden's protests.

"Yes Mum," Hayden squeaked playfully.

A new day dawned, the warmer weather just enough to start melting the top layer of snow. Card and board games only held their attention for so long before they gave in to idle chatter. Hayden and Paul bonded over a mutual love of cooking and immediately started planning an extravagant lunch. They worked easily together—chopping vegetables, debating seasonings, and arguing about the best way to cook the meat. He brought the conversation back to his harrowing experience with the mountain lion, grilling her about its behaviors and how often she'd run across it.

"Sorry—I can't help you with this one," she said, shaking her head. "Some kind of wildlife expert would be better suited for those questions," Hayden hovered over the oven, watching the meat thermometer needle creep upward. "My patients tend to be a bit less... dangerous," she flashed a smile his way, the pan full of chicken sizzling in her hands as she nudged the door closed with her foot. "That should do it!" she beamed.

They busied themselves—plating each dish, arranging them until they looked like edible art.

"Five stars. No notes," Alec sighed, sitting back and rubbing his stomach.

He reached for Clara's hand, pulling her back into her chair before she could push away from the table.

"You, my dear, won't be lifting a finger today. The kids and I can take care of this. Right guys?"

He winked as he began to gather the empty dishes with Hayden and Paul following his lead.

"I'm beginning to understand that I'll never escape that label," Hayden teased.

The company had been pleasant, the conversation smooth, and the food fit for a queen. But when the sound of a bucket scraping pavement echoed by, she felt a surge of relief. She needed to get her privacy back so they could have open conversation about what Paul's presence could mean. And there was also the pressing matter of his prophecy—for lack of a better term. She knew beyond the shadow of a doubt that it had been a sign, though she wasn't quite sure what it was pointing to.

"Looks like I can finally bring you back to your car!" Hayden said a little too cheerfully.

"She didn't mean that," Clara scolded. "You take care of yourself and make sure you go see a doctor for those hands. Don't mess around with frostbite," she fussed over him like a mother hen. Gathering his things and making sure that he didn't forget anything. "And don't you dare let that boss of yours take away your happiness. He doesn't deserve that kind of power."

"Yes ma'am," he agreed, a soft smile playing on his lips. "You sound like my Mamma. I believe that you and she would get along quite wonderfully."

****

He made them promise to keep in touch before trudging out into the blinding landscape once again. When he climbed into Hayden's truck and they turned out of her driveway toward his car, he felt a twinge of sadness. Until now, he'd forgotten how much he missed the comfort of belonging—with people and something bigger than himself. He'd been so busy trying to make his career happen, that he'd moved to a place where he didn't have anyone close by. He would have to fix that. His Mamma deserved that much.

The comical sight of his car piled high with snow—right in the middle of an otherwise perfectly plowed parking lot—sent them into throes of laughter.

"It almost looks like a page out of a Dr. Seuss book," he chortled.

After just a couple of days in Hayden's presence, he was well aware she wouldn't let him dig the car out alone. They panted, barely able to hold a conversation as they shoveled heavy snow into the growing piles the plows had started. He couldn't help but wonder how she kept going while he needed frequent breaks.

"Do you do CrossFit or something? Because I have no idea how you haven't needed a breather yet," he asked, one hand braced on his knee, his breath puffing out in little white clouds.

"No—better!" she laughed. "These mountains, almost twenty years of Jiu Jitsu, and being on my feet most of the day at work... I'm sure it all works together."

The last shovelful was finally cleared, and he was soon on his way back into town. He waved out the window, casting a final glance in the rearview at the idling red truck—and the woman leaning against it, her arms crossed.

Mystery surrounds that one. Ain't no doubt about it, he thought, just as the rolling hills swallowed her from view.

He absently rubbed the jagged scar on the back of his hand. It had been bothering him more over the past few months—worse than when he'd first gotten it—and his recent brush with hypothermia hadn't helped.

The looming office building came into view far too soon, dragging with it the familiar feeling of his soul bleeding positivity. This place fed on his spirit like a leech, making that freezing night in the forest seem more tempting by the second. He steeled himself against the worst as he trudged up the long hallway. He stopped just shy of the Captain's doorway. There was no way to avoid the tongue lashing that was coming.

"I suppose you expect some sort of hazard pay or something for that little stunt the other day," Captain Richard seemed distracted as he searched his desk for something and Paul couldn't help the thought that ran through his head.

If you kept things more organized, idiot, you might actually find something once in a while.

He grinned inside. Even thinking it made him feel a bit smugger.

"Well, I looked into it already," Captain Richard snapped, "and it doesn't qualify. But don't worry, you'll still get paid for the hours you would have worked," he slammed his hands on his desk in frustration, finally looking Paul in the eye. "I'm sure you've got some reports to write or something, so you'd better hop to it. Oh, and you told me you had to discharge your weapon, so make sure you get your paperwork squared away for that."

Paul politely nodded then made his escape back to his desk.

He plopped down in the worn chair. It squeaked in its usual way as he planned his next few hours. He grappled with the idea of whether or not to include his stay at Hayden's. But if he left it out, it would leave a suspicious hole in the timeline. He had no choice—unless he wanted to risk the career he'd worked so hard toward. Paul stared at the thick folder with the three autopsy reports, ran his hand over the needles on the pine branch, and pondered the idea of a murderous mountain cat moving outside its territory. None of it added up. Maybe he could unmuddy the waters with a phone call to Kent.

Or—he could take Hayden's advice and reach out to a wildlife expert. He picked up the reports, idly perusing them again.

"You've got to be shittin' me!" He whispered.

He snatched the phone off its cradle, dialing Freyja's work number with trembling fingers. He had to talk to her. She might be able to confirm his suspicion. Maybe the mountain ordeal hadn't been such a big coincidence after all.

<u>28</u>

A Difficult Discovery

Paul twirled the phone cord on his finger. It had already rung three times and with each additional ring, his anxiety only grew. Voicemail. Damn, he'd have to leave a message. It was too late in the day for lunch, so he assumed she might be in the middle of an autopsy.

"Gross!" He said quietly as the thought of both things together settled in his mind.

He nudged himself back into work mode, hoping to erase the disturbing thought. What other things could he look into in order to keep the ball rolling? Oh, right! He had those pictures of the claw marks.

"Who - do - I - contact - about - mountain - wildlife," he whispered as he typed. "Naturalist... dot org domain, aaannd... contact—there's the number."

His thumbs flew over the screen. The first number went straight to voicemail, the second rang endlessly, and the third blasted an ear-splitting "out of service" message into his eardrum. He was starting to feel slightly discouraged as he slowly dialed another. But to his relief, a friendly voice drawled a hearty hello.

"Yeah, I know a thing or two about the big cats out here. You said you had a run in with one?"

She sounded friendly and eager to help. Paul explained what he was after and why, tossing in a short snippet of his ordeal. She gave a low whistle, with surprise and a hint of awe edging her voice.

"That must have been real nerve wracking for ya! Well I sure am glad you got outta there ok."

Paul's mouth twitched in amusement—he hadn't expected someone quite so boisterous with the title of Naturalist.

"Why doncha send them pictures to my cell. That way we can stay on these here phones," a buzz sounded as the message went through. "Now that don't look right fer cougar-sized. And they're going in all the wrong direction too. Cougar marks go sky to grass and are longer than these. You'll see that when they're scratchin' trees sometimes to sharpen their claws. These are too close together and tipped more at an angle. How far apart did you say these two spots were?"

"I would say about 60 miles," Paul replied, lounging back as though he were talking to an old friend.

She rambled on, offering tidbits that weren't entirely relevant to the situation. But the conversation was pleasant, so he let it go on longer than he otherwise might have—taking notes just in case.

"One hundred and fifteen square miles. That's quite the territory," he said, raising his eyebrows. "Which leaves the two locations well within that range."

Still, even the naturalist agreed: a cougar wouldn't just wander into a populated area unless something was pushing it out of its home. He tossed the notes into the file. At least he knew more now than he had a few minutes ago and it was one more interview checked off his list. The Captain couldn't say he wasn't moving the case forward anymore.

Reaching for the phone again, he hesitated. His neck pulsed with the sudden spike in his heart rate, and his palms turned clammy. The butterflies were back. They'd arrived the first time he'd heard Kent's voice, and resurfaced every time he thought about their conversation. No one could find out he'd gone searching for him on social media. But he'd done it anyway–because he had to be certain he wasn't taking an interest in someone who couldn't return his feelings.

"Oh, this is ridiculous," he grumbled, forcing a breath as he grasped the receiver.

Paul's heart caught in his throat when Kent answered on the first ring.

"Hey there. How's my favorite detective doing? Did you find what you were looking for?" he asked, in that cheery, tempting voice.

"Well, I went to the place, and the snow—I mean, the car—there was a lion."

Paul was mortified.

Heat crept into his cheeks. He wished he could melt into the chair, never to be seen again. But he was a professional. So he straightened and did his best to smooth over the awkward moment.

"Um… wow. Let me have another crack at that," he said, letting out a huge sigh.

Paul heard Kent's chuckle at his blunder, which did nothing to soothe his already frayed nerves.

"Yeah, let's try that," Kent replied, his smile shining through his words.

Paul dropped his head into his hand, closed his eyes, and launched headlong into the story of the last couple days. Kent interjected at all the right moments, asking clarifying questions and sounding engaged, curious–even invested. The conversation flowed easily now, smoothing over the initial embarrassment like it had never happened.

"I think we should meet halfway if you can," Kent offered, and Paul's heart lurched at the invitation. "I know a long drive might not work for your boss, but what if you cut it in half?" He paused. "Of course, I feel it would be most prudent for me to confirm the tree species in person. For the record."

Paul heard the muffled grunt of a throat being cleared—like Kent had pulled the phone away to do it. He couldn't help the smile that crept onto his lips.

"I think I could swing that," Paul agreed, doing his best to keep any unprofessional excitement out of his voice. "If the boss doesn't OK it on the clock, I'll go anyway. This seems pretty important to the case."

He carefully set the receiver back on its cradle. He had to have imagined it. They'd only had one real conversation before this. Kent couldn't possibly be interested… could he? As luck would have it, Freyja called back just minutes after he'd ended the call. He needed the distraction to pull his heart back from the hope it entertained.

****

Paul stepped through the door, greeted by the earthy, nutty aroma of freshly roasted coffee.
They did it the right way here—at least, in his opinion. Roasting the beans on site made all the difference. Not only did it smell amazing—it made the coffee taste better too. The ambiance settled over him as he pulled the door shut, stepping fully into the warmth. He scanned the shop, relieved to see just one other person tucked away in the far back corner—half-swallowed by a circle of bean bags and deeply engrossed in a book. Good—no eavesdroppers. The things they had to discuss were of a sensitive nature, so it would be better without an audience.

"I'll take a large medium roast with a splash of oat milk, a couple dollops of maple syrup, and a pinch of cayenne if you've got it, please."

The barista nodded, turning with a theatrical flair to fill the order. The light caught a hint of glitter smeared across his cheek—and Paul smiled. It reminded him of his college days, and how much he'd once loved such things.

He tapped his leg, waiting patiently—when a fresh burst of cold air filled the shop. Freyja stepped over the threshold, looking nothing like the woman he'd met before. If her face hadn't been so distinctive, he might not have recognized her at all. Her bright pink wool coat and knit rainbow boots stood in stark contrast to the muted colors of the decor. Her grey hair no longer in a bun, flowed to her shoulders in soft silvery streaks, curling gently at the ends. Her glasses looked nothing like the ones she'd worn when he first met her. Those were plain, surrounded with a thin, barely there rim—but these? These had a personality all their own—horn-rimmed, sparkling, and shifting color in the light. An iridescent chain dangled from them, which disappeared into a black scarf. The stern look she'd worn a few days ago was replaced with one of mischief.

"You look absolutely bewildered, my dear!" she laughed.

It bubbled out of her with the ease of a sunbeam melting morning frost.

"I often get that reaction when someone sees either the work version of me or the real me—and then the other. Imagine being that dull outside of work! I think not!"

He pressed his lips together, cringing as he realized he'd been staring at her in open-mouthed confusion.

"I've been rendered speechless a couple times in the last few days," he smiled, raising an eyebrow at her. "Let's just add this to the count."

Paul stepped aside to let her order a drink—which much to his surprise, was a plain black coffee.

They found a booth, scooting in on opposite sides. Her eyes twinkled, daring Paul to question her as they both took their first sips. And Paul accepted the silent invitation, unable to resist.

"Love love love this look! But there's something else."

He tapped a curled finger against his lips, studying her face. Without a doubt, this version of her was going to be his new favorite person.

"I do believe that I detect a slight shift in your accent."

Paul winked, and Freyja giggled.

"Quite right," she said, setting her mug down with a tilt of her head. "I know it seems odd. But in my line of work—things can be rather taxing on the mind. This is truly who I am. I only bring *her* out for the serious matters," she jerked her head in the direction of the morgue. "I do hope you understand."

If there was one thing that Paul understood intimately, it was the need to be a chameleon.

"You don't owe me an explanation. I'm more than happy to roll with it. And I may just understand where you're coming from more than you realize."

Freyja wrinkled her brow, processing the unspoken admission. Her gaze flicked to the scar on his hand as the understanding in her eyes replaced a brief flash of pity.

"I'm truly sorry you have to go through that," she said, patting his hand in a gesture of solidarity.

He placed his other hand on top of hers. It was strange–this immediate, quiet connection with a stranger.

He pulled his hands back, wrapping them around his mug as he dropped his gaze.

"Now I feel bad asking you about work things when you aren't in work mode."

But Freyja waved him off with a smile.

"Oh pish posh! I don't mind in the slightest. What query do you have for me today that couldn't be asked over my mobile?"

Paul smirked. The way she seemed so completely at ease– that was the positive energy he sought out in friendships. They were, in his experience, the most trustworthy people. His thoughts wandered to his day at Hayden's, and he wondered if maybe–just maybe–the universe had finally decided to bring him something good.

"Right. To business," he pulled a folder from his bag and set it on the table. "I was reading through the report for the thousandth time this morning, and something caught my attention–something I must've skimmed over the first nine hundred and ninety-nine," he flipped through the pages. "You mentioned defensive injuries on all three victims. Let's see… Pete–fractured thyroid cartilage due to blunt trauma to the throat and trachea."

He shuffled the papers, searching for the next report. Freyja remained still–back straight, wrists crossed–but leaned in politely every time he pointed to another detail.

"Ah, here we go. Seth had a broken nose–which is pretty self-explanatory–and Sam… a ruptured eardrum."

He paused and looked up. "Could these have been injuries they gave each other before they died?"

Freyja sat back, studying him intently for a moment.

"Those injuries…" she said slowly. "In all my years as a medical examiner, I've only ever seen that kind of precision from someone who knows exactly what they're doing. A trained fighter, most likely," she tapped the pages between them. "If you read on, I do try to outline their physical condition. Not one of them looked like they'd set foot in a gym in the last decade. Which rather points to someone else being involved, doesn't it?" She paused, then pushed her glasses up her nose with deliberate emphasis. "But here's the thing—there were no fresh bruises. No scrapes. Not one defensive mark you'd expect to see from a bit of a dust-up. Nothing to suggest they turned on each other. Whoever did this… they were strong. Tracheas may be delicate, but they don't go just like *that*."

Paul slumped back in his seat. He had his suspicions, but they were too ambiguous to draw any conclusions yet. He still needed more evidence.

"I did, however, come across a couple of curiosities I chose not to include in the report," she said, her tone shifting just enough to make Paul lean in. "First–an unusual clumping of rapid-onset scar tissue on Seth's brain. It was smack dab in the middle of his amygdala. Just as if something frightened him so badly, it left a physical mark. And then there was the hair. Feline in appearance–but the test was baffling. Far too many markers spanning across species… including human. It didn't make a lick of sense. Then I examined it under the microscope and it was nearly impossible to keep in view. Almost as if it were… flickering. Slipping in and out of focus.”

Paul narrowed his eyes, scanning her expression for any trace of jest. But she was utterly serious.

“There's got to be an explanation, though. Right?”

Freyja tilted her head, then gave a regretful shrug.

“Oh, I certainly hope so. I reached out to colleagues I trust implicitly–not the sort to cart me off to a padded room, mind you. But no. No one had anything to offer. Not even a halfway reasonable theory.”

They spent a few more minutes tossing around ideas, grasping for some explanation that might make sense of the strange findings–but in the end, they were no closer to an answer rooted in reality. Paul thanked Freyja for her time–and this time, he was the one who promised to keep in touch. Then he slid behind the wheel and headed toward Sandstone Ridge.

Although the name made it sound like a cliffside town in the desert, Sandstone Ridge was nestled in a valley, surrounded by snow-laden peaks. A river curved along the southern edge, carrying chunks of ice that bumped against the shoreline and each other in slow procession.

Paul nearly slid into his parking spot as he fought the slushy roads. They hadn't gotten as much snow here, but the warmth of the last few days had turned driving conditions into a sloppy mess. He swung one foot out stepping straight into a pile of half-melted slush.

He cursed, inspecting his pant leg. Just a couple of splashes on the cuff. It could've been worse.

“Why is no one slowing down in these conditions,” he muttered through clenched teeth, flinching as another car flew by, far too close for comfort.

He slammed the door shut and scurried to the sidewalk, away from the spray of reckless drivers. Then, shaking off the negative energy, he pulled out his phone and opened his navigation app.

His destination was close—only another hundred yards or so to the front door. He pressed the pedestrian call button. **WAIT**. The electronic voice instructed. **WAIT**. He pressed it again. **WAIT**. Someone cleared their throat over his shoulder.

"Oh sorry—nervous tic," he apologized, startled and slightly embarrassed that he hadn't noticed him standing there.

The walk signal lit up, and Paul stepped quickly off the curb, eager to put distance between himself and the man who, he was sure, despised the very ground he walked on. Just then, a car skidded around the corner—sending a wave of slush, salt, and grime—splashing across the entire front of his coat and pants.

"Goddammit!" he gasped. "Just my goddamn luck!"

The cold seeped through to his skin as he shook the worst of the mess from his hands. The man hurried past, mumbling something about tough luck—and Paul was more than glad to let him put the distance between them.

If he hadn't just driven so far he would have considered tucking tail and heading back home. This was not how he envisioned himself meeting up with a specialist. He took great pride in looking professional whenever he was out in public—that was the reputation he wanted to build. Not this sloppy, slush covered version. Meeting anyone new in this condition was unacceptable—but Kent? The thought gave him pause.

"Nope. You're here for the case. Nothing else," he said, redirecting himself—then cast a quick glance around to make sure that no one had heard him.

"Guess I'm calling him," he grumbled with the reluctance of one who was desperate, but left with no other recourse.

Barely a ring this time, then Paul catapulted into his recently acquired predicament before he could change his mind.

"No way," Kent said intensely before Paul could get it all out. "I'm not letting you sit in discomfort for our meeting. Why don't you just come up to my apartment so you can borrow some clothes."

Paul was taken aback. He hadn't expected an invitation at all—let alone the fact that Kent had an apartment here.

"I can't ask you to go out of your way for this... but—hold up. Didn't you say you lived two hours south of here?"

He yanked open the door to the restaurant, realizing as he spotted the sign that it was part of a bigger apartment complex. It wasn't anything special. In fact, he was almost relieved to have his firearm on his hip as he took in the worn carpet and elevator buttons—pressed so many times, their numbers had long since been rubbed off.

"I'll tell you about that when you aren't soaked in road sauce," Kent promised. "But really and truly. It's no trouble at all. I have more clothes than I know what to do with—so if they fit you well, you're more than welcome to hang onto them. Just tell me your size—I'll pull some stuff that's close."

Paul pressed the button for the fourth floor. This trip was turning out to be so much stranger than anything he could have imagined in even his wildest version. He gave Kent his sizes, then leaned back against the elevator wall as it lurched upward. The lights flickered, and his mind wandered—bringing his thoughts to ghosts, iron, and salt.

The elevator doors squeaked as they peeled back, *reluctantly—like two lovers, loath to leave each other's presence.* Paul rolled his eyes as his thoughts flowed. All those books his parents had insisted on him reading... they did tend to give him a different perspective on the everyday, mundane things. The high shrill yap of a small dog echoed down the hall. He cast a glance down the long corridor at yet another dull and worn carpet. This one, though the treads were thin, still held a dizzying pattern—the kind that could make even the most sober person lose their balance. He shook his head trying to keep his focus on the walls. The pattern there was less upsetting, and the tacky design curled up where the edges met—made it easier to break apart the pattern—therefore easier to keep his feet in a straight line. With no windows to let the sunlight in, the lights dull, yellow glow barely pierced the darkness–despite the daylight hour.

"Do I even want to knock?" he asked himself. "I might be the next murder on the news. 'Unknown man goes missing.'" He waved his hand, punctuating the imaginary headline.

Before his meager courage could escape, he rapped his knuckles beneath the sign that read HAYASHI in all caps. The door swung open and he found himself immediately disarmed by Kent's smile.

"Come in! Come in!" Kent gestured, side stepping so Paul could pass.

The first thing Paul noticed when he stepped into the apartment was a drastic difference between the sketchiness behind him and the eccentric décor filling every nook and cranny of Kent's tiny space. He'd long ago dubbed this phenomenon, 'design shock.' When either person or place seemed out of sync with the style choice. But here–for the first time–he saw both.

"Oh my goodness! You sure are a mess," Kent said, sizing him up. "The outfit is there right next to the bag for your soggy set. I grabbed an undershirt, button down, pants, and socks. Unfortunately I didn't have any brand-new undershorts. Didn't think you would appreciate a used pair."

Paul chuckled. Kent seemed to have a way of relieving tense and awkward situations. He'd already expertly navigated two of them in their limited encounters, smoothing over what could have turned into the kind of embarrassment that Paul normally couldn't recover from.

The purple shirt wasn't typically a color Paul would've picked, but his beggar status prevented him from having a choice in the matter. He was uncomfortable. Even in the short ten minutes he'd spent under slush covered clothing, they were beginning to make him chafe almost anywhere they touched his skin. He grabbed either side of his undershirt–forgetting in his discomfort why he never did this in front of people he didn't know. Kent gasped quietly as the lower half of Paul's back was uncovered. Paul's heart dropped. This was not something he'd been ready to let him see. The ugly scars were enough to make anyone feel pity for him—and pity is the last thing he wanted from anyone. Least of all someone with whom he'd imagined a romantic connection with.

"I'm sorry you had to see that," he mumbled almost incoherently.

Then snatching the pile of clean clothing from the chair, he hastily retreated to the bathroom. At the very least, he could buy a few moments between the awkward one and the reason he'd come. He hesitated in front of the mirror, pulling on the pants that were just a little too tight. It would have to do. When he returned to the kitchen, Kent had busied himself washing the few dirty dishes in the sink and wiping down the counters.

"I don't know how to tie this," Paul said, the tie draped uselessly over his arm.

"You know, I'm not the best at it either," Kent laughed, turning to look as he dried his hands. "You look great without it anyway. Go ahead and drop it on the back of the chair again. "

And just like that, what could have turned into a difficult moment of asking questions and avoiding them, was one that once again was expertly smoothed over and swept under the rug.

Kent walked purposefully to the freezer—a small, nearly imperceptible puff of air escaping as he pulled it open.

"We can still go to dinner if you'd prefer... or we can make things easy and get straight to business with a mediocre pizza," he tendered, waving the frozen disc in Paul's direction.

"You're sure this isn't too intrusive?" Paul asked. He already felt like he was imposing—but what was more of an imposition? Taking clothing from the man... or a cheap frozen pizza? "Are... are you sure it's not too much? First your clothing, and then your food."

But Kent just dismissed his polite inquiry.

"Meh, don't you worry about that. Professional is in the eye of the beholder."

And without further question, he opened a lower cupboard, pulled out a pizza stone, and set the oven.

Their conversation moved back into the natural flow that seemed to come so easily to them. The mixed aroma of pepperoni, cheese, and tomato sauce filled the apartment, making Paul's empty stomach betray him with a loud growl.

"So, am I correct in guessing that you work two hours from home?" He inquired, hoping it would cover the sound of his hunger.

Kent laughed heartily.

"You get right down to the meat of things. But you ARE a detective, so that tracks," he said, a half-smile playing on his lips. "In short, my parents try to force me into their lifestyle. I pay for this place myself because I can't stand the richy riches that they surround themselves with. I'd rather live here, but much to my displeasure—my time must be limited. The life my parents require of me dictate that I can only stay occasionally in order to keep up appearances for them. And even then, they find themselves ashamed of my career path. Never mind the fact that I have a doctorate."

He tore open the cupboard door, slamming it backward as the weak hinges failed to stop the crash. His tone had become more strained the longer he talked about the expectations that he couldn't seem to wiggle away from. He drew in a deep, calming breath—placing the plates gently and intentionally on the table.

"Sorry about that—brief lapse in decorum. Are you a fork and knife man, or do you eat it the way the good lord meant us to?"

Kent rested his elbows on the table, gazing directly into Paul's eyes—making him shift nervously in his chair.

"I don't... really understand the question. Who eats pizza with utensils?" he guffawed, his answer sounding more confident than he felt.

The oven beeped, and much to Paul's relief, it distracted Kent—forcing him to release Paul from his piercing gaze. Any longer and Paul didn't think he would have been able to hold back the blush he felt creeping into his cheeks—a blush that he had no doubts would effectively show over his dark complexion. When they finally settled in to enjoy their food, Paul brought them back around to the real reason of their visit. After gleaning all the new information he could, they parted with a warm handshake—leaving Paul to mull over the additional leads.

He'd confirmed the branches role in his investigation. It was the kind of wood that Kent had mentioned from their first phone call— the most interesting detail being, that it was in fact used to make arrowheads. The kind that an experienced bowman might carve by hand. It was enough to confirm his earlier suspicion, just as it had been with Freyja.

The idea seemed almost otherworldly, coupled with the strange things that Freyja had also found. And there was just enough of *that* quality surrounding Hayden and her little crew to place his suspicion in their general direction. Never mind the fact that he found the claw marks near where he'd seen her and her animals before, the fact that she'd admitted to knowing martial arts—and then there was her phone. He'd looked up her number after she let him use her cell, and it placed her in the same parking garage the night of the murders.

The only detail that wasn't adding up—was timing. Her visit to the garage didn't fit in the timeline from the medical examiner on scene. Still, there were too many other coincidences. He hated to admit it—she'd been such a warm presence, and he'd hoped there was something there in the way of friendship. But he had a job to do—no matter how much he thought of her, she at least had to be brought in for questioning, and he'd need to get a warrant for her property. So with all this evidence stacked against her, why did it feel so wrong for him to pursue this route?

29

Initial Conclusion

Hayden's nerves were raw. How could she have been so careless with her words? She hadn't stopped kicking herself for offering too much information since they'd parted ways. If she could just know exactly what he'd already pieced together, it would put her mind at ease.

"The tree branch!" she exclaimed as she recalled it sticking out of his bag. "Why didn't we take it away from him when he was incoherent?" Hayden dropped her hand to her side, slapping her leg in frustration. "Because it wouldn't have been right. That's why."

The simple fact that he was carrying it made her realize how close he might be to the truth. She was all too familiar with the unique tree species—she'd been watching Cal harvest the branches for her arrows since she'd gotten her morphé back. Her steps were heavy as she trudged back into the living room, dropping her dead weight onto the couch, her hand resting on her forehead as she stared blankly at the ceiling.

"Ok, what's going on?" Cal's voice burst through their link. "We can tell something's off. What happened out there?"

If she thought she would be able to keep it to herself, she couldn't have been more wrong. This family of hers was too dialed in, too linked—for anything to get past them. She winced, the irony of the term slapping her in the face.

"We need to talk about me and my big mouth and where it may have landed us," she admitted.

This was quickly becoming the moment when she felt something shifting—a quiet push in the direction she'd been destined to go all along. Hayden laid out her thoughts, about the strange prophecy born from the throes of delirium, the branch and how it might lead Paul back to their door, and her frustration over not having any idea how to get them back to Dagrune. Then once there, she had no clue where she would even start. Who would follow her? A prophecy about a powerful lost child couldn't possibly be enough to rally people behind them. She rambled, chasing her thoughts around the twists and turns that had, until now, seemed out of reach.

Alec had listened to her self-doubt for long enough. He understood where she was coming from, but at the same time, he knew she struggled because she didn't know Dagrune like he did. It seemed like a story to her, even with the evidence that he, Cal, and Tor presented by being here—in this world. And so, he stepped into his role—the one that he knew was his to command from that fateful moment when he'd first stumbled into Jurtah so many seasons ago.

"If you think about every fork we've faced in our road," he began, "it has always led to something we needed. I found you that night after dealing with Tormaigh—that was no mere coincidence. There's a reason why Calliope followed Paul—and it's no small thing how an experienced mountain man found himself caught unaware by that storm. Then he channeled magic for that prophecy—there's no mistaking that. When the moment comes—and it will, you'll know what to do."

Hayden sat up. She stared into the flickering fire, wondering how—after all this time—she still wasn't prepared for this moment. It was no secret that Clara wouldn't be able to go with her, but she wasn't prepared to leave her alone either. Her chest tightened as her eyes traveled to the woman that had given her the gift of love. In a time when she'd conceded herself to living in fear, Clara had been a safe place to land—and the only woman she'd ever truly considered as her mother. It was going to be her biggest loss. She walked over and snuggled against Clara, resting her head on her shoulder.

"I don't want to say goodbye," Hayden said, her eyes misting until she could no longer keep the tears from trickling down her cheeks. "It's not fair that you have to be alone again."

Clara cradled Hayden's head, planting a gentle kiss on her forehead.

"Weren't you always the one to say that nothing is forever? That as soon as one allows themselves to get comfortable in their happiness—that it would change. Well this is that change. After putting all the pieces together—you were always too special for this world. You were always meant for bigger things—and I could see that from the moment I met that scared, ill-treated, and underfed little girl."

Hayden's body shook, racked with the sobs of finality. She didn't care that she felt like a child again, wrapped in the safety of Mum's arms as she worked through the pain. And Clara held her, rocking her as she'd done countless times when Hayden was a child. In the comfort only a mother could provide, her sobs finally faded, leaving the quiet hiccuping breaths of someone who'd cried all the tears they had.

Hayden wiped her puffy face, carefully dabbing at swollen eyes with the cuff of her sweatshirt. She pushed herself upright and looked into the eyes of each person in the room.

Tormaigh's—full of strength and determination.

Bérg's and his quiet, unrelenting devotion.

Calliope stared back with her familiar sarcasm—and beneath it a fierce, resolute affection.

And then there were Alec and Mum—both looking at her like she was something fragile, someone they still wanted to protect.

She felt the pull again—the same as before, but stronger. As if everything had been waiting for that moment of clarity. That heart wrenching final nail in the coffin of her time here on Earth.

"Mum–guys–I feel it."

She placed her hand over her heart, closing her eyes as the moment washed over her. There was something calling. Something she couldn't hear–but could feel. Behind her closed eyelids, she saw the boulder–split in two–just where she'd left it after her first burst of magic. She drew in a slow breath and the air began to shimmer around her. They could feel it–the buzz of her magic charging the space between them.

"I can see it," Hayden murmured softly.

There, flickering at the shore, was a wall of light–thin and elusive–like a mirage on a hot summer day.

She gasped, like someone underwater for too long coming up for air. Then gently grasping Clara's hand, she placed it in Alec's.

"Mum, Alec... it's time. I had my moment, now it's your turn. I brought you to each other, and it's on my shoulders that you're being torn apart. Go–spend time together. Alec, I'll pack your bag for you."

Clara tried to protest, but neither Alec nor Hayden would hear of it. They moved to Hayden's bedroom, where she could hear Clara softly crying. Hayden's heart ached, that in the end, she'd found a way to leave Mum with this gaping hole.

As she moved through the house, gathering food and supplies, she kept pausing–her eyes catching on the small trinkets and bits of her life she'd collected over the years. It all felt so pointless now. A long, cluttered procession of 'stuff' that meant nothing in the face of what came next. She sighed. Not for the first time, she reminded herself that destiny, in reality, kind of sucked. All those books–all those movies where the protagonist followed their duty–it always looked so noble. So epic. But living it? It wasn't romantic. Not in the way they portrayed it.

Thoughts of what was in store for them filled her head. At the beginning of this strange journey, she'd been unable to shake the doubts–whether or not she was equipped for the job. Tor, Cal, Alec... they'd grown up on Dagrune–so of course they would love it and want to save it. Their enthusiasm and love of that place was hard to ignore. But it was her home too—though she didn't remember its forests, mountain ranges, or its people. The doubts were still there, but purpose had crept in, making them smaller and less significant. Her hesitation melted in light of comparison—her childhood struggles versus what Dagrune had been left with: a world full of people afraid of an abuser doing what abusers do best—taking everything. Slowly at first, then more and more—freedoms... food... until the people were too afraid to fight back.

Someone had saved her from that bleak future and now it was her turn to save them... if she could. Every time she'd been forced into survival mode by the hell of her reality—those freezing nights on the back steps, the bruises left by brush handles, the screaming that rang in her ears long after the words had stopped—every time had led her here. She couldn't leave those people to live that kind of everyday horror. Because they were *her* people. And if her magic could help them—even if it ended in total failure—she had to try. Destiny had crept in, crowding out everything else—until there was no choice left at all.

Alec and Hayden put on their winter gear while Clara helped Bérg with his. There was a collective quiet, somber mood among them. Even Bérg's tail was tucked as he prepared to bid Clara farewell. She snuck in lipstick laced kisses, leaving their bright marks on his shiny white fur.

"I won't be a bad grandma and let you freeze, baby," she said, putting his third boot on.

Bérg waited patiently, thumping his tail half-heartedly on the ground. His devotion to Hayden had always included Clara. So he too, felt the weight of leaving her behind.

****

Clara steeled herself, holding her head high to keep the tears at bay. She waved as they disappeared over the hill. She'd stood here countless times, watching Bérg and Hayden vanish over that same hill—but there was a finality in this. One that felt more like a funeral than a simple goodbye.

Then came the crunch of tires, grinding to a halt in the driveway. Clara didn't need to look. She knew exactly who it was. So, wiping her hands on her apron, she prepared to stall him at the door. But the moment she pulled it open, her resolve melted at the bewildered look on Paul's face.

He blinked at her, his eyes unfocused—just as they'd been in his delirium—and in Hayden's, during the DriftLink. He wore the expression of someone fighting their own conviction.

"I'm not sure why Clara, but I think they need my help."

His brow carried the heaviness of a decision to follow his heart rather than the obligations of his job.

"You'll find the answers you're looking for at the lake," she said, seeing the sincerity behind his disorientation. "They have a good head start, so hurry!"

And as he too disappeared over the hill, Clara found herself bending the ear of an Angel she knew nothing about.

"Please help them and give them your guidance," she implored.

****

Pure instinct led him toward the lake. And now that he was once again alone with his thoughts—he let them wander—to the wild quality that seemed to ooze off Hayden and her odd posse of animals. From the strange colors and shapes in the eyes of both the cat and horse, to Bérg—so in tune with his Mom's every move. Then he considered Hayden's height and strength, and Alec—holding just as much mystery as she did. He followed the fresh footprints—piled one on top of another. Here and there, a hoof or paw print crept outside the stomped-down trail. And as he took notice of them, he found himself lost in a muddled state.

"Did she bring the cat too? No, that's not a cat. But there's also no way it's the dogs," he argued with himself at each new print.

They were too big to belong to a cat, but too narrow and light for the dogs. He tried to recall why they seemed familiar to him, and then, like a cog sliding into position; it crashed into him all at once.

"Holy. Fucking. Shit," he said, his voice trembling with a mixture of awe and shock.

His breath was ragged as he took out his phone and found the folder where he'd placed the pictures of the scratches.

"I mean, not an exact match I guess. But the size… perfectly on point."

And so he quickened his pace, now more eager than ever to reach them before they were lost to him forever.

In the distance, thunder grumbled. His heart rate quickened as the sound brought back the recent ordeal. But this time, through the thick of his hesitation, he knew that he needed to move toward it. The edges of the dark, billowy thunderheads were occasionally illuminated by a flash of lightning. And as the line of trees rose in front of him, so did the menacing clouds. Though they seemed strangely hesitant to blot out the moon. He gathered his courage, pushing aside the branches, and stepping through to the rock covered ground. Nothing could have prepared him for the sight that met him.

There, flanking Hayden, were two of the strangest creatures he'd ever seen. And suddenly, everything that Freyja told him about her bizarre discovery made sense. They were a species all their own—cloaked in shadow and mystery. As soon as he thought he could isolate their position, it seemed to shift. Just like the hair. Their eyes nearly glowed in the rising moonlight as they bored through him—daring him to come any closer. Bérg growled, a low warning rumble. Gone was the friendly, doe eyed goofball and in its place stood a dangerous force that no one in their right mind would challenge. Alec took up the outside of the line, his fists clenched and ready.

"At least now I know I'm not crazy," Paul breathed, glancing at the catlike creature he now knew to be Calliope.

Without the shadow of a doubt—the conclusion to his investigation stood right in front of him.

"Why did you follow us?" Hayden demanded.

Her voice was imposing, sending a shiver of compliance down his spine. The question hung in the air as he struggled to speak through his fear.

"I think I'm supposed to help," he said, the nervous crack in his voice betraying him. "I came to take you in for questioning, but when I got to your house... something changed. I was drawn here–not of my own will, but something else."

Hayden remained stiff as another rumble rolled through the sky. Paul cast a nervous glance upward at the moon–far larger than anything he'd seen in these hills. Lightning tore through the sky again and thunder answered, shaking the very ground beneath their feet.

The air thrummed around them, and then Hayden felt it again. That heartbeat that filled the air. A strange new connection. Then it dawned on her as Paul dropped to his knees and his eyes went blank. Words poured from his lips–and suddenly, it all fell in to place.

"The veil lifts. Use your mother's gift to come back to me. The lights will be your guide."

Tormaigh started, her eyes searching Paul's face.

"It all makes sense now!" she breathed, her voice edged with wonder. "The vessel. He is the *true* meaning of a vessel."

Paul slowly raised his arm, pointing to the sky at their backs. They turned as one, and an awed gasp escaped Hayden. In the emptiness surrounding the thunderclouds, the sky had come to life–exploding in crimson waves of light. They rolled outward, away from the storm, pulsating and swirling across the heavens.

Hayden forgot herself for a moment, marveling at the power around them.

"Never, did I ever, in a million years, think I would get to see the Red Northern Lights. But this..." She paused, eyes wide with wonder. "I've never seen anything like it. I don't think anyone has."

As she lost herself to the phenomenon, an unexpected warmth filled her palm. She opened it to see the bracelet glowing with a soft purple light. Then caging it in her fingers, the warmth grew—bursting from her hand, until it surround all five of them.

"She waits for you," Paul said, his eyes remaining unfocused. "When you learn how to use this vessel, find us."

With a grunt, he dropped to the ground, catching himself with his hands. His eyes were clear now, darting back and forth between them.

"Go!" he encouraged them earnestly. "If you're not here there is no way for me to bring in a suspect. And that way, I don't have to explain… all of this," he panted, still reeling from his brush with magic. "I don't know exactly what's happening, but I promise I will be a friend to Clara. She will be well looked after."

"Thank you," Hayden and Alec said in unison—and Hayden could sense no deceit in his promise. "That means more to us than you could possibly know," Alec offered gratefully.

The blues and purples, the moonlight and lightning, the crimson aura and clouds—all came together, just as they had during her awakening. Hayden's breath caught, paralyzing her with awe as they once again converged over her heart. Her magic swelled to a blinding glow and she opened her arms to welcome it. Her head snapped back as the flicker of an unfamiliar world shone through the thin wavering veil that was no longer invisible to her.

"Grab hold of me!" she cried breathlessly. "I can see it now. That's not the moon. That's our home!"

Calliope slipped her arm around Tormaigh's waist, keeping hold of Hayden's hand. Alec grasped Hayden's other hand and ran his fingers underneath Bérg's collar. Then they all heard a soft voice.

"*Farren,*" it whispered. "*Farren my child, it is time now. Come back home. Come back to me.*"

The mountains wavered as though a thick glass passed between them. All other light had faded, except for the soft glow from her bracelet. Something was pulling them—away from the fading scenery of the mountains. The violet light pulsed brighter, and as her eyes landed on the trinket, she realized it was this that pulled them toward a murky darkness.

"Water!" she tried to scream.

Much to her dismay she was unable to voice the warning as it rushed to meet them, leaving barely enough time to draw air into her lungs and brace herself for what she was sure would be a bone crunching splash. It took her by surprise, the gentle change from air to water instead, as if she'd done the perfect dive without making even the smallest ripple.

"Can everyone swim?" She linked in a panic. *"Tor! Cal! Can you hear me?!"*

She thrashed to get a better view. Although it was dark here, there was just enough moonlight to see each of them—swimming strongly toward the watery silhouette at the surface. Her arms and legs pumped with all the gusto she could muster, propelling her away from the crushing depths. But instead of getting closer, the moon seemed to stay just out of reach. She pumped her limbs harder. If she was having trouble holding her breath, the others were sure to be struggling more.

If I can get a fresh breath, I can come back for them. She thought, willing herself to go faster.

The sound of a gurgling roar brought her ascent to a halt. She torqued her body toward the muffled scream—and the large trail of bubbles where Tor had just been. Calliope stared at Hayden, her eyes shining with fear.

"What was that?!" She practically screamed through the link. *"Where's Tor?!"*

But something had turned their link to static. Fear of the unknown grew in the pit of her stomach. And when her eyes landed on Alec, she all but threw herself toward him as a huge frond wrapped around his ankle. It dragged him off as he also left a trail of bubbles in his wake.

Hayden needed no further incentive. She exploded into action. With what little air she had left, she surged toward Cal and Bérg. But it was too little too late. She could already tell that Cal was struggling through her last bit of air—and then she too was snatched away into the darkness. Bérg's powerful jaw clamped over Hayden's arm as she struggled after Calliope, but she was no match for him. His giant paws propelled them upward until, with a loud gasp, they finally broke the surface. Hayden coughed and gagged, gathering breath back into her lungs—until with a feral shriek, she shattered the stillness surrounding the lake.

"Bérg! I let them down," she cried, her voice thick with self-loathing. "I can swim but I'm not that good," Hayden slapped the water angrily, sending droplets flying, that fell harmlessly back to its surface. "We just got here and already I've failed them."

Another guttural scream tore from her throat, shattering the peacefulness of the night. She searched frantically for the shore in a lake so vast, it rivaled those in her mountains. They spotted a peninsula. It was close enough.

Their muscles burned as they worked together—Hayden's arm draped over Bérg's wide shoulders. And when they crawled onto the shore, they collapsed, leaning on each other in their exhaustion. Her chest heaved as she stared up at the full moon. It seemed to mock her as it bathed them in its gentle glow. The sound of water lapping at the shore did nothing to sooth her pulverized nerves or the accusations she threw at herself. She'd only just made it to this place that she had been sure was her destiny—and already, she'd managed to fail those closest to her.

To be continued...

Acknowledgments

As anyone knows, an author is only as good as the people who surround them. For me, there are many who made this book possible. If it weren't for their support, I'm not sure I would have made it this far.

To Jen, Kate, and Rebecca—the countless hours you spent reading, re-reading, and reading again... I can't thank you enough. Your cheerleading skills are immaculate.

To my kiddos, who listened attentively whenever I would finish a chapter, or an edit that I thought was especially good—and gave their input—your advice was truly priceless.

And of course, I would be remiss if I didn't mention my beta readers. You gave me such thoughtful, generous feedback, and I'm deeply grateful for your time and insight.

To the countless people in my life who inspired the characters in this story—it would quite literally be nothing without you.

And lastly, to anyone who picks up this book and lets these characters live in their imagination, even just for a little while—thank you. Your time, your attention, your curiosity... it means more than I can say. When I started writing this story, it was for me. Finishing it—that was for all of you.

But it's not *actually* finished yet, is it? It looks like I need to take a quick break and get to writing then. See you in book two!

Glossary

Of Magical Beings

Advisor

Human magic wielders whose power comes from the Angel and the sun. They use their magic to heal the mind, and their magical aura glows yellow.

Gworrdikan

Magical beings of the earth that draw power from minerals, and haven't been seen since the beginning of Lord Onyx's rule. Their magical aura is brown.

Lord Onyx

No one knows exactly how he got his magic. His magical aura glows blue.

Mender

Human magic wielders whose power comes from the Angel and the sun. They use their magic to heal the body, and their magical aura glows white.

Morphé

Draw their power from the shadows, morphing between their human-adjacent and animal forms whenever they desire. Each has a unique animal and possesses that animal's abilities.

Neidraium

Magical beings of the water that draw power from the moon, and haven't been seen since the beginning of Lord Onyx's rule. Their magical aura is pink.

Raxyief

Magical beings of the forest that draw power from the moon, and haven't been seen since the beginning of Lord Onyx's rule. Their magical aura is green.

Royal Family

Human magic wielders whose power comes from the Angel and the sun. They have the unique ability to manipulate the elements, and their magical aura is purple.

Sages

Human magic wielders whose power comes from the Angel and the sun. Using the elements around them, they are the inventors of the magical world, and their aura glows orange.

Of General Terms

Alchmene

Name of the resistance.

Annex

Lord Onyx's coup

BlackXard

Also called Xard. Humans who do the dark bidding of Lord Onyx.

Lore Keeper

Revered elder that keeps the history of a people and is a direct line to the Angels and Demons.

Noctorl

Group of people that creates and enforces regulations for magical humans.

Omphalos

Defiance headquarters in The Keep

The Keep

The resistances safe haven in the Lonhilnai Mountain Range

Trailfader

Someone who is trained in the art of leaving no trace when traveling.

Token

An item with magic imbued into it. Meant for protection.

Of Terms

Season Cycle

The turn of four full seasons.

Sun Cycle

A full day: from sun up to sun up. Almost two full hours longer than an earth day.

About the Author

Heidi Marine grew up in the heart of the Twin Cities but always dreamt of a quiet life in the country. Now living in the peaceful countryside she once only imagined, Heidi draws on that same sense of wonder and longing to fuel her storytelling. As a child, she devoured every story she could find, with fantasy quickly becoming her favorite—offering an escape from the ordinary and sparking dreams of adventures beyond the everyday. While real-life portals to secret worlds may not exist, Heidi found another way to chase magic: by creating it on the page. Drawing inspiration from her own life experiences, she writes stories that blend imagination with heart. Her hope is to craft books that resonate with readers and leave a lasting impact for generations to come.

Dagrune Awakening is her first book, but will absolutely not be her last.